For a time the only f[...]
over a hundred reporters have been killed by the military
government, Mike Bond has reported on revolutionary
war and human rights for a variety of U.S. newspapers. He
is now a Paris correspondent for the *Financial Times*
newsletters and has also been a journalist in Nairobi,
Moscow, and the Middle East. An award-winning poet, he
is the author of two travel books and two critically praised
previous novels.

Also by Mike Bond

Fire Like the Sun
The Ivory Hunters

Night Of The Dead

Mike Bond

First published in 1993
by HEADLINE BOOK PUBLISHING PLC

First published in paperback in 1993
by HEADLINE BOOK PUBLISHING PLC

A HEADLINE FEATURE paperback

10 9 8 7 6 5 4 3

ISBN 0 7472 4128 7

Printed and bound in Great Britain by
HarperCollins Manufacturing, Glasgow

HEADLINE BOOK PUBLISHING PLC
Headline House
79 Great Titchfield Street
London W1P 7FN

For Peggy, *compañera de mí vida*, and to the memory of Dr Jeanneth Mayra and the million martyrs of Central America.

ACKNOWLEDGEMENTS

I would particularly like to thank Lavinia Trevor, of William Morris Agency, my agent, and Anne Williams, my editor, both of whose energy, wisdom, and commitment made this book possible.

Special thanks also to E. Clapton and L. Russell.

And grateful acknowledgement is made for permission to quote from the following:

'Nighttrain', Guns N' Roses, Warner Chappell Music Ltd.
'Down to the Waterline', composed by Mark Knopfler, published by Rondor Music (London) Ltd./Straitjacket Songs Ltd.
'You're No Good', Ballard, Memory Lane Music
'Desolation Row', Dylan, Warner Chappell Music Ltd.
'Twilight Time', Ram/Nevins/Dunn, Warner Chappell Music Ltd.
'*Como Tu*', Roque Dalton, Copyright 1980, Editorial Universitaria Centroamericana

Y que mis venas no terminan en mí
sino en la sangre unánime
de los que luchan por la vida

ROQUE DALTON

They break down your door at midnight and shoot you while your children scream. They snatch you from the street at noon and cut your throat in an unmarked car. They torture you for weeks, sending you piece at a time back to your family.

You were hungry and wanted more for your children. Or you'd read the Sermon on the Mount and tried to do what it asks. Or you were young and like Roque Dalton knew your veins didn't end in you, but in the one blood of all who fight for life and bread.

All we can do for you is speak the truth.

I
House of
Jaguar

1

The mosquito hovered, settled on his cheek; the soldier raised a hand and squashed it, his rifle clinking on his cartridge belt. '*Silencio!*' hissed the captain. Another mosquito landed, another; the soldier let them bite.

From far away, beyond the wail of mosquitoes and the incessant chirr of nighthawks, came the snarl of an engine. 'Positions!' the captain whispered. One by one the soldiers squirmed forward through wet grass to the jungle edge, where the road glistened before them under the rising half moon.

The engine noise came closer, a truck grinding uphill round a curve. The curve coming out of Machaquilá, the soldier decided. Not long now. He fiddled with a scrap of electrical tape wrapping the magazine of his Galil. Wings swishing, an owl hunted over the road.

They won't be expecting us, he told himself. They won't be ready and we can kill them quickly and there will be no danger. The truck neared; he tasted bile in the back of his throat; his hands were numb with cold. If you don't shoot they won't see your rifle flash and won't shoot at you.

A beacon steadied on the treetops, fell on the road before him. A single headlight, the truck's, was coming up the road. He chewed his lip and blinked his eyes to chase away mosquitoes, rubbed his bitten wrist on the breech of his rifle. But if you fire fast and hard you'll help make sure they die at once and then they can't fire back.

The truck clattered closer, its headlight jiggling. Everyone will be shooting for the cab, the soldier told himself, so you must shoot into the back. 'Hold your fire,' the captain called. Transmission wailing, stockboards rattling, the truck rumbled past and disappeared into the night, just another cattle truck driven too many thousands of miles over bad roads on bad gas. 'Silence,' the captain said. From the jungle a howler monkey screamed like a dying child.

4

* * *

The Aztec eased down through five hundred feet, the jungle sliding under the wing like the floor of an immense dark sea. 'I hate it when you do this,' Johnny Dio said. 'Reminds me of that joke about the secret to safe flying is to avoid the ground—'

Murphy trimmed one aileron, watched the altimeter till it steadied at four hundred, the plane bouncing and banging on rising waves of jungle heat. 'It's so flat here there's nothing to fear, except the pyramids at Cobá.' He slapped Johnny's knee. 'And they're probably east of us.'

'Screw you, Murph. You know exactly where they are.'

'Unless the Mayans've built a new one since we were here last—'

'There could be some kind of goddamn TV tower, antenna . . . Even a big tree.'

'That's why we watch out. You *and* me.'

'It's so dark I can't see a goddamn thing.'

'Just as well. You'll never know what hit you—'

'Will you cut it out!' Johnny Dio shifted in his seat, fingers drumming his knee, his face glistening in the yellow instrument lights.

'The way you don't like this, Johnny, you should let me do it alone.'

'My gig,' Johnny said.

'Mine too,' Murphy said softly, and Johnny smiled at himself for worrying. If you had to be doing this, Murph was the one to be doing it with.

'You're right,' Johnny said, 'to be packing it in.'

Murphy stretched, rubbing his back against the seat. 'It's just habit, now. Got all the creature comforts I want.'

'You don't do it for money, Murph. It's because you don't have anything else . . .'

The glimmer of Chetumal began to bloom to the south; Orion was sinking into the west, Scorpio riding a half moon in the east, the Yucatán below darker than a midnight sea, the stars above like city lights. Murphy rubbed his face, liking the raspy stubble sound, closed his eyes and massaged them with his fingertips, still seeing the instrument panel, as if he could watch it directly from his brain, thinking of the lobsters he and Johnny had eaten in Mérida – he shouldn't have harassed the man because they were small – '*están cubanas*,' the man had explained. And Tecates. When this was over he was going to come back down to dive, sit

5

on the veranda and drink Tecates, lime and Tecates. He notched the yoke forward, the engine's pitch deepening in the soggy air, the altimeter sliding down to three hundred, two hundred and fifty. Light widened in the south-east. 'Corozal,' he said. 'Going under the radar.'

'I swear you like it,' Johnny sighed. 'You *like* this shit.'

The jungle reached up, solid rolling waves of canopies with taller bare ceibas clawing up like drowned skeletons, down to two hundred feet, one hundred and eighty, tipping the wings now between the tallest trees. 'One time in high school,' Murphy said, 'I was in a class play. Only had to say one word: "no". You know I blew it? I got so afraid I'd say "yes" by mistake, that when the time came, I couldn't remember which it was, and said "yes?" Screwed the whole thing up. Or maybe I was supposed to say "yes" but said "no" – can't remember—'

'You're not too bright, Murph. Always told you that.'

A great black serpent slithered under, sparkling with starlight. 'Río Hondo,' Murphy said. 'We're back in Guatemala.'

'When we get out this time,' Johnny said, 'I'm going to bag it too.'

'Figured you were.'

'I really like being with Sarah. She's easy, she's amazing. She loves me.'

'All that counts.'

'I really miss the kids, Murph. You were lucky, when you and Pam split, you didn't have kids.'

'Don't know what I would've done. What's Diana say?'

'She won't give them up, but if Sarah and I get married, she'll let me have more visitation.'

'Fuckin world,' Murphy said. The engines steadied, almost hypnotic, the jungle drifting closer, as if the Aztec hung suspended over the slowly spinning globe. Ahead, the land steepened into towering ridges of black stone with jungle on their crests. Deeper into a box canyon the plane droned, its echo bouncing off the cliffs that narrowed towards its wingtips. An end wall of vertical stone hurtled towards them; at the last second Murphy slid back the yoke, powered the throttles, and the nose lifted and the saddle swept beneath them and they floated easily into a wide valley under a bowl of stars.

'Fuckin cowboy,' Johnny said.

Several trucks were coming. Not from Machaquilá but the south.

The soldier wiped dew from his barrel with his hand, took a breath and held it, hearing his heart.

Lights brushed the pine tops and darted down the road. Headlights glinted round a curve – two trucks coming fast. The first roared past, a dark Bronco with orange roof-lights. Then a Ford pick-up with a camper top passed the soldiers, halted and backed off the road on to the shoulder. Two men got out and began to unload something from the back.

Half a mile down the road the Bronco's brakelights flashed as it stopped and turned. One of the men at the pick-up stood with a flaring lantern and began to pull crates from the back. From each crate he took another lantern and lit it.

The men placed a lantern on each side of the road. They ran up the road, stopping in front of the soldiers to drop off a second pair of lanterns, and turned back down the road towards the Bronco with the other lanterns. The Bronco was moving closer; it too was dropping off pairs of lanterns.

'Down there's Xultún,' Murphy said. 'A whole Mayan city – temples, schools, observatories, farms – all drowned in the bush.'

The jungle had flattened, tilting west from the Pine Ridge mountains towards the black defiles of the Río de la Pasión. 'Suppose they knew?' Johnny said. 'That it'd die, some day – their civilization?'

'Maybe they were smarter than we are . . .'

Johnny laughed. 'Can't lose what you ain't got.'

'Radar again.' Murphy dropped lower, skimming the trees, slid back the mini-window and the engine roar bounced up at him from the treetops. Little spots danced before his eyes, circles with black centres like the fuselage markings on British bombers. 'Petén highway,' he said, nudging the rudder to swing south-west along a narrow dirt road.

'There was a guy,' he said, 'in one of their myths, named Utzíl. He got tired of staying home so he wandered south through the desert, found an alligator dying of thirst and carried him on his back to a lake, went on to his enemies' lands, fell in love with the king's daughter.'

'Kind of thing you'd do—'

'The king's soldiers chased the two of them all the way back to the lake. He hid the girl in a cave and the alligator appeared and carried him on *his* back across the lake so he could get help—'

7

'Would you watch that fuckin *tree*!'

'It was five feet under the wing! You want to fly higher, so the radar picks us up and we get A37s all over our ass?'

'So what happened,' Johnny said, after a minute, 'to the girl?'

'When they got back the girl had died and he threw himself off a cliff into the water. Lake Atitlán it was, south-west of here . . .'

Black pastures and silver-thatched roofs flitting under, hearth smoke smudging the stars, the distant starboard glimmer of Dolores, the town named Sorrows; he swung west of the road to miss the Army outpost then SSE back over the road at Machaquilá, an Indian name for all Indian things lost, with its wan lamps and vacant streets, a sawmill and scattered tree corpses, the unfinished church gaping like a broken skull, the barracks school by the zipping road; and he banked right, then left, into the cleft beneath the two steep hills that always seemed like tits, ziggurats, the temples of Tikal, air rushing like a river over the plane's skin.

No shear now, he prayed, no crosswinds. The yoke was hot, vibrating in his palm, sweat tickling his ribs. He checked the landing gear: all down. 'There they are!' Johnny said. Murphy eased the engine into low pitch, dropped the flaps, notched back the throttles, lifting the nose, and flared in a near stall down through the trees towards two rows of lanterns with the rutted road between them.

2

Airspeed eighty, then seventy, the Aztec came down between the outreaching pine boughs towards the first lights, a man waving up. One wheel touched, bounced, caught a rut, yanking the plane starboard, pine boughs slapping the wing; Murphy gunned the port engine holding the nose high to pull it back till both wing wheels settled and the nose wheel dropped with a whump of gravel. Pumping the brakes he reversed the props till their roar shook the cabin, taxied back to the first lanterns, where the Bronco and pick-up truck were parked, and cut the engines.

Johnny let out his breath. He lifted a heavy daypack from between his feet and set it on his lap. 'Half-way home.'

Murphy leaned back in his seat, stretched, feeling the muscles snake up his thighs and back, popped open the door. The air was warm and watery, smelled of rotten vegetation. So natural up there, he thought, the ground's a comedown. He hesitated in the seat, not wanting to leave the familiarity of the Aztec's instrument panel and its worn controls, its sheltering cockpit and comfortable seat. 'Home's where the heart is.' He patted the instrument panel offhandedly, as though closing switches. A mosquito whined, touched his cheek. He slapped it, climbed out and slid down the wing, stood unsteadily in the glare of the lanterns.

The engines smelled of heat and avgas. There was a dent smeared with pine sap in the starboard wingtip.

'Murph – *qué tal!*' A tall, skinny man with a thick beard ducked towards him under the wing.

'Goddammit, Paco! You didn't fix the potholes!'

'The *what*?'

'The potholes – *los huecos – en el* fuckin *camino*! Now I got a dent in my fuckin wing!'

'Ah, *them*.' Paco kicked at the ground, '*Los baches*. If we filled them the Army would've noticed.'

9

'How many guys you got out?'

'Two at each end. Beyond the lights.'

'You got my fuel?'

'*Sí*, aviation fuel, as ordered.' Paco called over his shoulder, 'Ernesto – *los depósitos!*'

A man in a red bandanna and a Harley Davidson T-shirt pulled fuel cans from the back of the Bronco and lifted them up for Murphy to pour one at a time into the wing tank. Johnny Dio stood in the glare of a lantern inspecting large bags of grass that Paco unloaded from the rear of the Ford. Johnny broke open and smelled each brick, put it back in its bag and resealed the bag. He hooked a spring scale to the port engine cowl and weighed the bags one by one, writing down the weights on a note pad and passing the bags up to Murphy to load through the right-side baggage door into the cabin.

'Murph, he is getting crazy,' Paco said, 'seeing *huecos* – faggots, in this road here.'

'He must be *hueco con sus ojos* – proud of his vision,' Ernesto answered, pissing at the side of the road, 'to see faggots where there ain't none.'

'Maybe he means you, *hueco* – so zip your little mosquito back in your pants—'

'Fifteen hundred and twenty-three pounds.' Johnny shrugged the daypack from his shoulders. 'You can keep the twenty-three or throw it in . . .'

'What am I to do, *hombre*?' Paco said. 'Smoke it going home?'

Johnny gave him the daypack. 'One hundred thirty-five grand. All used twenties and fifties. *No hay riñas.*' Murphy bit a thumbnail as he watched Paco flip through the money in the all-encompassing hiss of the lanterns.

Paco came closer. 'Listen, Murph – you doing deals with anybody else?'

'You asking me that seriously?'

'*Sí, amigo*. People have been getting it – Flores, Dolores, Izabal. They fly in, everybody gets *extincto*—'

'By the Army?'

'Carlos says so. So you be careful, if you're doing any other deals.'

Murphy shook his head. 'We're *uno a uno*.' He stepped up on the wing. 'Anyway, I may be tying it up—'

'No more?'

Murphy shrugged. 'I'll let you know, through Lucia.'

Paco closed the daypack and looped it over one shoulder.

10

Johnny hugged him, climbed into the cabin and buckled his seat belt. *'Gracias, compadres!* Twenty-five thousand *norteamericanos* thank you also . . .'

Paco's grin, his hand half raised, the daypack slung over his shoulder, were caught in a burst of lights; standing on the wing Murphy saw it instantly – the glaring jungle, white plane and green Ford pick-up, Ernesto in his red bandanna with one foot in the Bronco's cab, the harsh, affronted jungle. He dove into the cabin and punched the starter, thinking, the starboard engine will be slow to start but I can run her down the road on one; if it's soldiers they'll shoot from both sides and we'll have to duck low and hope they don't hit the tanks; even if they do we can get a few miles if there's no fire. Over the whine of the starter a bull-horn blasted from the jungle, *'Están rodeados!'* and a shot cracked as the port prop lurched a quarter turn and halted. White smoke puffed from the port manifold, the prop spun slowly; Ernesto lay on his back, one foot still in the Bronco; there was a hole in the plane's windshield and Murphy thought, I have to stop or they'll kill us; the plane began to jerk forward but soldiers blocked the road. Johnny was yelling but Murphy couldn't hear over the crash of bullets caving in the windshield and the second engine catching. The plane picked up speed and the soldiers scattered as a pink tracer leaped out from the jungle and hammered the plane and Johnny jumped up as if he would smash through the canopy, punched Murphy's shoulder and fell against the stick. Murphy shoved him aside and the plane was moving fast now down the road with the bullets crashing through the fuselage past his face and knocking out pieces of broken windshield and sparking off the props, his whole body reaching upward to break free of the ground; smoke and flame burst back from the starboard engine, the cabin was blasted white with heat; the huge bang made him think the plane had been hit by a shell but it was the wing exploding; the plane cartwheeled off the road, smashing him against the roof and floor and stick, and Johnny was on top of him with flames coming up his sides and the door jammed, skin peeling like plastic off Johnny's face; he tried to pull Johnny through the windshield but one arm wouldn't work; his clothes were on fire and the pain was so awful he had to drop Johnny but grabbed him again but the seat belt was buckled and he crawled over Johnny to unbuckle it, then dragged him down over the plane's melting nose, bullets slapping into Johnny as Murphy dragged him towards the trees.

11

Johnny was screaming, then Murphy realized it was himself, not Johnny; a machine-gun round had taken half of Johnny's chest, bullets singing through the pine trunks, boots running and rifles crackling and the Aztec seething and sending up long spirals of superheated exploding air. His arm was broken – that's why it wouldn't work. Tracer rounds stitched up the road, spurts of dust bright in the flames.

Clasping the broken arm against his ribs he ran into the forest, seeing at first by the light of the burning plane, then deeper into the darkness. He smacked his face against a bough, behind him soldiers yelling, '*Por aquí! Por aquí!*'

He caught his breath, listening for dogs. Now that he knew the arm was broken it hurt awfully, blood spattering on the leaves. They don't need dogs, he realized – they'll track you by your blood.

He tore loose a liana with his teeth and with his good left hand twisted it round his right biceps above the bleeding bullet hole and the pieces of broken bone poking through the flesh. From afar, above the now-distant crackling plane and the yells and snapping brush, came a familiar flutter, a loudening chatter. He ran, vines snagging his broken arm, mangroves barring his way, lost a shoe in a bog but kept running, smashing into trees and branches, stumbling, falling, running again. The chatter grew to a clatter of downbeaten boughs and branches as the chopper's rotors flattened the treetops and its light darted down the trunks. A bullet whacked a bough; he fell, tried to crawl under a bush, but there were too many branches and he squirmed on his belly, dragging the broken arm, into a thicket of saplings. The chopper's light leaped over the thicket, dashed away. Soldiers ran past, boots shaking the ground.

The chopper swung east, its rotor roar hardening briefly as it crossed the road. Between the sapling stems he could see the firefly wink of soldiers' flashlights and hear the swish-chunk of their machetes.

'Is that you?' Right behind him the voice, in English with a Spanish accent. Murphy tried to duck but couldn't, hemmed by the thicket, his back expecting the bullet, the horrible pain. 'Is that you, Lieutenant Gallagher?'

Murphy bit his lip. Anything to live, even a moment longer.

'What you want? I'm over here!' Another voice, hoarse, American.

'It's Angel,' the first said. 'I got something!'

12

Now it comes, Murphy realized, the bullets crushing and tearing.

'Over here!' Angel said, still in English.

'I'm coming,' Gallagher answered. 'What you got?'

'Tracks,' Angel whispered. 'Hurry!'

Brush scraped and rattled as Gallagher neared. His flashlight danced round Murphy's thicket. But he did not seem to see, or he was waiting to swing round the thicket so he could shoot Murphy without hitting Angel.

'Where?' Gallagher huffed.

'Look down!' Angel whispered. 'See that?'

Someone gasped, fell, rifle clattering. 'No—' Gallagher gasped.

'*Sí!*' Angel answered. One set of boots stepped quietly away.

Seconds passed and no bullets came. Mosquitoes landed in Murphy's ear, on his eyelids, lips, cheeks, wrists, neck, and ankles. He did not move. The helicopter came and went. He rose to his knees and slipped from the thicket, tripped and fell over a soft log – a body, warm, blood spurting from the sliced carotid, a man in uniform. Murphy stood and found the Pleiades in a gap in the branches, and turned west through deepening jungle towards the Río de la Pasíon.

3

Lyman woke the instant the phone rang. He rubbed his face, cleared his throat, settled his elbows on his desk, and picked up the phone. 'Yeah?'

'Colonel?'

'Shoot.'

'Your Indian left Mérida at 0215 hours.' The caller's voice was tinny and indistinct from the scrambler. 'He crossed the Guatemalan border, Hondo River, at 0307. TD the Flores–Morales road seven klicks Sierra of Machaquilá at 0357 hours. Hey, what you think of that 'Skins game?'

'Impeccable,' Lyman said. 'Any other action, that sector?'

'Couple Guat slicks. You *see* that catch?'

'*What* slicks?'

'One on the LZ – he'd be your people. The other Cobán to Sayaxché – some general, probably, going for a beer.'

'Thanks, Lieutenant. I owe you one.' Lyman fumbled in his shirt pocket for his Marlboros.

'Negative. Don't sweat it—'

'I will. I hate to owe people.' He hung up, took out a cigarette, shook his head, put the cigarette back in the pack, picked up the phone and punched three numbers. 'Patch me through to Cobán.'

The phone's distant jangle sounded under water, slow and deep. It rang on and on. '*Sí!*' a man answered, sleepy and irritated.

'Identify yourself, trooper!' Lyman said in Spanish.

'Sergeant Almédio, Cobán Armed Forces Command, sir!'

Lyman waited a moment to let the man's fear sink in. 'Get me Vodega.'

'*Momentino*, sir, *momentino!*'

After a wait the man came back on. 'Capitán Vodega's not here, sir.'

'*What*? Where the fuck is he?'

14

'I don't know, sir.'

'He on that op?'

'What op, sir?'

'Forget it.' Lyman hung up, staring at nothing. Thousands of styrofoam cups had formed overlapping circles on the desk's mahogany veneer. Why would Vodega be on Gallagher's op?

He lit a Marlboro, remembered his resolve, stubbed it out, put it back in the package. He inspected his nails, brown in the quick and muddy yellow at the tips, evenly and tightly trimmed, fingers darker than the desk. He imagined nicotine travelling down his arm into the hand, staining the skin.

He reached for a styrofoam cup. The coffee in it was cold, the colour of used diesel oil. He emptied it into another dirty cup and poured a hot one. His hands would not stop trembling. He held the warm cup in his frigid fingers; reflected fluorescent light shivered on it.

Five forty-two. Eighteen more minutes and he could have a cigarette. Make it last till six-thirty. Then one more driving home. Yes, it was working – he *was* cutting down.

Dawn purpled the treetops, erasing the stars. Macaws stirred, began to crow; parrots and toucans screeched and battered wingtips in the branches. Spider monkeys jeered and threw down palm nuts; the cacophony of howlers followed Murphy through the jungle, making it easy for the soldiers to track him.

His stockinged foot slipped on a mossy log and he fell trying to protect the arm but it smashed against a bough and he cried out.

The soldiers had heard, were coming. Vines blocked his way, creepers and thorns, branches and saplings and trunks, madrones so tightly grown he had to scramble up and over them, his feet breaking through, the ching-ching of machetes and the yells of soldiers growing louder. Ahead were scrub and saplings, then a clump of thick brush that as he got closer he saw were treetops at ground height, trees growing up out of a sinkhole, a black pool glistening at the bottom. He slipped down into the sinkhole, rocks, dirt, and leaves tumbling with him, slid feet first into the water, took a breath, and ducked under.

The pool's rock sides were slick, he couldn't get a hold, pushed himself lower, already hungry for air. How many seconds? Twenty, maybe. Clouds of sediment rose slowly, began to settle. No, maybe thirty . . .

On the surface above him the leaves rocked slowly, stilled. Water stung his arm. Maybe sixty seconds now. You can do this. Dirt dribbled into the pool, shadows crossed it. The surface shivered as a hand cupped into it; a khaki knee rippled one edge. Eighty seconds, maybe. The soldiers' voices echoed, pebbles dimpled the surface and hit his face as they sank.

Not even two minutes. When you were little you did this. Sitting in school, holding your breath at your desk, the clock hand creeping. He sucked in water, coughed it out.

You have to go up and they'll take you and that's better than this, can't hold out any longer – go up there they'll reach down and help you.

Another soldier drank, his oval face protruding down. Murphy tried to remember how long it had been then could not remember what he was trying to remember, the light dimmed, he was heavy now, sinking into a dark chasm. In the distance a beam of light, drew nearer. It was true – at the end, you can see pure light.

He rose up a brightening tunnel towards it, no pain, no fear, and burst gasping and choking into an underground pool with a vaulted stone ceiling, sucking in pure sweet air, sweet lovely forgiving air.

A slit in the cavern ceiling cast down a column of clerestory light. Through it he heard the soldiers grunting as they climbed from the pit. He dragged himself half out of the water on an edge of stone and lay with his broken arm above water.

The light steepened; through the crevice came warm air perfumed with jungle, loud with monkeys and birds, the buzz of bees and cicadas.

He woke, confused, reached for the lamp on his bedside table, scraped his broken arm on the rock and screamed, the echo bouncing round him. Before him hung a phosphorescent green face with black eye sockets and purple lips, but when he tried to knock it away his hand went right through it.

His breath whispered off the dripping limestone walls. He sat up, head banging the roof. Just a *cenote*, this. A sacred Mayan spring.

The light shifted, dust motes tumbling in its sloping shaft. There was no sound of soldiers. The agony in the arm was unimaginable. You should have stayed in San Francisco, he told himself. You should have been happy with what you had.

The water dripping from the shaggy limestone ceiling into the pool was like countless tiny bells. If you pray for everything to be all right, he decided, then maybe it will be. It's just like you to pray only when things get bad.

He took a deep breath and dove back down the tunnel to the chasm, then back up to the surface of the sinkhole; he waited in the water but there was truly no sound of soldiers. He stood in warm sun, shivering; a lizard watched him from behind a trunk, darting its head from side to side. His broken arm was swollen and vermilion like the lizard's throat, his hand a mottled claw. He picked out slivers of bone and washed the wound with water from the *cenote*.

The bullet had come from the front side and had snapped the bone, leaving a small hole in his biceps and a larger tear with bone chips at the back. He was able still to move his fingers, and with great pain to raise the arm. He climbed from the sinkhole, found sticks and tried to splint the arm, but it hurt too much.

He focused his mind on the flight chart of the Petén as it had looked in the Aztec's instrument lights. The road where he'd landed ran up the middle, north–south. He must be twenty klicks already west of the road. If he swung northwest he'd hit the Río Machaquilá, could follow it to the Río de la Pasión. Maybe another fifty kilometres. On the *Río* he'd find a dug-out, anything; then only another hundred klicks downriver to Mexico. If he were very smart and very careful he might make it.

The last pines died out in an impenetrable lowland of hardwoods and thickets. Lizards and small green vipers were everywhere; scorpions scuttled, blue tails raised, over dead leaves. A weasel scrambled from a half-eaten rat; a boa swung at him from a vine-clogged limb, then turned away. Bees buzzed in an irritated cloud from a conical hive in the crotch of a dead tree aflame with white orchids.

Again a telephone woke Lyman. He sat up in bed, thick-tongued. 'Nancy!' he called. It kept ringing and he realized Nancy wasn't there. He ran down the hall to the living room and grabbed the phone.

'Howie?' Curt Merck's voice was nearly solicitous.

Lyman sat down, the leather easy chair cold against his thighs, trying to see the clock over the television. 'What's wrong?'

'They blew it, Howie. Gallagher's dead.'

'This line, Curt—'

'It's secure enough for this—'

17

'I'm coming in.' Lyman hung up, sat with the phone between his knees. There was dog hair on the carpet; he saw Kit Gallagher throwing a tennis ball in a long arc, the ball bouncing over the lawn, the black labrador bringing it back coated in slobber that Kit wipes on the grass before throwing the ball again. Who's gonna take the dog? Kit brushing dandruff from his tie, his rigid motions when he eats, jaws snapping like a trap.

Lyman went into the kitchen. Sun splashed the yellow flowered wallpaper, the ceramic trivet of a Dutch girl in a bonnet, the Mr Coffee with the 'Warm' light still on, the dishes in the sink where Nancy had put them before taking the kids to school, the wall clock — a Minnie Mouse seen from the rear, her tail showing the hour, her red-gloved hand the minutes. Twenty after nine. Blood flowing round inside your body then it stops. So many times you go out to meet death, and finally one time it's there.

He poured a coffee and picked up the *Post* from the breakfast bar, a corner of the first pages sticky with egg yolk. Words words words. If the assholes only knew. Does anybody? He returned to the bedroom, found a pack of Marlboros, lit one and stood in a patch of sunlight, sucking in the smoke.

4

A trail. Before him through the jungle. No wider than his hand. He looked up with thanks to the towering trees, followed the path till he met a long column of red ants carrying leaf chunks in their jaws, and realized it was they and others like them that had made the trail. The ants were stopping to touch jaws with others returning along the same way. He wanted to fall down, give up, but checked the sun and turned west again.

Soon the sun was overhead and he could not tell the way. He lay beside a tree. A blue motmot hooted from a branch and he wondered if it would eat his eyes. Long-tailed ebony *sanatés* flapped their papery wings, rustling and clacking in the palm crowns. Mosquitoes hovered with elegant patience. A huge fly bit his ankle; he waved at it and it buzzed round his head. Noon heat layered down in thick malodorous blankets, choking the narrow spaces between the trees.

He dragged himself in what seemed a westerly direction, drank at a puddle thick with mosquitoes, noticed the tracks around it, dug a stick from the mud and hid behind a fern clump. A vireo pecked at the water; he swung the stick and missed.

A small iguana crouched beside the puddle, its red dorsal fan raised, its throat pulsing. In his good hand Murphy raised the stick. It caught on a liana; the iguana glanced at him.

Like a whip the snake struck. The iguana leaped, rolling over and over but the bushmaster held, fangs deep in the iguana's neck, using its long thick body for leverage, till the iguana quivered and lay still. When the bushmaster had stuffed the iguana halfway down its wide, unhinged mouth, Murphy jumped out and clubbed its head again and again until it stopped writhing. The long curved pit-adder fangs hung open, one showing a tiny venom hole.

Murphy dug a stone from the mud and sawed off the snake's head, ripped its body lengthwise, tugged out its guts, held it between his knees to tear a chunk of body muscle from its back and swallowed it. It came up and he forced it down again. He pinched his nose against the rank raw taste and swallowed another piece. When the snake was half eaten he drank the puddle dry and lay beside it on the soft leaves.

Waking in darkness, he sat up to check for stars but none shone through the high canopy. Breath whistled in his throat, smelled of burnt, decaying flesh. His body was a vast hive of cells aching for water; water trickled on the wind and licked at his lips. He chewed the mud of the puddle; it only made his mouth more dry.

Moon shadows slowly climbed the black trunks. The darkness paled; swifts and swallows tittered, trogons stirred stuffily in the high, platy leaves. An ocelot screamed. Dawn came with slits of flame between the treetops, the birds chanting wildly with the joy of surviving another night.

He saw the arm would burst, the red infection, toxic as copper, sluggish in his veins. His tongue stuck, his jaw would not open. He crawled in circles looking for water, fainted, awoke, stood, turned his back to the rising sun, and pushed on.

Somewhere he had lost his other shoe; his feet were swollen with thorns and bites and ripped by rocks. Flies chewed his arm, their tiny feet stuck in the black blood.

He awoke on his back. Something feathery brushed his face, was tickling his ribs: a trail of ants crossing his chest like a red bandolier; they were feeding on his arm but he could not feel it. He sat up moaning and yelling, wiped them off with his other hand, lay down again.

The underside of a leaf glinted like a diamond. How pretty, how peaceful the sun was, the warmth, birds singing. Wind rustled at his cheek, stirred the leaf; the light danced. He pulled himself near, saw the puddle whose reflection had flashed on the leaf, and sucked it dry.

Ahead was a long low building draped in vines – a Mayan ruin, maybe – there could be water, a path made by robbers, archaeologists. Two eye sockets gaped through creepers. A great Mayan stone scorpion: water – had to be – somewhere.

Watching for coral snakes in the vines, he climbed, one-armed, up the front, looking into the sculpture's empty eye socket, where a fat, red-bellied spider hung in a web strung across the caved-in skull of a skeleton dressed in combat rags, the black nylon crossbelts still strapping it into the chopper's seat, the collective pitch and cyclic control levers jutting up rusty between its capless knees.

He backed away till he could see the one remaining rotor blade bent hanging from the shaft, the M60 mount in the port door.

He sat. It's true, he thought. You do get punished for every evil you've ever done. Your Huey, back from Nam. Waiting for you.

He jumped to his feet. A huge black panther stood ten feet away. Its red eyes watched him. He reached for a gun, a stick – there was nothing. The panther smiled.

Too far to the chopper. Nothing inside. Don't show fear. Smells the blood. Coming now. Your chopper from Nam, the black cat. Coming to claim you. Suddenly he laughed, had no fear.

The panther cocked its head, flicked its long thick tail. He saw himself eaten, inside the panther, bloody chunks. The panther circled him, sliding invisibly through the trees and brush, turned back and stared, unwinking.

He tried to go back the way he'd come but the cat slipped behind him, close again, snarling huge teeth. He backed away, the panther coming after him. It circled again and this time he followed it and it went on, just ahead, sometimes looking back.

The land began to slope. The panther stopped at the edge of mangroves by a wide, fast stream flowing west. Murphy had a sudden rush of understanding, wanted to reach out, touch the glowing black fur, the monstrous rippling shoulders, felt love, absolutely no fear.

The panther vanished in the mangroves. Murphy knelt and drank till he could drink no more, then waded downstream, the afternoon sun dancing on the current.

He killed a small turtle sunning on a log, tore off the back and belly plates, the beak and feet, and chewed down the lukewarm, tallowy flesh.

Night fell like a curtain. He dragged a dead bough into the water and tried to float downstream, but it caught on roots and sunken trees and he waded on without it. He could not remember how many nights there had been, at times could not remember what had happened.

He lay on a grassy bank. The ache of his arm filled his chest and shoulders, crushed his lungs; his fever made the blackness waver and buzz; thirst burned his throat no matter how much he drank. Sometimes the pain was so great he wept; at other times the arm seemed separate from him, its fate unlinked to his.

A blue sky and hot white sun gleamed through the trees. On the opposite shore a large-bellied girl watched him gravely; in the clearing behind her a hut of creepers and palm fronds squatted among plantains and dead corn.

He tried to wave, his voice a croak. The girl ran to the hut. A small dark woman came out and peered across the water at him, then ran along the bank to a clearing with other huts. She came back with several women; they waded to him and carried him across.

There was the sweet smell of woodsmoke, the murmur of women's voices, the hiss and crackle of a fire. An ancient, wrinkled face loomed down. 'Where am I?' he asked.

'San Tomás.' A hoarse voice, a strange dialect. '*Norteamericano*,' she said to the others, turned down to him. 'You're with the Army?'

'No – don't tell them!'

She smoothed a wool blanket up under his chin. He called out, tried to focus on the rain-stained thatch above his head, but the ground slid away beneath him and he dropped into darkness.

5

It took Lyman an hour on the Army C-34 from Guatemala City to Cobán. From the air the steep black-green half-jungled hills were peaceful and deserted, a miniature mountain landscape for electric trains. He tried to imagine *them* down there, the guerrillas, with their guns and fear and hunger.

The plane kicked up red dust landing at Cobán Airbase. Red dust coated the jeep in which Vodega and two sergeants waited. Vodega shook his hand. 'How was your flight?'

Lyman sat up front, forcing Vodega to the back. '*Any* flight that means seeing you, Captain Vodega, is a lousy flight.'

'It's not my fault, Colonel, that Gallagher couldn't protect himself—'

'I *want* whoever did it.'

'It must have been the pilot. He was the only one who got away.'

'You *let* him escape—'

'I've got a battalion tracking him in the jungle between the road and the *Río*. I got a platoon in three *lanchas* working up and down the *Río*, doing a "detailed inventory" as you call it in your manual, of every village. I got two Hueys on full alert twenty-four hours to intervene the first moment I hear of him. You think we *let* him go?'

'You're just like every other fuck-up. Instead of taking the trouble to do things right, you fuck them up and then you take much more trouble trying to fix them afterwards.'

'You are telling me you're different, Colonel?'

'Who is he, this pilot?'

'The deal that was to be made was out of San Francisco. His plane is too burned, no numbers. The flight plans out of Mérida were false.'

'Why'd you fire on him, goddammit? It all burned – the whole shipment? The money?'

'Yes.'

23

'You *fuck*-ups—'

'When my men yell to him he's surrounded, he jumps in the plane, tries to take off.'

'So you got no idea who they were—'

'Just what we know from before.'

'I want him *dead*, Angelo. But listen—' Lyman forced himself round in the jeep, stared into Vodega's boyish, acned face. '*I* want him before he's dead.'

'No one needs him going north, telling stories.'

'You don't have any fuckin idea who they were?'

'We identified one man, Paco Alguenes, from Jarha, in the south—'

'I *know* where Jarha is.'

'His wife was pretty uninformed—'

'Show her some pictures . . .' Lyman turned to grip the windshield rim as the jeep slid through a turn.

'She died too soon. The children knew nothing.'

The jeep halted before the HQ, a broad, yellowed building with tropical mould down its walls. Lyman got out, stood with hands on the fender, blocking Vodega. 'Why were *you* on that op?'

'Same reason you would have been, Colonel.'

'Pray tell what's that?'

'I was responsible—'

'And now you're responsible Gallagher's dead.'

'No. I'm responsible for wiping out another outsider. It's *your* people wanted Gallagher down here . . .'

'With good reason. And now I'm here to replace him.'

'I hope you fare better than he—'

Was there a ghost of derision in Vodega's glance? Lyman couldn't decide, filed it for later. 'We've lost a man – you know our policy on that—'

Vodega got out of the jeep. 'We know. We'll get this pilot for you.'

Through the hut's open door Murphy could see other huts, a boggy trail between them, a bit of stream bank. A rooster crowed; a baby was wailing. Hens clucked; two donkeys brayed back and forth across the village. The air smelled of fires, rotten vegetation, dank soil.

He shifted position and the earth moved with him. Turning on his side he tugged at the banana leaves wrapped round his arm. The pain and stench were horrible. With his good hand he fumbled for the tin cup of water the old woman had put on the floor by the head of his hammock, but it was empty.

Sunlight poured across the red dirt floor and over three clay pots and a white plastic jug, glinted on a half-loomed rug hanging from the centre pole. The old woman and a younger one crouched on either side of a firepit, both barefoot, in black cotton dresses and red embroidered ponchos. As the old woman spoke she rotated an iron pan on the coals, her flat cheek and wide brow sidelit by the sun, her silver hair braided down her back. She poured the pan into his cup. 'Drink,' she said in Spanish. 'Soon comes *la doctora*.'

The fingertips that touched his cheek smelled of jungle, smoke, and gun oil. The man's face was shadowed, only the long bridge of his nose, his thin lips and pointed chin visible. In the open collar of his shirt dangled a silver crucifix. 'What happened to you?'

'Plane crashed.'

'Who shot you?'

'Don't know.'

'Stop lying.'

A second man crouched down, black hair long under a camouflage cap, a white scar up his forehead. Two others standing in the door, rifles, one chewing gum. 'Why were you flying over the jungle?' the scarred one said.

'Taking a friend to Costa Rica.'

'I think you're CIA. Coming back from the raid on Paxtún that killed eighty-four people.'

The men stepped away. When Murphy woke again it was dark. Firelight tossed shadows across the thatched ceiling; green saplings hissed into the flames; the murmur of the river came with a cool musty smell through the door.

The old woman fed him bitter, hot drinks, built the fire till it crackled, her shadow dancing like a garroted man against the thatch. His heavy blankets were sodden with sweat. A glaring eye hissed down and he tried to get away but a strong hand held him. '*Tranquilo, tranquilo!*' a woman said. A lantern was hooked to the beam over his head. Cool hard fingers touched his cheek.

The woman wiped his face with a cold cloth, then cut away the banana leaves and washed around the wound with water smelling of peroxide. 'So you're a soldier.'

'No.' He realized she'd spoken English. 'Who are you?'

'The doctor.' Her voice neared. 'This will hurt, but is necessary.'
She slit open the arm; he groaned as the black blood spurted out.
'Who shot you?'

'I don't know – stop!'

The pain was unbelievable as she dug inside the wound for
splinters and bits of dead flesh. 'Rémito – Pablo!' she called. 'Hold
him!'

The one with the crucifix and the scarred one pinned Murphy
down while she cleaned the arm. 'Who were you meeting,' she
said, 'on the ground?'

'Not here,' he gasped. 'Costa Rica.'

'Don't give me that! You're a *narcotraficante*?'

'I don't care, what happens, on the ground. Oh God *stop*!'

'I'm sorry,' the doctor said. The backs of her fingers brushed
hair from his brow. 'Listen, gringo, I can't stay. I must cut off this
ruined arm and we'll send you downriver to Mexico.'

It surprised him he could move, sit up. 'No.'

She smiled, her face round and brown. 'You can't save it.'

Inch by inch he forced the arm up, made the fingers move. 'I
won't give it up.'

Her clothes rustled as she stood. The hammock rocked, the rush-
mat ceiling sliding back and forth. Across the room she was
speaking to someone – *'Delirante.'* There was a silence, the fire
hissing. Again she spoke. 'But we'll try.'

'Who is he?' Rémito said.

Dona Elena Villalobos rubbed exhaustion from her face, looking
down at the gringo panting with pain and fever. 'Probably flying
grass.'

Rémito snickered. 'Silly games.'

'Even with as much sulfa and bactrin as I've got he might not
live. Seven point six-three calibre, clean through, broken humerus,
but not shattered.'

'If you use the sulfa and bactrin now, one of ours will die later
without them.'

She stepped outside, let her eyes find the stars. 'I don't have
the right to refuse him.'

'You don't have the right to give him *our* antibiotics.'

In the dark she saw Rémito finger his forehead. The scar
worries him, she thought; it interests death. 'How soon can we
get more?'

'Not soon.'

'In five days I've lost two wounded who would've lived had I any place but these dirt-floored huts and water boiled over smoky fires. There's dirt everywhere, the flies feed on wounds while I work on them.' Her voice was gritty with fatigue; there was lethargy in her cells, grime beneath her eyes, an empty ache in her legs. 'Now these *campesinos* with their dying gringo. Did you ever notice, in our churches, all the angels have blue eyes?'

'He's CIA.'

'If he is I suppose you should kill him. But then why is he afraid of the soldiers?'

'Failed them, somehow.'

'He has old shrapnel wounds. In his chest and hip.'

'We should kill him.'

She inhaled the woodsmoke, rotten vegetation, and human ordure smells of the village. 'When I was younger, every odour had such meaning. Now they're just smells.'

Rémito took a deep, weary breath. He caressed her temples, massaged her neck. 'Whatever you do,' he said, 'do it quickly. So we can go. Before the Army gets here.'

6

Every time Lyman came down to Guatemala he hated it. Till he got here. Back Stateside he'd probably hate it again. He watched the rain fall in thick diagonal sheets across the parade ground, rubbed his shoulder where the holster had chafed it. Wet damn heat. Bugs chewing the rotten skin right off you. Worse than the Mekong. Didn't mind wearing this gun then.

Trouble's Nancy. Way she gets on you. In Nam at least there were women. Here what you got but monkeys? In Nam those girls would sell you anything. But Nancy never gave you any space without enlarging hers.

And now Kit Gallagher in a black plastic bag. Just like the old days. Except now it's him. Always said he'd end this way.

Admit it, Lyman thought, you just don't like her fucking other guys. You should be happy Kit's dead. But you're not. *It*'s what's rubbing you. Or you'd be eating it alive, down here. Guns, choppers, fear so thick you can slice it with a knife. Taste it, smell it, spread it on your bread. Fear in the night – the best kind, fear out of every nook and cranny, every crooked little street. Fear keeping everything alive.

This pilot still alive somewhere. Fearing too. Can *feel* him, Lyman realized. Wanting to live bad as I want to kill him. But always have to play 'what if': what if he made the road, at Machaquilá, got a ride somewhere? If he's in Chiapas already, on the MC-DC flight, hungry to tell his story to the world? What would he say? Who'd listen? What if Nancy's doing it right now, while the kids're in school, some guy's number in her mouth?

Forget Nancy. Let her get it off with other guys. If she does you'll dump her when you get back, go outside.

Nothing wrong with outside time. Set up your own deal. Anybody who has to show up five days a week can't call himself free. Can't call himself brave, either: only a coward denies his own needs. I used to tell her that, Nancy. But anybody who

28

has to explain things to his wife certainly isn't free.

The rain hammered into pools flooding the parade ground. With revulsion he went down the steps into the downpour that coated his face like warm syrup and melted instantly into his clothes. How had he forgotten a poncho? Now he'd have to ask Vodega for one – Vodega'd love that: 'Army of Guatemala', made in New Jersey.

He started the Jeep but it wouldn't shift into first, the synchro busted. Nam relics. Ghosts of gook chicks spreading skinny thighs across the back bench, American kids screaming out their shattered guts. Oh the dance of life. He nudged it into second and moved off slowly, the Jeep's bald tyres slithering in the crud. He had to snuff this pilot. When the pilot was dead, he'd break it with Nancy, get his black ass outside.

But Nancy didn't give up that easy. And did he want to, if she hadn't been serving it around? She always told him. One way or another. He flicked on the wipers but the blades were gone, their brackets scraping miserably. Hunched over the steering wheel, he drove one-handed, wiping at the glass.

Murphy sat in early sunlight beside a red achiote bush, his back against a warm adobe wall, cradling his splinted arm against his chest. Yellow chicks pecked at the dirt by his feet while the mother hen paced nearby. A little girl crawled into his lap, avoiding his arm, her long mahogany hair tickling his face. She tore bits of squash leaf and tossed them to the chicks, who scurried for them then spat them out. 'They're not hungry,' he said.

'Want corn.'

'Give them corn, then, Ofélia.'

'No corn.'

He nodded up at the cornfield on the slope above the village. The stalks were brown. 'Where's that corn?'

'They kill.'

'Who?'

'The first people come from corn.' She got up and moved away. The sun's heat danced between the huts. When I was young, he thought, I'd knock down a willow stem without thinking. Now every thing seems holy.

The old woman carried her blue plastic bucket up from the *Río* and filled his tin cup. From the hut she brought a lime and squeezed it into the cup. 'Keep drinking water.'

Towering clouds blocked the sun. Murphy stooped into the hut.

29

His arm throbbed; he moved it at the elbow. The pain was severe yet good. It was as if someone else wiggled his fingers. The old woman scraped *frijoles* from a *guacal*, warmed them in a pan on the fire, spooned them into his dish.

'I'm not hungry, Consuela.'

'How can you not be hungry?'

'What happened to the corn?'

'The Army poisoned it, and the beans and the rice in the *aguada* by the river.'

'That's crazy! Why kill the corn?'

'To make us move to the camps where you live inside hot wire, and if you try to leave they shoot you.'

'And if you don't go to the camps?'

'Sooner or later they kill you too, just like the corn.'

A noncom brought coffee. Carusi, the general's adjutant, clicked a pencil against his thumbnail. Vodega smiled steadily. General Arena had a cold and kept blowing his nose into a soggy Kleenex. Under the table Lyman wiped his palm against his thigh to cleanse it of the general's handshake.

'It's been a week and you haven't found the pilot,' Lyman said. 'Shall I remind you he killed our man on loan to you?'

'He wasn't on *loan* to us.' Arena tasted his coffee, wiped his mouth with his great dark paw.

'Shall I mention what this does in DC? You *do* read American papers occasionally? You *want* these jerks in Congress to smash us?'

Arena had a tiny, merry smile. 'Whether you get smashed or not has nothing to do with me.'

Outside the window, Lyman saw, the rain had stopped. 'Imagine, General, where that leaves *you*. When we thought some day you might replace Mejía Victores.'

'We have *your* democracy now. You can't just put me in or take Mejía Victores out, like in the old days. We have an "elected" president, same as you.'

'I mean Chief of the Armed Forces, General. The guy who runs things. To bring a little stability to this place—'

'Please don't lie so badly, Colonel, it's disrespectful. Stability's the last thing you want here. And please don't doubt the effort we've made to find this pilot—'

'I doubt everything, most of the time. Especially down here.'

'That's your job,' Vodega said, 'to doubt things. We don't mind.

We help you all we can.'

'So then help me by reconsidering the contributions thing, as Gallagher asked you. And don't be so goddamned territorial about the Colombians – we work with them – they're good people.'

'Your version of good and ours aren't necessarily the same.' Arena blew his nose, loudly. 'And, regarding this pilot – why do you want him so bad?'

'If ever once we leave a death unanswered, General, the whole thing begins to unravel. You know that.'

Arena wadded the Kleenex and put it back in his pocket. 'Then you'll be pleased to know that a few minutes ago I have word, one of our infantry sweeps, near Sayaxché, they turn up an old man who has sold corn to an Indian from Río de la Pasión. This Indian told the old man there's a gringo in his camp.'

Lyman jumped up, slammed his chair against the table. 'Then what are we doing *here*? Get the choppers, for Christ's sake! Are you people crazy?'

The general raised his hand. 'Moderation, my dear friend! No one knows where he was from, this Indian. The *Río*'s two hundred kilometres long, thousands of streams coming in . . .'

'This guy, who sold the corn—'

'He's not wanting to explain. So it takes a little while. But we cover every way out, Colonel. My men, they are hitting every part of that river, anywhere some Indian shoved aside the bugs and snakes to build his filthy little hut. If your pilot's on the *Río*, no way he gets out.'

'I remember other people,' Lyman said, 'being so sure of things. I had a CO in Vietnam, once, he was so sure he'd cleaned out a valley he got himself and half a platoon killed. I'm glad the gooks got him. Otherwise I would have.' He looked at Vodega. 'At least we should be up there, Sayaxché, somewhere . . .'

'That's in hand,' Arena sniffed. 'The next chopper north, you two are on it.'

Consuela ducked into the hut, her hair and poncho streaming rain. 'Placido's brought corn!'

Murphy stood, wrapped his blankets round his shoulders, bent to glance beneath the dripping lintel at the charcoal sky battering the earth with rain – the huddled huts, dishevelled path, and bent-down jungle drowned in grey-green aqueous light.

'I'll make tortillas,' Consuela said. 'There'll be food when the father comes.' From under her hammock she took a wooden

31

mortar and pestle, untied the sack of corn, poured some into the mortar, and handed him the pestle. 'You do it.'

He held the pestle under his left arm and began to twist it with his left hand into the corn in the mortar. 'Not like that!' she chided, 'keep it closer.' Gripping the pestle against her flat old chest she used the forward rocking motion of her body to crunch the corn down. 'This you can do, with just the good hand.'

He tried it, twisting the heavy pestle down into the kernels that popped back up the mortar's worn silvery sides only to fall under the pestle again. 'What does it mean, what Ofélia says – that the first people came from corn?'

'Not *the* first. Here, shove the pestle down and out. Push with your weight, not against it. In the beginning, the Creators wanted to have someone to thank them. They asked Coyote how to make people, and she said make them from earth. But these earth people weren't strong, they melted in the rain. No!' Consuela scolded. 'Can't you see you're pushing too hard?'

'I'm crushing the corn—'

'Not too much! So Coyote told the Creators to make people from wood, and *they* will praise you. The Creators whittled people from sapwood, and these wood people made many children and covered the earth.'

With his left hand Murphy moved his splinted right arm to hold the pestle. 'Don't use that hand!' Consuela snapped.

'This makes it stronger.'

'But then the Creators find these wood people have no hearts, no spirits. They do not remember the Heart of Heaven. They do not praise the Creators. "*De acuerdo!*" say the Creators, and bring down a black rain of flaming pitch to destroy the people of wood. This time, Coyote tells the Creators to make people from the corn.'

The rain was gone. Outside the door the village hunched stained and dripping under a slaty sky. Water splattered from the thatch and bled in ochre ribbons into the *Río*. 'Do the Creators think that the people of corn have hearts and spirits?'

'Not enough.' Consuela sat back on her heels. 'We suffer because we don't care about God. We do not praise the creation of life.'

Across the river the far dark shore loomed out of the mist. A tiger heron screamed, but he could not see it.

7

'I got already three House committees, two Senate committees, special prosecutors, all that shit, journalists, everybody, up my back.' Curt Merck's Slovac accent was burlesqued by the squawk box. 'And now you can't even find this guy what did Gallagher.'

'I'll find him, Curt. But we cut a deal.'

'Deal? The deal is you *find* him.'

'After I get him I go outside. With no recriminations. No callbacks.'

'After this you work the basement. In the library. You can cut the grass.'

'I didn't screw this op, Curt. It was screwed long before.'

'It's your ass now.'

Lyman checked his watch. The round clock on the signal room's yellow wall said two-thirteen – nine minutes slow. 'In eight minutes I jump the slick to Sayaxché—'

'You think this time you got the pilot tracked up?'

'Tracked down, Curt?'

'Up or down, just get him!'

'We got ten, maybe twelve villages to check. Off the Río de la Pasión, the Santa Amelia.'

'I don't need to know where, Howie. Just don't be visible.'

'You can't even *see* me in the jungle. Long's I don't smile.'

'You're never happy enough to smile. Make sure, this pilot.'

Lyman shook his fourth Marlboro of the day from its pack. 'I'm nobody's keeper, Curt. Not even yours.'

Consuela mixed the corn flour with lime and water and broke the dough into chunks she flattened between her palms, flipping one piece at a time on to a flat tin sheet on the coals. The tortillas as they cooked smelled like cornbread and caramel; he sat beside her, watching the pale yellow turn brown, swallowing saliva and clenching his hands.

When the first four were done she shoved them at him and started four more. He gave her two back. 'If I weren't here,' he said, 'you could eat them all.'

The hot rich tortilla flavour choked him. Unable to stop he swallowed the second, tried to stand but the room spun, making him sick.

She finished the new ones and gave him two. 'We'll save the rest for tonight.'

Clutching the two new tortillas he stooped under the lintel and went down to drink from the *Río*. A girl was gutting catfish to hang over a rack of saplings. *'Hola!* – it's you, *Guapo?'*

'Don't call me *Guapo.'*

'But you are!'

'How can you tell?' he teased.

She felt in her basket for another catfish, slit its belly and pulled out its blue-red intestines. 'Besides, Consuela calls you that.'

'How'd you know it was me?'

'You walk like a tapir – thump, thump, thump.'

'It's just the new sandals Danielo made me. They're loose.'

The tortillas were warm in his hand. I need them, he thought. Every family got the same. 'Did you get corn, Epifanía?'

'Yes.'

'Did you make tortillas?'

'My little brother's sick. We're saving it for him.'

'You'll get sick, too, you don't eat.'

She smiled. 'There's the fish.'

'That's Jesús's catch from yesterday – it's for the whole village.' The two tortillas were beautiful in his hand; never had there been anything so complete. Her face came up, lips parting as she smelled them.

'Here,' he said, 'I can't eat more.' She took them, fingers running over their edges, ate one and tucked the other into her dress. 'Is that for later?' he said, thinking maybe she wasn't hungry – he could have it back.

'It's for my little brother.'

'We've kept out some of the corn, to plant tomorrow.'

'Soon as it's tall I'll be able to see again.'

'Don't joke, Epifanía!'

'I *will*! I haven't always been blind. Only since the corn died.'

Beneath the Huey's open cargo door the jungle seemed to roll to the ends of the earth, the river down its middle like a great silver

34

tree of many branches. Even at three thousand feet the smells of jungle growth and decay and wet heat were stifling. Sun glittered on the treetops that each seemed to cup a sparkling bead of water in every leaf. A string of diamonds broke from the river and Lyman saw it was a flock of white birds the chopper had scared up.

The chopper's chattering thud thud thud thud shivered its bent, stained khaki aluminium against its missing rivets. Beside his hand on the door frame was an ancient yellow decal: 'Do Not Mount Machine Gun This Side.' Overhead the rotor shaft shimmied and wailed against the Jesus nut bolting it to the engine housing – you could go crazy waiting for it to snap, that bolt, Lyman remembered – how many had popped in Nam? When the rotors suddenly flew off and the ship dropped like a stone. Funny if that happened to him now, after all these years . . .

Steep palisades jutted black and treeless from the green jungle. Maybe they'd put the dam here – place with the biggest topographic drop, the Corps had said, with the biggest potential head. No, AID had told them, put it where it floods the most, drives these people out.

Vodega was crouched like a bat in the side door, bony shoulders tensed up around his neck, the machine gunner in a black T-shirt standing over him like a bulldog on a chain. Five soldiers sat bored in a clump on the vibrating cargo deck, one chewing on a cigarette he did not light. Sunlight through the rotor blades fluttered on their blunt, impassive faces.

Dona Villalobos shook herself awake, leaned over the dugout's side to wash her face. Rémito gunned the motor and ran the dugout up the bank. She found the gringo sleeping when she reached Consuela's hut. Such innocent faces they had, these gringos. She shook him. 'Time to go!'

He sat up instantly. 'Where?'

'Mexico. The Army's looking for you, checking the villages.' She gripped his hand. 'Press my palm with one finger at a time – I want to see how strong you are.'

Her hand was hard and smooth, cool. He pressed as strongly as he could, pleased when she winced. 'I can hide in the jungle,' he said.

'Too dangerous.' Quickly she unwrapped the splint, peeled back the dressings. 'It's amazing, how you don't infect.' From a US Special Forces pack she took a pair of scissor forceps, cut the black stitches sprouting like thick hairs from the bullet wound, and pulled them out of the pink, mottled flesh. 'If they find you they'll kill everybody. What's your word for it – "counterinsurgency?" – for shooting the men and women and driving the kids and old people off to the camps?'

'That's not *my* word.'

'What *is* your word for it, then? What your country does to mine?'

'I don't give a damn about words! You're fools, all of you! On either side. On *any* side.' He stood up, wanting to cut off the aching arm, lose it for ever. 'It's all the same, can't you *see*? Nobody's noble, least of all you.'

'You don't believe in war?'

'No.'

'Where did you get them, then, the shrapnel wounds? From loving peace?'

'You don't have—'

'I couldn't help seeing them. I was healing you, remember?'

'And I'll always be grateful to you.' The sun brightening her black hair made his heart plunge. Didn't she see *she'd* die too? And how senseless that was? Already he could see right through her thin envelope of skin, the nerves pulsing red and green tracers round the armature of her skull. 'I was a helicopter pilot, in Vietnam. I took out the dead and wounded. And brought the new ones in.'

'To do your killing for you.'

'A lot of them came right back, dead.'

'I was sure you'd die. I don't know why I gave you bactrin – it was a lost cause.'

'Some way I'll repay you.'

'I had no choice. I'm not allowed to turn you down.'

'By whose law?' He stepped into the warm breeze off the river. See everything in light of the eternal. Egret winging upriver above its own reflection, white cumulus in blue sky over green jungle, the light through strands of her black hair. What a lion must see, stalking through tall grass. She was so small and light-limbed, animated by a strange consistency. He could see through her, how no one can be replaced, should ever be forgotten.

'Is that what God is, for you?' he asked. 'The one who can't forget?'

'Someone's coming for you. In two days you'll be past Sayaxché, in three days Mexico. If you're caught you'll be tortured unspeakably, and when you tell them about this village everyone here will be killed, and everyone else who's helped you. When you cross the Usumacinta have this cast changed and the wound checked at Bonampak – the clinic there's used to Guatemalan wounds.'

'If I get caught I'll make something up, how I lived in the jungle.'

'They'll want to know who made this cast—'

'I did. I was a medevac.'

'Eventually you'll tell the truth. They always know. It's then they kill you.'

'It's crazy, what you do. You just make things worse.'

'For you?'

'*No!* For you, and everyone else.'

'Don't you see it's not enough, just to live your own life?' Strangely, she took his hand. 'Once I wanted to be a brain surgeon. I wanted to understand the mystery of thought, the genesis of life. And I wanted to live a good life. But soon I realized too many people were in pain or dying for the lack of the simplest medical necessities. That I couldn't turn my back on them. That living a good life means doing as much good as you can.'

'We all have altruistic reasons for what we do.'

'What are the altruistic reasons for what you do?' She stepped into the dugout, yanked the cord; the motor stuttered and caught. The man with the scarred forehead came down the bank, slipped his rifle over one shoulder and climbed into the bow. She revved the motor and the dugout pulled away, its wake still lapping at the mangrove roots after its noise faded round a bend in the river.

Conchita, Placido's granddaughter, was scrubbing clothes against the river stones and hanging them like multicoloured parrots on the streamside branches. 'She says you are better, *Guapo*? The *doctora*?'

'She's angry I'm getting better.'

'Don't mind her. It makes her sad so many people have been killed.'

'I told her to stop fighting.'

'She doesn't fight, that one. Anyway, it doesn't matter whether you fight or not. The Army still kills you.'

He sat next to Conchita beside the clear, soft-rustling water. What could he really do? If he was tortured, what could he forget? The *Río* rolled past on its way to the sea, and he saw how the rain made it and it made the sea and the sea made the rain, and they were all the same, each thing a symbol for every thing, and how to harm one thing was to harm all. The many-fingered

37

leaves of the *quiebrahacha* drew their mantilla of shadows across his shoulders; a fish leaped, momentarily mirrored.

A change in the wind brought village smells – smouldering fires, drying thatch, ordure, mud. He thought he heard a chopper and tensed to grab Conchita, but it was a bee, bumbling in a flower. He remembered cars, noise, buildings, money, television, city crowds. How could I live like that? he wondered.

Conchita finished her clothes and walked up to the village. Jesús the son of the widow Sonora came down, took a piece of dried catfish, and crumbled it into a bottle. He waded into the *Río*, filled the bottle with water, and laid it on the bottom. Minnows crowded the bottle's mouth, darting one by one inside where they twirled among sparkling catfish scales. Against the far shore a heron flapped upriver, wingtipping the water. A flock of snowy egrets settled in the shore branches, their white reflections rippling among white water lilies. Jesús took the bottle full of minnows and set it upright in his mother's canoe and poled out beyond the shallows, a dark form against the river's verdant sheen as he baited hooks with the minnows and cast them out. A kingfisher cried as it skimmed the surface and looped up into the cobalt sky. Jesús tugged a line and drew in a bright, writhing fish.

8

Fog alone and complete, from the edge of his skin to the ends of the world, cool damp encompassing fog.

In the centre it grew darker. A shape, a *lancha*, the pillar of a man with a pole. Gold against the grey as the fog thinned.

The *lancha* slid into shore and the man drove it high up the bank with a final thrust of his pole. A hawk-eagle cried, and Murphy wondered what it must be seeing, high over the grey jungle and the fog thick down the low broad belly of the river. The man stowed his pole, shouldered a small pack and stepped on to the bank. 'So,' he said in English, 'you're already waiting for me.'

'*Como?*' Murphy stood, thinking should I run back through the village, he'll have no angle to shoot, don't run along the river, there must be others – where are they? '*No entiendo—*'

'You speak Spanish?' The man stuck out a hand. 'I'm Father Miguel. The one taking you downriver.'

'Now?'

'No, no,' the priest chuckled. 'After dark.' He leaned back, hands in his pockets. 'So you're the guy who crossed a hundred kilometres of impossible jungle, barefoot, with a broken arm . . .'

'Seems long ago.'

'What did you think of? What kept you going?'

'Nothing. It sounds funny, but nothing kept me going.'

'Nothing doesn't exist.' Ofélia came running to him and the priest swung her into his arms. 'How is my *florita de Pascua*?' he laughed, bundling her against his shoulder. 'By its name,' he said to Murphy, 'it cannot.'

The fog was thinning. 'The Army's coming,' Murphy said.

'That's why we wait till dark.'

'I won't have you risk it, just for me.'

'I'm not.' The priest swung Ofélia on to his shoulders and

walked up into the village, the children flocking round his legs, the women running to hug and kiss him.

Dusk fell. Clouds of swallows skimmed the river; voices and fire-glimmer reflected over its sleek, darkening surface. Monkeys hooted; doves chanted and nighthawks cried.

Murphy climbed the bank and wandered through San Tomás, trying to see it all for the last time, the huts with fires glowing now through cracks in their thatch, the chatter of children inside, the odours of corn flour, tortillas, chillies, squash, dried fish, rotten vegetation, mud, the crouching jungle, the dirt between his toes.

Ofélia's father Manolo sat by the door of his hut cleaning a black powder shotgun, a gourd drum on the ground beside him. 'It's a shame you're going, *yanqui*. I'd have taken you hunting tonight, for *el tigre!*'

'What good am I with one arm, hunting for *el tigre*?'

'I need somebody to play this, to make *el tigre* come, while I sit in a tree to shoot him.' Manolo held the gourd in his lap, the deerskin cover facing up, reached inside it and pulled his pinched fingers down a plaited twine of burro hair which, covered with beeswax, made a deep, reverberating growl. 'See, it is something you can do one-handed.'

'And that makes the jaguar come?'

'When he hears this growling sound, he is very angry and comes to see what new jaguar is roaring in his jungle.'

'And in the dark you shoot him.'

'*Claro que sí!*'

'And if you miss he eats me?'

'Powder's too dear. I can't afford to miss.'

'And then you sell him?'

'I sell his skin in Sayaxché. The *yanqui* tourists in Tikal will always buy it.'

'They're not all gone, *los tigres*?'

'For two years I do not see a track. Then since you came this one's been near. He's very rare, a black one. Like you, out of the east. Last night he slept in an *aquada*, a mangrove swamp where last year I kill a tapir. Tonight after the ceremony I go and call him. Then we'll have money for more seeds – black skins are the most valuable.'

'How do you know he's black?'

'Black jaguars leave black hairs. Did you ever see one, when you were wandering in the jungle?'

'I saw nothing.' Murphy's arm was hurting, and he stood, to move around. 'It's dirty, your gun.'

'I keep it buried, like the Bible, so the soldiers don't find it. Wrapped in deerhide, with a plug of coconut in the muzzle.'

'They could come tonight, the soldiers.'

Manolo glanced out at the fog coating the river and slinking up between the huts. 'They come only in clear weather.'

Murphy massaged his arm above the wound, driving the ache back down. 'What does the Army care about the Bible?'

'You see that yellow flower? In our language it is *'estapu* – very pretty. But in Spanish it is *flor de muerte*. Christ says to love and help each other. Why would the Army want us to do that?'

The amphibious craft crossed the *Río* towards Sayaxché, its flat bow throwing up a broad wake that sparkled in the town's lights. The bow dropped with a muddy splash and two columns of men jogged up the bank, guns and packs clanking. Lyman's palms itched; pulse darted down his wrists like lightning. '*Usted!*' he shouted, grabbing a soldier.

'*Sí!*' the soldier yelled, startled, saluting. He peered at Lyman out of the dark. '*Sí, Coronel!*'

Lyman snatched the man's Galil. 'Where's your goddamned bayonet?'

'Here, sir!' The man slapped his belt.

'Mount it!'

'Now, sir?'

'Goddamn it, yes! We're going into battle!' He spun round, glared at the others. 'All of you, mount bayonets!'

'There's still the flight upriver,' Vodega said.

Lyman glanced towards the voice, saw Vodega's slender form on the dark side, by some upturned *lanchas*. He wondered what Vodega had been doing there. 'The men should be pumped. I want them hungry!'

'In your ardour, Colonel, don't forget they aren't your men, they're mine.'

'I pay for them. I pay for you too.'

'I pay my own way. Guatemala pays its own way—'

'By cornering the weed market? That's how your Army pays its way?'

'That's why Gallagher was here – that's what got him into trouble. Isn't it? Lieutenant!' Vodega called. 'Tell the men to dismount bayonets.' His voice swung back to Lyman. 'I don't want bayonets mounted in my helicopters.'

'*Your* helicopters? Shit!' Lyman turned away, boots slithering in the riverside crud.

José, Epifanía's father, had set up an altar of lashed saplings at one end of his palm-thatched shed which stood between the village and the *Río*. On the altar an earthen bowl sat between two candles on a white cloth; in the bowl were three tortillas. Stars gleamed through holes in the palm fronds. 'We're here to celebrate,' said Father Miguel, 'the life of he who was willing to give what is complete in him for what is missing in us.'

Some of the people murmured; a sense of agreement seemed to ripple through them. 'You have been gifted by a visitor to whom you gave the gift of life. Now he leaves but you live within him as he in you, although you may both forget this. Just as when he travelled injured through the jungle he says that nothing was with him, and does not remember. This is true of us all: we do not remember the gift of life—'

Murphy walked down to the river where stars rippled among the black grass stalks and the wide ebony water mirrored the pulse of the universe. It would not come back. Only pieces – a scrap of terror, lash of branches, bare foot torn and bloody, the pounding asphyxiation down inside the *cenote*, the hunger, snakes, the Mayan scorpion that became a Huey with his own dead co-pilot still belted in, a black widow nesting in his cratered skull.

Had there been a feeling? After the first day, something balancing the pain? A waiting? A willingness to suffer? For what?

Genetic. The ones without fear of death were selected out long ago, he thought. The longer we survive the stronger is the urge for life.

'This is the body of Christ.' The priest's voice was like the river. 'The lamb of God who takes away the sins of the world—'

After so many years, Murphy realized, it comes right back: the cold stone church floor against your kneecaps, wind sneaking like a cat under the door, stained windows patched with packing tape. Then door to door, the canvas bag of newspapers biting into your shoulder, snow like broken glass crunching underfoot, dawn turning purple over the black plains. But back then you thought God could take away your sins.

Now you're trying to bring yourself back inside. Like a reformed druggie teasing himself with the needle. A family man hungry for a hooker. Back inside the reason that has no meaning but the one *you* give it. But for you there's no reason at all.

The people gathered round the priest and he gave them each a chunk of tortilla. 'The body of Christ,' he said.

'*El cuerpo de Cristo*.' It was Erendria, the old woman, a great-grandmother whose men all were dead. Then Placido, who'd brought corn, who every evening gathered the children on the river bank to write Spanish words in the mud with pointed sticks. Then the children, ones who had sat beside Murphy in his pain and solitude, sung him scraps of song, told stories in Quiché, brought him limes and bits of melon saved out from their food. It seemed right to do it, silly as it was, and he waited in line behind Conchita, thinking that even her name meant little Immaculate Conception, she whose glossy black hair came up to his splinted arm; she bent and took her bit of tortilla and moved aside, and the priest held up a tan chunk of tortilla and said *el cuerpo de Cristo* and he answered *Amen*, remembering *amen* means *it is true*.

The piece of tortilla came down in the priest's fingers and as he took it into his mouth he understood, and remembered that he'd understood before, that this *is* the body of Christ, that a chunk of corn flour in the skinny fingers of a priest becomes the son of God who gives himself to us so we can become a tiny bit more like him. Crossing himself he turned away, anxious to be alone.

In the north was distant thunder. Rain tonight, Murphy thought. We'll get wet, going downriver. But the thunder was familiar, wrong. 'Choppers!' he screamed. 'The Army! Soldiers!'

They clattered down over the treetops and settled on the new-sown corn, black scorpions with long black M60D stingers, jet engines wailing, flares sizzling down on little parachutes out of the night. 'Get away!' the priest screamed at him. 'If they see us they'll kill everyone!'

Soldiers running along the bank. In the flarelight Epifanía's fish rack tumbling. The priest shoved Murphy ahead of him, down to the *Río* and along its banks, boughs lashing their faces, the clatter of rotors and their huffing breath and the splash of their feet loud in the flare-bright night. They circled the village on the jungle edge. Another chopper roared over, frothing the river and

battering down the mangroves. Under the glaring flares the soldiers circled, driving the people before them.

9

Three choppers had landed; one circled. The soldiers drove every-one to the centre by Manolo's hut. A small, slender officer was taking the people aside one by one and asking them something to which they all seemed to answer no. A soldier came out of Manolo's hut holding up the old shotgun. The small officer took out his pistol; Manolo shook his head, pointed at the jungle. Two soldiers tied him to a tree. The officer stepped back among the huts and spoke with another, much taller, black, who leaned over to hear, cupping his hand over his ear against the choppers' roar. Rotor wash knocked off his fatigue cap and he ran after it, came back banging it against his knee.

Ofélia ran to Manolo and he shoved her away. The small officer was yelling questions at Manolo and smacking him with the pistol each time he answered. Ofélia clung to Manolo's leg; the officer bent and spoke to her, patted her head, motioned her back. 'Even if they kill him,' the priest said to Murphy, 'do nothing.'

The officer pointed at Placido and the soldiers tied him beside Manolo. Consuela knelt before the officer, her hands clasped, speaking up to him. 'They'll shoot these two,' Father Miguel said. 'You must do nothing, or they'll kill them all.'

There were forty soldiers, maybe, plus the chopper still circling, and no way to crawl closer without being seen. Guns snapped; Manolo and Placido jerked back against the tree and slumped, Manolo's heels digging the dirt as if still trying to escape death. Flames climbed the side of Manolo's hut.

Sonora shoved Jesús through the circle of soldiers; they ran after her and knocked her down, two holding her wrists and two her ankles apart as another unclasped his belt and fell on top of her, keeping his face above her snapping teeth till another thumped her with his rifle and she lay still. Jesús ran back at them; they knocked him to the ground and tossed him over the bank, his body slapping down into the shallows. Two soldiers cut

45

Manolo and Placido from the tree and threw them into the burning hut; laughing, one wiped bloody hands on the other's back. The man on top of Sonora stood buckling his trousers and another replaced him.

'Stay here!' the priest whispered. He darted along the bank past Epifanía's fish racks, snatched up Jesús and ran back. 'Take him downriver to the first rocks and hide him in the mangroves!' Whimpering, the boy tried to squirm free. 'God keeps you!' the priest said. 'Go!'

Murphy carried Jesús along the river in the shadow of the bank, then waist-deep around the mangrove roots, searchlights skipping over the water. A rifle chattered and he thrust the boy under; nothing hit near them. Where Conchita had been washing clothes he shoved the boy into a crevice in the rocks. '*Stay* here!' He ran back upriver to the edge of the village.

He could not see the priest. Soldiers were pulling Conchita towards a hut but she broke free and sprinted across the dead corn toward the trees, her hair sailing out behind her, the stubble spurting with bullets as the flying chopper closed in. She sprawled but leaped up again, scrambled back towards the village, the chopper tilting to fire straight down but she zigzagged again for the jungle, a chain of bullets racing after her, and as she reached the first trees they hammered her down, her limbs tumbling, her red cape windblown in the chopper's wake. Guns thundered, the people screaming; Murphy ran across the cornfield, smashed into a soldier and grabbed his gun but the gun wouldn't fire and he bayoneted the man in the groin then the belly, lunged at another, tripping him with the bayonet then jabbing it into his throat but it stuck in his vertebrae and he couldn't pull it out; an M60 brayed, its roar smashing his ears; he grabbed the second soldier's rifle and fired at the M60; bullets hit beside him, shuddering the earth, spinning the bayoneted soldier. Soldiers were beating someone with rifles, forcing him into a chopper; Murphy saw it was the priest and ran after them. A white light tore into his skull and the ground came up and smacked his face but he rolled up and sprinted for the chopper, soldiers yelling and tackling him; the chopper took off; its lights caught him as he dashed through bright humming whistling bullets towards the village where Consuela crawled sideways dragging pink intestines, Ofélia's bludgeoned body lay in the flames, her hair sizzling, Erendria sat with her broken head clasped in both hands, Epifanía stumbled in circles, wailing; with the empty rifle he clubbed down a soldier, grabbed

46

Epifanía and ran for the jungle, bullets riddling branches, splintering holes through black-white trees; he tripped light-blinded over vines, bodies, stones, dived into the river and swam out beyond the lights, holding Epifanía in the crook of his broken arm.

He reached the rocks. 'Jesús!' he whispered; there was no answer.

Epifanía clung to him. 'Make them stop!' she screamed. 'Make them stop!'

Rifle staccato erupted in the village, faded into the snapping, crackling flames. Another chopper took off, the hum of its rotors deepening as the pilot changed their pitch. 'Jesús!' Murphy whispered.

The fireglow above the trees made the river darker. He hid the girl in the rocks, swam downriver, called, went further, called again. He went ashore and ran back to the rocks, trying not to slosh. As he reached the rocks soldiers came wading downriver, their lights flashing. He ran up the bank; someone leaped, knocking him down, pummelling fists, kicking. 'Jesús!' Murphy grunted. 'It's me!'

He led Epifanía and Jesús back through the mangroves, his shins and ankles banging on their roots, the mud underfoot cold, mushy, and tangled with rootlets. Epifanía bumped into Murphy and pushed ahead, moving faster than he through the darkness, waiting for him and Jesús where the mangroves thinned and they scrambled through saplings where he could see nothing, not even the branches before his face, tried to stand but other branches held him down, their leaves hissing as he forced them aside.

A flashlight glinted on the trees, neared, died. Murphy forced the children under a fallen trunk. A stick snapped against his leg; he reached for it and felt a snake's tail, rattles, the snake's head pinned under his knee.

'What's that?' a voice said.

'It's you, pissing your pants,' another snickered, hoarser.

Murphy pushed his knee down harder on the snake's head. 'Ain't nothing here,' the first voice said.

'That's why *we're* here.' A match rasped and flared.

'Disgusting,' said the first voice.

'More decorations for the *capitán*.'

Murphy felt left-handed down the snake's writhing body to its tail and snapped the rattles. 'Sickens me,' the first repeated. There was the smell of marijuana smoke, a sigh, the spatter of urine. Murphy slid his hand up the snake to its neck. Beyond the downed trunk a cigarette glimmered in a cupped hand, disclosing a sloped, big-nosed face.

Murphy gripped the snake's neck behind the wing-shaped bones of its skull and twisted. 'What *is* that?' the hoarse one said. The flashlight clicked on, its beam darting under the downed tree, boots crunching nearer. Epifanía tensed. Murphy tossed the snake over the trunk. 'Aiee, *serpiente*!' yelled the hoarse one. Murphy pushed the children further along the trunk.

'Who's that?' someone said, in front of them.

'Snake,' repeated the hoarse one. 'I've got him.'

Murphy led the children from the downed tree, behind them the soldiers' laughter and the thump of boots stomping the snake. Tendrils and vines dragged at the children's clothes; twigs and dead leaves rattled as small animals fled through the scrub. 'That you, Mico?' a new voice said.

'I'm here,' a gravelly one answered.

'Then what the hell's that?'

Murphy eased forward one foot, rustling a twig. A leaf snapped. He raised the foot, bumped a liana, sidestepped it. A tree was there; he leaned back and moved further right. Epifanía's hair caught on a thorn bush; the leaves rasped as she tried to free it. Murphy reached behind her and, holding the thorns, pulled her hair away. 'You're going the wrong way, Mico,' the gravelly voice continued.

'I'm over here, asshole! That's snakes you're hearing. Shine your light on them!'

Light shimmered through walls of vines, stems, trunks, and leaves, did not touch them. The gravelly voice and the one called Mico moved past. Murphy and Jesús followed the girl in a wide circle behind the village and upriver. Another chopper rose from the village and fluttered away, its throb fading. From time to time rifles fired like lone firecrackers long after a celebration has ended. The blind girl moved steadily, as if she could see through the jungle night, Jesús behind her, then Murphy with one hand held before his eyes to ward off branches.

10

Each time the Huey banked the priest's blood ran in streaks across the rattling deck; Lyman tried not to step in it. The scent up out of the jungle was like orchids, sharper than the jet kero vapour from the leaking fuel line or the charred cordite of the M60D.

The priest lay with his cheekbone crushed, his nose bent to one side, ripped open. His collarbone looked broken, too, one arm dislocated at the elbow and shoulder. The wrist was bent, too – clearly broken. Lucky for him, Lyman thought, that I was there to save him.

With his boot Vodega poked the priest's broken mouth. The priest pulled back his head; Vodega kicked him.

'Let it be,' Lyman said.

In the weird downcast shadows of the crew light Vodega's muddy, bloody smile seemed painted on, a mask. His boot squelched into the priest's face.

'Come on, Angelo, let him be—'

'It's between him and me,' Vodega said in English. 'He wants it – reliving the passion of our Lord . . .'

Lyman spat out the cargo door, the wind snatching it. The guy who'd run across the field, back there, he wondered – what if he wasn't a *guerrillero* like these goons think? What if he's the American – the one who killed Gallagher? And we let him get away—

The priest will know. Once we get him in the confessional the priest will want to tell us. And these goons were going to kill him.

He leaned along the safety strap to the M60D, slipped his hands into its grips. They felt good and tight against his palms, his fingers strong around them. He pointed down and squeezed a burst at the river, the muzzle leaping, red tracers diving fast into the jungle. He lowered the muzzle more and fired again, digging a row of black geysers up the moonlit water. 'Don't,' the door gunner said. 'Bullets are for people.'

49

Epifanía led them back to the *Río* then upriver in the shallows. A low moon bled across the water, fell behind the hills. Birds twittered, began to chant. The river brightened from mercury to silver as the stars died.

Over the din of monkeys, birds, and insects, there came no sound of choppers. Jesús led now, Murphy last. An alligator slapped its tail on the bank and dived past him, clawing his thigh. The far shore took form out of the darkness, till every leaning bough and tall crown stood clear above its jade reflection.

Over their splashing footfalls he listened for choppers. If the soldiers had come for *you* then *you* caused it, he told himself. Or if they *saw* you. But they didn't see you till after they started shooting. What if you'd just gone forward, surrendered? Would they have killed them then? But maybe they came for the priest, and it wasn't your fault. Except the priest came to take *you* downriver.

If you'd gone out to them right away, maybe they wouldn't have killed everyone. Except the priest told you not to. You figured he knew more than you so you did what he said. Maybe he was just covering for you. But you took him at his word.

Mist was rising off the river like smoke from flowing lava. The treetops of the far shore floated on a band of white, then were gone.

No matter what, they were looking *for* you. That's why they trashed everyone. So it's *you*.

An eagle whistled, far and faint behind them. The children stopped, spun round, Epifanía holding up her hand.

It came again, up the dark channel of mist. Jesús tilted back his head and screeched, the high bitter cry of an eagle, and the other answered.

'He's coming,' Epifanía said. 'He hears you.'

It was a dugout with an old man in the stern who jabbed his pole into the mud to stop. He spoke in Kekchi to the children and they answered simply, without emotion.

'He'll take us upriver,' Jesús said.

Murphy held the gunnel for the children to climb in. 'Tell him I'm going back.'

Jesús told the old man and he shook his head, clamped a hand round Murphy's wrist. 'It's no good,' Jesús said. 'He's been to the village. Everyone's dead.'

'Except the priest,' Murphy said. 'Tell him they took the priest.'

Jesús told the old man, who did not answer, steadying the dugout with his pole while Murphy climbed in and sat in the bow. The old man backed the dugout from shore and turned upriver, poling along the shallows.

Mist rose around them. The mangroves of the near shore faded. The air was thick and white. Water rippled past the hull, up and down the old man's pole. The canoe's prow grew hazy, vanished, the thwart and Murphy's hand atop it indistinct.

'Epifanía?' he said.

'*Sí?*'

'What did the little soldier ask everyone, at the start?'

'He was asking if they had seen you. They all said no.'

Dona Elena Villalobos snuggled down into her warm blanket, the hammock swaying gently. She raised her feet to swing the bottom of her tarp back under the blanket. The Galil lay beside her, its clip facing away, its barrel warm from her body.

Red sun streaked through the high, vaulting boughs. A drop of dew spiralled down layered beams of sunlight and hit her nose, spattering on her lip. She licked it, rubbed her nose against the blanket. How lovely to lie for a moment warm and peaceful, in the first magnificence of day.

11

Beyond the prow a dark line cut the mist. The water turned pewter, molten; the dark line was the shore, tangled mangroves, sun bronzing their leaves. The sky turned blue; sun beat on the water. The old man poled the dugout up a narrow creek, leaves lashing their faces. When they could go no further he tied up to a root, spoke to the children.

'He says wait,' Jesús said. 'Someone will come.'

'Where's he taking you?'

The boy asked the man, who said something then shook his head. 'Can't say,' Jesús said to Murphy. He came near and Murphy bent down and took him in his arms, then Epifanía. Jesús's eyes kept filling with tears and he wiped at them angrily.

'Can't I go with you, *Guapo*?' Epifanía said.

'Where I'm going it's too dangerous. Here there're people who'll look after you—'

'You'd look after me too. I know you would. I'll be a good help soon, soon I'll see—'

'He's going to fight the soldiers,' Jesús said. 'That's why we can't go with him.'

He held them both, sensing that whatever he did it would be wrong. 'I swear I'll come back for you. For you both. We'll go up north,' he said to her, 'and try to fix your eyes. And we'll go to Montana, Jesús, to the clear water mountains to fish for trout.' He stood, dizzy and nauseous, not wanting to let go. 'I swear it.'

The old man spoke; the children pulled away and followed him through a path in the bracken into the jungle.

Murphy lay on the mud by the canoe. Blood trickled down over his brow into his eye, across his nose, blocking it when he breathed. He lay on his back but the arm hurt too much so he lay on his side, his head tilted back.

The day grew hot and heavy. His bloody scalp buzzed with flies. He crawled into the creek, drank, vomited, drank, and vomited again. Once a chopper went over, quiet as a dragonfly. Jets passed, high up; he could not see them through the treetops.

He contemplated the canoe. There was the knob of a bough cut off half-way down the side; it had thirteen rings.

He could not help these people. He could not let them help him. He could not take the canoe. He could not get downriver without one. It was too far, from here, to walk through the jungle to Mexico.

He could make a raft. There would be lianas, logs, sticks. He let his head fall softly into the mud. When he awoke he'd build a raft.

When he awoke the fog was back, the dusk. Was it only last night the priest had come? He looked round the hut for Consuela, listened for children's voices. There was no hut, no voices.

A round-faced boy with a rifle came through the bracken. He was dragging a dead baby by the hand. Then Murphy saw it was a monkey. The boy tossed the monkey into the dugout. 'Let's go!'

'Go to Hell.'

'Hurry!' The boy pulled him up easily by the good arm and made him sit in the dugout. He poled back down the creek and out on to the *Río*. A string of cormorants scampered downriver and lumbered up into the gloom.

The pole plunked, sucked free, plunked, sucked free, the *Río* churning at the prow. Ticks were climbing from the monkey up the dugout's hull. Murphy trailed his fingers in the fleeting, cool water. A nighthawk screamed; a fish tail smacked.

After dark the fog lifted; the wind switched to the north, chilling his face. 'Let me pole now, Niño,' he said.

'Later.'

From the east a towering wind came whipping the treetops. A wall of rain roared across the water, driving icy needles into their necks and shoulders, poured down their backs and cascaded into the hull. The boy yelled something and tossed him a can and he knelt bailing as the boat filled with rain; the rain fell harder, shattering the river, emptying the sky.

Lyman took a taxi into Cobán and had a gin and tonic at the Hotel Excelso. The bar faced a dining room where no one sat. Beyond it was a half-lit garden where rain slanted across a Mayan pillar topped by four grinning jaguar heads. At the far end of the bar a tall, grim man in a too-wide grey suit and wet shoes stood with a fat, smaller man also in grey, their air furtive, as if even doing business together could get them killed.

Lyman downed another gin and took a taxi to the Little Pigs, a shack lit by kerosene lanterns, smelling of tobacco and spilt beer. The bar girl was short with a round Mayan face and body and wore a yellow dress that made Lyman watch her breasts.

'Lousy night,' he said to the barman.

The barman inclined his head.

'Can I get a beer?'

'Why else would I be here? El Gallo?'

'What else you got?'

'Nothing.'

'El Gallo, then.'

When the first was gone the man brought him another, a third and fourth. He watched the bar girl serving the four plank tables where a few peasants sat like cavemen waiting out the winter. He imagined holding the girl's naked ass in his hands. 'I'll have some rum,' he told the barman.

He raised the glass slowly, tasting the rim. Tonight one cigarette. He smiled, thinking how good that cigarette would be. How to make it *last*. How do you make *life* last?

Another fruitless day, he thought. Another meaningless night. At the end, do we get punished for all our meaningless days? Father, one day, barefoot, trousers rolled to his knees, a red cap on his head, had walked up a greasy road through the Mississippi woods and had never come back. And we had sat by the pond, Aunt Ettah and Lila and I, not knowing. He'd gone because I'd argued with him, said talking to me was like talking to a block of wood. And they all blamed me. And they all blame me.

The barman refilled his glass. 'Nice here,' Lyman said. Just keep changing – that makes life last. 'I'm going to Petén, for the temples. How's it up there?'

'It's fine,' the barman said.

'Fine for what?'

'Fine for temples, anything.'

'No danger of rebels?'

'Ask the authorities.' The barman nodded his chin in the direction of the Military Base.

'I'm asking *you*.'

The barman rolled up the wick of a kerosene lantern, stepped back to look at Lyman. '*I* have no idea.'

The rain stopped; the clouds parted; the last wraiths of mist slunk away across the water. At a bend in the river the boy turned ashore and tied up in the lee of a fallen tree. Bullfrogs croaked steadily. 'I just want a place to sleep,' Murphy said. The boy tossed the dead monkey over his shoulder and led Murphy uphill to a hut in a grove of banana trees. Lantern light shone through its rush walls; inside someone was moaning. The boy entered and someone came out. 'Where are you?' she said in English. 'I can't see in the dark.'

'It's you! What are you doing here?'

Dona reached out and took him in her arms. 'Oh, I'm sorry, so sorry,' holding him tight, her voice against his chest. 'I'm so sorry,' she kept saying, holding him, swaying with him, her hair in his face as he bent down to her and finally held her too, the two of them together.

'I did it,' he said.

She looked up at him. 'You? What do you mean?'

'They were looking for me. Like you said.'

'No!' She shook her head wildly. 'They killed everybody because it was a reprisal, for an attack on a convoy. They picked it because it's a village that refused to go to the camps. It's not you—'

'They were your people too.'

She held him tighter. 'It won't go away—'

'Nothing ever goes away. And nothing ever stays.'

She shook her head. 'Only the two children? No one else?'

'The old man went back. He says no.'

She reached up, held his face in both hands. 'You're so feverish! This is blood! You're hurt?' Quickly her fingers traced the edges of the wound. 'Come – let's get you into the light—'

'No.' He sat on the short, wet grass. 'They came for me, the Army. And I didn't know it was for me. So I hid, like Father Miguel said. I should've surrendered.'

She held his face as if to purge his thoughts. 'If you had they would've killed everyone, just as surely.' She held him one last time. 'Come into the hut. I must see this wound. We will give you something hot.'

'Twenty quetzales,' the bar girl said, cocky hope and fear in her eyes.

'Fifteen.' Lyman put his hands in his pockets so she wouldn't see them tremble. 'For all night.'

The silky, black top of her head did not come up to his shoulder as she stood beside him while he paid for the room at the Hotel Excelso. He followed her up the stairs, watching her thighs for the dark place between them. The room was long and thin as a boxcar, a window at the far end, a single bed across the middle. Next to the bed was a chair with a lamp and a stub of candle in a beer bottle. He lit the candle and put out the lamp.

She stood with arms folded while he tucked back her hair and kissed her neck. She smelt like fruit, like passion fruit. He could see umber nipples beneath her low halter. There was a nervous taste in the back of his mouth. He reached into the halter and played with a wide, flat breast.

She dropped her dress. Her breasts swayed like pomegranates. Her pale, stringy underpants sloped into her crotch. Her skin looked oiled in the viscous light. He took off his clothes and lay beside her, caressed her. He could not will himself to harden. She would not touch him. He thought of Nancy's thighs around a stranger's neck. He stuck his finger up inside the girl; she sucked in breath.

He mounted her but could not enter. She stared sideways at the cracked wall where the candle cast spiderweb shadows. 'Don't be sad,' she said.

He paid her twenty quetzales and the taxi. The night had chilled. A crescent moon was going down, Hydra slinking west. He walked out of Cobán towards the Base, his stomach eerie, as though his marriage had just died.

12

Inside the hut a fire hissed, a kettle on a pole across it. A woman lay on a mat, under blankets, knees drawn up. 'What do you mean, a reprisal?' Murphy said.

'The *guerrillas* destroyed a convoy, last week, on the Flores road. We think the government attacked your village for that . . .'

'Can I use the kettle?' the boy said.

Dona glanced at the woman on the mat. 'She'll need hot water.'

'She needs food more.'

'Put half the water in a bowl. Very soon I'll want the kettle.'

With a machete the boy slit the monkey's belly. The woman on the mat made a clenched cry and Dona went to her. '*Qué hubo?*'

The woman writhed, could not speak. '*Nada*,' she said finally. '*Lo mismo.*'

Dona felt the woman's swollen belly. 'It's never *lo mismo, cariña* – you're getting closer.' She stood. 'It's a breech birth,' she said in English. 'Caesarean, has to be. But I have no anaesthetic.'

'You'd do that here?'

'*Here* is not the problem. In the mountains, under a poncho in the rain, I have done brain surgery. Removing metal fragments.' She sighed. '*Why* am I telling you these things? Come, let me look at your head!'

He sat by the fire while she washed the wound with hot water that stung unbearably. Each time the woman had a contraction Dona went to her. The boy finished skinning the monkey, laid it over a log to disjoint it.

'The bullet glanced off this place where the two sutures of your skull come together,' Dona said. 'So maybe it's just broken the edges – I can feel them move.'

He pushed her hand away. 'It was fine till you messed with it.'

'That's true, it was. You just *don't* infect. Only a little, here,

57

up under the hair.' She soaked the blood and scab until she could pull the hairs free. 'Amazing you didn't break the arm again. Tomorrow, in the light, we'll make a new cast. But you have a monstrous concussion, I'm sure. You feel dizzy, very weak?'

The boy finished chopping up the monkey and set the innards aside. He poured some of the hot water from the kettle into a clay bowl and set the kettle back on its pole over the coals. He put the monkey's head and all the chopped pieces into the kettle, added fresh splits of wood to the fire, and took the innards outside. The woman writhed, relaxed, panting. 'It's coming, *cariña*,' Dona kept saying, wiping the woman's face.

'There is nothing you can give her?,' Murphy said, 'to ease the pain?'

Dona moved from the woman back to him, cleaning the wound. 'You think if there is something I would not give it to her?'

'I don't think it was a reprisal, my village.'

'They came because they were looking for you, but they killed everyone because of the convoy.'

He looked up at her kneeling above him, one half of her face firelit, the other shadowed. We all have two sides, he thought. 'Then we share the blame.'

'If you're hungry for blame there's always plenty to be found.'

'The government has its army, and you have yours. But it's the people who suffer.'

'Every person in your village was part of the *guerrilla*, fought for it every way she could, he could—'

'Even the children?'

'If you were a child seeing your parents killed, losing your older brothers one by one?'

'It keeps war going, that kind of thinking.'

'Every village in the Petén's the same. Everything the Army does just makes it worse. There'll be war till everyone's dead.'

'You like that?'

'I'm a doctor. I wish the war would stop. I think it's better to be a slave than dead. But the war's going on anyway. It won't stop. So do I go away and never think of it? Or do I stay and try to help?'

The boy came back with roots and the innards he had washed in the *Río*. He cut up the intestines on the log and put them in the pot with the rest of the innards and the roots.

'But you're *not* trying to help,' Murphy said. 'You're a *guerrillera*. A maker of war.'

'And I say to you, everyone here who thinks and dreams, everyone who's known pain, is a *guerrillero*.'

'Dreams always fail.'

'I have no bandages but will wrap this in a strip of clean *india*. You must wash the wound twice a day, with hot, boiled water.' She tied off the coloured cloth, pulling the last hairs free from under it.

'Why are they hunting me? At least ten grass planes fly out of the Petén, every week . . .'

'The Army's attacking other drug flights too. They're even killing the people who pay them for protection. But they are not suddenly against the *marihuana*, because they're still flying it themselves. Your friends, the ones killed when your plane got burned – they paid protection?'

'Every month ten thousand dollars, right to the top. Some General named Elena. Every shipper from Guatemala pays him the same.'

'Elena? There is no General Elena – Arena, maybe?'

'Arena? Arena. Yes. That's it.'

'He's the Director of Counterinsurgency. If an attack was ordered on your village, he was the one. Soon he's to be Chief of the Armed Forces.'

'*Where* is he?'

'He's in Cobán, sometimes in Guatemala City. But you won't find him. Better you go back to America, to the television, tell them what happened to your village. The Indian villages are napalmed, the people driven into camps to starve behind electric wires. Children shot in the street, women in the fields. For nothing. Because they are Indians. Tell them it's happening everywhere in Guatemala. That America must stop paying for the Guatemalan Army.'

'Their guns are Israeli – I saw them. Galils.'

'America passes money to Israel for Guatemala, to get around the ban of your Congress against sending too much money to Guatemala. Israel built a Galil factory in Guatemala City, sends all the napalm, other explosives. Israeli pilots teach the Guatemalans how to make low-level bombing runs on villages. Mossad taught the Army how to run the IBM computers it has in Guatemala City—'

'It makes my head hurt – your propaganda – everybody's.'

'It's even in *our* newspapers, and they're certainly not free.'
She turned to the boy. 'Soon I'll need the kettle, Pollo.'

'It's not half done,' Pollo said.

'There's the bailing can, in the canoe,' Murphy said. 'I'll get
it.' The air outside was cool and fresh after the smoky hut, the
stars a vast explosion of light. He went across the clearing down
to the *Río* and knelt to drink, the water rising up his wrist as
his hand sank into the mud. He filled the can, went back to the
fire, and set it on the coals.

When the water boiled Dona put her instruments in it. The
woman kept crying out. 'Sorry, *Doctora*,' she gasped. 'Can't stop.'

'We must choose, *cariña*. The baby's still blocked and I can't
get his head down. He'll die if he doesn't come out soon. I must
cut you open, the stomach, as I showed you. But there's nothing
I can give you, for the pain—'

'*Aguardiente?*'

'No, there's nothing—'

'Do it.'

'You will help me, gringo? First use a little of this soap to
wash your hands with some hot water. Then give me the instruments I ask for. And Pollo bring the water, when I say.'

The woman's belly was enormous. Murphy tried not to look at
her swollen, bleeding vagina. Dona washed the woman's stomach
with a piece of *india* and the tiny chunk of soap. She traced on
the skin with her finger, changing positions and looking at it from
different angles. The woman twisted up her body, clawing the
mat. '*Momentino, cariña*,' Dona said. '*Momentino.*'

She took the scalpel and cut a steady long diagonal down
across the belly. The woman shrieked, tears pouring across her
face, fists against her teeth. 'Take her hands, Pollo!' Dona said.
She made a second cut, blood spurting out black in the dim light
and pooling against the cloths she kept rolled round the cut. She
pulled up the skin, cutting beneath to separate it from the
muscle, then slit down into the muscle, the little cords popping
back. 'More cloths,' she said, tossing the bloodsoaked ones aside.
'He's moving, *cariña*, your baby's moving.'

The turgid womb beneath was purple-coloured. The woman's
mouth was bleeding; she's bit her tongue, Murphy thought.
'Check her pulse,' Dona said.

'It's steady. A little faint.'

'Keep watching it. Give me the number three scalpel now –
quick – wash this off before you put it in the water, hurry! And

string the big needles now, like I showed you!'

The scalpel blade sank into the bursting flesh. It's thick, the uterus, Murphy thought. The fire hissed and Pollo went to it, came back – 'It's almost done, the stew.'

The woman's hand in Murphy's was hot and weak, her breast throbbing. In the pool of sweat and tears in the corner of her eye the rush mats of the ceiling were reflected. Her whole body trembled; I've seen that, he thought, the tremor mortis. 'I have him!' Dona gasped. 'Slowly now he's coming.'

She raised a clump of bloody organs in her hands and he thought it was the placenta then saw its wizened Mayan head, the tiny gaping mouth, the twig arms and taut belly with the umbilical cord plunging down. 'It's a girl, *cariña*! A cloth, Pollo! Hold her, gringo, while I get the rest.'

The baby weighed nothing in his hands, a bloody bitter face choked with horror. This is what it is, he thought, making love. Where did you come from? 'Quick!' Dona said, held the baby's head down, sucked out her lungs and spat; the baby jerked, convulsed, wailed a high, tiny cry. 'More cloths,' Dona said.

'No more,' Pollo answered.

'My coat then, by the door.'

She wrapped the wailing baby in her camouflage jacket. 'A big needle, now, gringo. You're sure you've threaded three of them? And then the little ones. Remember – the light thread, not the black one. Take her, *cariña*, quickly, she needs milk!'

The baby gummed a nipple, took a breath and wailed, sucked again. Everyone's sacred, Murphy suddenly understood. Everyone's been through this mystery. Up out of the water into the air. Gasping, stunned, dragged like an innocent fish from the sea.

'The smaller needles now, gringo.' When she had finished suturing the uterus Dona gathered the muscles together one by one and sutured them with lighter needles and the same pale thread. Pollo took the afterbirth down to the river and then the cloths to wash them. 'The stew's done,' he said.

When she had finished the muscles she sewed up the skin with the black thread. Now that the woman's belly was less swollen the incision seemed smaller. Pollo washed her face and hands with the last of the hot water and brought her a cup of broth from the stew.

Murphy sat with Dona and Pollo by the fire, the bailing can half full of stew, chewing the last shreds from a shoulder bone.

61

The woman lay silent, the baby whimpering at her breast. Out of the kettle the monkey's eyeless skull stared up at them.

13

Lyman kicked at a stone, heard it skitter along the gravel and hop into the grass. You should've stayed with the girl, he reminded himself, stopped to piss by a clump of cedars, holding a branch for balance. Behind the cedars rose a broken stone wall. Ahead were more cedars and a white fence, then dark scrub, a moonlit meadow. Take away colour, he thought, you still get black and white.

The piss spattered on the rocks, sparkling. Rum and beer. Bad fuckin combination. And your combination doesn't fuck at all. But gets high thinking of other people doing it. People you know.

If your fly won't zip what if you leave it down? Why have a fly at all? To cover up your rod. Why have a rod? To make sure you're a God. Rocks stumbly underfoot, don't let 'em trip you. Half-way home. Fix the fuckin road, Lawd—

'Why don't they fix it in the road, Lawd—

'Why don't they fix the fucking road—

'Why don't they cover up their God, Lawd—

'Why don'—'

Horrible compression of air past his skull – he dived into the ditch as the sound of the shot crackled and banged up through the hills. In the ditch no cover, every stub and leaf sharp-cut. Clear ground uphill, a few bushes dark against the milky slope. Ahead a bare grassy channel, ditch shallowing to pale empty ground. Any way you go he's got you.

The pilot. He's followed. Wants you to fear before you die.

Close-cropped grass, a boulder, the far dark hollow of the road to town, distant streetlights on the church face. He'll hit you before the boulder or even if he misses he'll pin you at the boulder and you're worse off there than here.

Not a Galil, an M-16. Wind crossed the road, odours of mud, trees, cattle. He's in the cedars, behind the white fence. With a perfect field of fire.

You're going to cross the road and kill him.

'He's not the only priest in a Guatemalan jail. And even if he's still alive, there's nothing we can do . . .'

'I'm not going to leave him. In a sense he gave his life for mine—'

'That's what priests do. You can't change that.' Dona took a bowl of stew and sat across from Murphy at the fire, cross-legged. 'You're very good – the bandages, sutures. Where did you learn it?'

'The medics. I'd go in, to get some wounded guys, I'd get pinned or the chopper'd get hit, there'd be no medic or the medic would be dead or there's too many wounded coming in, so you learn what you can. While they die all around you.'

'And in hospital?'

'I was only there a month. Hawaii. Soon as my wounds closed up they shipped me back – they were short of chopper pilots just then.' He looked at the dirt floor, seeing the ward, the boys para-lyzed from the neck down, the blind, the maimed, the ones with brand new steel skulls begging to die. 'I learned there, too, how to care for people.'

She reached out, squeezed his leg. 'You see, you're just like me—'

He shook his head. 'I've learned every time you try to do good you just cause more pain.'

'And now you want to find Father Miguel. Isn't that trying to do good?'

'No. That's just settling scores.'

She sucked the marrow from a wristbone and dropped it in the fire. After a moment it began to hiss. 'Before Vietnam, what were you?'

'A kid from west Texas. With a grin and a pick-up truck. At least that's how I look in the photos.'

'And now you're a drug pilot.'

'Was. I don't have a plane any more.'

'You must have insurance—'

'They don't sell insurance for my kind of work.'

'And you liked it, that work?'

'It kept me alive. Like the signs on the cement trucks in San Francisco: "Find a Need and Fill It". Like vodka or Valium or base-ball or politics or television or anything else people want.'

'But what people want can hurt them—'

'Cars kill a thousand people every week in my country and

64

nobody says a word. Grass never hurt a soul. It's like music, it makes people happy.'

'And now?'

'That village was like my family. I didn't want to leave. I've walked into something I can't find my way out of.'

She held her ankles, knees up under her chin. 'Sometimes I think I've walked into something that even if I found a way out I couldn't leave . . .'

'That's war – you stay with it because you won't desert the ones you're with. But they're only there because they won't desert you—'

Lyman rolled to his feet, dashed up the ditch, spun round and sprinted down it then swerved sharp right across the road where moonlight snared every pebble and the thud of his boots was like thunder and the rush of his breath like the wind, feeling the bullets' whack against his ribs, smashing his skull, the loud blunt roar tearing out his lungs, then he was across, no shot, smashed down the fence then soft creeping on fingers and toes, close to the moss, the dirt, a breeze in his face, nobody, roots, stalks, lianas, creepers, bristle of pine tree, dead needles loud, creeping round it, still no human odour or gun or uniform or sweat smells. He laid his hand softly on a root and it recoiled and slid away.

He looked at her across the pale fire, her small body, her long hair, her lovely face with full lips and dark arched eyebrows with the lines of fatigue in the corners of her eyes. 'You look so tired.'

'Every death takes you with it.'

'Do you ever fear?'

'I used to fear for me; now it's that I can't afford it yet—'

'Afford it?'

'Death. Once you're in *la lucha*, you've don't have much time.'

'How did you start?'

'I was in love, with an intern, at medical school. They arrested him for going to the *barrios* to heal the poor. They shot him and six others the day the Pope came to Guatemala City. To show the Pope he needn't worry about liberation theology here. For three years afterwards I lived like a nun, finished medical school, did my residency in Mexico. When I came back I realized there was nothing else I could do—'

He wanted to lie down beside her, hold her. 'You're lonelier than I am.'

65

She smiled. 'In Vietnam, you weren't afraid?'

'All the time. Even on leave, I'd know what was waiting when I got back.'

'It doesn't bother you now?'

'I had some bad times and everybody I really cared about died, but now I never think about it.'

'Why?'

A rock in the fire cracked and he felt he could hold it together, keep it from breaking, despite the heat, the pain. 'It'd drive me crazy. If I really saw it how it was.'

'Then you are already going crazy. You just don't see it.'

His back was aching; he sat up on his heels. 'Maybe I still live it, all the time. Yes, I admit it – I do.' His ankles were tingling from his having sat too long cross-legged. 'After I came back from Nam I went down to Mexico, lived by myself in the desert, did a lot of drugs, thought things through. I learned there's no good in going over pain.' He took her hand, warm from the fire. 'Can't you see that?'

'It's not like that, *la lucha*.' She looked down at her hand in his, up into his eyes. 'Don't condemn what you don't understand.'

The fire was like a friend, softly rumbling to him in its red-golden depths. It doesn't matter, the fire said. You can choose to die and be with her. What else better could you do? 'Nothing's worth dying for,' he said. 'Except someone you love—'

'Then it just depends how far your love goes.'

He held the pistol against the palm of his left hand to mask the click as he pushed it off safety. Moonlight behind him, making him black and his enemy light. A stick twinged underfoot – *how* can I let that happen? He backed off, stepped round the stick. Shall I go to you, my friend, or wait for you to come to me?

'I never sleep in a hut, it's one of my rules. Nowhere they can surprise me. I always sleep in the jungle.'

Her skin felt so near, her eyes in his and his in hers, no distance between them. 'It doesn't spook you?'

'It did at first. I hate snakes. But if only once out of a thousand nights you avoid danger, it's worth it.' From her Special Forces pack she took a cotton hammock, two blankets, and a camo tarp. She lifted the freshly boiled instruments from the bailing can, wrapped them in dry *india*, put them in the pack. She handed him a blanket. 'Pollo will make you a place by the fire.' She felt his brow. 'You must terribly need sleep.' Her hand came down, caressed his cheek. 'Thank you for all you've done—'

'Done? What the hell have I done?'

'You fought the soldiers at San Tomás. You saved two children . . .'

'Out of twenty . . .' His eyes stung and he looked down at the fire, away from hers.

'You have to let it pass.' She squeezed his hand. 'If the woman has pain, or if the baby cries too much, Pollo will get me. You must sleep—'

He took up the camo vest and draped it round her shoulders, pulled it close around her neck. Her hair was fine, against his fingers. It's true, he realized, only once do you really fall in love. And right away you know.

She took up her rifle, but he slipped his fingers under the sling and eased it from her shoulder, bent down for the blanket she'd given him. 'I'm coming with you.'

14

To his right between the cedars Lyman saw patches of starlit
meadow. That meant the road was to the left, beyond the thicker
wall of trees. Ahead the cedars must narrow to a point fringing
the road: his enemy couldn't get away. His fingers touched stone
– no, three stones, one still muddy on the edge, just now over-
turned.

He put down the stone and checked that his knife was still
secure in its sheath at his ankle. A moth fluttered in his face.

An owl whirred down through the branches, swerved and
flapped away. Ahead was a big tree darker than the rest. Under
his hand the land sloped slightly left, towards the road. Was the
enemy still by the road? Or back in the trees?

The pistol caught in a spider-web and he tore it free, heard
the spider scuttle away. His fingers bumped a stinging plant. In
the darkness just ahead someone breathed out softly.

To step out of the hut was like falling into space; the stars vaulting up over the jungle were thick as atoms in a sea of light. Wind
came up from the water, tasting of fish and stone, rustling the
leaves of the banana trees.

They went down to the *Río* and drank. He dug mud from the
shallows and washed his hands and face, feeling the skin come
clean. Everything you give, he thought, you only get it back.

'I saved Ofélia's life once,' she said.

The name made him flinch. 'Nobody told me.'

'She had diphtheria. I waited it out with her, three nights. There
were no drugs but a bark tea we use, a salicylic compound, to
bring down fever. She came back—'

'You mustn't—'

'All during the Caesarean tonight I was seeing her, your people,
what the soldiers did. Over and over.'

He tugged the camo vest closer round her shoulders, the

smooth skin of her jaw against the back of his hand. 'You brought another life into the world tonight—'

'And I regret it.'

He kissed her temple smooth and cool from the *Río*, the thud of her pulse against his lips. 'You'll drive yourself crazy. For nothing.' He massaged her back; the muscles hardened then relaxed, her eyelash tickling the corner of his mouth, her cheekbone hard against his chin, her small breasts pushing into his chest, her hair soft over his fingers as he squeezed the muscles of her neck. 'You're hard as stone.'

'The muscles get like that – from carrying the gun.'

'Don't carry it.'

She shook her head, her face against his neck, her breath down his chest. Her arms were strong around his back, her hands gripped his shoulders. 'If I put down the gun it wouldn't change a thing.'

'It doesn't help anyone if you die.'

'You don't see what life *is*, in Guatemala?'

'It's still life.'

'It's what happened to your village – poverty, sickness, death squads, hunger. If you had children—'

'I'd get them out of here. Mexico, Belize . . .'

'They get sent back, and all the men and boys are shot.'

'Can *you* get out?'

'Of course, I've got Mexican papers. But never—'

'How long, here, do you give yourself?'

'It could be tonight. In a year.'

'All those years afterwards you won't be alive, to heal people.'

Her shoulders slumped. The *Río* was like a drumbeat, steady and deep. 'I'm sorry I was rude to you,' she said, 'when you first came.'

'You weren't rude; you saved my life.'

'No, but calling you gringo, and all that—'

'I barely noticed.'

'I say it sometimes now, but just to tease you.' She held the curve of his face, giving it form in the darkness. 'So many villages. San Tomás, Santa Teresa, Puychíl, Aguateca, San Juan Sayjá . . . I can see them all, every person dead and burnt, the children's bodies – all the hundreds of villages and towns destroyed, and I can still see all their faces—'

He hugged her tighter. 'You can make it go away. Everything goes away.'

'You're saying you don't care?'

'I'm saying I no longer care that I care.'

With a rustle of cloth the enemy stood. A click of magazine against the buckle of a sling. Black metal grazed by moonlight.

A beetle crawled up Lyman's calf. He did not make a noise breathing or licking his lip or shifting his weight as he dropped his left hand down to the knife. He held his thumb over the snap and slid his fingers under the flap and popped it free. The knife's ebony handle was soft and warm, the tang up each side cool against his palm. The knife slid by itself from the sheath.

With a crunch of cedar twigs the enemy turned to go. Doesn't know I'm here: a ravenous joy surged in Lyman's chest. He holstered his pistol.

The enemy was stepping lightly away, heading towards the cover of the trees, shouldering his rifle – doesn't even know I'm coming.

He switched hands with the knife, darted up behind and grabbed the enemy across the eyes, yanking his head back to slit his throat but long hair was in his way and the sentry screamed and Lyman twisted the knife aside, yanked the enemy down and fell atop her, the knife at her throat. 'Where's the others?'

'No one—' A girl, eyes wide with terror, flimsy hands at his wrists. 'Please no!'

'Why'd you shoot?'

'Just a warning, *Señor*, I'm supposed to warn you!'

'Warn me what?'

'Not to come up the road. We're stopping the road—'

'Who? *Who?*' He grabbed her hair and slammed her head against the rifle barrel underneath. '*Who?*' Pinning her arms under his knees he jammed the blade against her trachea.

She coughed, gasped a breath. 'The *compañeros* – I didn't mean to shoot you – I wouldn't shoot you – it's to warn you to stay back!'

'Why?'

'There's danger ahead. You were singing in a foreign language – I didn't want you killed, you're not a soldier.'

'I'm a goddamn tourist, and you shot at me!'

'I shot to miss you!'

The whites of her eyes and her teeth gleamed with fear and pain from his holding her hair and her neck jammed down on her rifle. Still pinning her arms he felt down her sides: no

70

revolver. He pinned her right arm, shoved his left under her head to hold her left wrist. 'Where's the other *compañeros*?'

'Please, *Señor*, don't kill me, please?'

'Tell me and I won't hurt you—'

'They're up ahead.'

'How *far*?'

'Beyond the hill, where the road turns . . .'

'How many?' Knife clamped in his teeth, he felt her breast pockets then down her thighs – no knife, a scrap of tortilla in one trouser pocket. He raised his hand up the inside of her thighs, clamped it there.

'Please, *Señor* – I was warning you only.'

'How many?'

'I don't know – I was told to stay here, warn off anyone who wasn't soldiers . . .'

He slipped the knife under her rope belt, twisted the blade and slit the trousers open to the knees.

'Please, *Señor*—'

He slid the blade under the front of her shirt, drew it down, cutting the buttons, gripped the knife again in his teeth and pulled the shirt apart. There was a black line down her right breast where the blade had nicked it. 'Please, *Señor* – I'm just seventeen . . .'

'You *tried* to kill me.' It was a stallion rising in him now, the delicious stinging joy, the hunger to absolve it. She had nothing under the coarse trousers, her mound little and warm as a bird in his hand.

'I could have killed you,' she cried. 'I didn't want to.'

'Stop making so much noise!' Dona whispered. 'You're like a hippopotamus!'

'I'm trying to keep up with you! Wait – I'm caught. There. Goddamn snakes. Don't know how you stand this.'

'The hammock's safe. Once you get in it.'

In the darkness ahead an even greater blackness. 'This the tree?'

'The ceiba?' She moved ahead. 'Yes.'

He put down the gun and backpack. 'I can hang my own hammock,' she said.

Her face was near; he could sense her form against the darkness, reached out, knowing exactly where she was, her arm already familiar in his hand. Maybe it was your healing me, he thought, engraved you on me. 'You got this goddamned thing on safety?'

71

'Of course, gringo – you are so crazy!'

'I hate it. I hate them so much it makes me sick just to see them.'

'Just because you had to fight for what you didn't believe in, now you think no one should fight at all . . .'

'You have guns – *they* have guns; you're just inoculating yourself with their disease.'

The girl was fighting to keep her legs closed but he jammed a knee between them, rammed her legs up and shoved in, her channel dry, too small, the rubbery membrane tearing, her cry, the channel slicker now with blood, and that's what it always takes, he thought, a little sacrifice to get things going, couldn't shove in deep enough with her writhing and flinching; it reared up like a stallion crashing down her velvet walls, driving far up, her insides imploding, in the sweet slick hot delight of everything coming to this and nothing more.

You could've made a baby. You always know. He drove the blade deep into her throat, blood spraying in his face, her body frantic then rigid then finally quiet beneath him. He grew huge again – I should have kept you, he thought, but it's better this way – and finally it soared out of him long and deep, from back there, the beginning, from way behind it, life, the end. He pulled out and rolled aside, wiped the knife and his hands and face on her rough-woven trousers. Oh Jesus, he thought. You bastard. But then again – she tried to kill me. He heard Nancy playing a Beethoven sonatina, the mantel clock ticking out its years, saw his son Joshua tossing up a tennis ball, not high enough, not hitting it at the drop. Joshua leaned forward, into the serve, and the pain of his death drove again through Lyman like a sword, Joshua beneath the huge tyre of the cement truck, half a boy's body in a lake of blood. Sheathing the knife and pistol he took up the girl's rifle, a battered M-16, short clip, only three shots left. He crept slowly to the edge of the starlit meadow and knelt looking for the best way across it and around the hill ahead, where the road turns.

She lay with her head on his left arm, her breath against his neck, her hands up between his arms and chest, the rifle lying at her back. He pulled the blanket down a little to see the angle of her cheekbone and the extra darkness of her hair. 'Your feet are too big,' she said. 'You'll pull out the blanket.'

He kissed her forehead; it smelled of smoke, jungle, and river.

72

Already she was sleeping, the barrel of her rifle cold with dew against his knuckles. Through a tiny high gap in the branches the Pleiades shone down. When he looked a moment later they were gone. But it seemed a good omen as he drifted off to sleep.

15

His voice came from the light. 'You can put it down.'

She held the weight tighter, was suddenly conscious of how it cut into her shoulder, made her back ache as if she carried concrete. She slid it from her shoulder and it thumped to the ground. She raised her arms, could see the jungle below and realized she was flying, dipping and diving naked through the winds, veering with the turn of a hand, air rushing past her body—

There was a warm tingling between her legs. Must have to pee, she thought. I'll have to get out without rocking the hammock, not waking him, and walk barefoot in the snakes to take a pee. But the feeling was hotter, radiating, a magnet between her loins and his, urging them together. For a moment she let herself imagine it. But maybe he doesn't want to. I'm heartless, wanting this, even thinking of it, after what's happened.

She recalled the woman in the hut, in pain but not crying out, the baby wailing at her breast. If I have to pee I'll check on her, she thought, though Pollo should be watching unless he fell asleep. Maybe she's haemorrhaged or the baby's sick and here I lie thinking about sex.

She slid one foot over the side. 'What's the matter?' he said.

'I was trying not to wake you. Must check María—'

He sat up. 'I'll go with you.'

'It's only a hundred metres through the jungle. Sleep.'

He slipped into his sandals, tossed her pack over one shoulder, took the gun. 'I'll go before you.'

From the clearing the *Río* was a canyon of stars. The coals still glimmered through the hut's rush walls. Pollo stood when they came in. 'She's been awake,' he whispered, 'but now she sleeps.'

'And *la chica*?'

'She drinks and sleeps. She's happy.'

Dona touched the backs of her fingers to the baby's face, the back of the woman's hand. She beckoned Pollo outside. '*Bien*, you know where to find me?'

'*Sí, Doctora*.'

'I'll come again at dawn.'

'Sleep well,' Pollo whispered, catching Murphy in the corner of his eye.

In the jungle she took the rifle from Murphy. 'Meet you at the ceiba.' When he'd gone she slid down her clothes and crouched, the wonderful feeling of it coming out, its warm smell rising up from the leaves. The rasp of cloth as she pulled up her clothes made her skin tingle. It was still there, the itchy feeling of having to pee, hotter than before. She bit her lip, saw the stone slabs she'd climbed as a girl, up Antigua's temple stairs. Yes, we called it church, she reflected, but it was *ours* from before, long before there was a church, when the stones that now make the church then stood in another form, for a different God – the sense of all this history *was* like God, this column of power. And he must like me a little bit, she thought, for he likes lying down beside me and kissed me and it's true as he says that I saved him . . . though maybe he would have lived anyway for he seems to live through everything, and in her hand she could feel how *he* would be, could not close her hand all the way around him. I will do it, she decided. I give up, he can have me. The Galil snagged on a creeper; she bent and tugged it free.

She was coming to him across the starlight filtering down through chinks in the rain-forest night – he could sense her, felt where she was, the motion of each limb, her face, each step turning, bending towards him through the trees. I've always loved you, he said to her inside himself. You're all I've ever cared for.

Just to brush her lips once with his was enough to last a lifetime but made him need to taste her mouth, her teeth against his lips, her odour washing him through mouth and face and hair and hand and every pore, her tongue like an orchid he'd seen once in the jungle deep in the crevice of a tree, her body hard against him like the Galil, her nails digging into the back of his neck, as if they were twins, two halves of one, dying of thirst for each other, drinking each other in.

She lay beside him naked, the hammock swinging softly and there seemed for ever, always, to do all this. To be naked, naked against her naked – how small, how lovely how slender how complete—

'This can't matter afterwards,' she whispered, as if someone could hear, 'we can't do it any more, just this once. Just this once I so need to, oh if you could understand how I need you—'

No wall between them, one skin, one blood, one body, to kiss her the only thing now, had ever been the only thing, wetting her rough smooth lips, his tongue inside them, against her teeth, her tongue warmed and curved and curled and wrapped his, drew back came forward and took him in again.

He reached down her slender body over the curve in her hips and between her thighs and she raised up one leg so he could touch her there, rub her there, anything he wanted she wanted, the two were one, and she held him, held his power, had forgotten how big, filling her hand as if it belonged there, completed it, her hand aching to envelop it and go up and down it and her fingertips around the tip and everything she did she knew how it felt for him as if she had the same sensation.

How small inside she was opening out, deep resonating petals, how slender her hips how small her breasts against him, and he saw how she would be heavy with child, everything, all time, was this, her body rising beneath him, her eager lips and teeth and tongue and breasts and belly reaching up, sucking him in, her knees locked round him, and he was coming into her, an arrow to pierce her so she could die and be reborn and this time I'll live for ever, she thought, in the glory of it deepening inside her, widening her, wedging her apart until its point hit high inside her, dead centre, making it all come true, she could not tell the smell of him from hers, his breath or hers, his skin or hers – we're twins, we just got separated young, for he was her body and she his, the great white sheet of night washing her away, and she saw that everything is twinned, has its reflection, is doubled.

She saw a rabbit crouched in the grass. It's mistaken, she realized, to think the eagle watches over it.

He could see all around as if the night weren't there, then realized that it wasn't, the raw boughs spiring into grey, skeins of creepers cascading down, bulging leaves and bracken, the fading stars. The jungle thinned with light, the trees tapered to carbon spars and blew away on centuries of wind, the soil chased after, flake by scurrying flake, the earth was bare – the entire earth – he saw how everything had gone, inhabited the stars.

16

Through a crack in the floorboards between his boots Lyman could see muddy ground. Roll a few grenades under these barracks you'd get everyone inside. Curling his toes against the morning chill he sat thinking how he'd attack the Base, as a guerrilla, how to draw strength to the north-east perimeter. But you wouldn't really be there, you'd fire across the middle, cutting it, hit the south-west from their back then when the north-east turns on you you hit them hard from the front, where you'd started in the first place. It was pure sense, pure guerrilla, and he thought lovingly of it for a moment, realized his toes were cold, and slid on his boots.

His body was stiff and sore, as if he'd played football, then he remembered he'd been drunk, had gone to town; his head was hurting, he realized – God what a fucking headache. Then he remembered he'd banged his forehead with hers, the girl, trying to escape, fighting him, and he remembered how easily the knife cut the trachea, the jugular, almost automatically, her body quivering one last moment in his arms. Was it true, he wondered, stood and lowered his trousers to see the blood in dark flakes on his penis, saw his shirt, the backs of his hands. 'Oh Lord Jesus Christ,' he said, rubbing his neck gently and shaking his head. But the headache wouldn't lessen, and he wandered towards the latrines to wash his face in cold water.

'This can't happen again. No more after this.' Her voice was hoarse, as if from too much talking.

'I won't let it stop.'

On her side, she drew one leg up over his hip, seeking him. '*La lucha* – won't let me. I don't want to.'

'To hell with *la lucha*.'

'You'd love someone who'd do that, leave those whose lives might depend on her?'

77

'And in *la lucha* people don't love, get married?'

'Married, yes.'

'Then we'll get married.'

She put her fingers over his lips. 'You mustn't even *say* that—'

With the swing of the hammock he rolled on to his back and she pulled up on her knees and knelt over him, the blanket sliding from her shoulders. She kept coming down and down and down atop him till he hit the place where he could go no more and she winced and pulled up slightly.

'You like this?' he said.

'God yes I like it. I'm not crazy.' Her hair slid up his chest as she came forward to kiss him, fell over him, breast to breast, skin to skin and sweat to sweat, her nipples hard against his ribs.

The dance of life was this, the yin and yang, the going in and coming out, one body and one blood, one core, one understanding – not thinking, far beyond it, the *body* doing this, the *body* knowing what is right.

'You look like you fall in a pit,' Arena said.

'Too much *aguardiente*.'

Arena took the coffee pot and served it around. He put it down and brought round a plate of biscuits. He's learned this at Langley, Lyman thought. This convivial serving of his guests. To lower their defences.

'Since when does rum scratch your face?' Arena said.

'I fell downhill.'

'That was very much rum.'

'That's all there is to drink in this Christly place—'

'Come now. There's El Gallo.'

When he's being convivial that means he's planning an attack, thought Lyman. Or has figured a new way to use me. Or knows how he can lose me. But when he is being convivial he's also at risk because he doesn't expect me to attack. 'You're still wrong, General,' he said. 'It *was* the pilot, at that village, who shot your men—'

'My men get shot by many people, Colonel—'

'And it's the same one who killed Gallagher. I saw how he moved, how he got in and out. He's a soldier, General, and a good one. I want him. And *you* still can't find him.'

'If that *was* him. This we don't think yet.'

'Just because the priest says it was some Kekchi. Trouble with you people's you can't drop the habit of believing your priests. No Kekchi looks like that guy. Kekchis aren't that tall – he knew how to use the gun—'

'You think Guatemalans don't know how to use guns, Colonel?'

'Not these farmers you keep killing all the time. Most of them can't even handle a plough. Excuse me for being blunt – I've got a hangover – but *I* could run Guatemala with a lousy military academy. How come *you* can't with a whole army and equipment up the rectum – excuse my Spanish – and all the counterinsurgency training you can swallow and a fucking spy satellite and twenty-four-hour infra-red overflight and six hundred million in military aid and three billion in slush funds and another ten billion you make off the grass and coke flights?'

'Talking to you, Colonel, is like talking to a recorder. We don't think the man at that village who shot our two soldiers was this pilot you are so hungry for. The priest has been to the point of death three separate times and this is what he begs us to believe. He has said some other things we know are true, so we are disinclined to disbelieve him.'

'Like what?'

'He has admitted he sympathizes with the revolution—'

'What priest *doesn't* sympathize with the revolution? Half your fucking Army and *all* the *campesinos* do! Probably even *you* do.'

'You're an expert now, on our society?'

'I'm paid to be. I'm not very good at it but I'm better than you. You don't have the fucking faintest idea what's going on—'

'And you do?'

'Give me a *lancha* and ten men, General. I'll show you how easy it is to find this sky pilot.'

Arena nodded slowly, watching his hands folded on the table before him, like the stubby fat prow of a ship, Lyman thought.

'Why not take your ten men and go up to Sayaxché this morning?' Arena said. 'Angelo Vodega will go with you.'

II
House of
Obsidian
Knives

17

Pollo blew on the coals and added resiny *ocote* twigs that flared up quickly. God give us peace, Murphy thought. Peace is love, came the answer. They heated the monkey stew, gave some to the woman, María, who was able to sit up and eat.

Globules of fat floated in the stew, between the bones. The monkey's flesh was wiry, the hairs nearly human – short, dark, and strong. The baby's wizened face seemed fuller, less frightened. You're getting used to it already, Murphy thought. Pollo took up his machete. 'I'll find some roots for María.'

Mice were chasing each other in empty corn husks by the door. Fog came up from the *Río* and under the hut walls.

He was conscious of every move she made, every breath, the pressure of her hand on his shoulder as she stepped past, how the light touched her black hair, the curve of her cheek. She stood beside him, warming her hands over the fire, and he held the inside of her thigh and kissed her there, between the thighs, smelling her through the worn jeans, her fingers combing his hair. Never, he realized, have I *ever* felt like this.

No matter how many times you see something it's never the same: now from the Huey the river with its coat of fog reminded Lyman of an old drunk sleeping over a heat grate, like a goddamn python, its jaws sucking in the world. He smiled at Vodega – in the company of villains and fools. I could've done anything, and look where I've ended up.

He waved the door gunner aside and took the M60D, the great gun swinging loose on its mount, grips tight in his palms. Truly nothing like this gun, nothing ever. No sense of power, purpose, like this. Treetops tipped past, birds scurrying. They're in among the fucking trees, the guerrillas. Millions and millions of trees. But their highway's the river. He punched the gunner's shoulder. 'Tell Ramón to drop down, follow the river.'

'*Es claro que es muy peligroso*,' the gunner said.

'I don't care how fucking *claro* that it's dangerous – do it.'

'We must go,' Pollo said, 'before the fog rises.'

'Unless you can wait, let her rest till tomorrow,' Dona said. 'That would be better.'

'Here it's too dangerous. Better she's among her own people. We can cross here and go up the Santa Amelia—'

'Go, then,' Dona said. 'Quickly while the fog's thick.'

'And if there's monkeys I'll shoot one to feed her.' Pollo took his Galil and went down to the *Río*, untied the dugout and brought it alongshore. Dona led the woman carefully down to the dugout.

'She's going to die,' Murphy said. 'She can't heal—'

'She's got no fever; at Santa Amelia she'll be with family. I have to leave today – can't go with her. In a couple of days I'll check on her.'

'*I'll* stay with her.'

Dona shook her head. 'You have to go downriver—'

They settled María on her rush mat in the middle of the dugout, the baby quiet at her breast, inside her red shawl. Pollo poled away from shore, the dugout slipped into the fog, first the bow, then the thwarts, till only Pollo standing in the stern remained, a glimmer fading, gone.

'You're crazy if you think I'm going downriver,' Murphy said.

She stood against him, warming her river-cold hands against his bare chest. He kissed her and kissed her, could not stop, get enough. Her body pressed hard against him. 'I've got work today,' she whispered.

He opened her shirt, making her hold him, her teeth nipping his lips, her breath fast. 'We're going to do keep doing this and never stop—'

'Let's go up there—'

'To hell with up there. We're going to do it right here.' He was unbuttoning her jeans and she was pulling him down when he felt it suddenly on his back, his neck – the sun, the air suffused with sudden brightness. Fog rose like a curtain from the *Río*; Pollo was *there*, half-way across, caught in sunlight, using his pole like an oar against the current.

They heard the noise and Murphy sprinted uphill for the hut, grabbed Dona's rifle and ran into the open as the chopper came sideways down the *Río* spitting tracer fire that hammered the water like a great sheet of glass breaking, loud as the whole world breaking, the dugout spurting up and knocked apart, and Murphy led the door gunner by half the space between him and the door, down the black channel of the Galil's sights, on his neck to be sure to hit his chest; the rifle kicked and barked as the chopper swung away and then came round in a quick arc and Murphy fired for the turbine housing then the motor head, knowing he was dead now, that the door gunner would kill him, and hunched over the M60D Murphy saw a black man, the black officer who had helped to burn his village; as he fired the chopper swung away and he had to shoot at the engine housing; the chopper jerked and pulled up, and the black man was gone, I've got to lead them away from her, he thought, running along the bank, huge M60 bullets whacking and whanging among the *boloconte* roots, in the smell of burnt wood and dirt and the horrible vacuum that bullets leave behind. The chopper's whine retreated; it was fluttering north towards Sayaxché trailing blue smoke from the engine housing.

Dona dove into the *Río* and swam towards the shattered dugout. Murphy checked the clip – six shots. 'I'll cover you,' he yelled, but she did not turn her head. He wanted to scream, tear his face, ran out into the *Río* till he could see the point far downriver where the chopper had swung round a bend, its smoke trail indolent in the wind. The water was stainless steel in the brilliant sun. Dona swam back, grabbed her rifle and ran up to the hut.

'Hurry!' she yelled, tossing her pack and blankets out the door. Wiping her face, coughing and crying, she knelt at the fire, blew it alive, tossed in more kindling. 'Watch outside – for more helicopters!'

'What are you *doing*?'

'Go!'

Outside there was no sound of choppers, no distant glint coming upriver. He stood in the hot shade of the banana palms, trying to catch his breath, the somnolent air searing his throat. He kept trying to check the rifle in his hands, but his hands were empty. She came out with a torch of kindling and held it to the thatch. 'What the hell?' he said.

'Quick!' They ran for the jungle, through the saplings and creepers and past the great ceiba where last night they'd hung the hammock, deeper into the jungle, up out of the *bajos* and into the hills.

* * *

The smoke got thicker and Lyman leaned out the door to breathe. The soldiers crouched on the floor, the dead door gunner between them. Lyman kept watching the engine housing but there was no way to know if it would hold, the Jesus nut rotating wildly, hot oil spattering the gunner's body. He stepped across the soldiers to the cockpit. 'Get down close to the river!' he yelled. 'When she dies we're going to drop like a stone.'

'*Bajo demasiado peligroso!*' The pilot craned round. There were cuts like red paint on his face.

'We tell you this already!' the co-pilot said in English. 'Now we going to ditch, goddamn you—'

Lyman made himself smile, nodded back at the Jesus nut. 'She'll hold. Just bring her down, first open place you find, so I can get my men back to that hut. We'll find them, get them for your gunner—'

'He's dead?'

'Through the head.'

'Goddamn you!' the co-pilot screamed.

Lyman swung back to the crew deck, glanced down at the river like a glistening concrete skin fifty feet below the chopper's skids. Fools, he thought, to take it serious. But it was him, the goddamn sky pilot, the tall guy with the blond hair and beard, the one who'd been at the village the other night. The same one. He killed the door gunner and blew holes in the motor housing. He tried to kill us all.

18

Her face, muddied, torn and bloodied by thorns, seemed a stranger's yet infinitely near. 'I didn't *want* you,' she said. 'We *can't* be together.'

He tried to catch his breath. 'Where're we going?'

'I must be somewhere tonight. That's why I couldn't stay, with María and the baby.'

The mud on her face, he saw, was just tears and dirt. 'I can get from here to Mexico. It's just jungle. But I won't leave you . . .'

She shook her head scornfully. He felt a moment of such pity and love that the earth shifted beneath him. He slid his fingers under the rifle sling to take it from her shoulder but she wouldn't let go. 'Everything you do – can't you see – just brings more pain?'

'Less than if I do nothing.'

'For you, perhaps.'

'That's cruel. And untrue.'

'If you hadn't been there to help María, Pollo wouldn't have died.'

She caressed his face, making him feel mean, selfish. 'You mustn't try to talk me out of what I do. Not when we both know I'm right.'

Lyman kept the river on his left, a glimmer through the trees. It could only be another mile, Jesus, till they got there. He kept the pace steady, running, ducking, climbing, crawling, pushing aside the jungle at each step, elbowing and dragging his M-16 through the walls of trees. He looked back, panting, could see Martínez, the sergeant, then the first man behind him. '*Anda!*' Martínez yelled, pushing Lyman with his rifle.

Lyman ran onwards, going to lose him now, lose Martínez, lose them all, the bastards, do it alone, run, run lose them alone, the words steady in his brain like a beat, a heartbeat, and you can always beat exhaustion, just run, just remember the American and how you're going to kill him for killing Gallagher and the door gunner, the two soldiers in the village, trying to kill you, thinking of how the bullet had skimmed past his head and whacked through the fuselage and sung off the rotor. Little piece of metal with your death on it. Run run run, with a little piece of death on it.

They came to a path going north and south along the first ridge above the *Río*. 'The burro trail to Cobán,' she gasped, holding his arm to keep from falling.

He felt the same sudden sureness he'd had the night before, going out with her to the hammock. He glanced up at the crack of light through the canopy. 'Choppers see us here.' Thoughts blizzarded through his mind; he could see the tree canopy from above, as if he were looking down through the chopper's Plexiglass shell, as if with God's eye he could see how the trace of the trail cut through the jungle, how to pick out a motion, gun it down. Nam, how it was, shredding people under white hot metal hail. He saw her dead, torn apart by .50 calibre slugs, saw her old, grandchildren round her, saw how that was false, would never be, saw the jungle crouching nearer, waiting for them to fail. 'Give me that goddamn thing.' He took the gun, swung it over his right shoulder, the backpack over his left. Sensing it might be the last time, he freed her lustrous hair from her collar, so that it fell down her back.

She wiped her face with both hands, a motion that seemed strangely like prayer. 'It's for *you* that I wanted you to go to Mexico.'

'How far do we go?'

'About an hour south. I'll tell you.'

'You're going to follow me,' he ordered, 'about fifty yards behind. If I hit trouble, you beat it.'

'The Army doesn't bother this trail, it's too far in the jungle.'

'If you hear a chopper get into the trees. Try to get under a log. Same if you hear me shoot . . .'

'Told you!' Lyman yelled. 'Here it is!'

Martínez scrambled up to him. 'There's fire.'

Lyman tried to peer through the brush at the clearing. 'Bastards're cooking.'

'No. Big fire.'

The men crept forward one by one through the jungle, exhausted, dirty, clothes ripped, faces bloody, Angelo last. 'So what you want?' he said. 'Cook lunch?'

'It's a big fire,' Martínez repeated.

'Spread out, Christ!' Vodega whispered. 'You want to get *extinto*?'

'They're gone, Angel,' Lyman smiled, enjoying it that Vodega didn't want him to use his first name, not in front of the men, Vodega already angry about the chopper, about leaving it back there in the clearing instead of trying to make Sayaxché. Pilots not daring to take off again, waiting for a Shit-hook to pull them out. World of cowards.

The men were spreading out in a line, down to the river and up into the jungle. Lyman crawled forward to the edge of the open space with three charred banana palms and the cinders and burned beams where the hut had been. Too goddamn small for an LZ or I would've had him, the American, he thought. Why was he here? Who was that with him, that had looked like a woman? He backcrawled to Vodega and Martínez. 'Burned their hut.'

'Told you,' Martínez said.

'I'm going around, find their trail. Hold your fucking fire.'

Vodega smiled. 'Think we'd waste *you*? Aren't you our ticket to Paradise?'

Lyman went up the line, Martínez's laugh behind him burning in his mind. 'I'm going in,' he said to each man. 'Don't shoot.'

He circled the open. His knees were trembling with fatigue and he forced himself to wait a moment till they stopped. Using the muzzle of the M-16 to prod his way between the branches and creepers he inched forward, waited, moved forward again. A khaki green and yellow bird hopped along the leaves before him, pecking at twigs, fluttered away when he got close. The jungle was like the bottom of the sea, too thick to breathe.

Ahead a big goddamn tree, didn't feel right, danger. They could be here, he warned himself. He lay in a fern clump watching the tree but nothing happened. Wind off the river brought the burnt smell of the hut. Why was he here, the American? Figure that out and you'll have him, he thought.

He moved round the tree, closed in. Scuffed leaves, broken ferns. Rope burn round a trunk. Something was tethered here, a burro? Nonsense – never get a burro through this stuff. There was a second rope burn on another trunk nine feet away. Or someone slept here, in a hammock, not in the hut. Why the Hell'd they do that?

Unless there'd been some people in the hut, the two we killed on the river, and another one out here. On guard? Didn't make sense.

He followed the tracks from the big tree down to the still-glowing coals of the hut. 'Angel!' he called. 'Just you. Come on in.'

Vodega came along the bank and up to the hut. 'One of them went along the river,' he said, 'then came back.'

'One of them slept up there,' Lyman pointed behind him. 'Under a big tree.'

'We're chasing *espíritus, fantasías*. People who sleep under big trees.'

'Who's your best tracker?'

'Chichito – the kid.'

'Get him.'

Vodega called and the boy came out of the brush, too small for his uniform, black hair in his face, his gun pulling down his shoulder, dirty toes out of worn sandals. 'Five hundred quetzales,' Lyman said, 'if you can track them down.'

Chichito dropped his eyes – he's too shy, Lyman thought. 'Three people here,' Chichito said, and Lyman realized the boy had just been checking the ground. Chichito circled the hut. 'Maybe four.' He raised his eyes, scanning the jungle wall, went down to the river, came back. 'Two left in the canoe,' he said. 'Two went into the woods. One man, one woman. The woman is *Guatemalteca*. The other wears Quiché sandals but he's big and heavy and walks like a white man.'

Joy cascaded down Lyman's spine. 'You see, Angel?' he smiled at Vodega. 'Oh thee of little faith?'

19

She followed Murphy at a run south up into the mountains, the trail overgrown in thick scrub under the over-arching boughs, tracers of day down through the canopy. It was crazy to let him carry the gun, the backpack – if he was killed how would she get her medical kit, the gun?

Murphy slowed to a walk but she couldn't see him in the brush, hunted his tracks through the snapped leaves and bent creepers.

She yelled in surprise as someone lunged at her but it was him, coming back. 'Lost the trail,' he said.

'Give me my pack.'

He held her shoulder, keeping them standing. 'No.' His head wound was bleeding. I don't care, she thought. I don't care for anybody's wounds. The blood was bright on her hand. 'I've got to sew this up again.'

'No,' he repeated, turned and spat into the brush.

'If they track us,' she said.

'That big canyon we just went round – not far from the *Río*.'

She nodded.

He took a deep breath, staring at the green wall of their back trail. 'I should pick out a good place, wait to see if they come.'

'With how many bullets?'

'Six, plus one in the chamber. You have more?'

'No.' She felt a wild need to protect, hold him. 'At the *Río* there'll be a canoe, to take you downriver.'

'You're coming—'

'Are you crazy? After all this? You think a quick fuck makes any difference? I have my job, other people here. They won't want you around. I have a man here – he'll be very angry if he sees you—'

He was breathing deeply, wiping mosquitoes from his face. 'You have some guy?'

'Of course!'

His face looked pummelled, defeated. She clenched her fists, the nails sharp into her palms. Do it now, she told herself, while you still can . . .

'The things you said, last night, this morning—'

She could do it one more time, touch his face, making it seem like condolence. 'I was heartbroken – the village, *your* village—'

'So you did it *for* me.'

She shrugged. 'Think that if you like.'

'Bitch.' He turned away, swinging the rifle ahead through the brush, and again she followed him, running harder, as he shoved through the thorns and scrub, shadowed under the great trees, this shred of still-unravaged earth, she thought, from way back, from the beginning. How have things gone so wrong, she wondered, why do things always go wrong? Go ahead, cry, he can't see you, he's far ahead, lost in his anger. That's why things go wrong, it's anger – striving causes pain, and striving's from a lack of freedom, the freedom not to die, and so it goes round and round and never stops and I must not get caught up, she told herself, must stay free to help those who aren't, for what good's freedom when others are in pain? But that's an old lie and you must promise yourself no more lies, not even the lie of love.

Chichito's back was bent as he ran, to watch the earth, sweat on his khaki shirt, the rifle butt like a brown animal under his arm, Lyman running behind, panting and trying not to show it, the others gasping and swearing and trying to keep intervals behind. Chichito halted, stood up; Lyman nearly ran into him. 'Good!' Chichito pointed his small finger at a leaf splashed red.

Lyman wanted to hug him. 'Head wound.'

'*Sí.*'

'Which one?'

'The tall one.'

'That's right.' With a stab of pain Lyman saw Joshua in Chichito's face, the boy's calm self-assurance, of one born too long before his elders. He looked back into Chichito's black eyes: this time I'll protect you.

The skein of things unwinds, then you have nothing. She tripped, not taking her eyes from his back, how he ran surely and without fatigue for hours, the rifle easy, part of him. The skein unwinds

91

and disappears. And when we're gone it never was. This is the decision she'd made long ago, after they shot Diego. To have nothing but *la lucha*. If you don't have it completely you don't have it at all.

The trail skirted a slope, half-clear, a view back over a hundred miles of jungle, the *Río* down its belly like a God. It's *all* God, she thought – and we betray it. 'The trail goes down,' he said.

'So do we.'

He snatched her arm. 'It's true, what you said?'

She looked at the ground. White rocks through the black soil, grass fine as a child's hair. 'Yes.'

She listened to him breathing. Sweat poured down her back. You'll never have this again, she told herself. And you're to blame. 'When we reach the cut-off for San Pedro there'll be someone to take you downriver.'

'I don't need anyone—'

'Without help you won't make it. We have a way.'

'I don't care for your ways.'

'You're being spoiled again, gringo. It's nothing – a man and woman making love – you don't do this, sleep with someone then go away, the next day?'

'It's all I've done, for years.'

'So what's so hard to understand?'

He smiled, shook his head. 'Forget it.'

'You'll go downriver? Or you'll be killed.'

'And you?'

'We'll split up at the *Río*.'

He grabbed her arm and knocked her into the brush, rolled up and crouched over her, scanning downhill. 'Christ – you didn't see?'

She tried to squirm free but he held her down. 'What?'

'You're blind as a fuckin bat! Soldiers – coming up the trail!'

Carefully she raised her head above the leaves. A string of soldiers coming at a run up the hill she and he had climbed ten minutes ago. 'Give me my gun!'

'Go! I'll keep them – it's easy, here, to pin them down. Tell me where to bring the gun—'

'You won't keep it?'

'I don't want your goddamn gun. I don't want anything that's yours.' He pointed the muzzle at her face, six inches away. 'You don't go right now and you'll be the very first one I kill.' He switched the selector off safety, jabbed the muzzle into her cheek.

'Then I'll only have six bullets for the soldiers.'

She had a throb of fear, seeing his face white with anger. 'In about ten miles the trail splits for San Pedro and Chinajá. There's a little valley. There'll be people there. They'll keep the gun. They'll take you downriver.'

Watching where the soldiers had disappeared in the brush, he settled himself in position, wiping bark and dirt from the Galil's muzzle shroud. She gripped his shoulders. 'Please?'

'What?'

She kissed him, tasting salt. 'Go, goddamn it!' he said.

When he looked again she was gone. Six bullets. And one in the chamber. Too many soldiers. Get a few and pin the rest. Or get one early and try to reach his gun.

He crawled backwards through the scrub to the apex of the slope where the trees grew thick behind him and there was an angle of fire downhill where the trail cleared at a bend, enough to hit the point, and if you had bullets you could rake the brush and try to hit the slack. But he didn't, so the slack would reach cover and open up as soon as he shot, and they'd spray everything up here and he'd have to pull back, then when they came forward he'd be able to get the slack unless they circled. Of course they'd circle, but if he swung uphill he could flank them and in any case they'd get him, it was just a matter of how soon . . .

Again he glanced behind but she was truly gone. You're such a fool, he thought, an abandoned puppy ready to fall for anyone, this crap of all these years without anyone means that's how it should be—

The first soldier broke through the brush, climbing fast, a small man in khaki with his rifle slung. Murphy rested the Galil stock on his left hand, elbow well propped, settled his shoulder and chest into the warm, soft ground so that the muzzle came up steadily, seeing down the barrel shroud to the centre of the man's chest, adjusted for the slope, and slowly squeezed the trigger.

20

Lyman had been thinking of his sons, how Joshua had never lied, didn't need to, except when he'd been very young, and Lyman had taught him not to, that it was bad for *him*. But that Jason lied constantly, almost a reflex – have I made him ashamed of himself? he wondered. Is he ashamed of himself because he's not Joshua?

The rifle's crack and Chichito flying back arms outspread were unreal because Lyman wasn't *there*, had to come back suddenly as he dived for cover and fired wildly uphill towards the sound and yelled for Martínez to spread the men. Someone was gasping; he realized it was Chichito; behind him someone opened up, bullets shrieking over and whacking into the knoll above. The firing stopped; from the knoll barked a single shot and below Lyman a man screamed. Several Galils answered back; their fire wound down and again from the knoll the rifle fired once.

'Stop shooting!' It was Martínez, yelling at his men. 'Eduardo, Camilio, Benito!'

'*Sí!*' one answered.

'Who?'

'Benito.'

It's him – the fucking pilot, Lyman realized. Up there with the *chica* I saw from the chopper. He doesn't have much ammo so he's letting us make the moves then picking us off. He's got the position and I've let us walk into what I said I never would.

Or he has the *chica* on his flank and when we try to circle she'll hit us. Or she's the one up there and he's waiting for us to come round. There was a far-off whine – Chichito, who must have fallen off the other side of the trail. There was no way to reach him without crossing open ground. Someone was thumping his rifle butt into the earth and Lyman was furious with him then realized the sound was his own heart.

* * *

There were three bullets in the magazine and one in the chamber. Murphy could not judge how much time had passed. Already soldiers were moving up through heavy cover to his left; he could hear them but couldn't risk a chance shot. When they got to the top they'd rush and he wouldn't get them all. He crept leftwards on his belly from the knoll into the dark jungle, down towards the soldiers.

A Galil chattered, uphill but not from the top. One of us, Lyman decided as he spun on to his belly and dashed across the trail and dived down beside Chichito who lay on his back, head low, feet splayed uphill. His mouth was full of foamy blood and Lyman sucked and spat it out, mouthful after mouthful, hammering his fist on Chichito's chest but not near the round wet hole in the sternum. Trying to stay low Lyman dug a compress from his pack and reached under the boy's slim light body, pulled out his hand coated with lung tissue and blood. 'Martínez!' Lyman rasped. Crumbles of earth bumped his knee and he saw they'd come from where Chichito's hands had clenched then relaxed. A breeze abraded the leaves.

'Sí!' Martínez whispered, down and to the right.

'We got to circle both sides of that hill,' Lyman called in Spanish, hoping the pilot wouldn't understand or maybe not hear.

'I sent the right flank,' Martínez said.

'You and Angel go left, cut off the back—'

'And you?'

'I'll stay with Chicho – cut them off this way. Remember, there's two of them . . .'

A dragonfly landed on Lyman's wrist. The wind ruffled the boy's hair against his sweaty forehead. A spider-web between a stem and branch cast prisms of sunlight. Lyman laid his ear against Chichito's chest, hearing only his own pulse.

Murphy crept fifty yards downhill, found a depression rubbled with limestone boulders, all around thick with trunks, limbs, stems, shoots, saplings, creepers, leaves, brambles. Like a rat something hissed on the damp leaves, twanged a thorn, moved uphill behind him. He waited, counting out a hundred in pulses, forcing his heart slower while mosquitoes battered at his forehead and face, while the wind teased the leaves, spreading the sound of moving men. Then he continued down, north, then up through ferns to a crevice of madronè that gave a view of the knoll where he'd been.

Leaves twitched across the slope, below the knoll; a soldier bolted up and dashed towards the knoll, another coming over the top, through the trees. They met at the top and scrambled for cover; he hit the first and missed the second who ran back for the first and Murphy blew his head off, his helmet bouncing into the scrub. Murphy squirmed back from his crevice as bullets sprayed and sang through the trees. He checked that there was one bullet still in the chamber and crossed over the top of the slope and down its western side, away from the trail and the *Río*, then turned south, paralleling the trail.

'He's not dead.'

'He will be. You're not going to save him by carrying him two hours in the jungle to an LZ.'

'How come you don't have any fucking LZs? How come you don't *own* this country?'

Vodega came running up the trail and ducked down beside them, lifted one of the boy's eyelids, shook his head. 'That's it,' he said. 'We're pulling back.'

'*Back?*'

'We have five dead out of eleven. Or out of ten if we don't count you. That makes six you've killed today including the chopper gunner.'

'You insubordinate little shit—'

'You're not my superior, Colonel. You're from another world and you're screwing up ours. As soon as we get back I'm telling Arena to send you home. If *I* don't get back, any of my surviving men will carry the message.' He turned half away to watch the knoll where they were bringing down the bodies one by one on a bough and poncho stretcher. 'We're not girls,' he spat, 'you can't cut our throats.'

The ridge of the knoll continued south, bending eastward as it dropped towards the *Río*. Murphy kept to the heavy jungle below and west of the trail, half-way between the ridge and its valley. The jungle seemed to thicken, then he realized it was night coming, everything falling into shadow. There was a grey glimmer ahead and he pulled back to skirt it, turning east towards the river. The ridge had flowed down into the valley and he crossed a trail and could smell woodsmoke and then the cool breath of the *Río*.

Voices were coming up the trail, several people running; he

ducked into the trees. Now, with only one bullet left, he would pay for shooting the last two soldiers on the knoll, for shooting the one who'd gone back for his comrade. The first person passed, running hard. The second passed, lighter on his feet. 'When we get to the fork,' the third one called in Spanish, 'we must spread out.'

'Doña!' Murphy called.

The running stopped; there was a snick of metal as someone dropped a safety lever. 'Dona – it's me,' he whispered quickly in Spanish, before they could shoot – 'I'm back.'

'It's him!' Her voice neared out of the darkness, her hands snatched his wrists, clasped his face. 'Oh God it's you,' she said in English. 'I was so worried, we came fast as we could – where are the soldiers?'

'Went back.'

'Pascual! He says they went back!'

A tall heavy man came to them, breathing hard. Dona dropped her hands from Murphy's arms. 'How do you know?' the man said.

'I hit several and they must have decided to carry back the wounded. After that I left the trail and went through the *selva*. They can't follow till tomorrow.'

'How many'd you hit?'

'Two. Maybe more.'

'*Mierda!*' the other man said. 'Is it true?'

'If he says it,' Dona said.

'I just wanted to give you time,' Murphy said to her in English. 'I came to get a gun and found these two and brought them. I kept telling myself I must not worry because you are truly difficult to kill, but this time I was sure you were dead.'

'And here I am.'

She felt perfect within the circle of his arms, her shoulders a perfect shape and size, perfect the touch and smell of her hair against his cheek, her neck against his shoulder, lovely the feel of her arms around his back. She leaned into him, her weight suddenly on him. 'Just let me stay here, a moment, like this . . '

21

'You're going to die here—'

'I *can't* go with you. Please, accept that.'

'Your people need medics – I'll stay.'

'You're too different – you'd be captured in a month. You'd give too many of us away.'

Swallows were skimming the *Río* under the rising moon, darting and diving after insects, crying their harsh cries. 'You're lying.'

She glanced round at Pascual, who stood a few yards behind them. 'Remember what I said – why I can't?'

'I don't care.'

'He's the one.'

'Shall I tell him what you said to me, last night?'

She half smiled, embarrassed. 'Go back to the States, tell the newspapers, everyone, what's happening here.'

'Dona – I saw it all in Vietnam. Nobody cares, up there. Long as it doesn't hurt them.'

'Tell them. *Make* it hurt them.'

'It's coming,' Pascual said. '*La lancha.*'

Murphy looked at Pascual, burly and bearded, hair curling down over his brow. 'Why don't you protect her?' he started to say, but the question was crippled by too many differences – Pascual would not think a man should protect a woman, give his life for her if needed and never spend hers for his because she was the holy mother of his children, because she was life incarnate, because no cause was worth the death of a single woman. He thought of Inquisition priests killing Indian children to save their souls from Hell – that they like Pascual believed in the efficacy of death. He saw how his whole life could be lived with Dona, and that it would not be.

'I'm sending a wounded *compañero* downriver with you,' she said. 'He was shot in the stomach two days ago. He's suffering

98

horribly. We're trying to get him to Mexico, to the clinic at Bonampak. Please stay with him – you were a medic – do what you can?'

From upriver a motor was approaching, a dugout canoe with two women in the stern, burlap sacks of corn stacked on planks atop the hull in front of them. In the shallows the women leaped out and shoved aside the front rows of sacks and lifted the planks, and in the moonlight Murphy saw a dark-haired man lying in water in the hull, under the planks. Dona bent over him, speaking softly, caressing his brow. One of the women grabbed Murphy's arm. 'Get in!'

Dona was gone. Murphy squeezed into the hull, keeping his face above the water inside. The other man groaned, and Murphy saw his mouth was thick with blood that ran down his neck into the water. You're not going to live, Murphy thought. Planks clumped down over their heads, the corn sacks thumping on them. He could see nothing; the bilge of water, blood, and gasoline eddied back as the propeller dug into the river, then came sloshing forward as the engine steadied and the prow dropped. He twisted up his face and tried to back his body against the hull to avoid bumping the other man.

The hull banged and slapped the water, bubbles rushing past the wood beside his ear. There was no air. The man coughed blood down Murphy's face. 'Water!' he gasped. 'Please, water!'

She lay in the hammock pushing it slowly back and forth with a stick shoved into the ground. It was like moving in a womb, protected by the blackness, the silence, floating in an invisible world. Her mother's womb, dark, enclosing, warm, complete – was she truly remembering it? Could she go further back, to the fusion of her father's seed and mother's egg, back down the tunnels of their single cells?

The hammock rocked gently, its mesh tight around her shoulders. Unimaginable that *he* was here, in this hammock, what we did. The skin of her neck prickled, flushed. It wasn't even *here*, then, this hammock. Nothing was here but *him*.

Sex is God. Why didn't I know that? she asked herself. Sex brings life and war takes it away. And look which one I've chosen.

The canoe's motor slowed; over its diminishing rumble grew a larger, heavier one: another boat approaching. Cracks of light flared down between the planks and corn sacks. The hull thudded into steel, the wounded man cried out as Murphy lurched against him.

'Where the hell you going?' a voice yelled down.

'To Sayaxché, Jefe.'

'Where from?'

'Finca el Paraíso.'

'Can't you see it's night?'

'They must be there by the morning! It's for the truck to Flores.'

'How many sacks?'

'Twenty.'

The prow dipped as boots thumped down on it. The wounded man sputtered as water sluiced over his face. 'You troopers,' the voice said, 'move those sacks.'

'You'll tip my boat!' one of the women yelled. 'I'll lose my harvest – who'll pay for that?'

The sacks groaned as bayonets thrust into them. Corn kernels sifted on to the planks. Lights darted back and forth through the cracks between the planks. Kernels plopped into the water. Murphy tried to raise his arms but the wounded man was jammed against him.

'Please, Jefe,' the woman begged. 'This corn is for the mill at Flores. To make tortillas. Everybody needs tortillas—'

'Don't worry, mother. Just checking you're not carrying something else in your sacks. Enough, men. Toss ten of them up here!'

'Please, Jefe! Everyone needs corn, everyone needs tortillas—'

'We do too, mother. It's your penalty, for travelling by night. You're lucky we let you through.'

Boots thumped back and forth on the planks as the soldiers lifted the ten corn sacks up to the patrol boat. Murphy tried to pull up his feet so that they would not show beyond the planks, but each time his knees bumped the wounded man's he moaned.

The other engine revved; the canoe's prow lifted as the boots rose from it. 'It's no wonder,' the woman wailed, 'you soldiers have trouble with the *campesino*.'

'Have the sense to be quiet, woman, when you've come out ahead,' the voice called down as the patrol boat pulled away. '*No critiquemos Guatemala!*'

'Water!' the wounded man murmured.

Again Murphy tried to free his own hands. 'You can't reach it?'

'Water!' the other said. Murphy twisted his face down into the water and blood, took a mouthful, and filled the wounded man's mouth. The man swallowed, then with a burst of blood coughed it up again, face contorted with pain. 'Water!' he gasped, 'please water . . .'

Nancy just won't play by the rules, Lyman reflected. It's because of her I go to other women. Just like it'll be because of the Agency if I go outside. If the Agency's bringing the Colombians into Guatemala, who says I can't work for them? You can only take so much, when you're doing all the giving. Like with Nancy – she's too sharp, too independent. Trouble with her being so self-sufficient is that someday *nobody*'s gonna need her.

He shoved the pillow aside and rested his head on his folded arm. With one blanket he was too hot, with just the sheet he was too cold. Shouldn't even think about Nancy, times like this. Surrounded by cowards and dunces, ignorant Arena and smarmy insidious Angel. Nancy's the past, while I create the future. A field man, scouting enemy territory ahead of the tribe. Standing on peaks they'll never even see.

Today wouldn't look so bad by the time the Agency reviewed it. Fucking Guats afraid of the jungle. How they gonna catch guerrillas with their chopper at three thousand feet? Fucking Guats afraid of a little patrol. Hit hostile fire and they run. One thing to burn down a village of kids and old people, another thing to fight somebody who shoots back. When it was only that pilot, and maybe too the *chica*.

The way he fights – something familiar, how he uses cover. How he came through us and fired down from behind, got the two guys on the hill. Or was that the *chica*? Now I'll never know. Unless I find them, alive, talk to them about it.

I can ditch Nancy and still stay close to the kids. No, that's just liberal bullshit. For the kids it's better if Nancy and I are unhappy together rather than being happy apart.

Can't ditch Nancy till I get back into the field. The Agency won't let me back into the field if I blow this pilot. And I won't find this pilot with these fucking Guats running away whenever things get hot.

If the priest would talk. A real confession. But Angel'll kill him, out of misplaced zeal. No moderation – that's the problem with these people.

The river slackened under the keel; the prow bumped mud. Feet splashed alongside the hull; someone dragged aside several corn sacks and planks. 'Hurry!' one of the women hissed. 'Here's the path to Sayaxché and the Flores road.'

The night air was cool and sharp. Murphy tried to pull himself up but his legs were asleep. 'The *doctora* asked me to stay with him!'

'It was her way to get you to leave. Now *go!*'

He clambered over the side. The *Río* was shockingly cold against his crotch. The gurgle of the canoe vanished in the raucous croak of tree frogs and the muted rush of the current along the bank.

He took off his poncho, shirt, and trousers, washed the wounded man's blood from his face, hair, and chest, wrung out his clothes, and put them back on. They sloshed and rubbed against his skin as he followed the bankside path north, downriver, till the half-lit hovels of what must be Sayaxché appeared on the far bank. Ahead the jungle thinned into a clearing where campfires flickered on the dun camouflage of armoured personnel carriers. A few soldiers were clustered, talking, around the fires, their rifles stacked in pyramids. He backed away and circled them through the jungle till he picked up the two muddy ruts of the Flores road. He waited several minutes beside it but no one came, so he followed it north till it rose up from the riverside jungle and crossed a huge, burnt forest under the vast bowl of the stars.

A charcoal dawn grew in the east. The road began to climb again and he left it to sleep in the scrub, awaking to bright hot sun and the nearing grind of an engine. It was not soldiers but a red Hino truck jammed with cattle, crawling up the last grade. As it downshifted to lowest gear he ran from the scrub and jumped on to the rear bumper, climbed the rack, and dropped in among the longhorns' swaying haunches.

The truck jarred steadily towards Flores, the cattle staggering at each turn, staring round at him, rolling their white eyes and lathering their grass-stained liverish lips, huffing him with hot, fetid breath. Beneath their bellies he caught flashes of rushing bush and cragged limestone. The brakes squealed, the axle shimmied and wailed, slowly the truck grated to a halt. Boots thumped round it. 'What you got?' a man commanded.

'Can't you see?' a voice answered from the cab. 'Twelve eunuchs spawned by El Negro, greatest bull of all Petén. On their way to Paradise – the San Benito abattoir.'

'Seen anyone on the road?'

'Several girls coming out of Sayaxché. One of them had tits I could've licked all night.'

'Beat it, farmer. You've never licked anything but yourself.'

The truck lurched along the dusty, rutted road, its crankcase clattering, stockrack rivets rattling, longhorns staggering and sliding on the manure-slick floor and slapping up at green flies on their bellies with dung-caked hooves. Three more times the truck stopped for checkpoints, the cattle lowing uncomfortably, the sun boring down like a blowtorch, crickets crackling like small-arms fire in the scrub.

The air smelled of charcoal and garbage; the truck wallowed from one pothole to the next; above the slats Murphy could see a radio tower then lampposts. He climbed over the back, hopped from the bumper, and walked into wide, gritty, unpaved San Benito.

Barefoot boys were playing tin-can soccer in the street. A shady sidewalk fronted a string of shops. In one window were hammers with black rubber grips, yellow-handled chisels, saws with gleaming teeth, wooden boxes of shiny nails, zinc pipes, bags of seed, an orange diesel pump from Japan, machetes with flaw-less gleaming edges, and behind them the weird image of a man in a rag serape and threadbare trousers, skinny dirty toes out of home-made *caites*, his tangled hair and short beard thick with dust, who he saw was himself.

22

Five soldiers turned the corner, sun glinting off their black rifles. Murphy drew his serape up around his face and stared down like a peasant at the broken stones and litter of the sidewalk, watching their dusty black boots as he stepped aside to let them pass.

Beyond town the road narrowed; the sun beat down. Dizzy hunger gnawed his guts. He walked and walked, but the distant hills drew no closer.

To the left the machine-gun nests of Flores Airbase were like huge concrete toadstools with black eye slits watching him. A pick-up truck took him to the junction of the Dolores road, then turned south, towards Machaquilá. He stood at the crossroads, the road to Machaquilá broad and dusty before him, and he felt it was the entrance to the path with heart, back into the time when he had flown at night over this same road, over Dolores and past Machaquilá and between the ziggurat hills and down between the lanterns to the bad landing on the pockmarked road, and he'd been furious because Paco hadn't fixed the potholes – and Paco had been right to fear the Army.

The dusty, still air blistered his lungs. If you concentrate, you can figure how long ago that was, he told himself. If you go down the road, it means you should go back to Dona. You're going down the road to your end. It was 13 September when you left San Francisco. You stayed over in Merida and left the next night, the 14th. After midnight, the morning of the 15th. So you got shot up and hid in the jungle on 15 September. It was two or three nights in the jungle, then a week, maybe, in the village before Dona came. Then two weeks more till the priest came to take you downriver. Then the soldiers attacked and it was that night in the jungle with Jesús and Epifanía, then the next night was Dona in the hut with the woman having a baby and we ate the monkey the boy had killed.

The night with Dona seemed like all his life, not just one night.

His brain seemed impossibly clear and he could see his life as if it were a skeleton, bared of flesh. What if it were true that he'd spent his whole life with her, because the only time he'd *lived* was that one night? To think of her was to feel the pain strike to the bone, a rod of steel down to his core, the huge weight of sorrow.

It was truly the path with heart, as Castaneda called it, to go back towards Dolores and Machaquilá, back into the past: it called him so insistently it could not be wrong. But what would he do in Machaquilá? Go through the jungle again to the village? It was now burnt and empty. Yet intensely the road drew him – who was to say you couldn't figure out your future?

A heavy truck came grumbling up behind him and he turned, sticking out his hand. It was an Army troop transport, more trucks following, and he pulled in his hand but the first truck stopped. 'Where you headed?' a soldier in the cab called down.

'Belize,' he answered, not looking up.

'Come here!'

The man who had called down had a round face and a swollen jaw, as if he were chewing tobacco. 'You're not Guatemalan!'

'I'm from Belize. I'm going home.'

'Belize is Guatemala too. The *Ingleses* just stole it for a while. Hop in the back.'

'Thank you but no. I've got friends to see on the way—'

'Come on! You stuck out your thumb – we won't hurt you. We're going all the way to the border. Hurry – or we'll lose first position and we'll be eating dust all the way!'

A soldier leaned over the tailgate to help him up. The truck crunched into first gear and jerked forward. He sat down quickly against the tailgate, the soldiers shouldering aside to make him room. More sat circling him on the floor, others along two benches; they watched him half curiously. They do this, he reminded himself, pick people up then execute them in the hills. 'Thank you, *compadres*,' he said.

'*De nada*,' one answered, turning to spit over the tailgate. He passed a sticky bottle. 'Have a drink – it's good for the dust.'

It tasted like jet fuel with a caramel odour. 'Jesus, it's strong!'

'It just *boj*, comrade.' The soldier had hairy nostrils. Flecks of tobacco stuck to his teeth. 'It's what the gods gave us when they took away our freedom.'

The bottle clung to Murphy's palm when he passed it on. 'Does anyone know what day it is?'

'Day? It's the Lord's day. You don't know that?'

'Yes, but what day of the month?'

'Luis, Franco – you hear?'

'It's 21 October,' a soldier said. 'It's Sunday.'

'How far is the border?'

The man who had given him the rum glanced at the sky. 'Till dark.'

'Maybe,' said a man with a bandaged eye.

'Since he got hurt,' the first said, 'Cíclopes here always worries about *la guerrilla*.'

'You never know when you get ambushed,' said the man with the bandaged eye. 'Especially in the first truck. These pigs,' he turned to Murphy, 'laugh at me because I'm not afraid to fight, don't keep my head down like them!'

Another soldier with a thick Mayan nose elbowed Murphy – 'But soon comes the bad part!'

Murphy glanced round the circle of faces. The bad part is when they take you out and shoot you. *'Guerrilleros?'*

'Hah-hah! It's when we pass the turn-off to Tikal – after that the road's no good. It's just paved between Flores and Tikal to impress the tourists.'

'It takes a wise man to stick his head up in battle,' said the hairy one.

'You should know, Valderrama. The only place you'll ever get injured is your ass.'

The truck dropped with a bang from macadam to a boggy track that narrowed and twisted painfully up and down the rambling green slopes, the truck bed whanging and wailing on the bumps and ruts, one torn fender flapping like a broken wing. At times there were strips of uncut jungle where thin waterfalls necklaced black mossy cliffs, trailing skeins of rainbow mist. Then came miles of slash-burned hills bleeding their cuprite soils into frothy brown torrents, the truck's dust coating the convoy behind it.

Checkpoint after checkpoint passed unheeded; Murphy sank down among his fellows, a chill breeze carving at his ankles. If they were going to shoot you they would've done it long ago. Unless they're playing with you. The road climbed through tangy pines flushed with sunset; he thought of chill Novembers in Texas Llano country, walking rocky ridges with his father through frozen juniper, a cold rifle in his hands, a smell of deer on the snowy wind.

Lyman kept the telephone close to his face, his back to the
Guatemalan soldiers in the Cobán signals room.

'You're not making things happen, Howie,' Curt Merck was
saying.'

'You want a new deal with Arena, you work it out.'

'What about this pilot, you're not getting him—'

'It's the Guats, Curt. They won't let me. They won't fly low, they
get freaked on hostile fire, and they're—'

'You're getting Arena pissed. We have too many irons in the
fire for you to do that. I'm sending down some people, give you
a hand.'

'Listen, we brought in a witness, a priest. Theology liberation
type. Vodega was gonna do him, and I saved him. Let me talk
with him a while.'

'How come you ain't already done this? You don't have your
heart in it, being down there.'

'I don't want any fucking D-team, Curt.'

'Stop goading me, Howie. I'm sending down Vaughan, a dozen
guys.'

'You telling me I'm not cleared? That you guys got some other
agenda?'

'You know what you know. When you get back here we discuss
it.'

The truck crested a long ridge of pines and halted. The cab door
slammed; a fist banged the tailgate. 'Get him out!'

It was the swollen-jawed man. 'Far as you go,' he said. The
second truck came grinding up behind. If they do it, Murphy
thought, this is it. Below was a narrow black valley speckled with
lights.

'Wait!' a soldier called from the back. 'Come on, you guys, let's
find him some food.'

They bundled bread and a chunk of pork into a paper bag and
handed it to Murphy over the tailgate. 'Sorry we can't take you
closer,' said the swollen-jawed man. 'But we're not supposed to
take riders. Those lights down there are Melchor. Got your Belize
identity card?'

'Yeah, somewhere.' Murphy fumbled at his clothes.

'Just have it when you cross the bridge. Or you get a ride in
another Army truck all the way back to Flores.'

He stood by the roadside gulping the bread and meat as the

convoy descended towards Melchor, mufflers banging and shooting sparks, headlights darting up and down the roadcuts. Soon all was silent. Guatemala was empty and dark behind him; the western breeze brought across Belize's plains and piney mountains the dampness of the sea.

23

He went down the hill into the sleeping town. A rusty statue slumped under a greenish street lamp; huts and hovels straggled along the river bench. The bridge and guardpost gleamed with concertina wire under yellow tungsten arclights. He turned south into a pasture past a clapboard hut roofed with straw, a pen smelling of pig manure and rotten mangoes, a hutch where chickens clucked fearfully.

At the pasture edge the jungle was a black impenetrable wall. He angled towards the river till he found a bankside path mushy with rotten leaves and occasionally the dung of donkeys. Fireflies were like shooting stars in the brush; mosquitoes whined in his ears; he kept wiping them from his face. Something pinged underfoot and he dived, expecting a mine but nothing blew; he rolled away and ran, tripped and sprawled; with a deep thump a flare burst overhead, trailing down radiant embers, cutting the jungle into black and white staggering shadows. From the guardpost came the growl of a siren.

He ran along the trail, stumbling on sapling stumps; another flare cracked, a third. The jungle was like day; he pushed through it to the river; the bridge was hidden by a bend. He squirmed into the water and began to swim across, coming up for breath. It's easy, he thought, I'll make it; then beyond the shallows the current snatched, him tumbling end over end, fighting up for breath and slipping under. The bridge swung into view, impossibly high and bright. With a crushing pain something huge and heavy hit him, dragged him down, he was caught in the boughs of a tree; the bridge was overhead now, black under the flares; like a sea creature the tree churned over and spat him to the top and he clung inside its branches, hidden from the bridge.

The river swung to the left, the tree bearing hard against the Belize shore. He swam to land, pulled himself up a slippery steep bank and climbed a clearcut slope out of rifle range to a ridge overlooking the black river and the bridge gilded by the arclights of the Guatemalan guardpost on the far side, where up and down the banks soldiers were beating the brush, their flashlights winking.

Below him the corrugated huts of the Belize border post were lit by one lantern in whose wan glow a single unarmed sentry loitered. Murphy ran down a slash-burned cindery hillside to the road climbing up from the bridge, and ran along it east, away from the river.

After perhaps an hour he began to walk. The road traversed a small town where a few dogs barked disconsolately; it climbed into bowl-shaped hills where huge stumps of recent rainforest jutted up like menhirs. There were no birds, no snakes, no insects, only silence and the shuffle of his feet under the wheeling stars.

Towards dawn a narrow moon rose over a distant ridge capped by a dark pyramid he thought might be Xunantunich, where Mayan astronomers once calculated the exact trajectories of the stars. After sunrise a rancher let him ride in the back of his pickup to San Ignacio, then gave him a Belizean quarter, 'for a roll, cup coffee' at a sidewalk vendor's. The black hot jolt of coffee and the sweetness of the roll made only *this* seem real, the rest seem a dream. So let it be a dream, he thought.

Beyond San Ignacio he washed his face in a ditch where gaily garbed women were cupping water into plastic buckets. He rode an empty cane truck to the outskirts of Belize City, then caught a lift north with a grass farmer in a new Bronco with quad speakers and fat steel tube bumpers for deliveries to the States. A warm breeze through the Bronco's window ruffled his beard and blew wisps of hair across his eyes. The farmer gave him a fragrant banana; he tossed the peel out the window and in the side-mirror saw it alight birdlike in the grass. The farmer lit a joint and passed it to him; the rich sweet smoke filled his lungs; he could *taste* the air, see every emerald cell of every leaf of the hunched jungle and spiky bunchgrass, the algal pools and stooping egrets, the flysore Brahma cattle with their concave white flanks, the bleached towering skeletons of mahogany trees tied by green lianas to the chipped and chalky soil. The Bronco hit a hummingbird that exploded in a rainbow of feathers and blood against the windshield.

At Orange Walk's rotting Victorian square the Bronco turned east, and Murphy walked uphill through shady rubber trees till

110

he caught a ride on a flatbed on which strips of mahogany bark writhed like bandages in the wind. He sat on the back beside a broken-toothed Mayan who shared a handful of pumpkin seeds, their legs dangling over the end as they spat the pumpkin shells on to the road rolling away beneath them. 'I just came from Guatemala,' Murphy said.

The Mayan licked a white flake of pumpkin seed from his lip. 'Guatemala? What is that?'

He got off the truck at Corozal Town and walked east along a dirt road fringing the Bay to a jungled spit with a white house in a grove of bananas and limes. A man was husking coconuts with a machete on a mahogany stump. 'Hey! Lovejoy!' Murphy called, not wanting to startle him.

The man looked at him a moment, buried the machete in the stump. 'What the fock happened to *you*?'

'They killed my friends, burned my plane, killed a whole village—'

'Who, mon, *who*?'

'The Guatemalans, the Americans—'

Lovejoy grabbed his shoulder, walking him towards the house. 'Let's get inside, get you a drink!'

'I don't need a drink. I want food, some time to think.' They went into the cool, thatched, sea-scented shadows of the house. 'I'm a little stoned, actually.'

'I believe it—'

'No – had a few hits off a guy gave me a lift.' He found a chair and sat. Safe now, he thought. Over. But she's still there. Going through it every day.

24

Lyman caught a limo from National, tense to be home, hating and wanting Nancy. Languidly the lampposts sauntered past, the sleeping suburbs where once there had been farms, once forest. Clumps of dead leaves were frozen to the streets; against the lights the trees lunged, black and spidery. 'Been gone long, sir?' the driver asked, but Lyman didn't answer.

They passed a restaurant, a man and woman walking on the sidewalk, his hand on her shoulder, then another couple arm in arm – the walking wounded, Lyman thought. Hobbling from the battlefield of life. He let the metaphor grow in his mind – as we get older, wiser, there's no more of this silly cuddling: we're the survivors, have learned he who fights best fights alone.

His house seemed caught out by the limo's headlights, the Norway firs on each side of the door leaning away, hungry to escape, the lava chunks of the walk loud like dry bread crunching under his shoes, the dry bread the children left but the birds ate it and the children never found their way home. The doorbell rang in the distance, as if new walls had come between it and him.

The light flicked on; he felt thin and childish in its glare, holding his bullet-proof attaché-case like a door-to-door salesman, his carry-all over one shoulder like an unexpected, unwanted visitor. Nancy's eye in the safety lens was huge and rotund. He held his breath, standing straight.

'Well hi!' Frowsy and sleep-fragrant, her hair rumpled, her silk nightgown warm with slumber, she reached into his arms and he felt how slim and light she was, how evil it would be to hurt her, feeling also as always the need to be cool, steady, almost devoid of emotion because she seemed to prefer it – who are you, anyway, he thought, to trot out your feelings?

'Why don't you ever *call*!' she said. 'We've missed you.'

112

'I've thought about you all the time.' Almost all the time, he corrected himself.

She was rubbing her eyes and trying to wake up and he tossed his coat on a chair, took off his shoes and held her, her perfume irritating his throat, her hair tickling his unshaven chin, her lips against his neck. She pulled back. 'Want something to eat?'

'No.' He went into the bedrooms and hugged each sleeping child, the girl mumbling a dream, the boy waking instantly and holding him tight in his arms and not letting go till finally Lyman made him lie down, go back to sleep.

He padded in stockinged feet across the broad living-room carpet, past the black stack of stereo equipment, the bookcase shelves of CDs in gleaming array, the leather couches, the marble side-tables, the French watercolours and tall tapering plants; they seemed all to belong to someone else whose taste was good but excessive. He undressed in the bathroom, laid his clothes on his dresser.

'Just toss them in the hamper,' she said.

'Not the suit—'

'So how'd it go?'

'Standard stuff. Inspection, drills, exercises, troop reviews ad nauseam. Lots of nights to read and stare at the barracks' walls.'

'What'd you read?'

'Oh, nothing – you know, magazines, that rot.' The waterbed sank under his knee. 'Detective novels, thrillers—'

'Any good ones?'

'Not really. In one mind and out the other.'

She smiled. 'You really could've called—'

'That's just it, Nan. I couldn't. Same old drill.'

'Same old drill.'

He lay down, punching up his pillow. She held herself along him, and he wanted her badly, thinking you shouldn't, she probably doesn't want to, she's not awake, not expecting this, but he couldn't help himself, and she raised her hip so he could slide up her nightgown; she turned her face from his breath as he shoved into her, recoiling then trying not to show it, and he thought the pain of it, the pain of it for *them*, while in him the fire was building, the gorgeous explosion, and she got up and went to the bathroom and he felt rotten and empty, as if he'd just spilt the last five weeks.

'You must be sleepy,' she said, getting back in bed.

He held her. 'Not at all.' Pretend she's a stranger, he told himself, tracing with a fingertip the line of her brow. Black hair, brown skin. 'One bad thing—'

The muscles of her neck stiffened; she made herself relax. 'What's that?'

'Kit.'

She raised up, pulling free. 'What?'

'He's dead.'

She spun away and sat. Her claw came out and raked his face. 'You bastard. You waited to tell me! Bastard!' She dashed out, nightgown sailing round her knees.

He followed her into the living room. She sat on the couch with her face in her hands. He wiped blood from his cheek and stared at it in the palm of his hand. 'It's sure?' she said.

'I saw him.'

'Who did it? Which of you bastards is responsible?'

'He was killed by a drug smuggler, Nan. I'm not supposed to tell you that . . .'

'I don't *care* what you're supposed to tell – your silly rules!'

'The reason I was down there so long was to try and get the one who killed him—'

'Which you failed to do!'

'It's not that easy, Nan.'

'I don't *care* if it's easy. I don't *care* anything about you!'

He looked down, realized he was naked. 'I've done a lot you never see. I'm a lot more than you think—'

She did not answer and he realized she was crying, quietly, into her hands. He felt cold and went back into the bedroom and climbed into bed.

Murphy was wading through a field of yellow flowers with a woman and a child. They were one flesh; he could feel what they felt and see with their eyes.

He was being hunted down a long hallway. He hid in the second storey of a warehouse stacked with cases of canned sodas; he took a can. 'Watch out!' Lovejoy yelled. 'It's explosives!' He laughed and tossed it over a wall; it banged loudly, waking him up. Those flowers, he thought, they must be *flor de muerte*.

Breeze stirred in the white muslin curtains; through the window came the cries of gulls and the mumble of bees. The room smelled of lime flowers, jasmine, and sea. The beeswaxed pine floor squeaked under his soles. He walked out on to the veranda and a flock of sparrows burst chittering from the eaves. He went back into the kitchen, drank fresh orange juice till the container was empty then squeezed more and drank it. There was bacon laid out on the counter and he fried it with six eggs and ate them with lime pie. He mixed a big cup of Mexican instant coffee and sat out on the shaded terrace in the warm wind off the sea.

Lovejoy came and leaned his yellow bicycle against the terrace wall. He carried a plastic bag of red meat into the kitchen. The refrigerator door opened and shut. 'You get enough to eat?'

'Just barely.'

Lovejoy came out with four Tecates and sat. He popped one can and squeezed lime into it. 'You slep' more, las' three days, than you used to in a month.'

Murphy stretched his right arm over his head, testing it. 'Feels good.'

'Goin' stay a while?'

Murphy patted Lovejoy's shoulder, let his hand rest there. 'Can't.'

'I think you oughta wait, find another cargo, drive it up.'

'Can't.'

'You los' your plane, mon. How you going to earn a livin'? Better you let me front you a load, I'll buy you a van, you drive it up. Then you got money to buy another plane. Simple as thet.'

'Don't need to earn a living any more, Love.' Murphy's head hurt and he wanted to get out of the sun, realized he wasn't in the sun.

'Get yourself a camper,' Lovejoy said, as if he hadn't heard. 'Tie in with one o' them American groups thet drives their campers through Mexico together – the Wally Byams – thet what they called? American Legion, or some kinda religious group, Protestants – thet kind of thing. Go through the border with them: you be home free . . .'

Murphy opened another beer and squeezed lime into it. 'I need you to front me a ticket and a driver's licence so I can go home.'

'Home don't sound like no safe place to be right now.'

'They can't trace my plane, can't trace me anywhere—'

'And what you goin' do when you git home?'

'Sort things out, maybe come back down.'

'Revenge don't work, mon. It take you with it.'

'I want to know why they hit my plane, killed Johnny and the others—'

'You never will know.'

115

'She said they're hitting other planes, even people who've paid protection. This General Arena – going to be head of the Armed Forces.'

'That's his job – wipe out the others, keep it fo' hisself. He be doin' a good job at thet.'

'And I want to know why that American officer was there – and why they killed him.'

'You's too curious by far.'

'Too curious by far!' Lovejoy's parrot repeated from its perch under a banana tree.

'If you fell for some woman like Dona,' Murphy said, 'you'd leave her?'

'Forget thet woman, mon. She not ever going to live for you.'

'And the people who burned my village – you'd let that be?'

'Like thet woman say, the best way to fix thet is talk about it in the States. But the moment you do thet you blow your cover and these people goin' come looking for you. Now what's the good o' thet?'

25

'They's a little too big for you, mon.'

Murphy looked down at Lovejoy's flowered shirt huge in the shoulders and the purple trousers rolled up at the cuffs. 'Your mother fed you too much.'

'They'll do till I pop over to Chetumal, get you some right ones. Shoes too. Today we takin' you into town, fo' a shave 'n' haircut—'

'I'll keep it like this. Covers up the scar.'

Lovejoy shook his head. 'One more inch to the right and you was gone.'

'Never hurt at the time. Only after . . .'

'Always meanin' to asks you – where you git thet star?'

Murphy glanced at the tattoo on his right arm, above the bullet wound Dona had healed. 'The Lone Star of Texas. Got it in Hong Kong.'

'Thet figures.'

'I was on leave. Rest and Recreation.'

'Thet's a trouble bein' black: can't do tattoos. You kin, but they don' show.'

'You ain't missing much.'

'Don't like Hong Kong. Use' to go there, in the merchan' marine. Didn't like it.'

Murphy went to the refrigerator and came back with more Tecates and another lime. 'Pick 'em off the fuckin trees.'

'Wha's thet?'

'Limes. Sign of civilization. No civilization where you can't have fresh limes.'

'Civilization's where the love's easy, mon. I thought a lot about it, seen a lot of places, and thet's the best indication I kin find.'

'Always thought civilization was sex, drugs, and rock 'n' roll. The Holy Trinity—'

117

'We's a lot wiser when we's young. We sure git stupid, growin' older.'

'All those days lying there in that hammock – limes saved my life. Dona told me, said they fight off the infection—'

'You believe ever'thing she say, this gir'l?'

The lawn in front of the terrace was white with sun. Through the beach palms Corozal Bay scintillated with blue fire. 'People been dead twenty years, Love, they came back to me – live, like you and me. When I was lying in that hammock . . .' Murphy stood at the edge of the terrace, the edge of the shade, breathing in the heat. 'My two best friends, in Nam, both got killed. We'd been living in death, seeing it all around us – there were days I remember seeing fifty dead or more, new ones, every day – but my friends – I would've gone crazy if I hadn't shut it down—'

'Tha's the trouble.' Lovejoy put an empty on the floor, opened another. 'You shut *thet* down, pretty soon you're shutting it all down.'

'For years I've hardly thought about them. Never realized what they've missed, since then – every day they could be living and don't they still suffer – and I don't let it hit me.'

'You lettin' it hit, right now.'

'My friend Okie sat on the floor beside the hammock and we talked, for hours. I told him I've loved him like a brother all these years, down inside my heart. He said I had to pull through, that he had come back mostly for that, to help me. That I mustn't feel bad because I'd lived and he didn't.'

'Yeah?' Lovejoy said.

'We called him Okie because he came from Oklahoma. He'd been a hippie, with a beard, before he was drafted. He would run right out in mortar fire to drag some guy in . . . bullets flying all around. He hated war. He just scorned it. So big and strong you almost thought he could take the whole war up in his fists and strangle it. He never let on, but it was eating him alive that his chick back home was screwing another guy – some guy who was too sensitive to fight, had a family that paid a shrink to write the draft board a letter saying he was crazy.'

'Then he probably was.'

'What?'

'Crazy.'

'Okie ran into a bunch of Cong on a path, he was going into the woods after a wounded guy screaming for help. He didn't have a gun or anything. The Cong just ripped him in half. I told him

118

I'd kept thinking of that moment, how he must have felt. He said it was pure terror when he saw them shoot and knew he was going to die, then being hit, horrible pain, being knocked back and you see everything close up and after your heart stops the brain keeps thinking for a while, sorting things out.'

'Then what?'

'He said you can come back to the people who knew you. That you can help them, that the same battle between good and evil that goes on in life goes on afterwards. That evil's stronger and usually wins, which meant I had to harden my character, become more honest, think more about death and life.'

'But what he say about *him*, since then? 'Bout where he been?'

'He just said you know what you know.'

Lovejoy shook his head. 'Shit!'

'He'd never known Clint, my other friend. Clint died before Okie came over. When I was in the hammock Clint didn't come as much as Okie, but sometimes they'd be there together and the three of us would talk, like sitting around a fire in hunting camp, thinking over past times. They became friends, while the three of us sat round together. Except I was in my hammock and it hurt to move and breathe and hurt even if you didn't and I was crazy with the pain and fever and they knew it and made allowances, and Clint used to tell me how to fight the pain—'

Lovejoy got up, squeezed Murphy's wrist and stepped across the terrace out into the sun, across the blazing grass to the shade of a papaya clump. 'Beer go right through you, on a hot day,' he said coming back. 'What he tell you, 'bout this fighting pain?'

'He said you can't hold it back, gotta let it take you. That sometimes you can change it a little by moving yourself or breathing or forcing yourself to think of something else. Said he'd lain for three days on a little hill with a neck wound – I'd never known what happened to him, we could never find them – and during the third night their position got hit by B52s. Thousand-pound bombs.' Murphy looked out over the terrace to the line of shore all green against the blue and white. 'I used to get so full of hatred about what had happened. I wanted to go back to the States, take all the people who voted for that war, the politicians and the people who voted for them, wanted to kill them one by one, have them feel what my friends felt.'

'And now?'

'I still hate them for being stupid. But now I think war's like

119

an earthquake or something. There's no way we can control it.'

'We jus' prefer war to other things, thet's all.'

'Clint's daughter, she's twenty-one now, she was born after he died. I got wounded again at the end, never went to Maine, where Clint came from, never saw his wife. Years later, I never called his kid. So he asked me to.'

'You going to?'

'Said I felt like one of those lousy fathers who never sees his own kid after a divorce, then suddenly when she's grown up he reappears, wants to claim her . . . he said it wasn't like that, that what keeps people apart is pain, not meanness. He said all meanness just comes from pain.'

'I'm very pissed you brought me back up, Curt.'

'It's not your business to have emotions.'

'How you expect a guy to do his best when you keep cutting his *cojones*?'

'I been behind you all the way, here. In this Agency, Howie, you got me to thank—'

'I got *me* to thank, Curt. *I* got me where I am.'

'With some help from your friends. Just like when I was coming up, I had people looking out for me. And what you got to remember is, afterwards you got to treat them well . . .'

The yellow of Lyman's fingernails irritated him, against the light chocolate skin, the fingers splayed out over the knee of his blue pinstripe. Spread fingers a sign of weakness, he thought, brought them together. Under the desk Lyman could see Merck's little feet hanging down from the chair, not touching the carpet. Little penguin feet.

'You got to accept when we wanted you out, down there, it's for good reason.'

'You mean latinos just don't like blacks—'

'That too. But that's why I always pushed you down there, pushed you in their faces, because you're better than anyone else and I wanted them to have to admit it. Now instead you screw up and get a whole buncha guys killed—'

'Six, Curt. Just six guys killed. And the reason the Guats don't take so many casualties is they're chicken. They'll burn a village, kill women and children, no problem. Just like us in Nam, the napalm raids. But at least *we* had the guts to go out in the boonies and hunt Charlie down. Blow his fucking ass off.' Lyman realized his arms were quivering, made them stop. 'You ask these Guats to get down on the ground, out in the bush, off the fucking trail? *Never!* A little recon? *Never!*'

Merck sat back, smoothed down one eyebrow, propped his elbows up on the chair arms. 'Howie, there's policies being decided –' his little hands came up and out, like a man rendering himself, Lyman thought – 'far above my head. Like you, I got to deliver . . .'

'Don't pull duty on me, Curt.'

'What you using your head for, Howie? Think *real* politik.'

'OK, I think it's fine we jacked down the crude oil price and pushed up the ante on defence technology and forced the Commies under. And like you've said, we got a different ballgame now in Latin America because the poor don't have any recourse any more but to eat shit. But bringing the Colombians into Guatemala – I don't see what it brings us.'

'That's why I'm where I'm at, Howie, and you're going to stay where you're at. Until you learn to see.'

26

'Soon's Miss Pru and Desirée come home I'll cook up thet conch. You want fritters?'

'Do I want fritters? What kind of question's that? But we're gonna need more beer.'

'Tecate he be all gone. Got to go back Mexico. They be jes' Libertad.'

'Jesus!'

'You have'n too much anyways, mon. You been beat up, got to rest easy.'

Murphy crossed the veranda and the grass cooler now in the late afternoon sun, stood barefoot in the water warm like warm tea. He stripped his clothes and waded in, sat letting the sea wash up against his chest. His head was spinning and he put it under the water and swam out underwater, the light pearly blue above and cool purple below, the rolling bay waves bubbling sunlight. You could drown like this, he thought.

Nancy took Lyman's coat and hung it in the hall closet. She glanced across the living room then came up to him, hands against his chest. 'I'm sorry about your face.'

'I know you don't love me. I know that and I accept it.'

'You don't need to hate me the way you do.'

'I don't hate you, Nan. You're all I've got.'

'You've got the kids—'

'Yeah, and they come from you . . .'

'They come from *you*, too! Can't we live with some affection – till they grow up?'

'They don't need me.'

'They'd need you if they had you. They just don't have you. And if you had them you'd need them, too. But you never spend any time with them.'

'I been too busy, Nan. Trying to make things easy for them. For you.'

'Let's make a new beginning?' She took his hand. 'Pretend we like each other, like friends? Pretend we're just living together, two friends?'

'How many times we made new beginnings, Nan? You're just saying that now 'cause Kit's dead, you got nobody to fuck.'

She twisted his wrist, nails in the skin. 'You're the *bastard* that started that – you *wanted* me to!'

'Because I knew it's the only way you'd come alive – that you couldn't get it from me!'

'I *married* you, didn't I? What more do you *want*?'

He caressed her cheek, realized it was a slow slap and pulled his hand away. 'We got married too many years ago.'

'The only thing that counts is a man love a woman.' Miss Pru put a big chunk of conch fritter from her fork into her mouth. 'Don' matter 'bout nothin' else – not to her.'

'She's got to love him too,' Lovejoy said.

'Of course. Otherwise she don' care if he love her or not.'

'I don't want any man to love me!' Desirée said. 'Who wants to have kids and everything – horrible! When instead you could be free?'

Pru was cutting more conch. 'Matters some day, honey. When you find you tired o' that ol' freedom. When it wearin' you down. But you got years to go. You git to finish your school first.'

'Then I'm going to be a doctor,' Desirée told Murphy.

He almost dropped his fork, bit his lip, raised his Libertad to her, a mock salute.

She shook her head. 'I'm *serious*.'

He watched the thatch, watched nothing; the pain went away. 'I'm sure there's nothing better you could do.' It sounded false. 'I mean it, honey.'

Pru leaned forward, big black sweaty elbows on the table. 'So I don' think you're right, Love – tellin' him forget her. He should go back there, *make* her come out here, to civ'lization, not live in the jungle like a monkey, like that—'

'He *can't* go back in there 'n' get her! They never let him back. They *kill* 'im if he try thet!'

'She won't go with me anyway, Pru.'

Pru put down her fork. 'Then she jes' a stupid gir'l.'

123

'No – she's right.'

Pru grasped the fork, shook it at him. 'She right not to love you when you love her?'

'No, not that. She's got another love, that came first.'

'You mean thet gorilla?' Lovejoy put in. 'Thet one she said she loved?'

'No,' Murphy laughed. 'She loves what she *does*, what she does for people, making things better—'

A wide incredulous *moue* creased Pru's face. 'What she doin' for you?'

'I've been thinking we should buy the McCormack house,' Nancy said.

Lyman poured the whisky into the octagonal glass and placed the one ice cube carefully, so it wouldn't splash. Wait twenty seconds, just enough for it to cool the whisky, not dilute it. The taste was like smoke, like fire, burning on the tip of his tongue then cooling backwards, oak fire flaring to ice up through his sinuses. He thought of hash in Vietnam, how the taste of it, the *feel* of it, had come up through his nose and into his brain. 'We can't stand each other. You want us to buy a house?'

'You're exaggerating, Howie. I agree, it's been hard. But maybe if we shared in something new, something bigger, an improvement? It would say something about *us*.'

'It would say we're out of our fucking minds.'

'You'll never *try*, will you, darling? It's always got to be Howie just the way he is, he never *tries* to be better—'

'I try to be who I am, Nan. That's hard enough.' He took another swig of the whisky but it wasn't the same, too much water now. The thought of a cigarette made his lungs ache. 'No, come to think of it, I don't try to be who I am. I never even know.' If he had a cigarette in front of her she'd think he was weak, that he couldn't shake it. Nine weeks now, down to five a day. He could get up and go into the bathroom, or say he had to see something in the garage, have a quick one. But she'd figure out. Smell it. He went into the kitchen, dumped the ice cube, came back and took another, filled the glass up. The whisky was like piss, yellow and oily. He thought of all the Scotch bottles in all the stores in the world, all the wine, the beer, champagne. Waiting to be piss. All the fine pastries and steaks and gourmet foods, caviar at fifty bucks an ounce, waiting to be shit. 'I bet if you try to learn about yourself, if *I* try to learn about myself – I bet I can.'

124

She took his wrist that earlier she'd clawed. 'I know you can, Howie. You do, and we can be together again. All the way.'

The thick air was musky with star jasmine and citrus, the indolent breeze off the Bay, the sweet-smelling cane fields. 'Coupla drinks, Murph, then I'm takin' you home.'

'I know the way back.'

Lovejoy took his arm, as if holding himself up. 'You liable to fergit.'

'You don' have any fuckin *beer*. Here I come to see you and you don' even have any fuckin *beer*!' Each time I think of her, Murphy decided, it's easier.

'I didn't know you was comin'.'

'Neither did I.'

At the end of the street a white house with wide steps. 'Them belly full but we hungry,' sang the music inside. 'A hungry mon is a hungry mon—'

They climbed the stairs, weaving between the men sitting with beers on the steps. Lanterns reflected inside off spilt beer on the table tops. Lovejoy got a cloth from the bar and wiped a table. Murphy sat; the table stuck to his elbows. Lovejoy took the cloth to the bar and came back with two beers. 'Belikan?' Murphy said.

'Belikan.'

'Jesus! The English ruined you people.'

'Not me, mon. I's from Ja*mai*ca—'

'I *know* that.' Murphy drained his glass and watched the dancing bright-eyed slim-dressed girls clapping cheap gold heels and bare feet on the beer-spilt floor. 'Going back, Stateside – I won't need a driver's licence. Just lend me money for the ticket—'

'How the *fock* you gettin' through the border?'

'Fly up, Monterrey, walk across.'

'You crazier 'n shit, mon. Border patrol going to have yo' *ass*. Then they going to start discussin' with you where you been . . .'

'You're afraid of the cops, Love. I really think you are.'

'Course I am. When you livin' fine and easy why should'n you be? When any time they kin take it all away?'

'You've got good distance. You're not in it.'

'The minute I stop paying I am. Or when they want to make an example. You always try to make sure they make an example of somebody else, but nobody ain't perfect.' Lovejoy leaned forward, clasping his beer. 'How much you shoulda made, thet trip to Guatemala?'

''Bout fifty.'

'You'll make more 'n that, driving it up.'

'It's too dangerous. I told you.'

'You's like I used to be, after twenty years at sea. I thought everything on land was dangerous. You been flyin' too long . . .'

'I don't want to go through no border with no half ton of weed.' Murphy realized he was talking like Lovejoy. It's just the beer, he decided.

'It's 'emetic, mon – all welded in. The dogs can't smell it and even if they strip down your rig they can't find it. You cross at El Paso, like I said, with some missionary types, you ain't ever got a worry.'

27

'Jason!' Lyman yelled. 'This yours?'

The boy saw the transparent film canister in Lyman's hand. Inside the canister a golden butterfly, crumbles of wing at the bottom.

'I found it one day. On a hike.'

'Well goddamnit keep it in your room. Stuff like this all over the house – no wonder we're all going crazy—'

'*We*'re not all going crazy, Howie,' Nancy said.

'C'mon!' Lyman yelled at the boy. 'Hustle! Hustle!'

'Howie –' Nancy sat on the edge of the couch, hands clamped between her knees – 'what's eating you?'

'*You're* eating me. *He*'s eating me. You're *all* eating me.'

She patted the couch beside her. 'Sit.'

Despite himself he sat. There was an ache between his shoulderblades, all the way up his neck. He wanted to say he was sorry but wouldn't.

She put her hand on his knee. 'I meant what I said, Howard. We're going to start a new beginning. I'm going to understand the stress you've been under and I'm going to make it better for you. And you're going to stop seeing me as some bitch and instead as the person you love, the mother of your children.'

He snickered. 'I'm not even sure of that.'

Her hand clenched. 'You're going to stop saying things like that, Howie. That's part of our new beginning. If I have to, I'll do this all by myself. But I'd rather do it with you.'

'You can't make me love you, Nancy.'

'You already love me. I know that. The one you don't love is yourself.'

'Got Irish whiskey?' Murphy yelled over the reggae to the fat woman at the bar.

She reached up a gold bottle. 'Black Bush.'

127

'That's Protestant whiskey, Bushmills.'

'You prayin' or drinkin'?'

He took the bottle and two glasses to the table. 'You goin' have a *bad* headache in the morning,' Lovejoy said.

'Wouldn't feel right without one.' He poured the glasses full. 'Don't make no sense.'

'It don' make any sense to me either, mon. So I jes' lets it alone.'

Murphy drank a second glass, not tasting it. 'You jes' love who you got,' Lovejoy said, 'an' you don' try to change the worl', 'cause the worl' been screwed up longer than you know.'

Four men in uniforms came in and sat by the door, waving at the bar. 'Those guys—' Murphy said.

Lovejoy screwed round in his chair. 'They's got a right to come in, get laid, jes' like anybody. On leave, prob'ly, from Honduras.'

'They're Airborne.'

'They's what? Hee, hee – I *know* they's born. Otherwise how they be comin' in here?'

'Like the ones who burned my village—'

'Tha's bullshit! Those was Guatemalans, you said.'

'There was Americans with them.'

The four Americans rolled up their sleeves, nodding and talking, the black girls gathering round them in the roaring reggae. One soldier, blond and broad-shouldered, beckoned to a girl in a lilac blouse and black shimmery slacks; she sat open-legged in his lap, drinking beer from his bottle as he bounced her loosely on his crotch, a cigarette hanging sideways from his red lips.

'Forget your troubles, and dance,' Lovejoy sang with the music. 'Forget your sorrows, and dance.'

Murphy walked softly across the noisy crowded floor to the four soldiers. 'Where you guys stationed?'

'Hi!' one grinned. 'Have a beer.'

'Where you stationed?' he said to the blond one.

'What's it to you?'

'I wouldn't have asked, mother-fucker, if I didn't want to know.'

The soldier watched him, chewing his cigarette. Murphy flicked it from his mouth. 'Ever been in Guatemala?'

The soldier slid the girl from his lap, stood. 'Well, look at this. I come in here to get laid and I get some asshole in my face.'

Murphy hit him square, the satisfying crunch of front teeth, agony snaking up his bad arm. The soldier went down in crashing tables and chairs, another's fist slammed into Murphy's chin and he flew backwards, sliding on his back across the floor, tables and beer bottles tumbling. He got up and with a red flash of pain a bottle exploded over his head and he spun to hit the soldier with the bottle wondering is it blood or whiskey running down my neck, another soldier swinging a chair but it caught on a toppled table and Murphy kicked him and the blond one grabbed him and they fell, Murphy twisting to grind him backwards in the shattered glass, the others kicking his ribs and a boot hit his bad arm and he screamed, rolled free, grabbed a table, a single still-upright Belikan bottle on it ricketing absurdly as he threw the table and the other soldiers backed away swearing; the blond one got up and Murphy hit him again, under the ear, and he fell face down in the broken glass. 'Get *out*!' Murphy screamed, a man behind the soldiers laughing white teeth, and suddenly Murphy saw everyone was staring at him, at the mess on the floor.

The blond soldier stood slowly. 'You're crazy.'

Murphy felt a sudden plunge of shame. 'You get out of here. You get out of *everywhere* down here.'

Blood was running down the soldier's forehead into his eye. There was blood in his mouth. 'We were doing nothing, just having a—'

'You musta done something,' Lovejoy said, 'to make him so mad. Be smart, mon, move on. They be 'nother bar down the street.'

'T'row dem white boy all out!' someone laughed.

The fat lady was sweeping up glass. People had set up the tables and were sitting again, laughing, animated. The barefoot girls were moving tentatively on the dance floor, watching for glass. Lovejoy grabbed Murphy's shirt. 'Why the *fock* you do thet, mon? This be *my* place! Grace!' he yelled to a barefoot girl in a yellow blouse, 'you take this crazy mon upstairs, see if you can *fock* some sense into him!'

Murphy rubbed blood out of his eyes. 'Go to Hell, Lovejoy!'

'They soldiers goin' be waitin' fo' you! You git you white ass up thet stairs!'

Grace pushed him ahead of her upstairs to a low room with a wretched mattress on a broken bed and a dejected table cluttered with empty Belikan bottles. She unbuttoned the yellow blouse, dark shiny breasts popping out, slipped down her black skirt, nothing underneath. The bed squealed and slumped when he sat on it; she found a cloth on the table and stood before him, wiping blood and beer and pieces of glass out of his hair, her breasts warm and full against his face, her cunt smell tangy. After a while he put his hands round her and licked her breasts, down her front and buried his face in her warm bush, the hair thick and silky, and she pushed him back on the bed and came on top of him, riding him slowly, saying 'Jesus', and his head was spinning and he was seeing strange places and dead faces and then it came out of him and he thought like pus, like purging some disease, and Grace a nurse, sister of mercy: how God was born, he thought, seeing the woman beside him, young and lithe, his seed inside her going nowhere, like all of us, seeing himself and Grace as God saw them – a woman and a man on a stained and sticky mattress, the floor with crushed palmetto bugs under a fly-stained bulb, mosquitoes clamouring through a torn screen, the laughter of drunks and reggae pulsing up through the boards,

> He who seeks of only vanity
> and has no love for humanity
> shall fade away, fade fade
> fade fade away . . . .

28

'Why you got a picture of *him* on your wall?'

'You should hear his new album, Dad.'

'He's a traitor to your skin, Jason.' Lyman sat on the bed, sneering at the poster on the wall of a premenstrual hypnotic bitch, suddenly wondering has this man suffered everything just to make himself what people need him to be?

His big flat hand felt strange on Jason's knee and he removed it, brushed the boy's fuzzy curls, *made* his fingers go into them. 'He even straightens his hair, that guy.'

'Like Christina.'

'She can't help it. She's going to do anything I don't want her to.'

'She's a girl, Dad. She can't be anything like you.'

'How d'you think she's going to end up? Really?'

Jason drew up one knee, hands clasped round it, thinking. Lyman glanced down at Jason's sneaker to make sure the sole was not dirtying the bed. 'Your mother has to wash that sheet,' he said.

'Oh – yeah.' The boy put down his foot. 'Sorry, Dad.'

'So what do you think?'

'About Tina? I think she's fine. She's nice to me a lot of the time. She takes me places, drives me to games when Mom can't.'

'You don't hate her for yelling at you?'

'She only does that sometimes. Mom yells at me too, sometimes, and I don't hate her.' Jason looked up at Lyman entreatingly. 'Sometimes even you yell at me . . .'

'Don't let's talk about that now. Sometimes you deserve it.'

'I got three goals last week.'

'You did? In one game?'

'No – one against Harmondale on Tuesday and two against Lincoln on Saturday.'

'You play forward both games?'

131

'At Lincoln I played defence the first half.'

'Shit! Why'd he do that?'

'Coach Larsen? He just did it, that's all.'

'Well, you went out and showed him. You got two goals.'

'He says everybody has to play offence and defence – that we're there to learn, not to win.'

'That's liberal bullshit. Don't you ever believe that. The only people who try to teach you that are the ones who want to keep control over you. That's a white thing to do, Jason. All that counts in life is winning. Morals and laws are to keep most people in line so a few can do what they want.'

'You've won a lot, haven't you, Dad? You've got this nice house and two cars – I don't know anybody else who has a BMW *and* a Mercedes.'

'The Mercedes's old,' Lyman smiled. 'You can't count that.' He leaned back, supported by his hands behind him on the bed. 'You ever feel out of place?'

The boy took off his shoes and turned round to face his father, sat cross-legged. 'With *them?*' He shrugged, pinched at the bedspread. 'There's lots of others at school, Dad. I'm not the only one.'

'You guys hang out together, all that?'

'Sometimes. I got white friends, too. I was just calling up Eric Baldwin, see if I can see him. Mom's going to drive me.'

'What do they think of you, do you think?'

The boy pushed out his lips to show ignorance. Nigger lips, Lyman thought. He wanted to slap him. 'I love, you, Son,' he said. 'Remember no matter what I do I loved you. That we all do what we think is best.'

'I think sometimes they think because we can run faster than them we must be stupider. But I don't think that.'

Lyman leaned forward, forced himself to brush the boy's hair. 'They used to think we were slow runners, too. But we showed them. We're going to keep on showing them till they all end up as manual workers. Like we once were. One thing you got never to forget, is what we *were*. Unless you keep that in mind, all the time, you're never going to be different – not inside your heart.' He punched the boy's shoulder, walked out, stopped at the door. 'And no matter what you think of them, or what they think of you,' he nodded up at the poster, 'never water down your blood.'

* * *

132

'You use' to say, we all pay for what we git.'

'I'm fine.'

'You look it.'

'Just my hand. This goddamn arm.'

'You head, it look pretty nice too.'

'I'm getting out of your hair, Love. Heading up north tomorrow.'

'You going walk roun' the Belize border? I'll take you—'

'I can find it.'

'I'll take you. Go up Cancún, get a driver's licence—'

'How much?'

'Maybe three hundred. But you ought to take a couple thousand. To have for the ticket and expenses, all that. I'll give you some pesos, too, for the bus . . .'

'Just give me a grand, some pesos. I'll send it right back—'

'Thet Mother Teresa – she real mad at you.'

'I'll pay her for the broken table, all that. Out of what you lend me.'

'She don' care 'bout thet. It's the *reputation* of the place, to have whites fightin' in it.'

'They had it coming, those guys.'

'You want a drink, or something? For your head?'

'My head just wants to sleep.' Squinting, Murphy crossed the metal-bright lawn and crawled into the hammock in the dark green shade of banana leaves. The air was like a warm bath, with the perfume of fruit and many flowers, the warble of the parrot and the susurration of birds, the rustle of the wind. Like Clint had said when he returned from the dead, the best way to fight pain is think of something deeper. Like the last time you lay in a hammock. When she said all those things, acted that way. Like she was lonely and afraid and you couldn't have her but if you did have her she would be for you alone.

The breeze had died. Gulls slanted across the paling clouds. He went down to the Bay and swam out past the buoy and Lovejoy's boat nodding softly on the swell. A fisherman was stretching nets over the gunnel of his rowboat and killing the crabs caught in it with a stick, the dull thunk of wood on wood drifting over the water. The Bay was warm, buoyant, clear as green glass sinking into black, tasting sweet with salt and dank with river mud. To the south stretched the flat green line of jungle with the hump in its middle of a buried Mayan city; to the east a red-sailed dugout sat atop the silver thread dividing sea from sky; before him a coconut bobbed on its stalk. He swam far out till the water cooled and darkened, saltier, and he kept looking down for the white shape of a hammerhead out of the agate depths; a rainbow school of needlefish shattered like glass, re-forming beyond reach. To the west the Bay narrowed, the palms and tilting white rust-roofed houses of Corozal Town reflected in its northern shore, beyond them a dark filigree of treetops against the sunset coals.

'All you need's a wife and kids. Thet's all thet matters in life. Your money ain't worth nothin' without thet.'

'You think I don't *know* that, Love? Why you keep telling me?'

°Cause I don' think you *know* it. If you did you would'n act lonely like you do.'

'So it didn't work out with Pam – it was too soon after the War, I wasn't settled yet, in my head. But that don't mean I don't want to.'

'Good you and Pam did'n have kids. Once you got kids you got to stay with them, no matter what.'

Murphy watched Desirée setting the table, her long glossy girl's legs, the ease of movement. 'I'd like kids.'

'Whyn't you come down here, get a place outside town? Swim every day, sail, fish, do what you want. It's not crazy like up there, San Francisco. I *been* to San Francisco—'

'How many times you told me about San Francisco? You think I don't know you been there? They *still* don't want you back.'

'They don' treat you right up there. People aren't warm. You should marry some girl and come down here. There's good girls right here, too – no need to go up there to find one. There's Dorita's daughter – Hey, Pru?'

'Yo?' Pru called from the kitchen.

'What's her name thet girl – Dorita's?'

'Tha's Missie.'

'How ol' she now?'

'She be comin' eighteen, finish' school.'

Murphy smiled. 'That makes her less than half my age.'

'She one pretty girl. Jes' as nice as they come.'

Murphy stood carefully. There was nowhere that did not ache. He watched the last sunset slip from the violet sea, the first razor-sharp stars cutting through. He imagined this girl, Missie, pretty and slender with a white lace blouse and desire that burned all night. Dancing and singing her way through life. Loving her way, on every level. How much better. Instead there was Dona, the cold fire of love eating up his soul.

'Le's eat,' Lovejoy said. 'So you kin head you way up north.'

29

The full white moon rose huge out of the sea, blocked the black horizon, its canyons and crevices wide as the earth. The motor's snarl was entrancing, barred conversation, barred thought, left the dream of the senses where everything was possible and nothing was unreal.

The moon climbed, grew smaller. The oily sea sparkled with snakes of light. Lovejoy cut back the motor as the boat rounded a point and the electric bonfire of Chetumal leaped out at them. Murphy turned away, closing his eyes, opened them slowly. The water was like burning crude oil; the air smelt of asphalt, diesel, decay, and rain-sodden rot.

They passed to the north of Chetumal, the city lights behind them. Lovejoy angled in to shore and killed the motor, letting the hull grate on the gravelly beach. 'You seen thet road? Going back to town?'

'That's the one?'

'Thet's it. You got maybe two hours' walk, jes' be at the bus station by midnight, for the las' bus for Cancún – remember, take first class!'

'You're like a mother hen.'

'I want you to come back 'n' marry thet Missie gir'l. Be careful you don' get checked by some police before you get thet licence in Cancún—'

'I'll do my best.'

'Take them new shoes off, goin' ashore – keep you feet dry.'

'I have, for Chrissake.' Murphy leaned over and hugged him. 'God bless you, Love.' He stepped over the bow on to the shallow shingle and gave the prow a shove out to sea. 'I'll send the money soon's I get there.'

Lovejoy started the motor. 'Bring it with you – when you come back!'

The beach was littered with plastic bottles and smelled of

seaweed. He put on his shoes and broke through the brush up to the shoreline road and walked towards Chetumal, scuffing his feet on the gravel to scare away the snakes that would be basking on the road's stored heat.

Occasionally there were houses crouched down by the sea. Once a dog barked halfheartedly. Once there was the smell of something dead at the side of the road.

More and more houses. Lights. The city ahead in dark and bright patches. Telephone lines, the sounds of cars. Dogs barking behind gates, lighted windows, human shapes moving behind lace curtains. Smells of pomegranates, lemons, orchids, roses, guavas. Disjointed streets with pools of lamplight, strung with wires, the ghoulish blue glare of televisions, a woman singing *'Y siempre volveras.'*

The bus station said *Autotransportes del Caribe* in blue. People stood in lines or groups in clouds of diesel smoke to board their buses. He bought a first-class ticket to Cancún and found a window seat at the back of the bus. The seat was velvety and soft. The bus smelled of oranges, disinfectant, and diesel exhaust. People were talking quietly in the nearby seats; squat dark-haired women in flowered blouses, children with gleaming hair, young moustached men in dark jackets. An unshaven old man in work trousers and an ancient tweed blazer sat beside him, took off his straw hat and put it in his lap. *'Hola!'* he said. He had no teeth and kept his lips over his gums. He took two oranges out of a plastic bag. 'Would you like one?'

'No thanks.'

The old man put one orange back and tore the other open, separated the sections and chewed them carefully, one by one, a faraway concentrated look on his face. 'It's a long way to go.'

Murphy turned from watching the terminal, the people coming, going. 'What's that?'

'Where you're going.'

'Como, viejo – how do you know that?'

'I was just asking. I have travelled too, in my life. I have been all over the Yucatán. Back then, it wasn't called that.'

'What was it called?'

'It didn't have a name. It was where we lived. It didn't have a road. Where we went we walked, or took our canoes, along the beach. We didn't belong to Mexico, to any other place. *Solamente estámos* – we just *were.*'

'It was better?'

137

'Of course. But that time's like a dead person. You can't ever bring them back.'

The old man went to sleep and Murphy watched the last buildings straggle past, the road then thin, straight and bumpy, the black hands of the jungle cupping round it. The steady strong roar of the engine came up from the back, lulling and eternal, as if this spindly aluminium carapace were not hurtling down a dangerous narrow road but through safe and empty night. Doesn't matter if I die: the thought seemed maudlin but he realized it was true.

'Tulum,' the old man said. 'Only forty-five minutes to Playa.' Murphy woke to look out at a scruffy station in the weak wash of a single street lamp. A clock said seven forty-five. That can't be true, he decided. Looking half-stunned and cold, a young man and woman with dirty long hair and variegated clothes waited for the driver to get down and store their backpacks under the bus. They gave him their tickets and climbed the stairs. There were no seats together so they sat apart. 'Too bad you can't go back,' the old man said.

'Where?'

'Playa.'

Murphy smiled at the old man's forwardness. 'That was long ago.'

'You don't see her any more, though.'

'See what – *la playa*?'

'That girl.'

'Just because I'm a gringo doesn't mean I always travel with a girl, *viejo*, or that I always go to Playa.'

'What do you suppose she's doing now, that girl?'

'I couldn't care, *compadre* – let me sleep!'

'That's not a word to use that way – *compadre* – unless you share somebody's fate. It's in Guatemala they say that.'

Murphy thought of the Mayan on the back of the flatbed truck from Orange Walk to Corozal Town: 'Guatemala,' he'd said, 'where is that? I've never been there.'

'Yet you wear a Guatemalan serape.'

'Anything can be bought, *viejo*.'

'True.' The old man took out the other orange. 'I myself have been bought many times over. Many women have bought me, only to sell me at a lower price later. My price keeps going down. That way I am freer and freer. When I'm worth absolutely nothing I'll be completely free.'

Murphy woke again as the bus decelerated then halted to pick its way through the potholes and ruts of the Playa del Carmen turn-off. It drove down Playa's long straight *avenida* to the sea. Everything looked the same but there was nothing he remembered. The bus turned round in the *Autotransportes del Caribe* station and waited, rumbling softly.

'There's time,' the old man said. 'We'll get a banana!'

'I don't want a banana.'

'Quick – come!'

He followed the old man out into the chilly onshore breeze. The *avenida* dipped down to the beach with the sound of waves crashing against it. To the right the half-lit ferry dock; across the horizon Cozumel was a string of far bright lights.

The old man gave fifty pesos to a boy at a bicycle stand for a clump of bananas. 'Why should I let you pay?' he said to Murphy. 'He would only overcharge you.'

'Out here, four o'clock in the morning, he should.' Murphy gave the boy a thousand pesos. The boy looked up at him, shocked, cocked his head.

'When you kill your love for one person,' the old man said, 'you kill it for everybody. I learned that when I was a boy like him, and the Mexicans killed my parents, and it has taken me many years to learn to love them and my mother and father too. He was right, Christ was. Love is the only way.'

30

The dawn was clotted with black floating flakes, the air pungent with burning plastic and rotten garbage where a line of trucks was waiting to enter the Cancún dump. Clouds of swallows careered through the violet air, feeding on flies, their bodies drumming like hail against the bus windshield. Half-naked children walked barefoot and old men rode burros or bicycle carts among tattered plastic, shattered glass, broken concrete, dead swallows, coils of rusty wire, and shards of derelict cars abandoned on the roadside. On the far, circling strand grey resort hotels were strung like half-illumined pearls.

Near the bus station a *jugatería* was already open; Murphy had two large orange juices, sweet rolls from a *panadería*, then in an early bar coffees and tequila. The sun had risen and heat was filling the streets. He took Avenida Tulum to a side-street that became a path through brush to another street that he walked up and down but could not see the place he wanted. Three streets further he found a tile-roofed blue adobe office building that was the right shape, but its colour was wrong. He knocked on its carved mahogany door. Jasmine flowers and dead bees lay on the steps. A bicycle passed, wheel squeaking; a jet rumbled over, gaining altitude. A sleepy-faced woman opened the door.

'Is this Nacimiento's office?'

'*Sí*. But he's not here yet.'

'The Nacimiento that sells insurance?'

'The one. You want to wait?'

The low front room was painted the same light blue as the outside adobe and smelled faintly of bug spray and perfume. There was a large modern black desk with two telephones, a brass lamp, and family photos. On the blue wall was a Mexicana calendar of a beach with palms. At a second, smaller desk a computer hummed softly. 'Can I get you some coffee?' she said. She had black hair and carmine lips and nails, wore a brown suit that emphasized her hips.

He drank the coffee and read *Excelsior*. She refilled his cup. The coffee made him need to urinate but he did not ask her if he could use the *servicios*. A car stopped outside; its door shut and Nacimiento came in. '*Buenas días*,' he said, shook Murphy's hand.

'The *señor* wants to buy insurance,' the woman said.

Small and compact, his hair combed back, in a light green suit, Nacimiento stood like a welterweight. 'How did you know to come here?'

'I've been here before.'

'I don't remember you.'

'A friend and I – three years ago. You found him a passport.'

There was a surge, then Nacimiento shook his head. 'I remember that, but not you—'

'We had a boat, big sailboat, out at Isla Mujéres. You got him a French passport, a good one—'

Nacimiento's eyes widened. 'That wasn't you.'

'It's just the beard. I've been on the road.'

Nacimiento took his arm, 'Have you been in *cárcel*? Sit down.'

'I've been sitting all night. I'm in a rush. I need a US driver's licence, any state, but current. Dependable—'

'If it weren't dependable I wouldn't sell it to you.'

'I know that. That's why I'm back.'

Nacimiento stood thinking, rubbing his palms. 'Probably I can. Give me two hours?'

Murphy looked round, could not see a clock. 'It's nine-fifty,' Nacimiento said.

'If you can, how much?'

'You know better than ask me that – what was it last time, two grand, when we thought it'd be three?'

'Eighteen hundred. Instead of twenty-five. You remember that.'

Nacimiento smiled. 'It really *was* you. You're not the same man. A licence, quick, even for you, it'll cost five.'

'Too much.'

'Times have changed. We're not the same little town. You want something that's been hot so long they pull you in first time you show it? For five hundred you get one so clean the owner still thinks he has it. All you have to do is change the picture.'

'You get me a clean one, before noon, change the picture for me, I'll go five.'

Nacimiento patted Murphy's arm. It still hurt, the broken bone, Murphy noticed. 'Get some photos,' Nacimiento said. 'Go to the bus station and turn on Avenida Uxmal – there's a booth. Four colour photos.'

On the way he stopped in the brush to urinate. It spattered off the dry soil, ants scurrying round it. On Avenida Uxmal the sidewalk was clogged with tourists – Americans with sombreros and loud voices, pot bellies, Bermuda shorts and sunburns; French and Germans all young and slender, the men unshaven and the women's long hair bleached by sun and tangled by salt and wind. There were schoolchildren in white and black uniforms, boys in rags holding out their hands. The Avenida was six lanes of buses, trucks, jitneys, Volkswagens, and campers; their fumes blued the air and blended with the bright odours of gardens and fruit-stands, the greasy tang of fried chicken, the sewery breeze from the Bay.

The angular, bruised face in the mirror of the photo booth was not his but simply a disguise. When he got home he'd discard it. The photos, too: four identical views of a tense, tanned man with a short beard, the cheeks sunken and the cheekbones far too high, the eyes receded, as if only to see out of and never into.

He took a taxi to the Hotel zone, tennis clubs and glossy cars, doormen, palm boulevards, and flashes of sea between shiny condo towers; in the Flamingo Mall he bought Levis and an ACA shirt and jacket and Nikes, a carry-on bag, underwear and socks, changed into the new clothes and put the ones Lovejoy had bought in the bag. He bought a cheap tennis racket and a can of balls, and opened the can and put them in the bag, then a beach towel that said, 'I lost my—' with a picture of a cherry – 'in Cancún', then a painted flat wood fish with a green head, orange fins, a maroon tail, a blue belly with a swan painted on it and a surprised look in its oval black-and-white eye. He bought shaving cream and a razor, toothbrush and comb, and shaved and brushed his teeth in a men's room reeking of urine, where a slim attendant paced, coughing quietly. He bought a cheap blanket and a kaleidoscopic shirt to fill out the carry-on bag, went upstairs and had a quarter pounder with cheese, fries, and a coke at McDonald's, bought a *USA Today* and a *Newsweek* and jammed them into the bag. He walked back to town through the traffic and harsh sea wind, scuffing the bag against palm trunks, rubbing his new Nikes in the dust.

142

'He doesn't look much like you,' Nacimiento said.

It was an Arizona licence, a reddish-haired man with a self-effacing smile and arched brows, ears too big and nose too little.

'Lamar P. Bultz,' Nacimiento said. 'That's who you are.'

The name sounded funny with Nacimiento's accent. 'Where'd you get it?'

'One of the guys working the dance clubs got it late last night. This Lamar P. Bultz, he's still sleeping it off at the Sheraton or somewhere – you'll be home before he knows it's gone.'

'If it's no good, I'm coming back—'

'Never you worry.' Nacimiento took Murphy's photos to the desk. With a drafting knife he cut carefully around the picture of Lamar P. Bultz and peeled it up from the licence. He cut one of Murphy's photos to match, bevelling the cut in towards the back so that no edge showed. He glued it lightly on the back with plastic glue and ran a slight coat of glue around the edge, and laid it in place. From a back room he brought a hairdryer and cling-film, heated the licence and laminated a new layer of plastic over it. Holding it along the edges he waved it to cool it off. He counted the twenty-five twenties Murphy gave him and put them in his right jacket pocket. 'You memorize the birthday and address, that stuff. So you know who you are – in case somebody asks.'

Murphy took a taxi to the airport and booked a window seat on the next flight to San Francisco, Aeromexico at three-thirty, via Mexico City and LA. He bought a book on Mayan ruins and sat waiting in the wide, bright terminal. There were blond, tanned families, young couples holding hands, college boys with spiky hair and football shirts, old men sweeping cigarette butts, cigarettes hanging from their lips. There was a smell of jet exhaust and flowers; the marble floor was sticky.

San Francisco International was cold and misty. The customs man glanced at his licence and nodded him through. He took a cab from the airport, lines of red tail-lights ahead on 101. 'Been gone long?' the cabbie called back.

'Couple weeks.'

'Nothing beats coming home, huh?'

'Nothing beats it.'

He had the cabbie drop him North Beach and walked the quiet midnight streets till he was sure no one followed.

San Francisco's cool, windy streets were wet and nearly empty, a few buses wheezing on the upgrades, whores in leotards and

143

fishnets chatting with two cops on a corner, men hand in hand under the tungstens, a bar disgorging laughing couples, a black dog running skinny and scared down a back alley past empty trashcans, once a gull coasting ghostlike downhill above the trolley wires.

He took another cab on Broadway out to the Richmond, got off at Twenty-fifth and Geary and walked down towards Sea Cliff, the trees dripping mist, lines of a song from the cab radio running in his head,

> and the only sound that's left, after the ambulances go,
> Is Cinderella sweeping up on Desolation Row,

in the chill of sea, the rush of surf, and the hesitant rumble of a foghorn rising up from the Golden Gate.

31

Twenty-fifth Avenue crossed Camino del Mar and narrowed to
a lane between two great stone pillars, then swept down and right
around a curve of broad lawns and Edwardian mansions. Between
the houses came the boom of waves against the cliffs below. He
went up the driveway of a white four-storey late Victorian house
with tall fluted columns and a great bronze knocker of a lion scowl-
ing at the street. The driveway followed the side of the house down
to the garage; he climbed the steps beside the garage to a deck
that swung out from the kitchen, then down the deck into the
garden. Sea mist and rhododendron smells blew up from the sea.
Under the back of the deck he popped a window and dropped down
on to the floor of the garage.

It was absolutely black. He moved forward, banged his knee
on a car bumper, swore under his breath, angled to the left till
his hand touched a hanging cabinet. He felt around it to the door,
opened it, and fumbled inside. At the back behind cans of polish
and oil was a clump of keys. He climbed out of the window and
walked back up the driveway to the front door with the scowl-
ing lion. He turned the latchkey then the deadbolt; deep inside
the house an alarm began to whine.

He ran down the entry hall through the dark dining room,
banging his knee on the double door into the sunroom, the alarm
loudening its yowl, fifteen seconds and counting, thirty more till
it lets go with everything – the old broad next door'll be fast asleep
but this'll bring him back to life – found the alarm and punched
in 32-42-47 but the alarm only whistled more menacingly, ascending through mezzo piano to mezzo forte, and he quickly tried 32-
47-42 but fumbled the 7 and had to do it again as the alarm hit
forte and suddenly halted; in the ringing silence he could hear
the slow bong of the bell buoy off Baker Beach and the steady
diesel thrum of a tugboat pushing a sludge barge out to sea.

The phone jangled. He went into the kitchen stubbing his toe on the edge of the freezer and dropped the phone on his foot, knelt and found the receiver. 'Yeah!'

'Who's speaking, please?' It was a black voice, official.

'You call up in the middle of the fuckin night to ask who's speaking?' He stood rubbing his foot against the other calf. 'Who the fuck are *you*?'

'Is this Mr Murphy?'

'Why?'

'This's ADT Security. Your burglar alarm just registered an entry.'

'Oh, sorry. The lights weren't on and I tripped over the freezer. Thanks for calling—'

'And you're Mr Murphy?'

'Yes.'

'Can you give me your mother's date and place of birth and maiden name, please?'

'Esther McCreary, Temple, Texas, 21 May, 1926.'

'Fine, Mr Murphy. Thank you very much—'

'No – I thank you. What if it hadn't been me?'

'That's what we're here for. Have a good night.'

He put on all the lights and walked like a peasant from room to room. In the living room he stood with his hands on the silken fabric of the couch back and stared at the ebony grand, the Pinchon of apple blossoms and the Seine hanging over the mantel, the endless meaningless books, the blood-red Kerastans on the gleaming oak floor. The ocean wind wailed down the chimney, stirring the ash; he went back to the front door and closed it.

The kitchen smelt shut-in and faintly of spices. Wreaths of mist dashed across the glass. He ate some pistachio ice cream and took a bottle of Dunphys upstairs and lay on the bed looking at the flat white ceiling, went out on the bedroom deck and opened the hot tub. It was swirling steadily, the water a little low but hot. He went back into the dressing room, rolled a joint, took off his clothes, and sat in the hot tub smoking and drinking the Irish whiskey while the mist flitted past like all the ghosts of history finally liberated from their graves.

'I drink water all day as you have said, *Doctora*. Still she's dying.'

'You've boiled guava root and mashed it for her?' Dona undressed the baby.

'As you said, with ashes of *Tusub cam* vine.'

146

Dona took a cloth and soap from her pack, poured water from a jug and began to wash diarrhoea from the baby. 'In Flores this could be stopped with a bottle of Kaopectil from the pharmacy.'

'You cannot get it, this miracle bottle?'

'We've lost two people this month trying to buy from pharmacies. The only way is to take it from the soldiers.'

The baby wrinkled her shrunken face and whimpered. 'If I had milk,' Dona said, 'I'd nurse her.'

'To make milk you first need a man, *Doctora*.'

'If there's milk anywhere, Roseta, I shall send it.'

'If there's never any milk how should it suddenly appear?'

'If we take some from the soldiers.'

Roseta waved her hand at the flies around the baby's face, and to Dona it seemed also a dismissal. 'You must drink more water,' she repeated, shouldering her pack and rifle. You must take more bone and tooth from your own body so your daughter may grow some day to feed her own frail calcium into her own daughter's mouth.

'Turn down the lantern, *por favor*,' Roseta said, 'when you go.'

The moon three days past full hung in the middle of the sky. Dona moved up through the village to the last hut and knocked.

'*Sí!*' An old man's voice.

She went inside. There was a single candle, a thatched wall with a crucifix. 'How is it?' she said.

'It was clear all the way to Concepción, *compañera*. Though some may have come since—'

'Could you see any tracks?'

'It was too dark.'

'And above?'

'One helicopter, very high, going south.'

'No sound of guns?' She watched the old man's face in the faint candlelight, exhaling softly when his face did not fall and he did not say, '*Sí*, to the west', or 'to the north', or anywhere.

'No, *compañera*, no sound of guns.'

'Roseta doesn't know Bautisto's dead. No one must tell her now, the baby's too sick—'

'The baby will soon die, *compañera*.'

The moon gave enough light to see the trail as she followed it up out of the village and crossed a steep range then down through thinning pines to the candlelit huts of Concepción perched on an eroded slope over a stream where stones rumbled and clattered. She entered an unlighted hut, rested her Galil by the door and dropped the pack from her shoulders. 'God, I grow old.'

'Your body doesn't show it.'

'It feels it.'

'Come, let me feel it.'

'Stop, Martín. I have no stomach for it.'

His hands clamped her waist, the hammock creaking as he pulled her to him, the pen in his pocket jabbing her breast, her face full of itchy beard as he kissed her eyes and cheeks and the tip of her nose, his mouth opening like a hairy peach against hers. He unbuttoned her shirt, his calloused hand flattening her breast. She backed away, buttoning her shirt. 'I don't want it, Martín.'

'Dona, it's *life*—'

'I want nothing to do with life.'

'Life's just who you love.'

'I don't love anybody!' She reached out in the darkness, took his hand. 'It's soon time.'

'I know the time.' His voice softened. 'That's why I wanted to.'

She could hear the fabric of his shirt stretch as he breathed. 'Forgive me, Martín. Another time . . .'

'They are well, your patients?'

'You know they're not.'

'And this plan, you think it's a good one?'

'There is no good plan for killing.' She went to the door, feeling suffocated by this hut, this village. Why am I always the one who must give reassurance? she thought despairingly. Like Roseta, draining myself to feed the doomed.

32

At two-minute intervals they moved out of Concepción – first
Manuel, a boy of twelve, no gun. Then Martín, then the Taliscá
brothers – the tall skinny one, Gordo, and the smaller heavy one,
Lupo – both carrying new Galils taken a week ago from the
convoy at Quimalá, where their youngest brother had died. Then
Margaríta from Chisapec, two women from Los Martíres, the
teenager Solano, Dona, and last El Caballo, a small man carrying an M60 machine gun light as a machete on his shoulder. Ten
in all, two minutes apart, they took the trail down the mountain
and entered the black jungle on an overgrown chicle road.

Picking her steps, Dona tried to balance the Galil so it would
not rub her shoulder. The mushy soil exhaled dank odours; the
stink of lianas and pungent bunchgrass was unbreathable in the
clammy darkness. Creepers and branches snagged the gun barrel
and snatched at her backpack. She stopped, legs shaking with
exhaustion, wanted to fall on the mud and cry. She made herself
swallow. Snakes will get you, she told herself. El Caballo's coming
up behind and he'll be angry. He'll think you're weak. She
unshouldered one strap of the backpack, hung the Galil from that
shoulder and the backpack from the other.

After two hours they broke out on a long ridge, the path dimly
visible through the thinner overstorey, the group tightening up
now that they were far from villages and there was less danger
of soldiers.

The ones ahead had halted; she came up to them, staying on
the edge. A cool breeze rode across the ridge and dropped into
the valley. She shifted shoulders with the Galil and backpack.
Martín's watch said 2:17. As they walked onwards the image of
the watch stayed before her eyes, three ghostly little numbers
with two dots between the first and second.

After many kilometres the trail descended and circled a swamp
where frogs croaked and insects chirred. It followed a stream from

the swamp down into a narrow valley smelling of old, damp cinders, past the charred spars of houses. An hour later they stopped where the trail dipped over a rise, in the south a cluster of lights. 'Them!' she said.

'Them,' Margaríta answered.

Dona dropped her pack and laid the Galil across it. Her body seemed to float. She lay down with her head on the pack. The night was spinning: one moment there was a tall tree before her eyes, then an open meadow, then the other *compañeros*, then the distant dangerous lights, the tree again . . .

Martín came up the meadow with another man whose glasses glinted from the lights. 'Ready, kids?' he whispered good-naturedly, and they laughed quietly and gathered round him. 'You've all heard the story . . .'

'They know it,' Martín said. 'We'll set positions before daybreak.'

'The hole is the proper depth and all the dirt's been carried away—'

'And every position is well protected,' Martín added.

'Just be sure you're out of there on time. Six twenty-nine for everyone, except six twenty-seven for Martín and El Caballo because your position's more exposed and you have further to withdraw. And again, *don't* regroup afterwards. When it's time, disperse fast in twos and threes. Each of you withdraw exactly on your assigned pattern. Never more than four together or the American heat-seeking planes will track you by body heat till the Guatemalan Air Force finds you.'

'You will overrun the Base?' Dona said. Her voice sounded hoarse, too quivery.

'If there's time, before the helicopters.'

'I need *all* their medicines. Not just what you can grab easily but *all* of it. Look in all the cabinets and in the refrigerators and in any closets and everywhere you see—'

'Guns first, *compañera*. Sadly, a revolution's not won by healing children.'

'Yes it is. Precisely by that. And each battle leaves more children to be healed.'

'Perhaps you chose the wrong battle?' He turned to the others. 'My squad attacks the Base from the east at five fifty-three, the moment the sun climbs above the ridge and its light strikes the Base: the soldiers'll have it in their eyes as they face us. Like us, *you'll* be looking away from the sun – up the road where the rescue convoy from Dolores will arrive.'

He half glanced back at the ring of lights. 'It will take between one and three minutes for the Base to radio Dolores they're being hit. It'll take Dolores eight to eleven minutes to get the troops into trucks and out the gate. It's going to take the trucks thirteen and a half more minutes to come round that curve below you. That's somewhere between six fifteen and six twenty-one. They'll be moving fast and looking for ambushes. But not where *you* hit them.'

'Because there's no cover,' Dona said. 'Because we shouldn't *be* there.'

'There's cover, *compañera*.'

'The soil's limestone and the scrub's too low.'

'If helicopters catch us,' Margaríta said.

'The choppers'll be cold,' he answered. 'From the moment we attack, at five fifty-three, it will take the Cobras forty-four minutes to scramble from Poptún. It'll take the Huey gunships forty-seven from Cobán. So the soonest they can be there is six thirty-seven, and more likely six forty. But you must be gone by six twenty-nine. El Caballo and Martín by six twenty-seven.'

'I am to risk the lives of nine people to believe this?' Dona said.

'*Ten* people, *compañera*. Plus all mine. Listen – all of you: under no circumstances remain one minute longer than your withdrawal time. If you come under concentrated fire – and you shouldn't, given our approach – be sure to break before the choppers come, in no case later than six thirty-five. If you're pinned, watch the time, and listen for choppers. When you hear them, no matter what, you run. Or you will die – do you understand that? You will absolutely die if the choppers find you.'

'We're not fools,' Margaríta said.

'When the trucks are below you the sun will be behind and above you, and in their faces. They'll be stuck on the road, with an open gully on one side and your slope on the other. You'll have a beautiful field of fire.'

'Who's across the gully?'

'We're not playing it that way. Too hard to withdraw.'

'If the convoy doesn't come,' Martín said, 'or if the firing stops at the Base, we leave, going in ones and twos as our friend has reminded us. In no case do we stay a second longer than our withdrawal times. If anyone escaping from the Base comes up the road we ambush them just as we would the convoy, *unless* we hear the convoy coming. Simple?'

A line of blood began to spread across the eastern sky, above the Base's frailer ring of lights. She felt the delicious coolness of death in her face, felt it coming down like Moses from the mountain with the engraved wisdom of God.

Reaching through the darkness, the man with the glasses touched each of them in turn, whispering, '*Vaya con Díos.*' It's like Communion, she thought as he squeezed her fingers, and she answered, 'Go with God, *compañero.*'

33

From her position Dona could see the brushy opposite slope
crowned by tree silhouettes against the lightening horizon, and
the pale ribbon of road that curved round its foot with the open
gully beside it then descended below her, swerving east towards
the valley with the lights of the Army Base at its end.

The stones beneath her had grown warm from her body and
she squirmed comfortably down among them. The rock on which
her Galil rested was sharp and damp; the cold barrel stung her
fingers. Thirty metres to the left was Lupo Taliscá's hunched form
and the faint glitter of his rifle. To the right, from where the trucks
would come, she could see neither Margaríta in her cover of
spindly trees nor Gordo beyond, guarding the flank.

It's just me, she realized, and Lupo, whom I don't know, the
two of us alone in this universe without time, without the sun
which will never rise and the convoy that will never come and
we will never shoot and that's what it feels like to be dead.

If it all goes well there'll be no bad wounds – she could hope for
that. But all wouldn't go well and she mustn't even say it. If all went
badly she had bandages and compresses for the easy bullet wounds.
And if they could get the wounded out she could operate later. But
a lung wound like García's, or Clemente's, and she'd lose them.

With a machine gun in the trucks there'd be some big wounds,
shearings and major tissue and bone loss and if the choppers came
there'd be rockets and much worse, and if there were A37s she
had nothing for the phosphorous burns.

A black jay fluttered down and pecked at the road's shoulder,
ran a few steps, pecked again. She thought of when she was a
girl and these *sanatés* gathered at dusk in the church tower outside
her bedroom window; leaning out of that window she had picked
figs from the ancient tree with its roots deep in the graveyard
below – it had always pleased her, this, the bodies of her ances-
tors feeding hers.

A red spot seared through the green dark east, widened, writhed up among the nest of branches into a white-orange ball whose heat came racing down the slope and slapped her face. Its light slipped down past the others' camouflaged positions, struck the opposite slope, and dropped on to the road where the trucks would come, then down into the gully, slid east past the rocks and madrone where Martín and El Caballo hid with the M60, paused, then poured down into the valley towards the Army Base, catching a line of yellow-leaved willows along an irrigation ditch, a pasture with two brown and white cows.

Once more she measured the distance below from the curve to where the first truck would stop: space for five trucks if they bunched up, or two if they didn't. Thirty-seven metres, Martín had said, from her position to where the first truck would be caught in the trench the other *compañeros* had dug last night; from that trench it was a hundred and ten metres to the curve round which the trucks would come. Behind her it was a hundred and forty-five metres to the crest of the slope where the real trees began – until then there were only thin trunks, thin chalky soil with sparse grass to her knees. Crawl like a snake through the grass, Martín had said, if you have to. She closed her eyes and tried to remember the position and curve of the road and the slope and every other detail then opened her eyes to check, closed them again and again until the picture inside her head and that before her eyes was the same. Again she closed her eyes and dismounted the clip of the Galil and remounted it and did it again, reached out to memorize the exact location of the second clip at her elbow.

Light raced east across the valley towards the Base, the sun heating her face as if she were leaning down to a blazing hearth, and as she turned not wanting to be blinded there was a far whammer-whammer-whammer of a chopper nearing fast then suddenly rounding the hill. It banked away and El Caballo's M60 spat hard and the chopper's tail rotor flew off; the chopper swung round and round like a stone on a string, the pilot trying to bring it down fast but it dropped sideways into the jungle leaving a sudden silence then the boom of its crash and orange flames billowing up oily smoke and a flare of magnesium and chatter of machine-gun rounds exploding in the heat.

'*Mierda!*' she screamed. '*Mierda! mierda! mierda!*' The Base gleamed silently in the new sun, columns of white smoke from cooking fires rising like the pillars of the sky. Out of the gully

154

rose the smell of burning foliage, flesh, and jet fuel. Voices came down the line; Lupo stood and yelled, 'Stay put!' and she called it on to Margaríta. Martín came running along the line. 'The outpost will come for the chopper – we ambush them – Miguel and his people attack the Base – reverse of the plan!'

'We must leave! This isn't the plan!'

'Fuck the plan! This is better!'

'Choppers never come alone!'

Sweat fell from his face on to her hand. 'They come, we retreat.'

'You mean run!'

'*Sí* – run!' He glanced at his watch, hers. 'It's now five fifty-seven. You still have to be out of here at six twenty-nine.'

'The choppers'll be here before then,' she said, but he was gone to Margaríta then up to Gordo on the flank before running back past her. From the outpost came the rumble and gear whine of trucks.

Clouds had thickened to the south; she kept hearing choppers in their thunder. But the choppers did not come; the sun inched higher; trucks came from the Base and stopped at the valley edge out of range, small and darkly backlit by the sun; soldiers ran from them into the trees and up the slope towards the burning chopper.

The M60 opened up; a soldier rolled like a cornstraw doll downhill, more running up the gully; and she shot twice as they crossed the road; one fell then the other but he scrambled for cover. A bullet flicked the bush beside her temple. Another soldier fell in a burst from the M60. Four helicopters in V formation dropped over the western slope, Cobra gunships with ugly jutting stingers; the M60 fired and one banked to spray it; Dona squeezed single shots at the side gunner and the Cobra turned on her, bullets shattering stones and spouting earth and she rolled up deaf and half-blind to fire back but her magazine was empty, the spare lost in rubble, her spine aching with terror as the chopper came at her, her legs begging to run, her fingers fumbling through the rocks for the magazine but it wouldn't mount and she saw it was backwards but now it jammed; a rocket battered her into the ground shrieking with fear and rage, the Cobra's machine-guns pummelling bush and stone, the air filled with flying rocks and dirt and branches and a great white heat sucked her in then slammed her down in raging white silence; there were cries like seagulls and the patter of dirt and stone coming back to earth; she realized it was herself crying, felt round but could not find

155

her rifle, scrambled up and sprinted for Margaríta's trees; the universe was panting, a great roar rasping in and out and she looked down to see if her chest had been torn open, if the noise was from there, but she was not bloody.

Margaríta lay on her back, no head, just red roots sticking out of her neck; someone was saying 'Jesus Jesus Jesus' inside Dona's brain and she grabbed Margaríta's gun and ran through splintered trees along the slope as the chopper returned for her, bullets shaking the earth as she ran, and she fell on her back to fire but it flitted past and she rolled up and dashed to Lupo dead beside a rocket's red crater and dived into the crater as the rotor's came back, bullets shivering and spattering the singed, reeking earth, and she jerked and lay out straight. Through her half-closed eye and the black half-veil of her hair she saw the door gunner in his flak uniform and helmet like an avenging insect as he tried to steady the hail of bullets on her and the chopper slid past and dived downhill towards El Caballo and Martín.

A black rod dropped from the chopper and flared, dashed against the rocks, a sudden white shock of heat exploding the trees, great boulders soaring like foam through gyrating phosphorous clouds. She clung to the crater, the blaze burning her back, kept holding her breath against the searing acid smoke, fumbled in the dirt for the rifle, waited till she could open her eyes then gasped a small breath that stuck to her throat like burning oil and she waited longer not breathing, waiting for the boiling white clouds to reveal the chopper hanging steadily above them like a snake over its poisoned prey. Still not breathing she aimed at the narrow black slot over the chopper's wiring channel and fired single shots that the chopper did not seem to feel till suddenly it lunged at her and she gripped the fractured earth waiting to die. El Caballo's M60 rang out, metal hailing the chopper and it dropped away as two more dived at El Caballo, dropping rockets side by side and the earth yanked itself from her and dropped her down ten feet away and she scrambled for the gun and fired at the new ones till the gun was empty and she ran past someone's shredded body to El Caballo half buried; when she knelt to him she saw it was just his head and torso, his pelvis and legs had been blown elsewhere, the M60 with them; Martín had crawled beneath a toppled trunk, his chest and face red, his beard gone – no, not gone, for his chin had been blown away so that the roots of his upper teeth grinned out at her. Not knowing his chest was gone he tried to speak, his larynx weirdly

156

working, bared ribs twitching. Something tugged her sleeve; soldiers were running uphill, their bullets snapping branches and sucking at the charred air; she reached beneath Martín's waist to the back of his ammo belt and yanked at the spare clip, the belt and part of his uniform and body coming with it, and she knocked off the other clip and mounted this one. A chopper was returning. She forced herself to check the clip then fired, a bullet hitting in front of a soldier but he fell anyway, perhaps from the ricochet, their bullets smashing bark and splinters from the fallen tree. Martín pointed to her rifle then himself. She kissed his forehead and his eyes, his bloody upper lip. He pointed at the gun then his heart. She shot him; he convulsed, legs quivering. She ducked behind him and fired into the back of his skull, emptied the rifle at the soldiers, and ran screaming into the jungle.

34

He woke in a strange peace. Familiar sun spread diamond patterns across the ceiling; through the open window drifted the sound of surf. The carpet was soft underfoot. He went down to the kitchen, the terracotta tiles cold, put water in the espresso machine, found coffee beans in the refrigerator, thawed a can of orange juice in the microwave, drank it, took a mug of espresso upstairs, set it on the sink and stood in the shower. Hot. Cold. Hot. Freezing cold.

The neighbour's poodle was barking; he finished the espresso, filled the mug with water, opened the bathroom window; the dog heard him and sprinted for its doghouse but the water hit it as it reached the door.

He grinned at himself in the half-steamed mirror, looked again, shocked by his rangy thin frame, the bony chest, skinny thighs with the long skinny pecker hanging down, the white puffy shrapnel stars across the gut and ribs – touch them, honey, feel the metal move – the right arm looked funny, too thin, the discoloured bullet scar like a hole left by a burning spike.

He rolled two joints, lit one and put the other in his right shirt pocket. He removed the inner sole from one running shoe, took a razor-slim knife from the drawer of his bedside table, slipped it into the shoe and replaced the inner sole. He found thirty-seven dollars and some credit cards in a kitchen drawer, and went down to the garage. You did right to come back, he told himself. This is the life for you.

The battery was dead and he pushed the car up the drive-way and down the street, running alongside, jumped in to pop the clutch in second. It caught, spitting black exhaust, the engine running ragged all the way across Golden Gate Park and up past the Haight and over the top of Divisadero. By the time he drove out along Castro to Noe Valley it was running smooth, the streets half-bright with sun through the fog.

Number 729 Diamond was a tall narrow Victorian house with leaded glass and three-colour trim. He picked the *Chronicle* off the bottom step, rang the bell. There was city scum on the Welcome mat. She smiled as she opened the door then turned hard and pale.

'Let me in, Diana—'

'Oh Christ oh please. You can't mean it.'

He brushed past her down the hall into the parlour with its couches and doilies, its jade-coloured marble mantel with the black marble clock, the soft reflections of ferns and wall fabrics, the distant KGO – 'your Bay Area news station' – she's like a lily, he thought, tall and pale and ready to bow at the first touch. 'Don't give me that, Diana. You guys were split, you've got a new old man—'

'How did you kill him?'

'We crashed. Hit a pine bough coming in. He never knew.'

'You bastard. You fucking lousy pilot. You'd risk anyone to make more money—'

'It was his life, Diana. His business. I didn't ask him.'

'*You* don't have to ask people. They're drawn to you. You feed off them one by one.'

'You want me to tell the kids?'

'You think *you're* going to tell *my* kids their father's dead?'

'Johnny had his own life. That's why you didn't love him.'

'What the shit do you know about love?'

'Or that's why he didn't love you—'

She gave him an upright look, coming out straight from deep inside, deeper than love or hate. 'Don't assume you understand anything, Murph.'

'You going to tell his folks? And he had a friend in LA—'

'Sarah Oldfield. An actress – he told me all about her. You've probably had her, too . . .'

He realized he was still holding the *Chronicle* and dropped it on a sofa and took her in his arms. 'Don't be like this, Diana. Just feel the pain. That's all we can do, is feel the pain—'

He sat in the car thinking of all the places he could go. He drove back down Market amid the traffic and the trolleys, white and black skyscrapers blocking off the Bay, through Chinatown to North Beach, parked on Grant, went into the

Trieste, ordered Italian pastries and cappuccino. Sun beamed through the tall windows on to faces and chrome table-rims, while the espresso machine rumbled and hissed through *fermate* in *La Donna e Mobile* and the wandering words of twenty conversations:

'He promised me Sri Lanka but we never got past Daly City.'

'That's Bachelard's mistake, subsuming dialectics in pure phenomenology . . .'

'After one night with her she was out on the street again.'

'I told him, "Darling, the standard deviation's just the square root of the variance—"'

He called the *Chronicle* and asked for Melissa Maslow.

'I remember,' she said. 'It was at a party somewhere. You're the guy who races motorcycles.'

'Just for fun. I used to. Listen, Melissa, I've got a story. Something you might use.'

'Everybody tells me that. That's why I hate this job.'

'I've seen the most horrible massacre—'

'You must've been on the Bay Freeway—'

'Central America.'

'People don't really care about Central America, Joe. Not like San Diego. But it's better than Africa. *Nobody* cares about massacres in Africa.'

'The Army wiped out a whole village.'

'Don't they do that all the time down there?'

'With American help.'

'What kind of help?'

'American officers.'

'Now that's interesting. You have pictures?'

'No. It was night. But I was there.'

'Come see me.'

'Now?'

'Can't.'

'Lunch?'

'I got a lunch thing. Two thirty?'

'Fine. But not at the *Chronicle*.'

'Across the street, then. The Rathskeller.'

'Till then, who can I talk to?'

'You could try Cyndi Wheaton – BACCA.'

'What's that?'

'Bay Area Committee for Central America.'

He waited till the espresso machine stopped steaming milk and called the BACCA. Cyndi Wheaton had a strong, friendly voice. He imagined her in white tennis shorts, a racket in her hand. 'I don't doubt what you've told me,' she said. 'It happens all the time.'

'But the American soldiers—'

'What do you think our advisers *do* down there? Teach knitting?'

'I'm going to the *Chronicle*, the television—'

'Before you do you'd better see me.'

The Bay Area Committee for Central America was one flight up over the Chevy dealer on South Van Ness. The receptionist was Latina but when he spoke to her in Spanish she answered in English.

Cyndi Wheaton was beautiful, about thirty-five, long golden-reddish hair curling in at her neck, slender high cheekbones and appraising blue eyes. She wore a long pleated plaid skirt and a pink mohair sweater and had little pearl earrings. 'It's too bad you don't have proof,' she said.

'That's what Melissa Maslow said.'

'But I'm going to get you together with our Executive Committee. And maybe some TV. Can you be back here at four o'clock?'

He drove home, dug through drawers in the dressing room and study, went down to the basement to a closet off the pool room and opened boxes till he found a worn brown address book. Under 'Cunningham – Willard and Mary', was a 207 area code number that answered on the second ring, an old woman's strong voice.

'Mrs Cunningham?' he said.

'Who's there?'

'My name's Joseph Murphy. I was a friend of Clint's.'

'I remember you, Murph. He used to write about you. He was very fond of you.'

'I'm sorry I never got in touch.'

'There was nothing you could've done.'

'How's Mr Cunningham?'

'We're getting along.'

'Clint's wife – wasn't she going to have a baby?'

'How'd you know that? He never knew.'

'Somebody must've told me. Is she OK?'

'The wife? I suppose she's fine. She got married again, some trucker. The girl, we don't see much of her.'

'Where is she?'

161

'Out in San Francisco. At least she was when we last heard. That was a while. Two years, maybe.'

'You have her number? An address?'

'Sherrie's? Probably not. Not one that works.'

'And his wife?'

'Lucy? She's over in Westbrook. Her name's Amato now. Married to this trucker.'

'You don't have a phone book, do you?'

'Just a minute.' The phone clunked to the floor, grinding as it swung back and forth on its cord. 'There's three Amatos in the Westbrook phone book. You have a pencil?'

He wrote them down. 'If I get in touch with her I'll phone you.'

'Clint was very fond of you. We have all his letters. We go over them. The time you landed in that lake, the time you boys went to Thailand . . . He always said he never would've made it through Fort Rucker without you—'

Lucy Amato was at the second number. 'Oh, hi,' she said. 'I remember 'bout you. That was a long time ago.'

'I guess we've both kind of forgot about Clint.'

'I'm married again. Been a long time. Prob'ly Clint's mom told you—'

'I heard Sherrie's out in San Francisco. That's where I am. Would you mind if I gave her a call sometime?'

'Wouldn't mind at all. If I only knew her number.'

'You got an address, anything?'

'Tell you the truth, Murph – that's your name, right? It's coming back to me now, that's what Clint called you in his letters – tell you the truth, we had no end of trouble with that girl. She always hated her new dad, even though she never even knew the old one – ain't that something for you?'

'Happens.'

'Hold on – I may have an address. It'll be an old one—' She put down the phone. In the background he could hear the wet hum of a dishwasher and an Eric Clapton solo, the pure music making the moment a lesson, for ever. 'You still there?' Lucy said. 'One fifty-four Alabama Street. That's all I got. Must've been six months ago, this. She wanted me to send some money – she was calling from a booth.'

'Other than this, Lucy, how you doing? I'm sure Clint'd like to know.'

'Not as if you could tell him, huh? God, what a time. But I'm fine now, me an' Mitch we got three kids – good ones, not throwaways like Sherrie. I don't like to say it, Murph, she's my own daughter. But that's all she is – a throwaway.'

35

One fifty-four Alabama was a tilting unrenovated Romeo near
the projects, Spanish names on the mailboxes. 'Hey, *niño*,' he said
to a boy playing marbles in the dank hall, '*donde vive la inglésa?*'

'Four,' the boy said. 'But she's got someone.'

It was up one flight of sticky stairs with broken linoleum, a
white door gouged by dog claws. The jamb had been split and
repaired with tin. From other apartments came canned laughter and children's screams. He knocked, then again.

A creak of floor, a woman's sleepy voice, 'Yeah?'

'Sherrie?'

'Who?'

'Sherrie Cunningham, I'm—'

'She's gone. I don't know where.'

'I'm a friend of her dad's.'

'She don't have no dad.'

'She did.'

The deadbolt opened, another lock shifted back. The door
thunked against its chain. The girl had a long slender face with
her father's palomino hair, a little freckled nose, wide lips in a
wide mouth. 'She didn't never have a dad.'

'I've got something for her. From him.'

Her face neared the door. 'What was his name? Her dad?'

'Clint. Clint Cunningham.'

She undid the chain, tugged her faded brown kimono tighter.
The kitchen smelled of leaking gas, ashtrays, crack, and heat.
She shoved beer bottles and dirty plates to one side of the table,
motioned at a chair and sat. 'I can tell her for you.'

'Cut the shit, Sherrie. What the fuck you doing to yourself?'

Her hand searching for a cigarette among the dirty coffee
cups was like a blind creature on the ocean floor. 'Who're you to
tell me that! I don't know you from nothing, asshole.'

'I'm Clint's friend. He asked me to come back—'

'You're just a little late.'

'It was in an old letter – I was supposed to read it if he died. But I got hurt and the letter disappeared and I just found it. I just talked with your grandmother in Portland, Mary Cunningham, and your Mom, Lucy Amato—'

'You some dick?'

'My name's Joe Murphy and I live here in San Francisco and I was in the 101st Airborne with your Dad in South Vietnam and Cambodia.'

'How's my grandma?'

'I think they all miss you. Want you to come back.'

The girl smiled and shook her head, hair rasping on the kimono. She tipped cigarette ashes into a cup. 'You got anything on you – coke, anything?'

He shrugged. 'A little weed—'

'Can you give me a few hits . . .'

He gave her a joint and she lit it keeping her hair back from his Bic, sucking down and holding in the smoke. She held it out to him but he waved it away. 'Your dad and me, we used to smoke that stuff all the time in Nam. They called our unit Celestial Airlines—'

'That's where it got him.'

He sat back. 'So it did.'

She waved the joint. 'This is good stuff. I could sell some for you.'

'It's my own. Not commercial.'

'Everybody should have their own. Victory garden.' Her pale lemon eyes canvassed the wall above the sink, yellow paint with big curling blisters showing a greasy tan beneath, the ventilator gummed black, a black cord hanging down, the single shelf with a rusty can of Raid and three empty Colt 45 malt liquor bottles. The eyes drifted back to him. 'What was he like?'

'He had hair like you and a small nose and broad shoulders – kind of an awkward, muscular build.'

'He was a runner, Mom said.'

'Yeah – that's right. In college.'

'I've seen a picture of him and you standing in front of a helicopter, at that place where you trained . . .'

'Fort Rucker.'

'Yeah. You don't look too much like you.'

'Reconstructive surgery by an Army intern. He had good intentions.'

'It's not that bad. You're cute. You got class. Normally I'd charge a guy like you a hundred bucks.'

'Because I'm white?'

'Because you look like you can pay it.' She nodded at his Levis, the old shirt, the black jacket. 'Not your clothes. You just *look* it.' She fixed him with the yellow tiger eyes. 'How you think my dad'd feel about me doing tricks?'

'I think he wants you to realize the magic of being alive before it's over.'

'That's how he was?'

'That's how he was. But he'd want you to give up the needle.'

'Who are you, cocksucker, coming into my house, criticizing me?'

'I had a friend who shook it. Took her three months. I'll help you.'

'Jesus. You walk in here, total stranger – tell me how to live!'

'I'm close as you're ever going to get to your dad.'

She stood, knocking back the chair. 'Well just fuck off!'

The door was greasy from generations of hands. 'Think about it. I'll come see you—'

'Get out before I wake Reno, in there, and he cuts you up bad.'

Murphy glanced at the black man face-down on the bedroom floor. 'Reno needs his sleep.'

Down the hall the TV was roaring for breakfast cereal, or was it toilet paper? Over the screaming children he couldn't tell. He held his breath till he reached the street.

Lila – was that her name, the one who'd kicked heroin? Dark hair, so slender, purple bruises up the pale insides of her arms. Who three months later jumped off the Golden Gate.

He turned left on Bryant and parked on Fifth. The Rathskeller was dark inside, after the bright street, and smelled of bourbon. There were bronze cups and photos of reporters on a shelf behind the bar, a few people still eating in the booths; he sat at the back with a double whiskey till Melissa came in. She was wearing a red and white checked suit and a white silk blouse with an open collar. 'You don't look like the same you,' she said.

'Everybody tells me that.'

'When was it, last spring? Why were you at Lily Tucker's party?'

'Friend of the bride.'

'That's what I heard. But gossip's not my beat—'

'I enjoyed talking with you. Would've called earlier, but I've been gone. Like I said.'

'So what happened?'

He motioned to the waitress for another double Irish. 'That's what I came to tell you.'

From the mountain Dona watched Concepción but there was no sign of soldiers. She lay in the shadow of a broad pine tree, on the soft scented mattress of its needles, the empty Galil beside her, her throat burning with rocket fumes and the singed stink of her hair.

In the village an old woman she did not know carried a basket of clothes down to the stream and began to scrub them against the rocks. A boy ran from the jungle with a dead wood rat and ducked into a hut. A little girl squatted on the bank and her pee trickled, glistening, into the water. On the hill above the houses a tan burro trotted in a circle, jerking at its tether.

Over her face a small brown spider had linked three pine needles with cables and was spinning a web between them. When the wind blew, shifting the needles, the cables tautened and relaxed, not breaking.

The spider did not know about the battle. She did not care about *la lucha*, the needs of the *campesino*. She was building a web so that she could kill other animals to eat and feed her children.

Cyndi Wheaton's office was full of people. There was a television camera in the corner; its red eye flicked on when he walked into the room. She beckoned him into the hall. 'This is for *now* – the evening news.'

'I wanted to talk to your people first – decide the best way to find out—'

'Find out *what*?'

'What I keep *telling* you: who the Americans were!'

'That we'll never know. The best we can hope for is a little exposure – the best for Guatemala . . .'

More cameras had arrived, more people with little steno pads and tape recorders, and it was easy to stand in their midst and look earnestly into the round black eyes with the blinking red lights, to answer the questions of the friendly men and women with the little note pads.

'Mr Murphy – Phyllis Steen of WFSF TV – what's your political viewpoint?'

'I learned in Vietnam not to care about politics.'

'But you must have a feeling now about Guatemala—'

'We should get out of there and let them solve their own problems.'

'Even if that means the Communists win?'

'I never met any Communists in Guatemala, just people.'

'You don't see them as a threat to our way of life?'

Then it was over and he was no longer news, the reporters talking about the mayor's six p.m. press conference. Cyndi Wheaton shook his hand and looked into his eyes. 'Stay in touch.' He walked up Mission Street in the milky afternoon sun, a lacy fog dropping over Twin Peaks, bringing a trace of California winter.

36

He was home before six and turned on NBC. At a corn auctioneers' meeting in Fargo George Bush was expressing his deep love for the people of North Dakota. Then came national sports; a left fielder who had just signed a four-million-dollar contract was explaining his philosophy of life. On national weather there were clouds over the west, rain over New England, and sun in the south. Then came California and local news, with good coverage of the mayor's press conference. He switched to CBS in time for the local news and carpet advertisements, then ABC for more on George Bush, the mayor, and the weather.

He called the Bay Area Committee, no response. He drove to South Van Ness through clogged and fuming traffic; no one answered the Committee's bell. At a Burger King telephone he tried to find Cyndi Wheaton's number but it was not listed. Don't rush things, he told himself. His meeting with the press had been too late for tonight's news; tomorrow there'd be a story in the *Chronicle*, then more on TV.

When he got home the phone was ringing. 'Mr Murphy?' An anxious, woman's voice. 'It's Priscilla Benson – your neighbour.'

'Yes. I remember.'

'It's really time we talked about your trees – they're getting worse and worse!'

'You're the president of the Sea Cliff Improvement Committee – if you want the trees along the sidewalk trimmed, then fine. Just leave mine alone.'

'How would it look with some trimmed and the others left to grow wild, like yours? My husband's a judge, you know, he sees these things from a legal point of view—'

The silver plate gleamed resolutely in the wavering candlelight, set off against the white damask tablecloth, the rich reds and blues of Royal Doulton, the silver-plated candelabra, Nancy's dark

169

dress and the oval of cultured pearls round her neck. Lyman thought of Kit Gallagher kissing her there, repressed it.

The heavy Kilkenny crystal felt good in his hand – how the claret sparkled, tasted like cooled, purified blood. He smiled at Jason sitting across from him with a napkin tucked into his collar; he felt it was a false smile, tried to make it true. Jason smiled, winked back.

He smiled at Christina; this time it was better; he wrinkled his brow inquisitively, asking her to smile back but she didn't. He had to admit he hated her, her teenage pout, plucked brows, and straightened hair, the diamond crescents in the ears he'd told her not to pierce.

Nancy glanced at him through the candles. 'Look at the grin on Poppa!'

'Just thinking of an old joke' – his standard answer, teasing her. Just thinking of what if all of you were dead, and I could walk alone on the hills where no one's ever been.

'Daddy never tells what he's thinking,' Jason said.

'Daddy never thinks,' Christina added.

'Daddy's buying us a lovely new house,' Nancy countered. 'So don't you hurt his feelings.'

'Daddy has no feelings,' Christina answered.

'Goddamnit, Jason – can't you hear the phone!' Lyman turned to Christina. 'And take those goddamn things out of your ears!'

'They're *mine*, Daddy. I don't have to.'

'It's for you, Daddy,' Jason called.

As he walked round the end of the table Lyman flicked his napkin hard so it caught Christina just below the ear, making him smile. 'Yeah?' he said into the phone.

'I need you to come in, Howie,' Curt Merck said. 'We've got good news.'

'It's my kid's birthday, for Christ's sake.'

'You had someone you were looking for, down south—'

'Yeah?'

'We think he just tried to get on TV, in San Francisco, tell his story.'

'Shit, no!'

'No news's good news. But you may want to go out there, discuss it with him?'

'Absolutely. Tell NoCal to stay out.'

'I can't, Howie, it's their turf. But I'm telling them he's yours.'

* * *

170

Dawn fog wrapped the house; the foghorn bellowed balefully. He dressed and walked up through the dripping, quiet streets to Geary, dropped fifty cents in a *Chronicle* rack.

Nothing on the front page, nor on page two or three. On page fourteen of the second section he finally found it, a small article in the gutter beside an I Magnin ad for see-through underwear: 'S.F. Tourist Claims Army Attack.'

San Francisco – A local resident who had recently traveled to Central America declared yesterday that US Army personnel are assisting the Guatemalan Army in its campaign against Marxist guerrillas. Joseph Murphy, 39, also alleged that US troops participated in a raid against a guerrilla-held stronghold.

In Washington, a Defense Department spokesperson, Joanne Quinlan, categorically refuted Murphy's claim, and explained that no US military personnel 'have been in recent years nor are now on duty in Guatemala'. Quinlan added that Communist revolutionaries trying to overthrow the country's democratically elected government often dress like soldiers and commit atrocities against the people, but that such incidents have been 'on the wane' in recent years due to the goverment's military successes against the guerrillas.

He threw the paper in the trash and crossed Geary through early traffic to Dunkin' Donuts, where a boy with pimples and a white paper baker's hat served him weak coffee and two jelly-filled rolls coated in powdered sugar.

37

He called the *Chronicle*, but Melissa would not be in until mid-morning and the operator wouldn't give him her home number. At nine-thirty someone answered the phone at the Bay Area Committee.

'It's OK coverage,' Cyndi Wheaton said. 'The *Chronicle*'s the best in the country for Central American news—'

'They didn't *say* anything! They acted like it was made up!'

'Wasn't it?'

'I don't follow—'

'I got a call last night at home, from the DEA. They say you're a drug smuggler and your plane got shot up by the Army and you've made up this story to get them back.'

'What'd you tell them?'

'That I didn't know where to find you.'

He was waiting for Melissa Maslow when she arrived at the *Chronicle*. 'When do I get the whole story?' she said. 'Now, or when you're in prison?'

'I told you the truth!'

'It's a sign you're guilty, saying that.' She led him across a wide low room of people hunched before green screens. The air smelled of warm newsprint, electricity, Coffee Mate, and cigarettes. She took a chair from another desk and put it beside hers, snapped on her computer terminal. 'Tell me about the drugs.'

'Turn it off,' he said. 'You tell me.'

She flicked off the computer. 'After we talked at the Rathskeller I called DC. They denied any US involvement, blamed the Communists.' She picked up a pencil, ticking it against her teeth. 'By the way, my story was much longer. It got cut up there—' she pointed at the ceiling. 'Editorial.'

She leaned back in her chair, playing with the pencil. 'DEA called last night, wants to talk to you about some drug shipment from Guatemala . . .'

172

'That sucks! I was down there looking at El Ceibal – there's ruins all up and down that river—' Murphy glanced round, making himself relax. 'What about this General Arena – the Guatemalan grass shipments?'

She ignored him. 'And you're just a San Francisco real estate investor – don't even know how to fly?'

'Of course I know how to fly – taught free of charge by Uncle Sam. That doesn't make me a drug pilot.'

'DEA said I should talk to some guy in City prison who just got nabbed with four million in coke. I saw him this morning, brought him photos of ten men, including one of you taken at yesterday's press conference. He picked you out instantly—'

'Who is this guy?'

'Normally I wouldn't say, but it'll be in tomorrow's paper. Carlos Bonaventura, originally a Cuban from Miami. Why are you making such a fuss, instead of running for Panama, Colombia? DEA has you *made!*'

He glanced at the room of people clinging crablike to their desks, their hands raised in adoration before the flickering green screens. 'What would you do?'

'Turn myself in – or leave. Fast.'

For a low-profile place you couldn't beat the Oasis. Three hundred units in two long, two-storey barracks at the junction of the Bayshore and Monterey Highways, forty-nine dollars cash for colour TV and two double beds and a shower with a massage head that sometimes worked depending on the room, with couples in cars in and out at all hours, nobody seeing anything but sex or money or getting somewhere down the road. Lyman checked in as Tim Merriweather but left no trace of himself in the room, got back into the Accura he'd rented at the airport and drove downtown, parked on O'Farrell and walked up Polk to a girlie joint, dark and sour-smelling after the bright street. He paid ten dollars for five tokens, locked the door of a booth behind him and put the tokens in the slot. The floor was sticky. A black plastic wall before him slid up and there was a Turkish-looking girl with heavy thighs and purple nipples dancing on a little plate turning around in an octagon of mirror windows. She smiled rotten teeth to welcome him and pushed her cunt against the window. He showed her a five and slid it into the slot and when the little plate came around again she shoved herself up and down his window. The timer buzzed and

173

the black wall came down and he stood waiting for a moment then went out of the booth and down the hall to the end through a door marked STAFF ONLY and up narrow stairs to a suite of offices on the third floor. A fat man in a Scorpions T-shirt was talking on the phone with his feet on the desk. He finished his call. 'You again.'

'I want a PPK and a hundred rounds,' Lyman said, 'and this guy's picture and address. And I want you to stay out of my way.'

The pay-phone was beat up and didn't work when Murphy put two quarters in it. He walked down California till he found another. 'Steele and Feldman,' a woman said. He asked for Saul Feldman.

'He's in conference.'

'Please get him out. Tell him it's Joe Murphy.'

A minute later Saul came on. 'Murph – what's the rush?'

'I want you to sell Sea Cliff and every other piece of property I've got in forty-eight hours—'

'You fucking nuts?'

'Sell it to CMC, Bayview, anybody, best price you can. Spread it around, not in a lump. Don't tell anybody the whole show—'

'You're out of your mind. You're going to get creamed.'

'And I need you to hire movers to get all my stuff out of the house by tomorrow night. In storage. And draw up an affadavit that all my stuff belongs to a woman named Dona Villalobos – I'll spell it—'

'I'm not doing this, Murph. Don't jerk me around, I got a client waiting.'

'Who the fuck you think I am, the paper boy?'

'You really want to do this?'

'I *was* a paper boy once, actually, in Texas. Yes, I really want to do it.'

'Even the Porsche?'

'Yeah. No – keep that out. That and my bikes, and the Ford three-quarter ton. Sell the rest.'

'Why? You're going to get creamed there too.'

'I got the kind of problems we always talked about.'

For a moment Saul said nothing. 'Damn.'

'All cash, Saul. Everything. And one last thing—'

'Let me tell my secretary, tell this guy to wait—' Saul came back on. 'Murph, you gotta think this over.'

'Everything sold in forty-eight hours. Then within twenty-four more hours you wire it all to the regular setup in CI? I'll take it from there.'

'You're really screwing me up, Murph. I was taking Chris kayaking tomorrow, out at Point Reyes—'

'Tell him I'm sorry. Tell him if I ever get out of this I'll take him hunting in Montana, whatever he wants—'

'You ought to drop all this, come with us.'

'One more thing – you're going to hate me for this—'

'Probably.'

'Can you go see a chick named Sherrie Cunningham, lives at 154 Alabama? Write that down – 154 Alabama. She's about twenty. A junkie. I need you to offer her money, support her if she goes back to school, gets into de-tox, goes straight—'

'You shouldn't fuck junkies, man, you'll get AIDS.'

'I'm not. Don't go there alone.'

Lyman drove out Geary through Golden Gate Park till he was sure there was no tail, then cut across to the Sunset, parked in an Esso garage and stuck the PPK and hundred rounds up behind the Accura's firewall. He took the trolley downtown and rented a Dodge from Asia Rentals with a licence and credit cards in the name of Lucian Hayward, registered at the Hyatt Regency under the same name, drove out Mission to Noble's Gun Shop and bought a used Zastava 9mm and forty rounds for four hundred and fifty dollars, using the same ID.

The sun was a thin orange disk sinking into grey beyond the rooftops. He drove down Twenty-fifth Avenue into Sea Cliff, passed by the house, parked two blocks further, and walked back on the far side of the street. The gun was heavy in the holster under his armpit, slippery with sweat. The houses were white and vast, no one in sight. Murphy's house had tall pillars like the Jefferson mansion, no lights. This can't be the guy, Lyman thought. He sat in his car for several hours till a car pulled into Murphy's driveway. It was low and lean but Lyman couldn't see what kind. He started the Dodge and drove past the house as the garage door came down. He idled to a halt. Lights came on in the front rooms. He parked and jogged back along the sidewalk, keeping his left arm against his ribs.

'Murph!' she said. 'How sweet of you to call! It's only been what, six weeks?'

'Lay off, Angelica. I've had a bad time.'

'Sorry to hear. Who is she?'

'Can I come over?'

'There's some people here – little party. What the hell—'

He went down to the garage and started the Kawasaki, let it run for a few seconds then pushed the door button and roared up the driveway, turned left and accelerated to the corner, passing a tall black man who turned round suddenly, running back down the walk – somebody's servant, maybe – never seen him before. He gunned the bike round the curve and up Twenty-fifth Avenue, swung left towards Pacific Heights, burning the lights.

From its curving driveway her house cascaded on levels down through lemon trees, rhododendrons, acacias and palms, to a lower lawn with fountains, all overlooking the gingerbread gables of Pacific Heights, the Marina, and the Bay. There were cars in the driveway and up on the street. He hugged her then sat on the kitchen counter watching her green eyes. Music thundered from the faraway front of the house. 'Got anything to eat?' he said.

She poured him coffee and set it on the counter with a Sara Lee cheesecake and a bottle of Bushmills. 'I've got people to take care of, in there—'

'I'll be right in. How's Eric?'

She glanced at the clock over the sink. 'He's had his book and he's already in bed.'

'Can I go see him?'

'Just for a bit.'

He drained the coffee and filled the cup with Bushmills. 'You're going to an early grave, Murph,' she said.

He lit a joint and passed it to her. 'I've already lived longer than I ever thought I would.'

'That makes you attractive to women but not necessarily a good prospect.' She inhaled the joint, held it. 'I've given up waiting for you.'

'You've been balling every guy in town while I've been gone—'

'My fuck rate's far lower than yours.'

'Like that morning in Cleveland when you screwed the Sam Colter Band? All five of them?' He put the Sara Lee box in the trash under the sink. 'AIDS will make us all virtuous again.'

'There's other ways to whore yourself.'

'You should know.' When she said nothing he looked up, but she was lighting the joint. 'This isn't life, Angie.'

'You've always said that. You've just never found anything better.'

176

Footsteps came through the hall and sunroom into the kitchen, a tall man with a black beard and a bit of a belly, black leather jacket and grey slacks. 'Murph!' he extended a hand. 'When she didn't come back, I should've known it was you.'

'Hello, Mitch. Angie's been telling me my fortune—'

'Shouldn't take long,' Mitch said. He glanced at Angelica. 'Just kidding.'

'Murph thinks I fuck too many people,' Angelica said.

Mitch took a film canister from his breast pocket and tapped some coke on to the counter, scraped it out in a line with a book of matches that said *Enjoy Life . . . Eat Out More Often*. 'Guests first,' he smiled.

Murphy shook his head. 'How's the new album?'

'She's losing her voice.' Mitch bent over the counter to sniff up the line. 'Too much coke and Benedictine and parties. Now this album's done, she takes a year off, raises her kid, lives a normal life.'

'Fuck you, Mitch,' Angelica said.

38

He climbed the stairs to the third floor, went into Eric's room, the purple glow of a fluid oscillator sliding round the walls, a fish mobile banging his head as he leaned over the racing car waterbed. 'How you doin', amigo?'

'Murph! Where've you *been*?'

'Travelling. Had to stay a while.'

The boy sat up. 'You get hurt or something?'

'Nothing bad. How's you?'

'Doin' fine.'

'Feelin' alone?'

'Never.'

'Everybody does, some of the time.'

Eric glanced at the door. 'You don't act so lonely, Murph.'

'It's a mask, amigo. A charade.'

'What's that?'

'When people dress up to be somebody they're not.' He brushed the boy's pale hair, short and crisp. 'Pretend they're happy when they're not.'

'Mom's happy when she drinks.'

'Yeah, I know about that.'

'What's drinking change?'

'Makes everything worse.'

'Mom says my dad was a lush. I asked Mary what that means and she said a drunk.'

'I never knew your dad. But he made beautiful music. Music to make people happy.'

'Like drinking does?'

'No. Not like that.'

The boy snuggled down. 'I was worried about you, Murph.'

'No need to.'

'Mom isn't going to stay with you, is she?'

He patted the boy's arm, shook his head.

'She never stays with anybody, does she?'

'You and I can still be friends.'

'You're awful thin, Murph. You wreck your bike again? You sure you're OK?'

'Guaranteed. You get some sleep now. And Eric—'

'Yeah, Murph?'

'If I don't come around for a while, that don't mean I'm not missing you . . . I'll be back, soon's I can.'

The boy had drifted off to sleep and Murphy went downstairs. The living room was crowded, more people on the stairs going down to the sunken parlour, Guns 'N' Roses thudding pyrotechnic solos off the walls – to be able to do *that*, Murphy thought, what the needle gives – pure perception of beauty, untainted? He thought of Sherrie Cunningham, the blue-black marks on the inside of her elbow.

'Murph!' someone called. 'Bring your axe?'

''Lo, Tiny.' He leaned into the man's face to speak over the music. 'Not going to compete with this dude.'

'He *is* amazing.' Tiny gulped a glass of red. 'Listen to that shit – how he fills it in, doubles up on the E—'

'It's not that, Tiny. It's that he's so *clean*.'

'Like Clapton.'

'Different. A different vision.'

'Heard you had some trouble,' a woman bent forward to be kissed. 'Down in Costa Rica?'

'Hi, Laura.' Her lips tasted like cold cream and raspberries; she shoved against him. He clung a second, nipping her, pulled away. 'Where'd you hear that?'

'Paper.'

'It was Guatemala. All over now.'

A girl came by with a silver salver with lines on it and a silver tube and Laura put down her wine to take one, her face sharp then melting into a smile as the coke hit her.

> I'm on the nighttrain,
> Ready to crash and burn—

The girl offered Murphy the tray; he shook his head. 'Oh what the hell,' he said, sucking in one line, switching sides, then the next. It was a cold blue blade of perception: he could see individual lamé filigrees on the girl's neckline, her big soft tits beneath, nipples poking out the fabric that clung all the way down to her

179

mound and slender thighs, could hear the drummer's quick ripple
tossed in for free and the guitarist's fingertips quicksilver down
the neck, in and out of blues, playing *for* God, *to* God only, could
taste the wine and the rooty soil and chromium sulphate in it, taste
Laura's lipstick on his lips and the lilac perfume of this girl with
the silver salver, see every black and silver curly hair of Tiny's
beard, smell Tiny's breath of garlic and weed, his armpit stench
and the Ban under the girl's shaved pits and when someone
knocked over a plant on the glass table by the piano he saw it fall
in slow motion, the awkward frightened leaves, the dirt rushing
out when the pot hit the floor, stems snapping like soft wet bones.
'Shit!' someone said, stepping back into the dirt, the stems squelch-
ing. Someone hit two piano notes, an F and G, discordant, making
him look up, but it was just a wine glass, sitting on the keys.

A rocket took his brain straight up, his body far below on the
launch pad but still he could feel every cell and the fire climbing
from his legs and roaring in his sex and soaring up into his chest
where every breath was made of ice. He met the girl with the silver
salver in the dining room and she gave him two more hits and he
held the salver out to her and she did also, and we're completely
in touch, he thought, her body absolutely part of his so when he
rubbed her breast he could feel not only its soft smooth heaviness
but also how the tingle from his hand made her breast feel hot inside,
the nipple's stinging need to be touched, touched softly, fingered,
could feel the ache racing down into her guts and through her groin
to him, her teeth sharp into his lips, her hand round him moving
back and forth, and as they went upstairs he raised her dress so
he could see her long thighs rising before him, bending at the knee,
her crotch in white lacy underpants and he put his hand there as
she climbed the stairs, feeling the wet hairs through the silk and
wondered, is she that hot already or is it from someone else? In
Angelica's room he held her against the shut door and shoved the
underpants down, her spine against the jamb and her legs around
him; he gripped her thighs and shoved into her, her arms squeez-
ing his neck and her teeth hard against his cheek till she came
sobbing, leaning back her head, red mouth open, wide large teeth
agape with a thread of shiny saliva between them. He carried her
to the bed and pushed her legs up around his neck to go in deeper,
feeling her every cell, his own, every molecule he breathed.

'I've got to go back,' she said. She went holding up her dress
into the bathroom and squatted on the toilet. 'Barney asked me,
keep everybody stoned.'

'I could fuck you all night.'

'I gotta go back.' She wiped herself, holding her thighs apart
and looking at the toilet paper. 'Barney said he'll get me a part.'

He followed her down, sex on fire. 'I don't care if he *had* Scuds,'
a woman was saying. 'That's no reason to nuke him.'

'We're not getting single time,' another said.

> No money in our jackets
> and our jeans are torn
> your hands are cold
> but your lips are warm

He went into an atrium of lime and jasmine trees enclosed by
a silvery cedar wall overhung with purple wistaria. There was
a pool with a rock fountain, a lone dwarf maple stooping over it,
red carp in the water. I'm just like them, he thought.

'Lovely tonight.'

He looked at the voice – a slim man with spiky hair, an earring,
and a black leather jacket. I'm supposed to know your name.

'You've been out of town, Murph?'

'Few weeks.'

'Must be nice to travel. Like that.'

'You should try it.' He went back inside and met Laura in the
hall and she kissed him hard, pushing her pelvis against him,
but would not go upstairs. 'Sleeping with skulls,' he said.

A guy in black jeans and cowboy boots took her arm. 'How's
your horses?' Murphy asked him.

'You got the wrong guy,' the man smiled patronizingly. 'I don't
have any horses.'

'Then what you doing in those boots?'

He was talking with a smaller girl in jeans, sandals with little
red-painted toes, her blouse open down the middle. She gave him
two capsules of Ecstasy. 'The more I reach, the further things
recede,' she said.

'Don't reach. And everything'll come to you.'

She laughed. 'Don't be nasty.'

> You're no good
> you're no good
> you're no good
> baby you're no good

He reached out to the girl's lovely breasts inside the open blouse but she batted his hand away and walked back into the living room.

Downstairs was an enclosed terrace and a redwood tub full of people, and others sitting on the sides with their feet in it. The water burnt his skin; he sat with his back against a nozzle pumping hot vibrating water. There was a noise in his head like a jet landing but it never landed, just kept getting deeper and louder. The people beside him were fucking and trying not to show it, till the girl came and wilted on the man, her long hair down over his shoulder into the frothing steamy water. When she moved up and away from the man Murphy slipped up to her from behind and she was angry for a moment then widened her legs and let him come inside and began to move up and down while the guy watched her. Finally she came again, gasping face down, hands on the rim of the tub, her hair stringy in the water.

The small girl with the red painted toes came in. She had a dark appendix scar across the right side of her belly. 'What happened to your arm?' she said. After a while she let him come into her but again he could not come and she took him hand and hand out on the grass under the gentle cool rain and sucked him softly for a long time but he still could not come. With a numb desolation he kissed her goodbye and got dressed and went back up the stairs where two men were kissing, one making little girlish sighs, the other's hand on his crotch.

He started the bike and roared up the driveway, slowed for the sidewalk, the bike skidding. Watch out, he reminded himself, liking how the yellow turn signal flicked – its steady dependable bursts, controllable. Long as you watch out you're fine.

He spun out on to Pacific and tore down the block, letting the front wheel go up, feeling the back shimmy. The bike wanted to flip but he wouldn't let it. Keep it under control, he told himself – then you can have fun with no danger.

He coasted through the Stop and dived down the steep drop of Steiner, engine screaming, up to eighty, let it back off, muffler blaring, the intersection coming up like a head-on collision but he eased the brakes not skidding and there was no one going through the intersection so he made it, sliding sideways down the next block, bouncing slow motion off a light pole, missing a parked Volvo and spinning to a stop.

He looked up ashamed, as if everyone in the apartments nearby had seen him risk his life. The bike had died; he kicked

it alive and rolled downhill and swung left on Lombard, beating
the last lights and accelerating through the long, wide approach
to the Golden Gate bridge, passing a Mercedes that flashed
behind him in a blur of shrinking headlights, a Scirocco far
ahead whipped past, the bike screaming the roar of pure truth
and he reminded himself be cool, don't let it trick you, saw the
needle bouncing at a hundred and forty but didn't dare look
down to be sure, the handles vibrating with road ripples, the curve
straightening towards the bridge, a patch of mist and moths spattering his face, headlights the other way flying past like comets,
wind thunder yanking his hair, the grey concrete wall a blur beside
his knee.

The bridge was a rising metal wave, the far tower climbing
inside the near one, orange cones separating oncoming lanes and
he wove among them; a pick-up flashed past blowing its horn.
He went up the hill under the Rainbow Tunnel and down into
Mill Valley, took the exit to the sea, through rainy hills where
eucalyptus scent dripped from the trees and sebaceous snail
tracks slicked the road. A white owl flapped up from his headlight, a rabbit in its claws. The night was thick with manzanita
and wild roses, thunder and smell of the sea cascading up the
cliffs, rain washing his face.

The bike was wild with anger to go faster, screaming up
through the long Slide Ranch curve in third, a hundred, hundred
and ten, slipping sideways on the dew-wet road but he could hold
it, go as fast as it could go, he could hold it, the Ecstasy hitting
now, bringing everything in one and he loved it all, the speed,
the world and all its night odours and sea crashing and all the
girls and the engine roaring between his thighs as he tilted into
the turn, and there was a cop car across the road and nowhere
to cut and he swerved from the edge and the bike went down and
soared off the highway and he slammed across the gravel shoulder and crashed into the manzanita.

The world was spinning over and over, slapping him; he stopped
and lay looking at the stars. An enormous noise, the smell of dust
and crushed ice plant and manzanitas. He could fall between the
stars. He went down to the *Río*, realized he had dreamed her and
she was gone, gone for good.

Deuce Harmony had dumped his Triumph in the rain and got
decapitated by a Stop sign. Bikers who'd loved speed were spend-
ing their lives in wheelchairs. He touched his neck, head, arms
and legs, could feel them all, stood carefully. No special pain. Voices

and people coming down the hill. He pushed through the manzanita to the edge of the cliff but could not find the bike, climbed up to the highway, saw the CHP car and remembered.

'You crazy fucker!' he screamed, running at a cop.

More cops from all sides. Another CHP car. Cops with guns. 'Cuff the son of bitch!' one yelled.

He tried to back up, too late. They pinned his arms behind him, hard metal biting his wrists. 'You assholes tried to kill me!'

'Stupid maniac – you were doing a hundred and thirty on that curve!'

'I *had* it. I *knew* what I was doing! You assholes! Don't you know *anything*?'

'When you get him to San Rafael,' one said, 'be sure to do a drug screen.'

A plain car slid up, idling hard, a brown Dodge. Tall black guy, three others. 'Thanks,' he said to the cops. 'Y'all have a good evening, now.'

'You really want him?'

'C-6. No questions asked.'

The tall guy grabbed Murphy's bad arm and yanked him towards the brown Dodge. 'Wait a minute,' Murphy said.

'Wait nothing!' One of the other plainclothes guys popped open the Dodge's trunk. The two CHP cars revved and pulled away. The tall black man took something small and black out of his jacket. A gun.

'Wait!' Murphy screamed. The black man gripped the gun in both hands and smashed it down on his head; pain exploded inside him and he fell, grateful to be nowhere.

39

The Huey fell in a pocket and he pulled back the collective pitch lever but it didn't respond and he shoved the cyclic to drive it sideways but the ship kept dropping and green tracers leaped up from the treetops; he kicked the pedals but the tail wouldn't swing, the Huey spinning as the tracers closed in and he screamed, 'Take it!' to the co-pilot but the co-pilot was hit, blood spraying everywhere, wounded grunts screaming in the back, the cockpit filled with smoke and the jungle of dark killers reaching up for them.

The ambulance surged forward, the differential whirring beneath him. He tried to change position on the stretcher but found he was bent backwards, wrists pinned to ankles. Not an ambulance, a dust-off. Shot down but the medevacs found us. Tied down so won't fall off. Must be shot in the head – can't see.

Hard to breathe. Not an ambulance. Trunk of a car, this. The car bounced on a bump and pain crashed through his head. *They* hit me on the head. CHP, the tall black guy.

He bent himself harder backwards to reach his ankles, grabbed a shoelace but dropped it, found it again but the knot had tightened. He kicked the shoe loose but it fell beyond reach.

The engine slowed. He gripped the shoe with his toes and pulled it towards his hands, tugged out the inner sole but it was the wrong shoe. He yanked the other off and pulled out the knife, cut the cord round his ankles. The engine roared; the car swerved, dropped from macadam on to dirt, gravel spattering the underside.

The car was climbing through S-turns, springs jouncing in the ruts. He dropped the knife and doubled himself up to slide the cuffs under his buttocks, tearing his shoulder sockets, the metal cutting his wrists. He slid his cuffed hands forward under his thighs and feet, had them now in front, squirmed round to pick up the knife and held it in his teeth. The brake drums squealed, the trunk's interior glowing from the brakelights. He found his shoes and shoved them on, with one hand squeezed the knife under the trunk lid and popped it open, keeping it down with the other. The car halted, he leaped from the trunk, ran through a wire fence across a mucky ditch towards a low white building, men shouting, the car's tyres shrieking after him, its headlights bouncing over the ditch and he ducked into the white building's ammoniac darkness of screeching chickens, his nose smashed something hard – a perch – and he darted out the back door across a dirt road, sprinting awkwardly with his hands cuffed before him, dogs snarling along a fence, the car gaining as he jumped a corral fence and dashed uphill into an orchard and above it a pasture; the dogs poured out of the kennel and came howling up the hill behind him. There was a cyclone fence; he climbed and wriggled through the barbed wire on top and down to a chaparral slope, the dogs hitting the fence, their fangs clanging steel.

He ran up a rolling meadow, the stars bright above, to the ridgetop. Headlights far below wound sleepily along a country road, over a bridge past a cutbank then a small white house with an orange pick-up in the driveway, illuminating a stone wall along the shoulder, a yellow curve sign, then slipping around a ridge out of sight.

Voices and dogs coming up fast. He ran downhill and splashed across a creek, climbed through alders to the road as more headlights came up fast behind him. A Ford slid by, a pebble ticking in its hubcap, its searchlight raking the slope and bouncing off the red alder trunks inches over his head. The Ford passed the white house, the pick-up truck, the stone wall, and vanished round the curve.

Dogs were baying down the hill behind him; he ran along the road past the white house, up the driveway to the orange pick-up, its cab light flashing as he leaped inside. He shut the door, ducked under the steering wheel to cut the ignition wires. Two men were running up the road, a big dog bounding before them. He linked two wires but they were wrong so he tried the first and third, the dash indicators gleamed, he shifted into reverse, the dog crashed into the door as he rolled back, popping the clutch, the dog snarling at the door handle, three men spanning the road. The engine backfired and died.

The dog leaped on to the hood, beating its teeth against the windshield, a Doberman, the three men running for the truck as he bent again under the dash, found the starter wire and touched it to the others; it caught; he raced the sputtering engine, shifted into first and drove at the men who dived for the hard shoulder, the dog squealing off the hood and whacking the pavement as Murphy took his hands from the wheel to shift into second. A spiderweb of cracks spread across the windshield; there was another *tick* and glass spattered from the rear window down his neck, another star in the windshield, and he spun the wheel weaving the truck. *Tick*: another then another hit the windshield and it collapsed into his face, cold air crashing in; another ping of metal then only the truck's uneven roar as he peered through the gaping windshield at the unlit road, flakes of glass like snow flicking past his cheeks.

Safely around the first bend he took his cuffed hands from the wheel, holding it steady with his knees, and fumbled at the dash till he found the lightswitch. Valves chattering, transmission yowling, headlights jolting, the truck wound up to eighty-five but would go no faster; ahead was a straightaway suddenly familiar – Olema's scruffy store and few houses. Headlights jumped into the mirror and he shut off the truck's lights, stomped the emergency brake and skidded up an alley behind the store, jumped out and hurdled a fence into a eucalyptus grove as the Ford roared through the Stop southward on Highway One towards Bolinas.

He ran to the truck and cut the tail-light wires. The Ford came flying back through the Stop, going north towards Point Reyes. He started the truck and drove fast south, flicking on the lights after a mile; at the Bolinas turn-off he swung uphill on a narrow road into the Coast Range, no guardrail between the edge and the chasm on the right where redwood tops flitted past; near the top the truck began to gasp then died. It would not start; the gauge showed empty. 'Damn!' he yelled. Below, three sets of headlights came fast down Highway One. At the turn-off they split, one continuing south, one swinging west towards Bolinas, the third coming up towards him.

Everything took place very slowly but there was no time. He rolled the truck back, swerved it round till it was pointing downhill, pushed it forward. The car's lights came darting uphill; the truck gained speed. He dived out of the truck's door as the car accelerated round the last curve; the pavement spun up and slapped him in the face as the car's tyres screeched and the truck slammed into it.

He got to his feet. The awful howling inside his head was the car's horn. He wiped his hands; they were stuck with gravel. He found the knife and ran uphill; from the wreck the Ford's horn wailed like a primeval beast.

He reached the crest. More headlights came up the road and halted behind the wreck. In the columns of light he could see men running uphill, the dark shadow of a dog bounding before them.

Holding the knife carefully before him, he pushed from the road down the far side of the coast range, through prickly low firs, stumbling on roots and fallen branches, the needle-thick slope slippery, across a meadow where a deer snorted and bounded away, into a marsh, the dog's bark nearing.

He ran down a steep ledge, Mill Valley's lights two thousand feet below. Now he could hear the dog's fast patter through the brush. Snarling it slammed him down, a horrible Doberman crunching his arm, fighting for his neck. He drove the knife straight up under its collar and yanked; it cried, gurgled, teeth sunk in his wrist, dragging him; it fell dead. He unbuckled its collar and ran along the ledge and threw the collar over the cliff, heard it hit moments later. The brush crashed as the men neared; he ran up the slope above the cliff, dug a rock from the moss and hid gasping under a juniper.

The first man came panting through the trees to the cliff. 'Here!' he called. Two others scrambled through the scrub. There was the sound of static, a high, steady beep. 'Dog's down there,' the first said.

'He ain't moving?'

'He's got him down . . . Go uphill and around and down this cliff. I'll take the down side, with the receiver. Charlie, stay here, coordinate positions. Watch our lights and keep signalling.'

The flashlights parted, one moving downhill along the cliff edge, one remaining, another climbing towards Murphy. It passed, the man exuding smells of sweat and cigarettes.

When the two had climbed down the sides of the cliff they signalled three flashlight blinks up to Charlie. One step at a time, Murphy edged along the cliff towards Charlie, who was scuffing out a place to sit. 'Charlie!' one called from below. 'Charlie!'

'Yo!' Charlie called.

'Dog lost his collar. It's here, caught on a branch.'

Charlie stood, flicked on his light. 'I'm coming down.'

'Go the uphill way. It's easier.'

Charlie came towards Murphy, switching his flashlight to his left hand, parting the bushes with his right.

40

He hit Charlie with the rock and Charlie fell in a clump, flash-light clattering; Charlie was twitching and moaning; in his pockets Murphy found a gun, a wallet, and a thin aerosol can that made him gasp for breath.

Charlie whined, tried to sit. Holding the spray can in his left hand, Murphy shoved the knife against his throat. 'Quick! Why you chasing me?'

'My head . . .'

Murphy shifted the spray can and squeezed a burst into Charlie's face. Charlie choked, coughed, tried to pull back. 'Tell me fast,' Murphy said, 'or I'll empty this whole can in your face. Then I'll kill you.'

'Syndic,' Charlie gagged, 'wants you—'

'The dealers?'

'No! The *big* guys. Please don't—'

'That place you took me – what was it?'

'The ranch.'

'*What* ranch?'

'Congregation – I'll tell you, just don't—'

'Charlie!' a voice called from below. 'What's keeping you?' Charlie lunged for the edge and Murphy sprayed the Mace full into his face, up his nose, Charlie writhing, choking, fighting him off. Holding his breath, Murphy hit him again with the rock, grabbed Charlie's wallet and gun, ran away from the cliff, half blinded by the Mace, through the trees and along the meadow and down a great rubbled cirque.

Beyond the awakening lights of Mill Valley, Highway 101 was swelling with early traffic. The Bay gleamed gunmetal under the waning stars, the East Bay hills powdered with lights, their crests stitched with redwood tops against the lavender, orange east.

At a stream he washed blood and dirt from his face, and finger-combed his hair. Charlie's gun was a lousy little Grendel .380 – it would be loud and nearly useless. He pocketed the knife and pulled his jacket up over his shoulders from behind and down over his arms to cover the cuffs and gun, holding the jacket against his front as if carrying extra clothing too warm to wear.

In the first street of houses a dog came barking, making him jump, but it was only a spaniel on a chain. Next came a line of unfinished apartments, the lawns bulldozed and littered with scraps of redwood siding, a pile of uprooted apple trees along the kerb. 'Early Occupancy', a sign said, 'Apple Grove Condominiums'.

Cars began to trickle down the streets, into the larger roads that poured into the river of 101 carrying them to San Francisco. An empty *Chronicle* truck idled smokily outside Johnny's Stop 'n' Go; Murphy ducked under the canvas rear-gate, clambered over bundles of fresh papers and hid under plastic and old newsprint near the cab.

Lyman drove fast up the ridge road past the wreck of the truck and Ford to the top where two more Fords had pulled off the road. A NoCal man came out of one. 'They want you on the horn, sir!'

'Let the assholes wait!'

'Whatever you say, sir. But it's HQ.'

'I said *let* them wait,' he seethed into the man's face – a kid, crewcut, anxious. 'You guys can't wipe your ass without getting it all over you – *why* should I talk to any of you!'

'Regs require response to radio traffic when response is possible, sir!'

'You little asshole!' Lyman shoved him against the car. 'Don't *you* talk regulations! Just take me to where he got away.'

The NoCal man pushed himself up from the side of the car where he had fallen, wiping his hands on his pants. 'He beat up one of the Syndic guys. The guy's still out there, and another one with him.' He nodded at the gun in Lyman's hand. 'So be careful with that rod.'

The NoCal man opened the car door, spoke into the radio, shut and locked the door, and led Lyman through the woods and across a meadow. They came to the top of a cliff where a man was sitting against a rock, his head bandaged, another man sitting beside him, smoking. The cigarette drove Lyman wild. 'Go

191

back to the car and order up a medic,' he told them.

'We did,' the NoCal man said.

'Go *get* the medic, I said. I want to talk to this dude.' He took Charlie's hand. 'Howya doin', big guy?'

'OK. Fucking head.'

'What'd he ask you?'

'Ask me? Nothing. Nothing, boss.'

'C'mon, don't pull my string. I need to know where his head's at.'

'I didn't say nothing—'

'I *know* that. Just tell me what *he* said. C'mon, good buddy—'

'Well, he wanted to know why we was chasin' him . . .'

'Yeah?'

'I didn't say nothing, boss.'

'What else?'

'Wanted to know where it was we took him, that's all—'

'You told, didn't you?'

'No sir, I didn't say. I swear . . .' Charlie strained at Lyman's arm. 'That's why he hit me—'

'Relax, I'll make it better.' Holding Charlie's forehead steady with his left hand, he gripped Charlie's neck in his right and jerked hard. A few moments later he stood, inspected Mill Valley far below in the blue-golden dawn, and walked back to the cars. 'Cancel the medic,' he told the NoCal man. 'Your boy's had a haemorrhage.'

'He's *dead*?'

'It's a homicide now. Give the CHP and the Marin and Frisco cops Murphy's full details. Remind them it's C-6. That they are responsible for maximum silence. Say he's armed and very dangerous, probably headed back to San Francisco.'

The *Chronicle* truck's door slammed and the truck lurched into gear, halted minutes later. The door banged, the canvas gate grated aside, a bundle of papers slapped down on the sidewalk; the door slammed again and the truck lurched into gear. After a dozen more stops the truck rattled on to Highway 101 towards San Francisco. It crossed the Golden Gate Bridge, wheezed to a stop for the toll-gate, and took the Embarcadero towards downtown. When it stopped for the light at Columbus and Bay, Murphy hopped out and walked up Columbus towards Chinatown, ignoring the occasional passer-by who turned to stare at his torn face, the strange way he carried his jacket inside out before him over his clasped hands.

41

Chinatown's sidewalks bustled with housewives carrying straw baskets of fish, vegetables, and poultry on their elbows, with slipper-shuffling old men hugging Chinese newspapers under their arms, with chattering girls in red parochial skirts and solemn boys in blue cardigans hustling to the parochial school of Notre-Dame de Victoire.

Up a dead-end off Mason was a motorcycle garage. A German shepherd sitting in the open door wagged its tail as Murphy approached. Inside a man knelt over a disassembled Suzuki. He stood up slowly, put down his wrench. 'Did you dump?'

Murphy glanced round the shop. 'Anybody else here?'

'Not now. I better be getting you to a doctor—'

'Close the door, Ray. You got some cable-cutters?'

Ray Lin whistled the German shepherd inside and pulled down the door. Murphy sat on a car seat that served as a sofa, raised up his arms to let his coat slip back from the cuffs.

'Jesus, Murph! Who put you in those? What are you doing with that dink little gun?'

'I need you to get me out of them.'

Ray bent over him, checked the bloody wound on his skull, the scratches on his face and hands. He went to the wall of tools and took down a large pair of cable-cutters, made Murphy hold his hands on the concrete floor and broke through the hardened steel chain linking the two cuffs. Murphy raised up his hands with a dizzying sense of freedom. 'Oh God, what I've been through.'

Ray sat back on his haunches. 'You going to tell me about it?'

'Let's get these cuffs off first.'

Murphy stood by a bench vice and Ray clamped the cuffs one at a time in the vice and cut them with an electric hacksaw. Murphy told him about the CHP car blocking the road, the black man with the Dodge, his break-out from the Dodge's trunk, stealing the truck, the man named Charlie, the escape to Mill Valley—'

'I don't see why they do all this just because you were speeding—'

'Where's Susan?' Murphy said.

'At work.'

'Can I go upstairs and take a shower, lie down? I've never felt so bad in all my life.'

The phone rang; Ray answered it briefly, came back. 'I'll make you some coffee, something to eat while you take a shower, then you have a sleep. When you wake up we'll sort this out.'

'That's the problem, Ray. There's nothing *to* sort out.'

When he woke rain was falling steadily against the window. The slightest move agonized his head; every muscle and bone hurt miserably. There was a little round carpet on the floor; if I can get my feet on that and stand, he told himself, I'll have it licked.

In the bathroom he took four empirin with codeine and stood again under the shower, careful not to let it hit his head, till his muscles loosened and the pain became reasonable. Back in the bedroom he could not find his clothes, went downstairs. Over the thunder of Fleetwood Mac was the shriek of a grinder; he waited till it stopped. 'Ray!'

Ray came to the foot of the stairs, grinned up at him. 'You're one ugly specimen. What happened to your arm?'

'Where's my clothes?'

'Just a minute.' Ray put down the grinder and came upstairs. 'I washed them, put them in the dryer.'

'Thanks. What time's it?'

'Two-thirty.'

The clothes were still warm from the dryer. 'Hungry?' Ray said.

'I need a drink. Took some of your codeine.'

Ray poured him coffee and brandy, went out and came back a few minutes later with three hamburgers and a six-pack of coke. 'Tell me about the Syndic,' Murphy said.

'We don't mix with them. They're selling all the coke now, trying to take over the weed.'

'*Who* are they?'

'Mostly Cubans from Miami, and the guys that got thrown out of Nicaragua when those Sandinos got in.'

'Sandinistas.'

'A spic's a spic.'

195

'Ever hear of Carlos Bonaventura?'

Ray shook his head.

'Ever hear of some place in Marin, up by Olema, called the Congregation Ranch?'

'Don't ever go to Marin. No Chinese people up there.'

Murphy found the wallet he'd taken from the man named Charlie. Inside was a driver's licence in the name of Hector Alvierez, 1449 Paloma Terrace, a scrawny face squinting at the camera. He handed it to Ray. 'Ever see him?'

Ray gave it back. 'Never.' Also in the wallet were Visa and Master cards from Southern California Federal Savings, a bowling league card, a mini calendar from Southern California Federal, a polaroid of a dark-haired, chubby woman and a teenage girl sitting on a floral couch, the camera flash reflecting in the dayglo painting above their heads. There was a business card with a federal seal, US Bureau of International Development, Hector Alvierez, Senior Program Evaluator, a condom, and three hundred-dollar bills and seven twenties.

'I got those valves to finish grinding,' Ray said. 'Susan'll be home at six – we can go up to the Jade Palace.'

Murphy stood carefully. 'Got to make some calls.'

Ray nodded at the living room. 'Phone's in there.'

'Rather do it from a booth.'

'Shoot yourself,' Ray said.

The rain had ceased. From a Powell Street booth he called Melissa Maslow. 'I never expected to hear from you,' she said.

'I need to ask you some questions.'

'Questions? You out of your mind?'

There was a drift to her voice that bothered him. 'Where you calling from?' she said, offhand.

'I got beat up by some cops last night and put in a trunk and taken to this place east of Olema called Congregation ranch. Ever heard of it?'

'I used to think you were a nice guy. What the Hell'd you do that for?'

'Do what?'

Her voice was on edge, distant. 'Kill that guy.'

A woman was walking past the phone booth, tugging her little boy by the hand. He was sucking a lollipop and staring at Murphy out of almond eyes. He was wearing shorts and had skinned one knee. Across the street a panel truck was trying to back into a

space too small for it. When Melissa had finished he made her
repeat it. 'I didn't hit him that hard,' he said.

'He's dead, Murph. And there's an all-points out for you. You
didn't know that?'

'Please listen to me—'

'I don't want to get involved, Murph.'

'Please, listen to me?' He told her about Charlie, the Syndic.
'Do me one favour? See if you can find out about the Congregation
ranch, this US Bureau of International Development, find out
who got to that guy Carlos Bonaventura in prison, made him say
what he said about me—'

'You telling me you're not a dealer, Joe?'

'Not the kind that guy would know.'

'I'll make you a deal?'

'What's that?'

'I'll go down to the *Chronicle*'s morgue, talk to some news
people, check this stuff out for you. On the condition that when
you get arrested I'm the only reporter who gets your story.'

'Can't you get it through your thick head, Melissa – they're not
going to arrest me! They want me dead.'

There was the click, across the phone, of her hitting her teeth
with a pencil. 'Call me at six.'

A black and white police car eased down Powell, two fat cops
watching through shut windows. He bent down in the booth,
pretending to speak into the phone; the car slid by and turned
the corner.

When Lyman checked Murphy's house there were two moving
vans out front and a black BMW in the driveway. Men were carrying furniture from the house into the vans. A Mercedes and an
Olds station-wagon pulled up in the driveway; a bearded man
in a grey suit came out of the house, shook hands with the
people, and led them inside.

Lyman strolled along the sidewalk and stopped to watch. After
a minute he spoke to one of the movers, then walked on, came
round the block, got in the Dodge and drove downtown.

'I could care he's moved,' said the fat man at the desk on the
third floor over the girly joint.

'He's going to vanish. We need coverage.'

'*We?* A day ago you didn' wanna know us.'

'We're supposed to keep distance – you know the drill. But the
Congregation needs him. And you just lost one of your golden

197

boys. Don't you *want* this guy?'

The fat man peeled plastic off a toothpick and shoved it in his mouth. 'We're just the ugly girl you fuck when there's nobody else.'

'You should be so lucky.' Unbidden, Lyman sat. 'I need you guys to crank out a contact list, spread the ID on his vehicles – there's a Ford pick-up and a silver Porsche 944, licence MZG 505 – I got all the details. I need *you* to find him before the cops do.'

'Cops?' The man laughed a raspy smoker's cough. 'If you think *they're* going to find him then you're one bright boy.'

'And I need you to stay in touch with the media – make sure he's not talking to anybody. We don't want divergent stories.'

The man shifted his toothpick. 'One truth. That's all there is. Under God. Indivisible.'

'I went back to see Carlos Bonaventura,' Melissa said. 'But he made bail.'

'Damn!'

'No! Don't you understand? Here's this nobody crack dealer, suddenly makes two hundred thousand bail, the day after he identifies you for the papers—'

'Where'd he get the money?'

'I have no idea. But I'm going to find out.'

'Be careful, Meliss.'

'We need to talk. In person.'

'You're not going to run me in?'

She laughed. 'I'll keep my side of the deal.'

'Meet me somewhere, then.'

'I'm working late. Edinburgh Castle at midnight? It'll be safe for you, and it's on my way home.'

42

The rain had died; runnels glistened on the streets. Everything was sharp: faces in passing cars, shirts stacked in shop windows, cutlery on tables in closed restaurants, a Sprite can in the gutter. A cruiser tailed him up Polk then veered away like a shark sensing fresher blood elsewhere. A half-moon burst through towering black clouds, tainting them silver, vanished. The rain returned.

The Edinburgh Castle faced O'Farrell with its back on a narrow unlit alley where cars crouched along one side against grimy brick walls. Rain beat on cobblestoned puddles where the macadam had worn away. Stairs with dripping, rusty rails descended like gruesome mine entrances. Over the rooftops came the murmur of traffic from Polk and Geary; beyond the dark end of the alley was a Fish 'n' Chips stand with two distant skyscrapers looming out of the fog above it. The rain hammered his shoulders; his socks sloshed, his feet were numb. A cat scampered between trash cans, something wriggling in its jaws.

A car's lights leaped into the alley, the engine roaring, and he stepped between two parked cars to let it pass. It slowed, tyres rumbling the cobblestones; he saw the rectangular Ford grille and dived behind a parked car down slippery stairs to a locked door, broken bottles grinding underfoot, fumbled for the latch but it wouldn't open, and dashed back up the stairs to see the Ford continue down the alley, brake at the end, and turn left on Larkin. He rubbed a scraped elbow and stepped back into the alley. Fool, he cursed himself, even the normal betrays you.

Another car swung into the alley, headlights making him a dancing bear's shadow down the oily cobbles; he stepped aside, waiting for it to pass; it slowed, a searchlight hit his face, a megaphone: 'Police! – You behind that car – Get out here!' He sprinted along the wall, knocking over trash cans and ducked past the cop car as it screamed into reverse after him and he leaped a car's

199

hood on to its roof and up a fire escape, his bad arm wrenched with pain, a cop clambering up behind him, cruiser lights painting the buildings blue and white. He jumped the parapet and dashed across the puddled rooftop, leaped a gap between two buildings, a ghastly emptiness sucking at him, made the far side and crossed the next rooftop, reached the end and swung over the edge, the cars far below on Larkin casting little cones of light, people like ants on a strip of sidewalk tiny as a ribbon between his feet.

The cop had halted at the gap between the buildings, yelling into his radio, his shiny bulk silhouetted by St Mary's gleaming cross. Murphy dropped free, landed on the top rungs of another fire escape, ran down it five floors; more police cars screeched through the Geary red light a block away; he jumped the last storey to the sidewalk and slipped into a bar which stank of whiskey and cigarettes.

Biker women in black jackets and chains stared him down as he hobbled towards the johns, reversed his jacket to its pale grey lining, grabbed a yachting cap off the coat rack and ran into a storeroom of aluminium kegs and beer cases. A dead bulb banged his forehead as he stepped into the alley where the blue globes of police cars blinked beneath the fire escape that three cops climbed intently, their flashlights darting up the walls. As though curious he watched them for a moment, then went down the alley to Larkin and around the corner to the Edinburgh Castle.

In the men's room he wiped his ragged hair and torn, bloody hands with paper towels, staring at the stained sink, stinking urinal, and carious scribbled walls as if even they would betray him. At the bar he rubbed whiskey into his hands to stop the bleeding, set the yachting cap tighter over his wet hair. Two cops came in, cloaks brilliant with rain. One stayed by the door while the other talked to the bartender, who nodded, thumbs in the pockets of his plaid vest, and jerked his chin down the bar at Murphy. The cop ambled over, splay-footed and chubby, cloak trickling. 'Just come in?'

Murphy pulled back his sleeve to inspect his watch. The crystal was scratched. 'Jes little while 'go.'

'Got some ID?'

He nodded, as if finding the question confusing, knocked back his whiskey and fumbled at his pockets. With the coat reversed it was hard to get at the wallet; he finally got it out and laid it laboriously on the wet bar, holding it open with one hand, and pulled out the Arizona licence in the name of Lamar P. Bultz. The cop took it in pink cold fingers and held it to the light.

Murphy held out his empty glass to the bartender, beckoning for another, waiting for the cop to put the licence down quietly and pull his gun and walk him handcuffed out of the Edinburgh Castle. He imagined Melissa coming in as they left, her astonished look—

The cop put the licence down in spilled whiskey and glanced at Murphy's cap. 'What's the name of your boat?'

'The hat says SS *Miranda*. But I don't have a boat.'

The cops left and he finished the second whiskey and ordered a third. The clock over the guns and sabres hung behind the bar said twelve fifteen; a couple trudged out hand in hand into rain gusting yellow across the lights. Twelve eighteen. Melissa wasn't coming, but in a few minutes the cops were sure to return.

'You're a bit laid back, aren't you?' Melissa sat on the wooden bench beside him, blonde hair dripping down her yellow anorak. 'For a wanted man?'

He took her damp, cold hand. 'Thanks for coming.'

'I wouldn't be doing this, except I remember how you were, that one night we met—'

'I was going to call you . . .'

'You just weren't the kind of person to do what they say you've done—'

'I *have* flown weed, Melissa. That was my schtick – no big thing. I was going to tell you. What I told you about the village is true. And about the American soldiers—'

She leaned against him. 'Kiss me, quick – two cops came in.'

Her mouth was small, cold, a girl's. He kissed her again, her hair wet against his hand. She backed away. 'They've gone!'

'You're going to catch your death—'

'I'm going right home, hot bath.'

'What did you find, in the morgue?'

'Not much – a recent *Examiner* story about the CIA's *contras* getting busted for ten million in coke – the funniest part was that federal prosecutors gave the money *back* to the *contras*. Anyway, you asked me about this US Bureau of International Development. I called some friends back east who've done a lot of FIA stuff – Freedom of Information Act – they said it's been described in classified State Department cables as a CIA group operative.'

'What kind of "group operative"?'

'Formed by President Bush when he was Director of the CIA.

201

He did a bunch of them. Its purpose was to build links with right-wing groups in developing countries, to funnel so-called "bank loans" to start up commercial enterprises as a cover to channel funds for arms and paramilitary operations, death squads. In Central America it works with fundamentalist Protestant groups, façades. Its top man in El Salvador was Leon Rivera Morales, a close friend of Bush and a campaign manager of Robert D'Aubuisson. He was arrested when his private plane crashed a couple of years ago in Arizona, on its way up from Salvador, carrying four million in coke. After that the Republicans had to stop calling him the Abe Lincoln of Central America.'

'And the Congregation Ranch?'

'I asked our Marin correspondent. It's twelve hundred and seventy acres west of Nicasio, a private religious retreat. The Congregational Church of Christ Pentecost, very fundamentalist Protestant. Lots of missionary work in Central America – they've got an office in Guatemala City, Avenida las Americas. Where'd you hear about it?'

'This guy Charlie who told me about the Syndic—'

'The one you killed—'

'I didn't kill him, Meliss. I didn't hit him that hard.'

'Tell that to the Coroner . . .'

'Charlie said that ranch is where they took me.'

'Then there's a connection. If the late Charlie was in this CIA front group, and they took you to this Congregation Ranch—'

'And the Syndic?'

'I wanted to ask Carlos Bonaventura. But he miraculously posted bail. The Syndic is just the Syndicate – the new word for an old plague – organized crime. The Mafia, that's what we used to call it. It's nobody's secret that the CIA's worked with them for years – like Air America's drug flights out of Laos and Cambodia.'

'Air America was the CIA airline in Vietnam, the one that used to ship heroin out of the Golden Triangle—'

Melissa rubbed her hands, trying to work warmth into them. What a marvellous gift human flesh is, Murphy thought, how *alive*. 'Interesting thing,' she said.

'What's that?'

'Southern California Savings and Loan, that's being bailed out after losing three billion in government pension funds – they and the Syndicate were laundering money for the Colombian drug cartels—'

'That's what banks are *for*, to launder money . . .'

'It holds the mortgage on the Congregation Ranch . . .'

An old woman had put money in the juke box, the slow rising strains of a bagpipe surging forth,

> I once was lost
> but now am found,
> was blind
> but now I see.

'Southern California Savings and Loan was Charlie's Visa card.'

'Don't leave home without it.'

'I still have it.'

'And the nice thing, the even *nicer* thing, is that Southern California Savings and Loan is in a similar situation to Silverado Savings and Loan in Denver. They're being bailed out to the tune of three billion by the taxpayers.'

'Bastards. Goddamn crooks.'

'And guess who's on Silverado's Board of Directors? Neil Bush, whose father was director of the CIA before he became president.'

He stared at the bar, the British colonial sabres and muskets, the regimental colours from Scottish regiments, the tartans and plaids. 'If all this stuff can be discovered, why doesn't the media reveal it – why don't they *track* this stuff?'

'The American news media is a big cartel that doesn't like to cover what people don't want to hear. They depend, after all, on advertising. That's why when you go to another country the news is so different.'

'I don't *care* about the news—'

'And more than a few journalists – well-known ones, even, have close ties with the CIA. When the Agency was founded one of its first administrative goals was its media programme. There's people with strong Agency connections who've used these connections – access to sources, insider information – to become prominent in newspaper and TV journalism, serving partially as a funnel for what the CIA wants to have said. If you watch the papers over the years you can tell who some of them are—'

'All I care about is getting the story straight and protecting the people in Guatemala.'

'You're crazy if you go back.' Melissa slipped into her raincoat.

'What's with Angelica Newton – I thought you were living with her?'

'We couldn't stand each other.'

'Drug-dealing murderer throws over famous rock star for woman doctor in darkest Amazon – that's the kind of story the media loves.' Her cool small hand caressed his face. 'Don't be down – we're making progress. Tomorrow I'll interview some Syndicate people, talk to my editors about an investigation of the Congregation Ranch . . .' She wrote two telephone numbers on a piece of paper. 'The first is another number at work, a better one. Just ask for me. The other's my home number.' She put ten dollars on the table, 'Just hold tight. We'll move on this, fast as we can.'

They walked to her red Colt. 'You have some place to stay?' she said.

'Thanks. I'm fine.'

'Don't take chances.' She smiled up. 'Take care.'

He kissed her again and it was different this time, just a lovely kiss with the promise of more, some day, if there ever were a some day, if he ever wanted. He had a quick sense of how badly he'd wasted the first time he'd met her. How you have to be in pain to sense good. But even though he was the one in danger, she seemed the one needing reassurance, proof that the conventional order is not corrupt, that justice can survive, that evil does not invariably conquer good. Her kiss was salty, her grip against him strong, her body almost offered – yes, offered, unknowingly, in the guise of needing reassurance. I've hurt everyone I get near, he thought, and pushed away.

Her car turned the corner towards Van Ness and the Golden Gate. A passing taxi stirred the kerbside puddles. Across Larkin he saw the building where an hour ago he'd run down the fire escape and fallen to the sidewalk, and he felt fear again.

He walked through waning rain over Russian Hill, the city lights spread out in the mist below like the answer, the gift, of something at last found and understood.

'I once was lost but now I'm found, was blind but now I see.' The Syndicate and the Agency, hand in glove, in San Francisco and in Guatemala, tied to the people that had run the United States ever since John Kennedy was killed in Dallas and his brother in LA – why should that surprise him? If they could kill the Kennedys with total impunity, what could he do against them?

Watching for cops, he walked down into Chinatown and let himself into Ray Lin's, and fell warm asleep on the couch in Ray's blue sleeping bag.

Ray shook him awake at eight, pointing at the television where someone was saying that Joseph Murphy, already wanted for the murder of a man yesterday on Mount Tamalpais, was now sought in a second gruesome killing in Pacifica of a San Francisco *Chronicle* reporter, Melissa Maslow, last seen alive with Murphy in a San Francisco bar. The camera closed in on Melissa's red Colt, found deserted at three a.m. on the coast highway south of San Francisco. The camera switched to a silver Porsche owned by Joseph Murphy that had been found an hour later in Pacifica, Melissa inside it with three bullets in her brain.

43

'They're going to kill you, man.' Ray went to the stove, picked up the coffee pot, came to the table and started to pour it then realized there were no cups. Still holding the pot he got two mugs from a shelf and put them on the table. 'They want you so bad, how they're doing this—'

He put the pot on the stove, sat down, picked up his mug, shook his head. 'Out of my fuckin mind.' He went back to the stove and got the pot, filled the mugs. 'You was back here long before she got killed.'

'She was—' He tried but he couldn't talk about her. 'I've never known anything to keep happening. Like this.'

'Thinking like that don't get you nothing, man,' Ray said.

'She had that cocky way of acting like she was cute but not really believing it – trying to be tough, but you could tell she *cared*.' He walked down the hall, boards creaking, came back and sat. 'What am I going to do?'

'You're going to skin your ass out of here—'

'No! I mean about *her*.'

'Murph – you plan to die today?'

Murphy laughed, looked out the lightwell at stained concrete. 'You better decide, man. I can testify you was here at one a.m. I can testify anything you want, but they're not going to believe me, I'm already on the wrong side . . .'

'You'll just get accessory, Ray. You'll get ten years.'

'No I won't. They'll kill anyone who's touched you. I wouldn't make trial.'

Murphy stood, feeling the room's weight on his shoulders. 'I've done all this.'

'Think of what you did in Nam, man. You never did a thing to hurt people.'

'Oh yes I have.'

'You even used to even drag in the fucking gooks! I've seen you

206

– run across a fucking field of fire to pick up some dumb dink—'

'You just didn't like the dinks because they've got slanty eyes like you.' Murphy hugged him, turned, holding the door jamb. 'How safe is this bike?'

'It was wrecked and sold for parts and there's no way to trace it. Calvin Wong doesn't exist.'

'Who the fuck is Calvin Wong?'

'He's your friend – the name DMV has it registered to.'

There were no cops on the Bay Bridge and none on 580 going south, fields of pale tomatoes to the horizon. At noon he filled up at a truck stop near Coalinga, empty plastic cups sucked along the greasy parking lot by passing trucks, transmission lines like giant mantises across endless rows of beet and cauliflower. He bought a six-pack of Coke, sandwiches, maps, and two five-gallon jerricans, filled the jerricans with petrol and strapped them on each side of the bike, beneath Ray's blue sleeping bag, spare clothes and poncho.

Highway 46 East was two flat lanes across half-irrigated fields stretching to the smudged horizon where oil derricks rose and fell like the heads of feeding vultures. There were white houses in willow groves and dusty pick-ups with gun racks, windblown soil and scummy sloughs, the air greasy with herbicides, crude tar and methane.

East of Mojave he loaded the first jerrican into the tank, but that made the bike off-balance so he stopped again and poured half the remaining can into the empty one. Out on the highway the cars were beginning to flick on their lights; in the south grey rainbursts slanted across a slug-pink sky. His arms were queasy with exhaustion and his feet stumbled bluntly over the volcanic soil.

Barstow ahead seemed like danger so he dropped south on 395, a straight black line pointing at Mexico, trucks shaking him as they roared north, casting a fine spray that kept him wiping his eyes with the back of his arm. He turned east through Twentynine Palms and Earp and into Arizona at midnight, the cars and trucks fewer now, the stars like points on a great pinball machine.

Mountains and constellations rose and fell. There was just the rumble of the bike, the white lines zipping beneath the wheel, now uphill, now on the level, now going down, nighthawks and jackrabbits darting from the headlight, semis rolling north like dinosaurs, crushed rattlers like red ropes on the highway, once

207

a doe in a mass of blood and guts, remnants of a fawn beside her, saguaros beyond the headlight like shadowy hanged men. There was no feeling in his hands, no feeling in his arms, no sound but this freezing air screaming through his brain, his body locked into the seat by immovable legs, and he moved the bike by leaning only, tipping this way and that through the curves, the white lines flicking under, the tyre's tread a continual blur in which endless detail could be seen, the fluorescent green fuel gauge sinking from half to quarter, the speedometer needle jiggling between a hundred and twenty and a hundred and forty – if you hit anything this fast, he consoled himself, you'll hardly know it.

South of Gila Bend the horizon grew lighter, and then the ground was rolling waves of boulders and cliffs like bone chips from which the dawn rose like yellow oil. A sign flashed past: *Luke Air Force Bombing Range. Stay on Highway.* Grey rubbled mountains hunched over thorn and cactus and chipped soil. As he floated over a long easy rise with dawn mirages on the pavement, there were suddenly two cruisers across the road between narrow cliffs, and he hit the brakes looking for a way out, the bike skidding sideways towards the two cops – one running for his cruiser, the other with a shotgun. He spun to a stop and stood, twenty feet away. 'You're moving too fast out there!' the one with the shotgun said.

Maybe they don't know, Murphy decided. 'Wasn't anybody around.'

'*We* were around.'

'Sorry about that.'

'Let's see your licence—'

US Air Force was stamped in gold on their cruiser doors. Not cops but MPs – maybe they didn't know. He handed them the Arizona licence.

'From Flagstaff,' the other one said. 'Hell, I used to live in Flagstaff.'

'Where you headed?' the one with the shotgun said.

'Ajo.'

'What's there?'

'My sister's ex-husband. We're going hunting.'

'Where's your gun?'

'He's got the guns.' Murphy dropped the bike into gear. 'I'll take it slower.'

'We're out here looking for drunk Indians,' the one from

Flagstaff said. 'But we catch you again we'll pull you in too.'

He accelerated slowly, watching in the mirror for them to turn and shoot, then for them to leap into the cars and speed after him, but the two cops and the two blue cars diminished in the mirror, stationary in their wobbling, shrinking reflection, the sunlit mountains climbing up behind them.

Ahead the road rose steadily into the vermilion sky scented with desert morning; soon he could kill the headlight, in an hour Mexico. In the mirror he caught a flash of blue – blue cop lights – the two cruisers were coming fast and there was only long straight highway ahead with no place to hide; he stood on the brakes and spun the bike off the road, whanging over the borrow pit and slamming through thorns and cactus. He glanced back to see the cruisers smashing through the brush behind him and he roared up an arroyo to shake them but one kept coming, banging and snarling up through clattering rocks and with a great *ping* like a ricochet the bike's chain snapped, the engine roaring wild. The bike fell over, pinning his thigh to the arroyo rocks, the car smashing towards him as he broke free and ran back downslope before the cop could shoot or turn round, then he cut left across the slope, above the other cruiser, out of pistol range, now out of shotgun range. Looking back he tripped on a saguaro root, needles in his hands, kept running, through rolling, bowl-like hills, already too hot to breathe, the sun melting over the ridge.

44

He ran upslope towards a saddle with a tan peak behind it. The ground was sloshy with lava gravel but open between the desert thorns and cactus so he could run quickly, pacing it, the cruisers now a thousand feet below, and still he could keep the pace, trying to reach the shelter of the tan peak before the planes came.

The arroyo crested into a shallow valley of white boulders, the tan peak above on the right. He ran part-way up the valley and then uphill between huge boulders with spiky cactus in the crevices between them. It had been fifteen minutes since the cops would have radioed. Planes could come any time now. If they were fixed wing he could hide among the rocks and maybe they wouldn't see him. If they saw him he could still run – but if they were choppers, once they saw him it was over.

The slope turned to lava talus, a furnace of rock. His legs ran with no feeling. He crossed the ridge, looked back; no one had reached the valley below nor its far lower end dropping down into the arroyo. On his left rose the tan peak. To the north-west, back the way he'd come, was purple desert to a crotch of distant dark mountains with raw, pale peaks. Behind him, south, stretched a string of ridges with long sweeping saddles between them, boulders, cactus, sun-tortured brush.

Nearly half an hour, still no plane. Now he could put on the miles, stretch out the legs, nothing but running, running and thinking. Running and listening. If I get out of this I will be happy no matter what deaths have happened and how much I'm to blame, he promised. I will force myself to be happy.

There was a tiny airplane whine, a bug maybe. No, a spotter – the nasal blare of its motor as it came upridge hugging the slope. It was still far; he crawled into a clump of greasewood and saguaro and as the plane flitted past it crossed him with its shadow.

It dived over the ridge down towards the bouldered valley. He ran as if the land behind him were on fire, down the long sweeping saddle from ridge to tilting ridge, the planes coming and going behind him in widening circles, lazy-sounding as bees seeking honey.

The saddle toppled into a plain of red-flowered cactus widening towards low mountains. All the way across it he stayed ahead of the planes, then up the low mountains through a sharp and craggy canyon with cooler air in pockets in the shade of its great slabs.

From the low mountains a vast chalky mesa tilted southward, millions of cactus pinioned against it, scrub and brush and desert grass and burnt arroyos. He ran in a trance now, knew he could run till night unless his body broke, his heart stopped. Several times there was a white glint of plane behind him, never close. After midday there were no more planes, the land levelled then rose and fell again; in late afternoon he stopped on the bank of an arroyo to look back; still there was no one, no planes, just an immense white land of crevasses and canyons and dry bouldered river-beds across the rippled sand.

Standing still made him dizzy so he ran again but could not lose the dizziness till he fell against a cactus and the pain made him sharp. He ran on, the setting sun on his right, saguaro shadows darkening the brush, ran till it was too dark, then walked, watching Scorpio rising in the east to point the way south.

At dawn he could smell smoke and water, day rushing across the desert as he followed a goat trail down into a rocky valley with some palm trees and a stone hut with a palm-thatched roof and shed and a turgid pool. There were fresh droppings on the trail. An old woman came out of the hut, wiping her hands. 'Can I have water?' he said.

She seemed frightened of him but brought a pail of well water and a clay bowl to drink. He made himself stop drinking after five bowls. 'Where is this?' he said.

'This? It is San Jacinto.'

'But what country?'

She turned from the ground where he sat. 'Felipe! This is what country?'

'It is the Sonora,' an old man said, coming out of the shed. He had a knife in one hand and a chunk of cactus in the other. 'The land of the San Jacinto people—'

Murphy forced his hand from the bowl of water. 'It is Mexico?'

'It is not the United States and it is not Mexico. Which one are you running from?'

'I was hunting with my friends, got lost. Two days I've had no water—'

'You're going the wrong way. Go north, the way you just came down.'

'Can I buy food – *frijoles* – anything?' He reached into his jacket for his wallet but it was not there. He felt all his pockets, waiting to discover the wallet so he could relax and stop this horrible sudden fear that he had no money, that he'd lost the wallet when the bike broke or somewhere in between. The wallet was truly gone, only the false Arizona licence left in his other shirt pocket.

'We can give you *chiles*,' the woman said. 'Some cactus *tamale*.'

'No thank you,' he said. 'I have plenty.'

'You have nothing and no money,' the old man said. 'She did not offer to sell them to you.'

The woman took the cup into the hut and brought it back with sour goat milk and *chiles* and a cactus *tamale* with beans inside it. He ate the cactus shell last, breaking it in pieces with his teeth. He tried to remember where he might have lost the wallet but could not. He would have to go back, at least as far as the border.

'You should stay,' the old man said. 'Leave tomorrow. We will feed you.'

He drank more water, turned back up the hill the way he'd come, up the goat trail whose droppings were now drier and harder in the sun. At the top of the arroyo he looked out on a wide canyon-land of broken, buttressed cliffs and rolling stony plateaus. A distant plane buzzed, nearer – a hummingbird at a cactus flower.

This moment would decide his life but he could not tell which way to go. Go back for the wallet and probably he would not find it and probably he would be captured. To go south without money or food or water was death.

The old man was riding a burro up a switchbacked trail on the far slope. Murphy watched him till he crossed the ridge out of sight, then ran back down across the arroyo above the hut and climbed the slope after the old man. When he reached the ridge the old man was far ahead, an atom of black and white among the towering cactus. The trail grew firmer, other paths coming in, became a pair of ruts, rolling over a mountain shoulder and down to a barbed-wire fence with a gate and a few miles ahead a *rancho* with a silo and metal windmill, thin Brahma cattle stand-

212

ing motionless in its corrals. Next to the house was a creosoted pole with a telephone wire going from the house past the corrals and down the road. The old man was tying his burro to the porch. In the distance were the silver flashes of cars on a highway.

Murphy circled the *rancho* to the south and followed a fence-line east and reached the highway at dusk. Swallows were darting after moths; somewhere cattle were lowing. The cars on the highway made a low, cadenced hiss.

He followed the highway south to a town. Trucks were parked at a bar smelling of frijoles and steaks. He stood in a dark street watching the back of the bar. A boy came out and scraped plates into a bucket. Murphy waited till the boy went inside, then crept closer to the bucket, but a dog came snarling and rattling its chain, so he went round the bar to where two semis were idling, facing south at the edge of the highway, one driver standing on the ground and speaking up to the other. One was closed, a refrigerator truck. The other was a flatbed loaded with large shapes covered with blue tarps; he came up behind it and crawled under the tarps; there were huge chunks of steel, pieces of turbine or motor of some kind; he squeezed up inside them. The voices tailed off, someone laughing, '*Arriba!*' The two trucks revved and Murphy's slid forward, bouncing and jouncing over the potholes and out on to the road.

45

The truck rolled endlessly through darkness, gearing up and down for the hills, tyres roaring against the tarmac, the huge iron segments jiggling rustily, the tarp and steel cables whistling in the wind. He was sick from the goat milk the old woman had given him, crawled to the back to throw up over the end when there were no headlights behind. Once there was a shower and he lay with his head in the open, drinking the oily rain that funnelled off the tarps.

They went through a big city, green lights reflecting against the pavement, the truck starting and stopping, the iron lurching and squealing against the truck's pitted bed. Watching through a crack under the tarp he decided it was Hermosillo. The truck was still heading south.

He woke to a blue-grey light filtering through the tarp, the truck gearing down through sloping long curves, diesel snarling, brakes hissing, tyres grinding gravel off the edge. He took off his shoes and repaired the laces that had been frayed by cactus thorns. Again there was a city, stop and go traffic, car engines on all sides, their exhaust collecting up under the tarp. Beyond the city the truck geared down, ground into second and rumbled off the highway across a gravel lot. It pulled into a space where the sound of its engine echoed closely. The engine died; the cab door opened and shut.

He waited what he thought was two minutes but may only have been a few seconds, squirmed to the back and looked out under the tarp. Trucks lined up all around, oil and dust, a distant radio. He could see no one, dropped over the side, walking unsteadily on the pockmarked ground, walked around and between the trucks till he found a building with a water spigot that said *no potable* but he drank it anyway, long deep cool luscious liquid gulps that made him vomit but then he could drink easily and it was good. A man in boots with pointed toes and worn-down heels, Levis and bow legs, silver buckle and red check shirt, tanned small face with a black moustache and thin black eyes and a black cowboy hat looked down at him. 'That's for radiators,' he said. 'You should ask at the café.'

'Oh.' Murphy stood.

'Where you going?'

Murphy said nothing, watching him. 'Why?'

'I saw you get off the truck.'

'Going south.'

The man reached in his pocket, took out a fold of bills, flattened it and pulled one off. 'Get yourself a little cleaned up and get something to eat.' He gave Murphy a bill. 'You'll be OK.'

Fifty thousand pesos, a wrinkled blue bill in his palm. 'Jesus!' He kept looking at it but it was still fifty thousand pesos. He ran looking between the trucks but could not see the man. He went into the café, steamy and warm and full of the smell of men and hot food and coffee. The toilet was filthy but he washed with water from the tank above the toilet and combed his hair with his fingers till it lay straight. He washed mud, oil and dust off his black jacket and shirt and jeans and shoes with wet toilet paper that left pink shreds. He had tortillas and beans and coffee at the counter for five thousand pesos, found two empty plastic cola bottles and filled them with water, and walked out into the new bright sun.

In late morning the truck pulled off the highway again, halting among others in a huge lot rimmed by hog wire and wind-stunted dusty trees. The driver got down but came back in a few minutes, climbed up and shut the door. The truck did not start and after a few minutes Murphy decided the driver had gone to sleep.

He climbed out the back and walked awkwardly among the other trucks. Most of their cab windows were open, the drivers sleeping on benches up behind the seats. He found a rig with DF plates carrying thick concrete pipes with canvas on each end. He put down his water bottles and crawled up underneath to feel the engine. It was cold. He crawled to the back, picked up the bottles, climbed up under the canvas into a pipe and fell asleep.

After a while the heat woke him and he could not breathe under the hot canvas. The engine started and the truck shook but then it sat for a long time with the engine running. Then the door slammed and the truck creaked out on the highway, the concrete pipes grinding against their chains.

The truck travelled all day. Zacatecas, a sign said, then before dark another, Aguascalientes, where it stopped for diesel and food. Murphy was waiting when the driver got down and he followed him into the restaurant, a roly man in sneakers and a yellow Caterpillar hat. The man went into the toilets then sat at the counter and Murphy went into the toilets and looked into the mirror.

Dirty, dusty and sunburnt, thin-faced and hungry: the look that draws cops like sharks. He smoothed and washed off his clothes, his face and scabby hands with their red infections where tips of cactus spines festered. 'You look like shit,' he said to the man in the mirror, who smiled, revealing yellow teeth with brown chunks between them. He brushed his teeth with toilet paper and hand soap, went into the restaurant, ate quickly and paid, watching the roly driver across the counter, returned to the parking lot and climbed back inside the concrete pipe.

Dusk came, dawn went, the air was thick with diesel fumes then thin with the high pine taste of the hills – the truck kept rumbling on, the whirr of the wheels sewing and dismembering, keening and snickering over the curves and downgrades, over the moments and hours that stretched and contracted, appeared and disappeared, phantasms and nightmares, and is this death he wondered – how can you ever tell if you're dead?

Howard Lyman sat on the edge of the bed watching dawn burn down across the Oakland Hills. Strings of headlights trailed down their sides; below them, square squat buildings were lighting up along the Bay, the Bay Bridge a grey filigree of half-lit steel bearing a serpent of headlights into San Francisco. He made himself a cup of instant and Coffee Mate and sat on the bed again; it burned his lips.

Soon it was cooler but his tongue kept stinging. He looked down at his naked arms with the tendons and veins sticking out – come near me if you dare, they said. He stretched his shoulders out and up, arms in a cross then vertical, the sleepy muscles stretching like awakened cats, the pectorals hard as steel, smiled to think there was not a single thing in this room he couldn't break with one hand. Sipping the cooler coffee, he began to do his wake-up stretches.

The east grew bright; a tallowy fog coated the Bay. He showered, dressed in Levis, work shirt and worn leather jacket, went downstairs to eat, then walked up Market Street to Tenth and across Mission to Alabama Street, entered 154 Alabama and climbed to the second floor. A television roared behind thin walls, a puppy was squealing. He knocked hard on Sherrie Cunningham's door.

III
House of
Fire

46

Footsteps at the door. 'Yes?' – a girl's voice.

'Sherrie? It's Steve Williams – I'm a friend of Joe Murphy's – Saul Feldman asked me to come—'

Her face in the door. 'Saul Feldman?'

'The guy who came yesterday. The lawyer.'

'Oh yeah!' She opened the door, looked up at him. He shut the door behind him. She went to the sink, wiped her hands on a T-shirt. 'What can I do for you?'

'Can I sit?'

She nodded at a chair. 'Sure.'

She had on new black Levis and a bright blue sweater that came down to her wrists. 'How are things?' he said.

She smiled, a kind of off-sides grin. 'They sure have changed—'

'Been celebrating?'

She shrugged, shoulder-blades up into her long straight hair, sat at the table, smoothing an edge of vinyl tablecloth. 'A little bit . . . I bought some clothes, paid my rent. He sure was astonished, the landlord, to have me paying the rent.'

'What'd you do before, give it to him on the side?'

Again she shrugged. 'He said that wasn't enough.'

'You have enough now, don't you—'

'When Saul gave me the money – that's his name, right? – I couldn't believe it. I sat here a long time, right there where you're sitting, saying to myself, "Sherrie, you don't deserve this. You've been mean and hard and you don't deserve this."'

'Sure you do,' Lyman said.

She looked at him, surprised. 'I sure don't. But I've promised myself I'm going to make myself good for it, that I'm not going to let him down.'

'Saul?'

'No – Mr Murphy.'

'What else he tell you?'

'Mr Murphy?'

'Yeah—'

'Nothing.' She cocked her head, appraising. 'You're his friend – ask him.'

'He won't tell me why he did it, just wants me to watch over you, give you a hand. So what's up – why'd he do it?'

'You a cop?'

Lyman chuckled. 'Me? Never.' He watched her fingers, nervous on the table-top. His own hand rested against his cheek, like a cleaver ready to fall. 'Just tell me why he's giving you the money – not just for a quick fuck?'

She looked hurt, then angry, stood. 'Maybe I ain't saying.' She walked towards the door but he jammed his foot across it, reached up and yanked her down, hand across her mouth. 'I *want* you to tell me.'

She watched his eyes. He loosened his grip. 'He said he was a friend of my dad's, in Vietnam. My dad died. Mr Murphy wanted to take care of me a little, that's all . . . I'll give you the money if you want—'

Softly he massaged down her slim neck, her breast, felt the little nipple harden. 'That's not all I want.' He shoved her against the sink, face down, her hands on the edge. 'One sound will kill you. Otherwise you'll be fine.' He unbuckled her belt and pushed down the black Levis and underpants, licking down the inside of her thigh as he knelt to yank her pants off one leg, bent her over the sink and pushed into her; she gasped and he reached up and broke her neck.

Murphy came into Villahermosa after midnight in the driving rain on a flatbed carrying a yellow bulldozer, crouched under the bulldozer's dripping engine, between its two massive treads, half sheltered by its blade. Roots, creepers and dirt clods hung down from its treads and made a muddy trail of windblown rain across the flatbed's deck. A heavy, cold spray came over the blade.

He was hoping it would stop but the truck drove straight through Villahermosa's pale concrete boulevards and cheap international hotels, through the *barrios* stinking of open sewers, the stinging haze of crude distillation, vegetation's sweet rot.

On and on it rolled through the Campeche lowlands. Tree frogs chirped in scraps of jungle; the rain stopped and the moon was a silver stain down the middle of the highway. At dawn roosters brayed from roadside hovels in the grey wool of cooking fires and the smell of asbestos brake linings, red mud, and warming asphalt. Once there was a mighty mahogany tree towering over hills of brush and stumps. They crossed a wide river, the bridge shivering under the truck's weight. An hour later the truck rumbled into Escárcega; when it halted in heavy traffic he jumped from the back of the trailer, a woman in a pink Passat staring at him as he stepped round her bumper and walked to the kerb. The light changed and the truck lumbered with the traffic towards Campeche, trailing its yellow bulldozer.

He bought tortillas and oranges for three thousand four hundred pesos and walked out of Escárcega in warm morning sun. Where the road went into the jungle there was a black-water marsh with cattails growing, and egrets; he washed his clothes and himself and dried in the hot sun, then ate tortillas and oranges, woke with the sun in the middle of the sky. He hitch-hiked a ride with a small, bearded priest in an old hearse all the way to Nicolás Bravo, another on a farm truck to the Chetumal turn-off and Belize border.

He waited till dusk then walked an hour west in jungle along the Río Hondo, past the last trails, swam the *río*, walked back to the highway and hitched into Corozal.

'I told you this'd happen,' Lovejoy said.

'Not like this.'

'You was goin' up there with a hard-on and you was goin' to get it cut off and handed to you – yes you *was*. Did'n matter what I said . . .'

'Fuck off, Love, that's past now.'

'What the Hell did'n you jes' let be 'lone? What you gotta go makin' trouble?'

'Don't be angry at me, for Chrissake—'

'Who else I s'posed to be angry with? Ain' you the one what did it? Jes' like you wen' in Mother Teresa' place breakin' every-thin' all up. Fightin' with those Americans – Murph, when you goin' *up*?'

'So you would've said nothing, up in the States?'

'What? 'Bout thet Guatemala stuff? What the Hell good thet do? Other 'n make *you* feel good 'bout yourself? What difference thet make to them Guatemalans how much you talk on American television? You can be a TV star for all they care. You just get yourself kill', that's all!'

222

'I made it down here—'

'An' you fuckin' lucky to do so! Is'n no thanks to you you made it – you had the breaks—'

'Once I wire some money from CI, I'll be fine—'

'You got enough to live on over there?'

'Enough to buy another plane, go somewhere, start again.'

'Minute you get a plane they find you. You still tryin' to fock up you life, ain' you? And you better get thet money out of the Channel Islands fast before DEA track it down—'

'They can't find it—'

'Anythin' DEA want to find, it find.'

Murphy stood on the terrace watching the stars rise out of Corozal Bay. 'Ten days ago I stood here and didn't know what was going to happen. That someone would die just because I went up there, trying to tell people . . .'

'What I told you, Murph, is don't walk in death's way. As it is, it goin' come get you far too soon—'

'What would you do?'

'I certain would'n go after thet doctor woman. You ain't goin' change *her* mind. You certain ain' bringin' *her* no luck. Shit, I should'n get you any money – then you can't go back to Guatemala—'

Murphy smiled. 'I'd go anyway.'

'Thet's the thing about you, Murph. I think you's the stupid-est person I ever seen.'

'I told those kids I'd come back for them. Would you leave Desirée?'

'I'm keepin' you damn money.'

'I don't need money to get in, Love. It's just safer to have it when you're inside.'

'You make it sound like ice, Guatemala.'

Murphy shrugged, biting his lip.

'I was inside five years, in El Paso.'

'I know. For sticking that dude.'

'Lucky he lived. So I didn't get life. Thet prison was the bottom of Hell, Murph.'

'The House of Fire—'

'Whas thet?'

'The Mayan Hell had six houses. The House of Fire was the worst.'

'Them Mayans, they should see Guatemala now.'

'Guatemala's a tourist destination, Love.'

47

Lovejoy drove the needle in and out of the ripped knee of his trousers, pulling the thread through. 'It's for you I'm worried. Not thet I get back my money.'

'It'll clear on Monday from CI to Kingston. There'll be fifty extra for me, for when I get back.'

'You ain' goin' come back.'

On Corozal Bay the wind was scraping white riffles off the blue water. A string of cormorants laced eastwards. The air was warming and redolent with soil and grass and sea salt and jungle. 'Would you leave her, someone you cared about, in Guatemala? Not try to talk her into coming out?'

'Comin' out wit' you? What kind of safety is thet?'

'And that General Arena – he's the *one*, Love! My friends paid him ten grand a month. It was *his* soldiers that shot us up and blew away my village. *He's* the one who sent the word up north, got Melissa killed . . .'

Lovejoy tugged the thread tight, circled the needle twice through it and bent over and bit it off. 'You know thet trail there, one that goes into the jungle?'

'Out back? Yeah.'

'Luther Tallow, thet lived up the road, he had a woman in Revelation Town, used to take thet trail through the jungle to go see her. There was this crazy Mexican, Willie the Fireman, lived back in the jungle, gone crazy on wood alcohol. Willie hated Luther, used to wait for him in the brush with his machete, try to cut him up. I used to say Luther some day he goin' get you, and Luther said he's always too drunk and I ain't afraid of no Mexican.'

Murphy stood, stretching his back. 'You're so full of shit, Love!'

Lovejoy spread the trousers over his knee, smoothing down the mend. 'Willie's dead now. They chase him in the Bay and drown him. After he killed Luther Tallow.'

Lyman sat in the kitchen with a cup of coffee in his hands. The
Minnie Mouse clock showed nine-thirty. The dishwasher hummed,
amber light on. An icicle clinked as it fell from the window.
There were blue sky and white clouds, bare maple branches and
the spikes of Normandy firs beyond the double glass. A squirrel
ran along a bough, a blue jay called; under Lyman's feet the floor
rumbled as the heater in the basement kicked on.

He shivered, in undershorts and T-shirt, bare feet cold on the
yellow, tile-patterned linoleum. You let Nancy go free, he told
himself, she can fuck anybody she wants. At least married she's
got to hide it. Say she's not doing it.

He stepped into the shower, let the hot massaging water eat
into the back of his neck. Oh Jesus good. He rubbed himself hard
with the thick new towels Nancy'd bought for when they'd move
into the McCormacks' house. Yellow and green. With Nancy
everything has to be yellow and green.

He flipped on CNN but it was just another white face looking
earnest about some shit. So sickeningly tiring all these white faces.
After a lifetime of trying to be nice, have to admit they suck. Even
Kit Gallagher. He winced, seeing Kit Gallagher sucking Nancy's
cunt.

The reason I hate them. But I've always hated them, and
setting Kit up with Nancy was just giving myself another reason.
To see if she would do it with a white man.

Now that I'm older and wiser, I see so many reasons, but
where's the *truth*? Was I trying to keep distance from Nancy by
enticing her to screw a white man? Or is she right, that I was
trying to live out my own desire for Kit through her?

That's just Nancy's psychological bullshit. Marrying Nancy was
giving myself another reason, because she doesn't hate whites and
even likes some of them. A triumph of integration, Nancy.
Bringing up my kids like pigs. Little white pigs.

He dressed in the same Levis and work shirt he'd worn when
he'd offed the junkie hooker in San Francisco. Who wouldn't say
where Murphy was.

He could see Curt Merck sitting there, his desk, little white
penguin feet hanging down. Saw himself standing before Curt
in these clothes he'd killed her in. Free and strong as an animal.
Smart as an animal. Curt like a little white toad as the wolf circles
round. Breaking the rule that says you have to disappear the
clothes you do a job in. Completely disappear them. Fire and the

river. Out to the sea. Never a shred of fabric to recognize. Telling Curt what he was wearing. Watching the little penguin stutter. You're done, Howie, Curt Merck will say. You can cut the grass.

But Curt won't ever let you cut the grass. Doesn't even like to *talk* about the grass. About how he gets his cut, the Agency's. Hilarious that liberals in the States never realize the grass they smoke pays for guns to kill liberals in Central America. How what goes around comes around.

Little white penguin with his Bratislava accent on his little pointed tongue. Little fingers in his pockets. Little white flippers. Who doesn't dream I'd break the silence. If you're not loyal to us, Howie, you're not loyal to yourself. And the moment you tell the story the Congregation's lifeline drops dead. Along with you, Howie. And a lot of other people.

You hauled us over here in boats, Curt, but it was *we* who built this fucking country. The one you own.

Lyman bent up his leg to put on the running shoe, liking the feel of power round his shoulders and down his arms. Skin like black oil, tendons and muscles rippling. Not like steel – mahogany. Black heartwood.

Curt Merck weighing the odds in his little white paws. Kill me or just send me outside. When you have something on a man, don't let him know. Until you need it. Like a sudden stiletto between friends.

He shrugged into the leather jacket, reminded himself to stand straight. 'Keep your shoulders *back*!' his father used to say. Before he'd gone away for good. 'You don't have no burden, son, bowin' you down.'

He turned to scan the house. Wide rooms and carpets, sense of warmth. Pictures on the piano, everybody smiling. Never trust a smile.

In the garage he revved the black BMW, dropped the window to inhale warm exhaust. A few good breaths is all it takes. Never did anybody that way. But do it right and it has a nice twist – the shame of a dead man who took his own life. He pushed the garage door button and drove up the street, singing

Left my little blue-eyed darlin'
down by the sewer-side

Curt won't kill you here. He'll send you away somewhere. Guatemala. Like he did to Kit.

He jerked the car off the road, staring across the steering wheel and tinted glass and down the long black hood to leaves and macadam and rough beech trunks umbered by winter and pale grass and cyclone wire and a schoolyard where boys and girls ran in winter clothing. It had been Curt's idea to send Kit down there.

No, but Curt didn't kill Kit; Murphy did. Murphy who's disappeared into the Sonora desert and they think he's dead. But I know him too well, Lyman thought. Only *I* can kill Murphy.

Lyman ran his fingers over the leather steering wheel. But I've got to write it down somewhere. A record. A tape. About the Congregation, Guatemala. About all these things. So somebody can hear it. In case I die in a car wreck, have a sudden stroke. But who to give it to? Who'd keep it for me? No one.

At Langley Merck did not invite him into his office but instead led him up two floors through three coded doors to a place he'd never been, a closed corridor with deep green carpet and polished hardwood doors and wainscotting. He thought of it all being brought up, this antique-style hardwood, to be stuck inside tunnels of iron and concrete.

It was a little room with an oval maple table and maple chairs with plush green arms. The table gleamed with spray polish. There were video cameras in every corner and in the middle of each wall. 'Take that one.' Merck nodded at the chair where the cameras pointed.

Lyman sat, folded his big hands before him, hating their yellow palms. He reminded himself not to bite the side of his mouth. Sweat trickled from under his arm down his ribs.

'We hear your trip to San Francisco was not an unmitigated success.' The voice came through the middle of the ceiling. A Virginia country club voice.

'I didn't find this guy—'

'Not just that. You caused too much commotion.'

'It wasn't my fault, the girl!'

'Which girl?'

'That reporter—'

'Ah. Then whose fault *was* it?'

'NoCal's.'

'*How*, pray tell,' said another, slower voice, rumbling out the words, a Brahmin voice, 'can you imagine it might have been theirs?'

'They have the people. I don't know *anybody*, out there. And their people got mad when the Murphy killed their man, up on that mountain—'

'They swear they didn't do the reporter, Howie. And we believe them. That leaves you—'

Lyman lurched forward in his seat, looked into the camera. 'Then Murphy did it!'

'Murphy's the least likely part of this package,' country club said. Lyman could see him as a courtly, cragged face, unruly black eyebrows and silver hair, an ancient assassin promoted to top management.

'Murphy's a minor drug pilot,' country club said. 'He also did two tours in Vietnam, got a Silver Star, two Bronze Stars, and two Purple Hearts. You got through Vietnam without any wounds *or* medals, didn't you?'

'In those days white guys got the medals—'

'How many tours did *you* do?'

Lyman got out of his chair and stood at the end of the table. '*You* know how many tours I did!'

Like cobra heads the cameras turned towards him. 'We just don't understand your *thing* about Murphy,' country club said. 'Under other conditions, we wouldn't even mind having him here, working *for* us.'

'He killed Kit Gallagher.'

'We think not.'

'Then who did?'

'We're not yet sure. Maybe the fates caught up with Kit. Maybe he'd drifted way beyond his role, wouldn't change in a changing world. Or he was ad-libbing, like you.'

'I've stuck to your script when I can see holes in it for miles.'

'Like?'

'Like—' Lyman turned, sat down. This is where they'll have you. 'I just want to do my job.' He put his face in his hands, reminded himself not to look through the fingers. 'I have this naïve, absurd idea that if I just do my job, defend *us* as I would my own family – the rest of my life'll be all right.'

'How *is* your family, Howie?' It was a third voice, New York intellectual, professionally interested.

'We have our ups and downs. Like everybody. But I think we're the centres of each other's lives.'

'That's a nice answer.'

'And I'm trying to move the Guatemalans on this contributions thing, on the Colombians. And I tell them, look, you've got to cool

228

it on this death squad stuff. But they say, look, we were tougher than El Salvador and now they've had to have elections and we're still in charge.'

'And you've told them?'

'Straight policy. That we don't want to interfere in their internal matters but we're concerned about image. And to stop knifing me in the back every time I start to make progress.'

'Maybe they don't want *too* much progress. Maybe nobody does. Maybe you're just not reading things right.'

'You know how far it is from Guatemala to Mexico, Howie,' said country club. 'How'd you like to see a bunch of revolutionaries running Pemex? You think that'd be good for *us*?'

'We all agree on the death squad thing,' Lyman said.

'Human rights is the buzzword for the moment,' country club said. 'It will pass.'

'Did you like being in California?' the Brahmin said.

'Sure.'

'You stayed in the Oasis, all that?'

'Sure.'

'We understand you doubled up on us.'

'That's shit.'

'We *know* it's shit. And we don't like it.'

'I didn't do any doubling up.'

'You weren't happy to be Tim Merriweather at the Oasis, with your pretty new blue Accura and your PPK from NoCal's friends on Polk Street.'

'*That* fucking cunt joint—'

'*You* seem to like it there.'

'Why'd you run the double on us, Howie?' Curt Merck said. 'The room at the Hyatt Regency and the Dodge from Asia Rentals? How stupid d'you think we are?'

'That was *for* you.'

'If you don't understand the fault of your own gestures,' the Brahmin said, 'how are you going to understand our needs?'

'My needs have always been whatever yours were. That's the problem. Yours keep changing.'

'Do you want to explore that a little bit for us, Howie?' New York said.

'I wasn't running a double. I was keeping you clean.'

'Even in your soul, Howie, we don't want private agendas—'

'I don't have a soul. That was the first thing you removed.'

'You had no soul long before you came here. Or you wouldn't have done us any good.'

'When we want soul, Howie,' New York said, 'we pay for it. And it wasn't in your contract.'

'What *do* you want from me, then?'

'Go back to Guatemala. Hold Arena's hand. Try to move him towards some understanding on the contributions thing. About the importance of working with Medellín and Cali. For everybody's good. About removing all this nickel-and-dime competition. These little guys. Remember, Arena's our *ally* – try not to be so judgmental. And let's avoid private agendas—'

'Everybody's got a private agenda or two . . .' He looked into the camera.

The amused Brahmin voice: 'Tell us about them.'

He could see him there beyond the camera somewhere, an attenuated pale man with nervous fingers. A secret homosexual, unknown even to himself. But probably not to the Agency. Look at a sample of your blood they can tell everything you've ever done, you'll ever do. 'I have no idea. No interest. I just want to do my job.'

'And what, pray tell, is that?'

'Finding Joseph Murphy.'

'If he reappears down there, won't you be the first to know?'

When Lyman left it was after dark, twin lines of tail-lights trailing away before him in the Virginia slush. God, just to drive to the end of the night, the end of your soul, till you and everything you know is washed away.

48

'It was a waste of lives,' Dona said. 'Everything we do's a waste of lives.'

'There was no way to predict those helicopters,' Principio said. 'It's the only disaster we've had in this sector in over two years. In war you can't plan everything. Even in life you can't . . .'

Dona stared away from Principio's angular features at the dark wall of jungle painted with shreds of firelight. Everything he did angered her – his skinny ankles with their long thin hairs, his sandals and long toes, his clean worn uniform, his fingers folded like a priest's, a priest who has his eyes on people's souls, not on their lives. And what is the soul except an excuse to fall back on when one fails to live? 'I won't do it any more,' she said, wanting to wound him.

'Any of us can go, at any time. But don't blame yourself, not for the accident, nor for wanting to go . . .'

'I do, you fool! You! Acting so holy!' She threw a stone into the fire, realized it was at Principio she'd wanted to throw it. 'Five people we lost! Four rifles, a machine gun—' She saw Martín and the others dead again and she fought the tears, waited till they passed. 'What good do you imagine it did – their sacrifice?'

Principio drew up his knees with his arms around them; this infuriated her. 'It's the most people we've lost in one fight in thirteen months—'

'It makes us weaker!'

'We're getting stronger!'

'That's *mierda*!' She wanted to scratch him, mar his calm assurance, realized she was very hungry and the hunger was making her tense. 'We don't even know what we're offering any more! Why die for us?'

'It's not for us we're dying – but for a chance for everyone . . . free education and health care, land to grow your own food, enough to sell if you want. No more fear of death squads, freedom to say what you want, live how you want: we've been over this territory, every person in *la lucha*, a thousand times, Dona – you know it all by heart!'

She stood, too angry to stay. 'All I know by heart is sorrow!'

Once again Murphy looked down from the clear-cut Belize hills to the Río Mopan and the guardpost under tungsten lights on the Guatemalan side. It was like going back into a dream where everything had gone wrong but now he could change it, go back into when he'd come this other way, swimming across the river in the night, before then coming down the mountain after the Army truck had let him off, before then the trip from Flores with the soldiers, the cattle truck, the Río de la Pasión, the dugout canoe with the boy who now was surely dead, his hoarse, 'Water, God please, water!'

He could go all the way back up the Río de la Pasión to the first moment with her – when she'd peered down through the lantern's aureole and he'd thought that she was death, but it had gone wrong long before that, when he'd landed on the Machaquilá road, when he'd flown out of San Francisco with Johnny Dio – even long before that, the first time he'd flown for money, the first time he'd flown – but he could not understand how to make it happen differently.

In his mind's eye Dona was looking sideways, to his left, sun gleaming off her Indian-black hair, her smile wide, the slender body strong under the loose shirt. Then her body was naked and he inside her, back down the tunnel of life into the whorl of the universe: all you can do is do what you like, because it's the only message you can trust.

He went down the steep, cindery slope in darkness, listening for the hiss of vipers or the rattle of a cascabel. The river seemed impossibly fast and the water too cold. He put all his clothes and his shoes in a double plastic bag and tied it off and shoved it in his shoulder pack and stepped naked into the hard, chill water. With the pack on one strap around his neck he swam the river, came out on a sandbar way downstream, got dressed in his dry clothes, squirmed carefully up through the riverside brush and steadily and patiently climbed the mountain.

A wedge of orange moon rose out of Belize, outlining the pine trunks and their knobby roots that jutted like old men's knees up from the needly ground. He reached the ridge, turned south to the saddle where the road crossed it, and followed the road down the long, piney slope he'd ridden up in the Army truck. As he walked he tried to count the days and got to twenty-four but knew that there were more since he'd sat in the back of the Army truck and smelled the rare fine scent of the pines and remembered clearly the smell of Texas pines and deer rut and the sweet tang of gun oil, seeing his father's boot heels rising before him, dropping their sharp snow imprints along the long llano ridges.

At dawn he climbed from the road and slept high on a piney hillside at the edge of a clearing where sun shimmered all day on the yellow grass. Bees and hummingbirds fed on rainbows of flowers, hawks and falcons keened far above, the hubbub of birds and crickets constant as an air conditioner. The sun poured into the crack in his skull where the bullet had creased it, into the dent the black man had made with his pistol, into the mended bone of his arm, softening wrenched tendons and bruised skin, relaxing the muscles of his back when he lay face down in the grass, tiny spiders running across his nose. At sunset he ate half his day's rations of bread, canned meat, nuts and dried fruit, waited till darkness then dropped down to the road and walked all night, leaving it only twice when cars came out of the darkness like furious, preying monsters.

After midnight the next night he passed the turn-off to Tikal where a month ago he'd wanted to turn south towards Dona, towards the long straight road through the pine forest beyond the ziggurat hills where once he'd landed the Aztec.

Near San Benito he slept in the brush and walked into town at dawn. Women waded knee-deep in translucent Lago Petén Itzá, unloading corn sacks from dugouts that had come across from Flores. He walked out of town along the dirt road he'd travelled a month ago with doomed cattle in the back of a red Hino truck.

He was hungry and stopped to eat *frijoles volteados* and tortillas in an open café with a thatched roof on four posts, drinking milk from a green coconut with its bottom slashed off and a straw stuck in the hole. At another table a man and woman played happily with a baby; the man got up, went to a blue Jeep parked in the street, and came back with a baby bottle. On the Jeep's front bumper, above the licence, was a metal plate:

US ARMY FLYING SCHOOL
Fort Rucker, Alabama

Murphy pushed aside his plate. It was a crime to waste food; he pulled it back. Methodically he scooped the *frijoles* with a tortilla. The man paid; he and the woman stood; she held the baby to her shoulder. *'Con permiso, Señor?'* Murphy said.

The man looked at him, surprised. *'Sí?'*

'You were at Fort Rucker?'

'I was just there. For six months.'

'You fly a Huey, then.'

'Sí.' As the man approached, Murphy saw his face was badly scarred, a map of Guatemala, almost – the Petén high and jagged above his left eye and down his cheek from the ear to Puerto Barrios at the mouth, the Tenangos and the Pacific coast torn and mended along the right side of his chin.

'How is it, this war?' Murphy said.

'Very bad.'

'And the rebels?'

'The poor always dream of a better world. It's just a dream—'

'You'll win?'

'We'll never beat them, but they'll never win.' The man almost smiled. *'Es una tontería, la guerra.* War is stupidity.'

There seemed less danger now so he rode in the back of a pick-up to La Libertad and then walked twenty kilometres to El Subin, a town that was nothing but a steel bar across the road and a fortified gun tower and a few *tiendas* and children begging money. He caught another ride to Sayaxché as late afternoon fog drifted downriver, blurring the soldiers waiting by a row of armoured personnel carriers on which the US Army stars had been painted out. He crossed the *Río* in a dugout with six soldiers; the town came grainily into focus, its streets broken and gritty, garbage and plastic showing the high water mark, the shore stinking of sewage and dead fish.

There was a hotel overlooking the river with four rooms and hammocks with mosquito netting and a WC at the end of the hall with a pipe that dropped straight into the water. He counted forty-seven bullet holes in the door of his room. Up the dirt street there was the Temple of God and across from it a restaurant where he ate *pollo* and rice while through a loudspeaker the minister of the Temple promised everyone that the sorrows of this world will be recompensed by joys in the next.

After a long while he gave up trying to sleep and sat watching the black muscled *Río* ripple northwards towards Mexico. If she was dead he would still go through with the other part. No, there'd be no point. If she were dead he could see himself shrinking into how the world saw him – a fleeing killer – no hope, no future, trying uselessly to change into someone else.

With the smell of cooking fires and the ashes of dawn over the *Río* he ate hot tortillas and drank strong coffee in the restaurant, went down to the river bank and rented a dugout with a five horsepower Evinrude from a man named Vaquero, who insisted on five hundred quetzales deposit. 'But I'm just going to El Ceibal,' Murphy said, 'for the ruins.'

'The Army doesn't mind if you're a tourist,' Vaquero answered. 'They shoot at you anyway.'

For hours he steered through fog too thick to see the prow, listening for the change of propeller pitch to warn him when the boat neared the shallows. Then the white disk of the mid-morning sun burnt through the mist and the river suddenly appeared – a wide tilting sheet of flowing silver, edged green with reflected jungle.

A string of ducks rose before the prow, settling ahead till roused again by his approach; a blue heron plodded upriver with steady, whistling wingbeats. A log ahead became an alligator that rolled over and vanished with a slap of its tail. The river narrowed, filled with floating islands, sun-spangled, vibrant with birdsong; the propeller snagged often, forcing him to tip up the motor and clear away weeds. He came round a bend in the river and ahead was the cove where Jesús had fished from his mother's dugout and where Epifanía had gutted catfish to hang on racks of saplings.

49

There was nothing to come back for, ash and broken pilings of huts and cinders of palm fronds scattered among bones the vultures had dragged from the fire where the bodies had been burnt with helicopter fuel. Digging in the rubble of Consuela's hut he found a twisted spoon and the glob of plastic that had once been her water jug. There were scraps of black jerky on the branches where the soldiers had hung the faces they had cut from the bodies before they burned them. He kicked over a chunk of half-burned wood and saw it was the charred mortar in which he'd ground the corn Placido had brought upriver, that had made the tortillas for the Mass Father Miguel had said before the choppers came.

A macaw shrilled, dipping its scarlet tail for balance and peering at him sideways as it jounced in the unscarred top branches of the yucca under which Ofélia once had played with Manolo's goat in the yellow *flor de muerte*. Stand this, he told himself, and nothing can touch you. A flock of blue-crowned parrots argued, shaking the branches of a ceiba beyond the ruined corn where the soldiers had shot Conchita down, her red cloak flying in the choppers' wake.

As he poled the dugout from shore a buck broke from the brush and bounded high-antlered into the jungle. The sun sank below the tallest western trees, throwing shadows across the water, lagoons of coolness where flycatchers swooped after the first mosquitoes of evening.

Night fell with the malevolent yowl of howlers from the lowering hills, the slap of fish tails against the steely water, and encroaching mist from which herons glided like heralds of an afterlife, the rabid chortle of spider monkeys, the lament of wood owls, the dipping, chittering whirr of bats, the surprised snarl of an ocelot fishing belly-deep in the shallows. Trees merged into fog, only the horizon of their peaks still visible, then all was black.

He switched gas tanks and travelled all night, till a chill down-stream breeze cleared the fog, the vast star-blazing river sinking northward toward the Great Bear, a violet stain widening in the east.

The banks steepened, closer. Under widespread *bolocante* boughs was the mouth of the narrow creek where he'd left Jesús with the old man, and where round-faced Pollo with the dead monkey had come to take him upriver to Dona for the last time. He cut the motor and poled up the creek, its leaves lashing his face. Where the old man had tied up his canoe the root was still velvet green where the rope had abraded it.

He followed the path through the bracken and up the mountainside. It led to a corn and bean patch with a hut where, in its shade, a woman was weaving at a stick loom.

'I'm looking for *la doctora*.'

She smiled. '*Está bueno*.'

'She's well?'

'*Está bueno*.'

'Where is she?'

'*Está bueno*.'

He spoke louder. 'Do you know Spanish?'

'*Tixtxol castiy*,' she smiled.

'You could learn Kekchi.' Behind him, woman, pointing a rifle. M-1. Young, an Indian, short-haired, jeans and sandals.

'Don't shoot, goddamnit, I haven't done anything!'

'That won't keep you from getting shot.'

'I was at San Tomás, brought the boy here, Jesús—'

'Why are you back?'

'The *doctora*—'

'You don't belong here.'

'She's OK?'

'I have no idea.' She shouldered her gun and led him round the corn and bean patch up into the jungle and a steepening valley walled by reddish cliffs, her feet rising steadily before his eyes, clods of dirt and leaves breaking under her sandals and skidding past his wrists down past his feet. She laughed when he rubbed mosquitoes from his face. 'Too much meat you're eating! It attracts them!'

'Please tell me how she is!'

'Where we're going someone might know.'

The valley peaked in a wide saddle of sparse, tall trees. She crossed the saddle and turned down another canyon of rumbling

237

wind and water, down between dark escarpments to a spattering stream of gloomy tall trunks. Three men in bandilleros nodded, ascending; woodsmoke came up the canyon. Trogons were gathering in the high leaves, croaking and scolding. By a firepit a camouflage tarp linked three trees, with four bodies on raised stretchers beneath it; beside it stood a woven sapling table with instruments on a white cloth. A stone scuffled – a small thin woman was coming up the trail.

'You!' he said, seeing the joy and pain in her face at seeing him. And seeing it was love.

Stuck in traffic, Lyman drummed fingers on the steering wheel, punched the Platters into the CD and popped them out again. Couldn't be worse to have a cigarette than breathe this shit.

He reached for a Marlboro but his pocket was empty. Seven days without nicotine. Forty days in the desert. My bound and bloody wrists. At three hundred and eighty thousand dollars Nancy was calling the McCormacks' house a good deal, sure to appreciate. Getting it from them at a loss. What Nancy knew about white people and about money could be put in a very small space.

The cars ahead inched towards a flock of red and blue flashing lights. He glanced across the road, thinking of going back, but there was too much traffic the other way and no way to turn. The accident grew closer, its boxy ambulance and massive fire truck like two animals feasting on a third – a baby-blue Thunderbird upside down in the ditch, a blanket-covered body on the grass, a Raggedy Ann doll sounding flump-flump under his tyres. No seat belt – how could anybody be that dumb? He would not think of Joshua's red frothy pool under the cement truck. He would not think of it, clenching hard fingers on the leather wheel, thinking of a cigarette, of Nancy in Kit's arms, her coming twice, one right after the other, when with him she never came more than once. Or did she come at all – was *that* a lie too?

The accident eased past, the traffic took a breath and hurried onwards, back to business. Lyman punched in the CD

> heavenly shades of night are falling —
> it's twilight time,
> deep from the dark your voice is calling

He should have been a singer, riding up and down the harmonies like this. He could sing as good as these guys – why hadn't he?

'You can't just walk right in and kill him,' Principio said. 'There's a thousand soldiers around him all the time.'

'And when he goes to his *finca*, like Dona said, down on the coast?'

'You'll never get close, not even then.'

'Even with a helicopter?'

'What helicopter?'

'The one I steal and fly in there.'

'It's been years since you flew one,' Dona said.

'I can fly it in my sleep.'

Principio scratched at mosquito bites on his ankle. 'And you would do all this, probably get killed, just for Arena?'

'It's not *just* for Arena. It's for the people who've been hunting me – here and in the States. This Syndic . . . Anyway,' Murphy pulled back, not wanting to push, 'there's no need to get killed. With the chopper we'll be out of there before they know what's happened.'

'It's not your battle.'

'It was *my* village. When I was nearly dead in the jungle they're the ones that saved me. You don't think you owe debts like that?'

Principio recoiled; Murphy sensed he'd wounded him, that Principio thought of almost nothing *except* what he owed to those who'd died. Principio smiled, and Murphy saw his upper front teeth were gone.

'Also the reporter in San Francisco,' Murphy said. 'The Syndic killed her.'

'Over a hundred journalists have been killed in Guatemala in the last five years,' Guadalupe said. 'She was doing her job.'

'And my friends who were killed when my plane was burned – to you they're nothing because they were drug dealers but to me they were good people and one was a friend.'

'To avenge the murders of all the good people in the world you would be very busy,' Principio answered. 'You would have to be God.'

Murphy leaned across the fire, brushed a coal from his knee. 'These were *my* people.'

'You mean if you'd never come down here they'd all still be alive?'

'That too. That most of all.'

'After Vietnam,' Principio said, 'what did you do?'

'Went back to the States, got spat on by war protesters. Took all my pay and sat in the Sonora desert for six months.'

'That is where you learned such good Spanish? Then what?'

'When the money was gone I went back north and worked on a cattle ranch in Montana. For a couple of years the oil thing was good and I worked on drilling rigs in Oklahoma. When that gave out I drove trucks, Salt Lake, Boise, Billings, went to San Francisco and worked – how do you call it, "jackhammer" in English – the thing that breaks up stone—'

'*Uno martillo*—'

'—went back to Mexico, down the coast. One day I started flying again. San Francisco was wide open – I flew weed out of Mexico, Belize, made good money . . .'

'It's a crazy scheme,' Principio said.

50

How they irritated him, her patients. Craving, in pain, dying, taking up her time, leaving none of her for him. Boys spilling out their guts, women with breech births, babies slated to die under a chopper's guns in the middle of the river – couldn't she see that sooner or later they'd all die?

She came back, putting on her camouflage jacket against the night's chill. 'How are they?' he said.

'One will die but the others are getting better.'

'That's good—'

'That's *good*? The one who lies dying there, he's an engineer – a chemical engineer! What happens to a country that kills its best?'

'It's something we all do. I don't understand why.'

'And now you want to kill some more.'

'Only one.'

'You don't think others will die when you go for him?'

'I'd kill any of the soldiers who attacked my village. You wouldn't?'

She crouched beside him at the fire; he sensed she saw more clearly than he ever would. 'Most of those soldiers are farm kids.' She squeezed his wrist. 'Like the boy from Driftwood, Texas, who went to Vietnam.'

He took her hand; her fingers laced quickly into his. 'I don't ever want to cause another death,' she said. 'I told Principio I'm against your idea.'

'I don't want you in it.'

Her two hands came up his ankles, warming her fingers. 'I'd go away with you, right now. No killing, nothing. Just go.'

'Going away with you is all I've dreamed of. For weeks.' He eased his fingers back through her hair, massaging her neck, felt the muscles soften and bend. 'And now I see we can't.'

'I don't care they're after you.' She smiled. 'I'm used to being hunted by the Americans.'

He sensed her naked, skin to skin, her lips opening, he could taste her, breathe her in. She drew back, reading his eyes, his face. 'We're going where I can be a doctor and you can do whatever you want.'

'I have enough money. You don't ever have to do anything.'

'I'm a doctor. It's my life.'

'We're not going anywhere.'

'I've already told Principio.' She held his face in her small, chilled fingers. 'I can't do it any more. Even without you, I'd go.'

She returned to her patients; he could see her moving like a doe among them; one raised his hand briefly to her and it seemed a benediction.

Before dawn, the chemical engineer died, he who had raised his hand; the others slept. She lay beside him in the hammock, silent, curved within his arms. He felt strangled by a horrified joy, that of one who thinks everyone in his family dead in an accident, then finds one is still alive.

The stars were fading through the distant canopy. Three times she had been up to check the wounded; each time he'd gone with her. Sleepless, he dreamed of the past, seeing the young bodies tossed into his chopper, bodies that had laughed and hoped just hours before, boys who last night had sung 'Blowing in the Wind' to a cheap Taiwan guitar and had smoked too much grass and drunk too much Jack Daniels, who wore peace signs on their dogtag chains, but when you yanked off the dogtag the peace sign fell lost into the mud and blood; battle-spent boys who didn't know why they were there, who'd just written home, 'Don't worry, I'm not seeing any action.'

Lyman rose stealthily so as not to wake Nancy, got dressed and went outside into the new snow. It caped the Norway firs and lay on the maple branches and twigs and half-way down their trunks. It squeaked softly underfoot, like mice. He shook it from his loafers, went back into the kitchen and took five slices of bread outside, tore them up and tossed them on the snow, but no birds came.

Dona came upstream with two men carrying shovels. They carried the chemical engineer's stretcher up through the trees to a flat place with seven mounds. The two men dug and when one was tired he gave Murphy his shovel. The soil was soft and damp but corded with roots that were difficult to slice. Sweat ran down his chest, attracting the mosquitoes. His arm ached too badly and he gave the shovel back. When the hole was three feet deep they took the tarp off the chemical engineer and laid him in the hole. He had on a white T-shirt and his chest bandages were soaked with blood. His eyes had turned up into his head and his mouth was open, showing a silver filling. There was a wedding ring on his finger and a cross around his neck. More *compañeros* came and one read from Ecclesiastes: "'For in much wisdom is much grief, and he that increases knowledge increases sorrow.'"

Dirt pattered like rain on the body. Going back to camp one of the men took a banana from his shirt and gave it to a wounded *compañero*.

'It's stupid to risk good people to kill Arena,' Principio said. 'When Arena's dead there'll only be another.'

'But it's justice. If you won't help me, I'll do it alone.'

'Even that we oppose. If you were successful it would lead to great reprisals. They'd kill hundreds of people. Women and children, students, nuns, nurses, teachers – anyone they have a grudge against.'

Murphy looked at the dirt he crumbled in his hand, little flecks of mica or quartz in black duff. Again he saw the dirt falling on the chemical engineer's chest. 'That changes everything. I hadn't thought of it.'

'Every year for the holidays Arena goes to his family *hacienda* in the south, near El Salvador. He keeps a chopper there.' Principio turned to two others, Guadalupe and Pablo. 'What if you captured him?'

Guadalupe, tall and slender, with an upturned nose and haughty eyes, was the kind of person, Murphy decided, you instantly don't like; she had a way of preparing the world for each step she took. She tossed her head to one side, a rejection.

Pablo was chewing a twig under his moustache. 'You think we could get in, and get him?'

'He does dove hunting. Out of season. Riding by himself in the brush.'

'Why not just go in there on foot?' Murphy said. 'Why use the chopper at all?'

'To get him out. Or they'd have us in hours.'

'To take him where?'

'A place would be ready,' Principio said. 'It's nine days to the Feast of the Dead. He'll be there then, Arena, for the Feast – at his *finca*.'

'How much is he worth?' Murphy said.

Principio's delicate fingers slid down his trouser seam, as if the answer could be harried out, like lice. 'Hundreds of people.'

'I'd rather kill him. But seeing that's impossible, that it would lead to reprisals—'

'Like your village,' Dona said.

'—then I'd be willing to steal a chopper and fly in there, to get him. To *try* to get him.'

'Right now,' Principio stood, 'we're just working with an idea. A lot depends on people elsewhere. If there were an operation and you were in it you'd learn little about it. It's probably impossible.'

'If you were tortured,' Guadalupe said to Murphy, 'how long could you hold out?'

'Probably not at all.'

'If such an operation were done, and at any point you could be captured, those surviving must kill each other. It's absolutely standard practice. If, despite that, you *are* captured, the rule is to hold out for forty-eight hours. That gives other *compañeros* time to realize what's happened and make adjustments. Under torture, forty-eight hours is an eternity . . .'

'And you know all about it?' Murphy said to her.

'Yes.'

An animal scurried through the brush. Overhead the leaves lisped; a spider danced across a web in which a single star was caught.

This night was colder. The burlap poncho over them crawled with centipedes and chiggers. He dreamed he was surrounded, put Dona's rifle to his temple but could not shoot. 'Do it!' Guadalupe hissed. 'For your own good!'

The burlap was soaked with dew, the stars sharp as stiletto points between the high, tiny leaves, the universe clear and cruel, nourishing some and crushing others.

A shape moved past and knelt beside another sleeper, who rose, took up his rifle and departed; the first lay down in his place. Another came and changed places with a different sleeper who shouldered her Galil and stepped away.

A scream made him jump then he realized it was only a *jaguarondi*, hunting; he thought of Father Miguel perhaps still alive in an Army torture house. If they got Arena, Miguel was one who might go free . . .

244

The *jaguarondi* called further west – it must have crossed the stream. Was it calling for a mate in a world where there are no more *jaguarondi*? He thought of Epifanía and Jesús walking steadily before him in the shallows of the Río de la Pasión. If he died here trying for Arena he'd never come back for them as he'd promised. Maybe that would be the biggest sin of all?

Beside him Dona turned, on her shoulder; he had an instant's repressed vision of her turning in the grave, getting comfortable, laying her face to the earth.

Between the trees grew a lighter darkness. There were footfalls, the snapping of twigs, someone blowing on a fire, a bony face tinged by bronze as the coals caught.

51

A-37s stood in sunbright silver rows when Lyman landed at
Flores to catch the Army propjet for Cobán, each fighter with twin
pods of jellied death beneath its wings, like the weeds in the fields
– you break them and the seed spreads on the wind, Lyman
thought.

He saw a napalm pod as it would strike the earth, its onrush
of fire, people running, coated in flame. America's backyard
barbecue.

Vodega extended a hot wet palm. 'He's back.'

'Where!'

Vodega raised his hands – a crucifixion, or ignorance, it wasn't
clear. 'Shit!' Lyman screamed.

'A *patrulla civil* recognized his photo . . .'

'Why didn't you *grab* him?'

'My dear Colonel, you *just* sent us his picture! Anyway, we heard
you'd got him, in San Francisco.'

'That's shit! Who told you that?'

Again the smarmy shrug. 'It's a small world.'

'Advise all the *patrullas*. Spread the photo, the checkpoints . . .'

'Every drunken little civil guard in the mountains has his
lousy photo.'

'Put a hundred thousand quetzales on him.'

'Yours, Colonel? Or mine?'

The propjet gained altitude fast to avoid fire. From far below,
the refracted sun off the Río de la Pasión blinded Lyman, but
he would not turn away nor look at Vodega. To the south the
hills were like storm omens, steepening dark waves. Murphy's
down there, he thought. If I can figure why he's back I'll have
him.

He went down to the *riachuelo* and drank. The water tasted of
rocks, moss, cool sand, the humus of leaves. Water spiders skit-

tered away; black beetles chugged along the bottom raising tiny trails of silt. A water snake uncoiled past his hand and slid like a slender twig downstream.

Naked he scrubbed his body with silt, sitting in the stream to wash it off, lying back and drinking the cold water as it flowed over him. It was sweet-tasting from the guavas that had fallen from a tree; the tree's blossoms floated on the surface.

He stood on the bank, letting the sun dry him. How long have I lived in buildings and walked on concrete, he wondered, yet spoke of being down-to-earth, of having my feet on the ground?

'With your knowledge of helicopters it is a very unusual chance,' Principio said. 'But we should never do it with such short notice, not knowing you.'

'And I don't know you,' Murphy reminded him.

'You're more danger to us than we to you.'

'Perhaps.'

'We're willing to study it. We think the four of you should go down to the coast as two happy couples – you and Dona, and Guadalupe and Pablo. Quickly. If it seems possible, to do it.'

Murphy watched the stream roil round its polished stones, tiny flies shifting before it in skeins of light. Caught by the current, a fern frond ducked and rose, tugged constantly downstream, constantly reasserting itself. Till one day it would break.

It's actually in the Bible and you've missed it. Not that you cared about the Holy Book. But you knew what it said.

Outside Lyman's window a large buff spider with a yellow belly sat in the centre of a web full of dead insects. As each new insect landed the spider leaped on it, bit it to death, and returned to the centre.

The walls were barracks yellow, the door and trim dark. There were voices in the hall; he hoped no one would knock. He shoved the Bible into a drawer and shut it. The Bible was just another handbook for mass control, social management. A storehouse of tactics. Like any effective tool, it had to have enough truth or it wouldn't sell. But, thought Lyman, when it says, 'Thou shalt not kill', is that what it means?

They walked south all day, a hundred yards apart: Lupe in the lead, then Dona, then Murphy, without a rifle, then Pablo. The trail was rarely visible through the jungle understorey. After

247

sunset they crossed a ridge with the jungle falling away in a great sweep to the south. Lupe looked at her watch, shifted her rifle. 'We have to close up, move faster.'

'Christ! We've done forty klicks in seven hours!'

'More,' she smiled. 'Nearly fifty.'

'How many to go?'

'Sixty.'

'When you escaped through the desert, *hombre*,' Pablo said, 'you didn't walk like this?'

It *was* like the Sonora desert, but jungle. Running all night through the thick, tangled, humid blackness, seeing only rarely Dona's shade flitting before him, or Lupe's before her, hearing occasionally Pablo's soft pad and steady breathing behind him. Each time he fell he rolled to his feet and kept running, Pablo slowing, giving him slack, then closing up again.

'Four-twenty,' Lupe said. He could smell her and Dona and Pablo, and himself, each separately, hear his own heartbeat in his temples and their hearts thumping in their chests, the whistle of breath in his windpipe and the rush of their lungs.

'Christ!' he said, bent over, holding his knees, needing to vomit, to spit, but nothing would come out.

'Well done, *niña*,' Pablo said.

Lupe moved against him, whispered something, they kissed. Pablo turned to Dona, kissed her on each cheek, turned to Murphy, his hand coming out of the gloom. 'Well done, comrade.'

'You're going?'

'Just stick with them.' Pablo moved on ahead and took a trail breaking to the right. They went straight, slower now, for two hours, till dawn cut in nearly horizontal layers between the tops of the trees. In the distance a rooster crowed; a truck was climbing a hill. The trail grew clearer; Lupe picked up speed, her black mane bobbing far ahead, Dona's behind her, Murphy, angry now, trying not to fall back.

They laid up, panting, in a cave on a rocky, jungled slope with a tan glimmer of road cut visible above through the trees. 'Bathroom, whatever you have to do,' Lupe said, 'do it now. We don't move outside all day. I'll take first watch, till noon, Dona till three, then Gringo, then me.'

He woke to the sound of a car coming along the road. It was dark. The car paused and seemed to come downhill towards them, stopped. 'Let's go,' Lupe said.

The car waited, no lights, on a trail below the road. Someone was there. *'Listos, amigos?'* he said. It was Pablo.

Lupe drove with no lights, her rifle slanted loosely across her chest. The road was narrow and terribly rutted and potholed. Trees had been dropped in it to fill the biggest holes, and the car jounced and clanged miserably over and round them, slithering, stuck then stuck again as they pushed knee-deep in mud, the wheels spraying them, the blackness harsh with the smells of overheating radiator, crushed vines, and oily mud searing on the exhaust. The road climbed a plateau where she drove faster, branches and boulders clanging and clunking the fenders, rocks pinging on the chassis, brush and trees ducking past, thorns screeching at metal; the transmission kept popping out of fourth so she held the gearstick and drove one-handed.

'Chopper!' Pablo yelled; Lupe skidded into the brush and they dived out, scrambling for cover. Lupe ran back to slam the doors and kill the dome light. The roar loudened, three choppers in formation slid across the stars, a beacon slashing up and down the road. They rumbled westward, their thunder dying in the mountains.

'How the hell you hear that?'

'Natural selection, *hombre*. The ones who don't hear them die.'

'We were very dumb,' Lupe said. 'About the light.'

'Before this it didn't work,' Pablo said. 'I thought it was cut, but we must have bumped the wires. I'll take out the bulb.'

'And the brakelights?'

'Already I've taken out their bulbs.'

They drove back down the ridge into forest. Then Pablo walked ahead, holding a cigarette for Lupe to follow its light. They crossed a stream on foot which Lupe drove through fast, then climbed a mountain and broke out on a savanna studded with thorny trees, the grass barer, the calciferous soil like a tilled grave-yard.

There was a thump and a body rumbled underneath. 'Damn,' Lupe said.

'Jabali,' Pablo said, then to Murphy: 'Mountain pig.'

'No,' Lupe said. 'Armadillo.'

Three times they stopped so Pablo could walk forward to scout for soldiers or civil patrols, driving on cart tracks around each checkpoint. After midnight Pablo drove and Lupe slept, her head thumping against the window.

Dawn hinted in the east, ahead lay the lights of a town. 'Fifty kilometres to Guatemala City,' Lupe said. 'We've circled the last checkpoint.'

The road coiled ahead through grey hills tinged with reddish-green daybreak and loud with chattering birds and roosters. People were walking on the roadsides – women balancing bundles of corn or water-jugs on their heads, old men and boys with tall firewood stacks slung from tumplines round their foreheads, a naked little girl with a black puppy on a string. The air stung with the smoke of green hardwoods, smouldering rubber and burnt oil from the worn diesel engines of the trucks labouring up the hills, the seared asbestos smells of their brakes and clutch-plates deepened by the occasional rank stench of pig manure where a family fence ran close to the road.

At sunrise they crossed the Río Las Vacas bridge into La Ermita and the Guatemala City smog, turned up Calle Martí behind a rusty red truck whose back doors clanged their chains each time it jerked forward.

Lupe drove through the city and across Río Barranca down a long slope of packed shacks, with the river valley falling off steeply below. The road turned to garbage and mud thick with citrus skins and cardboard, the air bitter with charred litter and plastic, naked children and bony dogs staring from between the tin and cardboard huts. She parked amid broken cars and trucks, where a man with a Galil kept guard, and led them down the slippery, stinking slope of a dump where people lived in caves burrowed out of the garbage and trash, alleys loud with the music of competing tinny radios, the voices of strangers calling each other.

In a lane of rotten detritus and reeking urine Lupe turned suddenly aside and banged on a plank door hinged by two rubber straps to the corner post of a chicken-wire shack covered in newsprint. There was no answer and she opened the door. 'Stay here,' she said to Murphy. 'If no one comes by dawn tomorrow, go home.'

52

Inside in the igloo-like light he could read the advertisements on the newspapers of the ceiling and walls. Clouds of flies clustered on a black, stinking fluid that percolated from the upper wall across the floor; there was a crucifix and a God's Eye over the door.

He tried to lie where the black stream would not touch him. Exhaustion was thick as vomit in his stomach and his eyes would not stay open. He thought of eating some of the newspaper to slow the gnaw in his stomach. As the sun rose higher the hut grew hot, the smell horrible. He went outside and sat in the half-shade of an upturned truck seat; three boys were playing soccer with a shred of tyre; a woman brought a skinny rooster out of her hut and cut off its head on a car fender, catching the blood in a chunk of coconut bark.

He had diarrhoea and tried to find a hidden place among the walls of trash; there was nothing to drink and his tongue stuck in his throat. He went back into the hut and slept, curled in a corner in the reeking heat.

'Let's go!' Dona was shaking him. It was dark. They went up through the aisles of trash to the car. She wore sports clothes and carried a handbag.

'I've had enough of this,' he said.

'It's just you and me.' She gave him the car keys. 'Take the Periférico.'

'Where are Lupe and Pablo?'

'We'll see.'

He drove up the long hill of garbage. Kerosene lanterns glowed on faces in the crowded huts. 'Where we going?'

'I have a Mexican passport. You are this American – Lamar Bultz – where do they get such names, these people? We're on vacation – listen, now, we must practise the story of what we're doing here . . .'

251

The traffic was light – a cattle truck with two men in the back holding M-16s, a Jeep, a BMW with dark windows, the dim roadsides empty of life as he and she rehearsed past times and presents, lives in which she was Maria Iturbo of Oaxaca and he was still Lamar Bultz of Flagstaff, and they were in love.

She directed him south on Central America Nine, towards Villa Nueva, past Lago Amatítlan, flat as mercury under the moon, black buttresses above one shore.

Sickness felt like a snake in his stomach. One by one the checkpoints passed, at each Dona pretending to wake, rummaging sleepily in her bag for her Mexican passport, while the soldiers thumped their rifle butts on the ground. The road narrowed, slinking through curves in rolling hills silvered by a setting moon, no lights in passing huts and villages, occasionally a truck or car the other way. Several times he pulled off the road and waited, twice doubling back, but no one followed.

The moon fell down; there was sea smell in the air. She pointed him down an overgrown lane through miles of dunes and salt-brush to a village square with an adobe church. They left the car in a grove of wind-stunted cypress behind the church and went down to a narrow beach and a broad estuary scattered with stars, beyond it a hump of sandspit and the shuddering roar of the sea.

'We have three days,' she said. 'I'm not supposed to tell you, but now you know.'

'I don't like having the truth dribbled out like this.'

'How else would *you* do it? The less we each know—'

'I won't be pushed around by Lupe.'

'We have three days. Let's just live with that.'

They took off their clothes and washed in the estuary's liquid silver; it felt like a magic shield they could wear; he drank the salty, algal water, and it felt good in his stomach.

At dawn a boy took them in his dugout across the pale estuary reflecting pink, tumbled cumuli. The church tolled six, the bell quavering across the still water. A line of snowy egrets undulated away like a broken necklace. The dugout crossed the inverted reflection of the sandspit's palm huts, and grated ashore. Beyond the huts was a streak of platinum that was the sea, then the lightening blue pit of space. 'Twenty centavos,' the boy said.

A woman in a black dress was cooking *frijoles* on a chunk of tin over a ring of stones. Smoke from the driftwood fire contorted

252

in the breeze. A man came out of a hut scratching his chest. '*Sí,*' he said. 'I have rooms.'

It was a hut with a plank door and tiny padlock, a driftwood floor and rush walls, two woven willow sleeping mats raised on posts, a wooden chair. Beyond the door was the curl of the beach then the great blue shoulder of the sea. 'You want breakfast?' the man said.

It was coffee from fresh beans heated over the fire then crushed with a rock and boiled in a black pot, black *frijoles* covered with green salsa, bright yellow eggs from hens run wild, tortillas charred on their edges. When they could eat no more they took their coffee cups out and sat on the newly warm dune going down to the waves that hissed and darkened the sand with foamy wet fingers.

A bony, lion-coloured dog burrowed in the sand, trying to escape his fleas. A salt-corroded red and white sign, COCA COLA DA MAS CHISPA!, banged in the wind. Gulls cried, blown eastward; waves slapped the strand, blue fingers frothing.

The sun reddened her black hair. 'How did he die,' he said, 'your fiancé?'

She raised her head from the sand to look at him. 'That doesn't matter now.'

'It always matters. It never *stops* mattering.'

'He was one of seven people captured by Mossad's new IBM, the one the Army was given to watch the flow of water and electricity in Guatemala City. They found them all in one house, and shot them the day the Pope came.'

The waves broke suddenly and late against the steep beach, shaking the dunes so that sand avalanched down them.

'I was such a kid,' she said. 'Twenty-three, first year of medical school. Wild with studying so hard and trying to keep my head above water, working in the hospital from midnight to six as an orderly to pay for my room and food. Diego was so bright, alive, a cardiology intern. He thought that if we've learned how to heal the body we can learn how to heal the soul—'

Looking southward the beach was pure as cocaine, stretching out through blue sea and sky to a horizon of low clumped trees hazy at the world's edge. In both directions the line of white sand fled beyond the ends of the earth. 'I wish I'd known you then. I wish I'd always known you.'

'Silly!' She pushed him. 'Then you'd be bored with me by now.'

'I've always wanted to walk this beach. From Alaska to Chile.

253

Funny to realize you'll never do the things you always thought you'd do—'

'Down there's El Salvador. You'd never get through.'

'El Salvador,' he said. 'The Saviour. Who said do unto others what you would do unto me . . .'

She put a finger over his lips. 'Let's try to live through all this, and raise children, get old and tired of each other, like normal people?'

He smiled, pillowed in the warm dune, tasting the sand that the wind blew into his face. The sun, like a hot abrasive sponge, seemed to cleanse his skin. 'Better to die for something than nothing,' he said dreamily.

He must have slept, woke remembering a vision of atoms, atoms uniting in paramecia, ants, bears, humans – each a coalition of atoms defending their union from dissolution, all hungering to continue.

53

The huts were a tiny hump on the beach behind them. The sea slung cool foamy tentacles round their ankles, crabs scurried sideways along the waterline. Far ahead a pebble became a thatched shelter, a blue-painted dugout drawn high up on the sand below it at the edge of the dune grass.

The shelter was empty, the windy sand trackless. The other side of the dune went down to a fringe of thick trees along a *riachuelo* paralleling the beach, with flat, low jungle behind it. Her ankles and the rolled-up cuffs of her jeans were white with fine sand.

A tern slanted across the cobalt, white-capped sea, its cry familiar as a language he'd forgotten. From further down the beach they could not even see the huts or the shelter and blue boat in the misty distant silver curve behind them; ahead the tree-topped cape of El Salvador seemed no closer.

They swam through the warm salty froth beyond the waves, down to kelp raising willowy arms like drowned men, the water turbid, colder. In the shallows the waves washed cool silk between them, lightening and lubricating, welding them to each other and to the soft sea, the sand, the sun.

'We should be more careful,' she said. 'It's here the choppers drop lots of bodies.'

'They won't bother us.'

'It's the sharks – they have a taste for human flesh.'

Carrying their clothes they walked naked, the breeze like warm water against their salty skin. Terns dived, crying over feeding mackerel. Along the water's shifting edge, countless millions of tiny embryonic creatures wriggled up the damp sand, battling the swell, trying to reach dry beach, most already dead, here and there one succeeding till the next wave bashed it down, the universe crammed with worlds hungry for life; from time to time, he thought, one survived, but not for long.

They grew thirsty and went back to the huts, sat with bottles of mineral water at a roughsawn table. The sun had sunk past the thatched veranda that a pig was shaking as she rubbed her pink flank against a corner post. Loose fronds of thatch tossed in the breeze like a woman's long blonde hair.

Beyond the hump of beach they could not see the shore, only the sea rising and sinking like a sleeping woman's breast, the casual rumble of each wave drowning the chatter of Radio Tropicana from a portable radio that hung from a beam. He realized he could see the earth's curve in the wide arc between the sea and sky, thought how small it was, and how many people were on it. '*Hay que vivir*,' sang a Mexican love song, '*Vivir el momento* . . .'

The sun sank, round and scarlet, into a sea of blood. A fisherman was mending a net, a web of gold that shimmered as his fingers moved across it. The sun's last blaze ignited a strip of red plastic, half buried in the sand, the scuttling shreds of paper, strands of thatch, the riffled dunes. Gulls slid by; the sky thinned, magenta to crimson, violet to emerald, to manganese, to the copper-grey of ashes thrown on snow. Between their toes the sand was rivuleted by infinite tiny capillaries of sea, as if they flew at a great height over a land of many rivers.

The man, Felipe, brought them *morrachos* grilled with lime over palm fronds, rice with *chiles*, raw white cabbage with tomatoes covered in salt and lime, tortillas, and El Gallo beer. The *morrachos* had transparent, needle bones. 'They're from the river,' he said, pointing to the estuary. 'Now it's sweet water, but at midnight, when the tide comes, it's salty.'

The woman, Carlita, sat with another by the fire; children swung in a fish-net hammock hung between two beams. Felipe chopped green coconuts with a machete and tossed the chips to the grunting, butting pigs. Murphy borrowed Felipe's cracked, peeled Mexican guitar and played, and the children came closer. After a while he could feel the music start to go out of him, out of his heart and down his arms through this beaten old guitar to the end of the night where all the music goes—

'Jesus, that's beautiful,' she said. 'Where did you learn that?'

'It's just the blues.'

'Do again that part that goes down and then way up . . .'

'It's all I've ever wanted to do, this,' he said. 'Sit on the beach with you and play the guitar.'

'Your fingers move so fast! *Madre*, it is beautiful!'

'You should hear the good ones. The ones who know how to play.'
'I am getting drunk with your music and your beer.'
'We're going in the hut to make love.'
'I won't let it happen yet. First I am going to drive you crazy.'
'You already drive me crazy.'
'We are going to get drunk and crazy. We are going to be like normal people, with all the time in the world.'

A slim moon had risen, silvering a great dark cloud over the sea, low in the middle and raised on each end, that looked like the crouched form of Chacmool, the messenger between the worlds who, holding his tribute of fresh human hearts, ferries his burden of poor human souls across the great divide.

In the main hut a candle flickered against the thatch and beams. He unlocked the padlock and they went into their hut and hooked the string behind them and took off their clothes, his jacket folded for a pillow with Dona's .357 beneath it.

54

He was travelling through rough country and kept looking for water but all the streams were dry. Even the cactus were dead; he pushed one and it snapped and crashed to the ground. It wasn't the cactus banging but guns; he snatched the Magnum and shoved Dona to the floor; someone scrambled over the wall and he fired, the sound enormous in the tiny dark room; a cat snarled and rushed away; there was another boom and a rattle of guns; he yanked open the door and sprinted for the beach, pushing her before him; they dived into the dunes as another string of shots erupted and he saw across the lagoon that it was fireworks, their bright cinders twirling down.

'Good God, we're stupid.' She stood, brushing sand from her stomach. 'The Night of the Dead – that's all it is—'

'I shot that poor cat.'

'Perhaps the shot just scared him.'

Inside the hut he lit the candle and found the burnt hole of the bullet high up in the thatched wall, went outside but could see no blood. 'Felipe, he's going to be pissed.'

'He doesn't care. We'll tell him we brought our own fireworks.'

'We have no dead to feed tonight . . .'

A curlew called, morose from sleep. A baby cried; the sea rose up and slapped the beach, recoiled, rose up and fell again. The moon strode glittering over the waves. He retied the door string and put the gun back under their heads.

When she slept he held his hand warm on her warm cheek, feeling the soft skin. How magnificent life. How can it die?

How deep love, how absolute. Her skin so smooth, her forehead clear, how soft the fine hair of her eyebrows – all so holy, pure, and death so present, the awfulness of it when there's so much to lose.

He'd never thought of it when it had seemed far away, death. But it was never far away – it's always here; we're always dying.

It isn't going to happen some day; it's happening now.

You could see the skull beneath the smooth soft skin, the sockets behind sleeping eyes, the gaping jaw within the lovely lips, moving so gently now in a dream. The awful aching endless silence of death.

Her coppery face seemed loving, without care. The peace that passes all understanding. Oh Lord make me understand, he prayed. Do this and I will love you always. Give me a chance to understand. One hand beneath his head, his wrist against rushes and hemp, the other arm under her neck and round her shoulders, he watched the hewn rafters and their burden of crossed saplings and thatch, each frond lashed to each alternate sapling in the simple harmony of Indian handiwork. Each of us contributing his or her handiwork to the structure of infinity. Harrowing a meaning, order and pattern, a shelter for the future, for others and ourselves.

There was coffee on the roughsawn table in the cool morning breeze off the sea. Up and down the beach, for ever, the hot sand and wet waves. El Gallo in the evenings, too many, laughter coming out too easily from under the stone of his heart, while he knew he couldn't afford to laugh and told himself not to care. When she laughed her small nose wrinkled and the sides of her eyes crinkled, her laugh both deep and high as if two bells rang at once. To make her laugh he told her stories, of Texas rabbits big as coyotes, drunken hookers in the Oklahoma oilfields, forty-five below in April on the Montana Highline, carrying newborn calves into the ranchhouse to warm in the bathtub, all the truck-stops to get sick at between Elko and Salt Lake. Deliberately exaggerating, he played the joker, anything to see her smile, hear her laughter as he'd always heard it down inside a part of himself that had been deaf and dumb.

She told him about bringing the goats up to pasture in the early mornings with Venus going down over the Sierra Madre, the cold spring between ancient carved pillars where a black jaguar sometimes slept on the low broad branch of a *chicozapote* tree with a deer carcass beside him, the magic plants the old women used to heal the ill, liven the spirit, and even, in the case of some, look forward into time.

'Did you ever do it, take them?'

'I tried the mushrooms, when I was fourteen.'

'And?'

'After all the laughter and fun I suddenly realized I was able to look into my own brain. It was incredible. How it worked and where the pieces are. In medical school, years later, when I finally opened one, it was exactly as I had seen, way back then.'

The priest had the odour of old cloth and tobacco. The veins on the backs of his hands were distended and blue. Although his left hand was still, his right kept twitching, as if beckoning Murphy closer. 'Come back in an hour,' he said. 'Bring Felipe and Carlita.'

Murphy took the dugout back to the sandspit. In the hut Dona was brushing the salt out of her hair; it hung way down her back. 'Do I look all right?' she said.

He could not speak. It came upon him, now, the wonder that she would be his wife and that this lasted for ever, because it is part of the Mass, the Sacrament. And the Sacrament is that which cannot be undone.

'Carlita says that after we have children we must come back here so that they can grow up in the countryside.'

'Felipe told me the same thing.'

'It is kind of them to do this, they don't know us.'

'It does them no harm, a quick trip to church.'

With Carlita and Felipe they took the dugout across the lagoon. The priest threw open the church's eroded plank door. Inside was musty and chilled, dead fragrances, incense, and candle wax. 'You have the rings?'

'Jesus,' Murphy said. 'I never thought—'

'I will not do it without them. Quickly, go see the old man, Pepe Domingo, in the last street by the dock. I hope he's there.'

He ran through town to the last street, sweating in the sudden sun. Pepe Domingo had a purple snake tattooed round his neck. He lived in a hut whose rush walls had been coated with clay and whitewashed. He had a window but it had no glass. He made Murphy wait in the path then had him come inside. He had seven rings in a rusty tin can. Fresh dirt clung to the can. On the wall behind him a dayglo St Michael, face full of hatred, was spearing a dragon.

'*Con prisa!*' Murphy said. '*Con prisa* – I'm getting married!'

'No need to rush.'

He tried on the biggest. It pinched but he could wear it. He picked another, smaller one. 'How much these two?'

'They are gold, very expensive gold.'

'How much? How much!'

'Well, that one it is white gold, the most expensive. Twenty-two thousand. And the other, well, it is fine gold, but, well, eighteen thousand.'

He put them in his pocket and ran back through town, dust rising under his feet. The church door was open but there was no one inside.

He ran out into bright sun. 'The falcons took them,' said a woman in a *tienda* across the dirt street.

'The *what*?'

'The death squad. Your woman and Felipe and Carlita and the Father. In a black Jeep with a Guatemala City licence.' She was weeping. 'What are we going to do,' she said, 'without a priest?'

He fell on his knees, looked up at the sky, the yellow tower of the church. Somewhere birds were singing.

'You should never have bought rings from Pepe,' the woman said. 'He gets them from the *camposanto*. From the dead.'

55

He ran to the car but had left the keys back at the hut. He ran to the boy's dugout and poled to the sandspit, smashed down the hut's door, grabbed the keys, their things, raced back across the lagoon. '*Which way?*' he screamed at the old woman.

'Towards San José. But you won't catch them now.'

He drove like a madman, dust, rocks, trash and coconuts flying from his path, turned towards San José, down the middle of the road as fast as the Nissan could go, other cars and trucks screaming at him as they dodged out of the way.

'No,' said the advance guard at the San José Paratroop Base. He looked nervously back at his comrades in their machine-gun nests on both sides of the road. 'I haven't seen a black Jeep coming in here . . .'

'You're sure?' Murphy grabbed money from his pocket. 'Here – I'll give you fifty thousand – anything – you tell me—'

'Sorry, *Señor*. I cannot take your money. I haven't seen a black Jeep.'

'Panchito!' somebody called from the machine-guns.

'I got to go now, *Señor*. You too, or we have to shoot you.'

He stopped only for gas, at Escuintal, making the four-hour trip to Guatemala City in an hour and forty minutes. Before the towering stone gates of the Army Headquarters, four soldiers with Uzis manned the barrier, machine-guns to each side. He parked half-way down the street and shoved the Magnum under the seat.

'No,' said the first man with an Uzi. 'You can't go in there.'

'I have an appointment – General Arena.'

The soldier had a dark face with flat cheekbones and black eyes under heavy brows. His hand caressed the trigger guard. Murphy thought of the heavy bullets, how they smash through you. Happening to her now. He jammed his fingers into his pockets to keep from grabbing the Uzi.

The soldier smiled, walked inside the stone gates. The others watched Murphy without interest. Cars and trucks rumbled and banged on the Avenida. A chopper came up from the south and landed inside the Base, rotors clattering. Again he thought of shooting his way through them but there was no way to make it to the machine-guns and if he made it to one he'd never get across open ground to the other and even if he did they'd close the gates and shoot him to pieces from the walls. The soldier came back. 'You make a big mistake. No General Arena here.'

'You don't know where he is?'

'I don't know of any general like that. Anyway, you not stay here. Go.'

'I'm a reporter, American. I need to see the commanding general.'

'No commanding general. You're getting in trouble now. Why not just go?'

'Listen, I *have* to see him. I have information, on the guerrillas—'

The man's head jerked back. 'You better go your own embassy for that. Up the Avenida, to Ocho Calle.'

'I have to see the CO—'

The man stepped back, dropped the Uzi. 'You're exactly one metre from death, *amigo*. Step forward and you get erased . . .'

He returned to the car, feeling their gun barrels aimed between his shoulder-blades. He drove into the back streets and sat. He could see it all, the guns, the knives, what they were doing to her right now, each second.

In a corner drugstore he borrowed the phone book and found the Iglesia Congregacionale del Cristo Pentecostal, 112 Avenida las Americas. It was a two-storey white building set in a palm garden. Around it was an ornamental iron fence topped by barbed and electric wires. He rang the bell. '*Sí?*' a woman said through the interphone.

'I'm Will Daley,' he said in English, 'from the Church in Marin.'

'Marin?'

'Near San Francisco.'

'Just a moment.'

The interphone went silent, then a man's voice: '*Who* are you?'

'You want a conversation on the sidewalk? Open up!'

A crew-cut man in black horn-rims opened the door. Inside was a square vestibule with three blank white doors and two television monitors high on the walls. 'Explain,' he said.

'The folks at CCCP in Nicasio sent me down about a flying job.'

'This is a *church*, fella. We don't have flying jobs.'

'Bullshit. I got two thousand hours in Nam, I'm rated from dusters to jets and I came down here to fly in and out of Petén—'

'Our office in Marin *told* you this?'

'Of course. What's the hitch?'

'Stay here.' The man went through the middle white door and came back three minutes later. 'Nobody's ever heard of you.'

'I fly all the way down here and now you guys jerk my chain!' Murphy snatched at the door, spun round. 'Let me talk to the top guy, we'll sort it out—'

'There *is* no top guy. This's a church, remember?'

'I was promised a job! Listen – I flew for Renamo, Angola – what more you want?'

'Calm down!' The man spoke up into a TV monitor: 'I'll take him uptown.' He led Murphy through the left-hand door and down a white corridor with no windows or doors to the rear of the building. There was a Van Gogh print on one wall, beached boats with an arched stone bridge and women washing clothes. The man took a plastic card from his wallet and slipped it into a slot beside the rear door, punched a code into the keyboard above it. The door opened. They went down the stairs to a walled alley and a white Plymouth Aries with diplomatic plates. 'One,' the man told the driver.

'I've got information,' Murphy said, 'about the guerrillas.'

'Kill it,' the man answered, nodding at the driver.

They went north on las Americas round the Costa Rica oval, crossed Ocho Calle in front of the US Embassy, and pulled into the driveway of a three-storey beige building with a forest of antennae on the roof.

The driveway was guarded by a burly man in a red blazer who carried an Uzi, and by four Guatemalan soldiers who saluted hurriedly as the car drove down to the basement garage, stainless steel doors opening then shutting behind it. In the garage were several new cars with diplomatic plates and three Suburbans with Guatemalan plates. They took an elevator to Two then down another white empty corridor into a little room with no window. There was a grey steel desk and chair and two grey metal folding chairs before it. A big man with a rectangular red face, his lavender tie undone and his sleeves rolled to his elbows, came in and sat behind the desk. He snuffed out a cigarette in a glass ashtray atop the desk. 'So what's up?' he said.

'This guy says NoCal sent him down for Southern Air, out of Petén.'

The big man looked with interest into Murphy's face. 'Impossible.'

Murphy stood. 'You guys've really screwed me up!'

'Hold it, trooper!' the big man rumbled genially. 'You got to start from the States if you want to fly for Southern Air—'

'Listen, I got data, too, on the guerrillas – I need to talk to somebody.'

The man rubbed his jaw. 'What *kind* of data?'

'I'll make a trade – I need to interrogate someone, who's just been captured, on another matter – I'll trade some data—'

'What other matter?'

Murphy looked into the friendly, blank face. 'Drugs.'

The man looked back at him, and Murphy saw the black widow he'd seen in the chopper pilot's skull, in the jungle, so long ago. It was big and very black and moved on dancing spinnakers from side to side. 'Nobody trades info here, trooper,' the man said. 'I'm beginning to think you're in a real bad place.'

Murphy stood. 'Then you're just wasting my time.'

'You can't hop down here, just run all over us. You got to play by the book, trooper. Channels, like anybody else. Who you think you are, Galahad or something?'

Not waiting for them Murphy went back into the corridor and down the elevator to the main floor, stepped into an anteroom guarded by Guatemalan soldiers with MAC-10s and Uzis. There was a steel box at one side with a woman answering a telephone behind bullet-proof glass. 'What *is* this place?' he said.

'*This?*' She had a pleasant Alabama accent. 'Why this's USAID. ROCAP.'

'What the hell's that?'

She looked at him in surprise. 'We're foreign aid. We organize urban work, agricultural self-help, educational projects.'

Behind him Murphy heard the elevator open. He went out the front door and down the marble stairs guarded by Guatemalan soldiers, through the electric sliding gate.

In the shade of great trees on La Reforma there were Indians selling flowers, blankets, and willow baskets; chubby men in hundred-dollar running shoes jogged past skinny kids hunting the sidewalks for butts and gum, past lovely fifty-dollar girls and hobbling old women, the road full of flashy cars, and Microfé vans with their windows crammed with faces. There were rattling smoky buses tilting their ragged human burden, children pushing bicycles stacked with Coke crates, black-windowed Jeep Wagoneers and Chevy Suburbans, symbol and tool of the death squads.

56

A cindery sediment was silting down between the buildings that wobbled in the ochre heat. He drove across the Río Barranca and down the slope of shacks and garbage, left the car and ran through the dump with the caves of rotten garbage and the trash huts, found the chicken wire shack where he'd stayed. It was empty; he climbed up through the trash to the next hut and knocked on the wall. A skinny little girl looked out, up at him.

There were two babies on a blanket on the floor, no one else. She did not know where her mother was. He went to the next hut, recognized the woman who had killed the rooster, days before. 'I don't understand you,' she said. 'There's no *compañeros* here.'

He tried three other huts, then in an alley asked a wiry girl with a scarred face. 'Don't talk about it,' she said. 'Go back to your hut and wait.'

He stood by the plank door of his shack, out of the way of the broken sewer. After perhaps an hour Lupe came in. 'If you've lost her I'll kill you,' she said.

His hand itched to take out the Magnum and shoot her. He told her about the priest, the rings, the death squad. 'You're insane,' she said. 'You deserve to die.'

'What are they doing to her?'

Lupe held her face in her hands, her back to Murphy. She knelt down on the ground, and he did not know if she was crying or praying or simply thinking. 'They're torturing her,' she said. 'When she tells them everything they'll kill her. Unless she figures out how to kill herself first.'

'We can still get Arena – trade him for her, the others!'

She shook her head, her face a mixture of pain and fury. There was perspiration – or tears – in her eyes. 'It's too late, now – you were supposed to meet others—'

'Let's go, meet them!'

267

'It was for this afternoon. By now Arena's on his way back to Guatemala City.'

'We'll meet him here then.'

She stood. 'Stay here.' She went out the door, came back. 'You're just worrying about her! Don't you realize every word she says will cost a life!'

'So hurry!'

She vanished up the path and he stood at the end of the alley, watching the hazy sun sink behind black pillars of trash smoke, the first breeze of evening rising through the dump of huts and tunnels, bearing the chatter of children, a woman's laugh, the odours of garbage and tortillas, the wistful songs of radios and seagulls, and the chirr and swoop of swallows after flies.

He realized he was incredibly thirsty. Hungry. The world of your body goes on, he realized. Each step, everything that had happened, he could see how he'd done it. Even the rings. Each step had made sense at the time and each had led to ruin later.

After midnight Lupe came with a bottle of water and two tortillas. 'Sorry, this's all there is.'

'What next?'

'You have clean clothes?'

'In the car.'

'Go up and sleep in your car. In the morning wash and shave with some of this water and change clothes. Make yourself presentable.'

'And?'

'Wait.'

Where the car was parked, the sewers from the City above had backed up into pools where mosquitoes bred, so he had to sit with the windows rolled up, sweating, barely breathing.

At dawn he washed and changed. At ten Lupe and Pablo came down the hill behind him and got in the car. 'Drive,' Pablo said.

He drove back across the Río Barranca into Guatemala City. '*¡No critiquemos Guatemala!*' screamed a yellow billboard above a highway abutment.

'Get out on the next corner,' Lupe said. 'Three corners ahead you turn left on La Reforma and walk to the El Camino Real Hotel. It's a big building on your left in one kilometre. Use your Arizona licence to register. They don't file room booking data by telecom so there's no danger for forty-eight hours. Take a room on the south side with a clear view of the pool, at least four floors up. Don't take *any* room that doesn't meet all three of those qualifications. *Stay* in the room. *Don't* go out. When you're hungry use room service—'

'What the hell for?'

'Someone'll get in touch. If in three days nothing happens, go home.'

From the window of Room 708 he could see the long aqua pool and its ramps of sunbathers like dead seals flayed over deck chairs, others sprawling under palm-frond umbrellas, white-coated waiters wandering among them like medics looking for survivors on a battlefield. Beyond the pool a thick wall shut out La Reforma. Between the buildings the noon hung thick as lead.

The room had two king-sized beds and a colour TV and a red telephone and a desk and a bar with a small refrigerator. On the coffee table was a bowl of fruit and fresh orchids and a fan of brochures for the hotel sauna, coiffeur, massage, tennis, room service, luxury shops and chapel. In the bathroom were double sinks set in a long pink marble slab, a pink marble bath and a separate marble shower with a rubber floormat, a bidet, toilet and white telephone. There was a complimentary kit of shampoo, a shower cap, laundry bag, shoe polish, sewing supplies, tooth-paste and tanning lotion. Over the faucets a sign said 'Purified Water' in English.

He turned on the TV, CNN on death in the Middle East. He pushed a button and a college football player was speaking about today's game: 'It's life and death for us.' The player leaned down to speak into the microphone, his shoulder-pads blocking out the light. If it's college football, Murphy decided, it must be Saturday.

A man in a red jacket and cap brought him eggs and bacon and tasteless white bread and a thick steak with coffee, orange juice, milk, and a lime pie. He slept till three, ordered news-papers and magazines from room service. 'GUATEMALA KILLINGS RISE,' said a *New York Times* headline, 'BUT OVERALL GAINS NOTED.' *El Grafico* listed yesterday's twenty-one known deaths of the death squads, another article on a visiting US official:

'The democratizing process operating in Guatemala is extremely significant,' said Democratic Congressman Stephen Solarz of New York yesterday after visiting Armed Forces Chief, General Mejía Victores. 'It is imminent and sure the US government will extend new military loans to Guatemala . . .'

On an American game show, housewives grovelled for kitchen accessories. The phone shrilled.

'*Sí!*'

'*Señor* Bultz?' In the man's accent it sounded like 'Bullets'.

'No – *Sí!*'

'This is reception,' the man said. 'May the maid clean away your lunch?'

He held the Magnum hidden under a towel when he answered the door. The maid was a little Indian woman with a bowed back and a smile. He went into the bathroom to put the gun back in his belt, under the shirt. In the mirror it swelled his stomach.

He turned on the TV. The city of Ponchatoula, Louisiana, was burying its pet alligator. A thousand citizens, many weeping, marched in the funeral procession. A new alligator had already been caught to replace it.

He paced the room, twenty-seven steps from bathroom door to far window, round the beds and coffee table and back again. She could be dead now. Maybe they just shot them and didn't torture them. You could always hope for that. Whatever Lupe and Pablo were doing they'd better do it fast. Or what? What was he going to do?

The daylight failed like a bad dream. Car lights were like snails' eyes on La Reforma. Three sharp knocks on the door. He ducked into the closet beside the door, aiming the .357 through the wall. Again three knocks. '*Sí!*'

'*Señor* Bultz? It's Guadalupe.'

He let them in, Lupe and Pablo, she in a short silky pink dress and black stockings, he in a tuxedo. 'Arena's downstairs,' she said. 'He may be coming up, with me, to another room one floor above this . . .'

'That's nuts!'

'You have to wait up there, outside the window – there's a little ledge, you and Pablo—'

'We'll never—'

'He's here often – the bar's full of Americans, from the Embassy. He likes the hookers here, always likes new ones; he's never seen me before. If I can get him to come to the room upstairs, we'll try to take him out the window, down to this room, then down to the car. We're keeping you with us, in case we need the chopper, a way out . . .'

270

He backed away, to see them better. 'You've been working this all out, never letting me know?'

She brushed his hair forward, almost affectionately. 'What *good* would it have done, except cause you more suffering if they ever catch you? And other people too—'

'I won't do it unless I know what's going on.'

'She's told you what she can, *hombre*,' Pablo said, 'take it or leave it. We're not even sure we need you.'

'Where's Dona?'

Lupe took his face in her hands, looking right into his eyes, like a mother with a beloved, belligerent child, and he saw with shock how beautiful she was, how deep her eyes were, how her presence glowed through her skin. 'We don't know.'

'You *must*!'

'We think she's been taken to Cobán for interrogation. The three others we think were found this morning near Escuintla.'

He could hear his own words through a thick fog, as if he were alone in the room. 'You think?'

'There's been over twenty found today. Most of them don't have heads.'

There was no air to breathe. 'How do you know she—'

'There've been only five women. They all were bigger.'

He couldn't move, couldn't speak, seeing the five headless women found today, thinking of their lives, thought how willing we are to trade others' lives for those we love. 'She's dead. You just haven't found her yet.'

'The people who took her – they'd have identified her right away – just bringing her in is worth ten thousand quetzales.'

Everyone was ordered to hold out for forty-eight hours after capture, to give the *compañeros* time to adjust, but no one could. Very soon you told your interrogators everything – anything, to stop the pain. They'd know she was trying to hold for forty-eight hours, and would find a quicker way to break her. Right now. Right this very second. Every second.

Lupe went to his window, left it open. 'Let's go! You still have bullets for the Magnum?'

'Eleven.'

They took the stairs up one floor to Room 809. Lupe opened that window. 'Wait on the ledge, here. Watch carefully. Come in when I call you, not before. Remember this: if I don't call you, don't come in. If Arena is here, do nothing. His bodyguards will be waiting for him outside the room door. If anyone comes in, I will pretend to faint if there's danger. If I do that then shoot everyone you can except me and Pablo.'

Lyman watched the chick come down the wide stairs into the bar, with her short pink dress showing lovely long legs in black stockings, half-way up the thigh. There was something about the way she walked that let him imagine her cunt right there, under the silk, moving as she walked, and he could feel it warm in the hollow of his hand.

She gave the room a professional glance and sat at the bar behind him. '*Gin y tonica*,' she said – a girl from the *barrios* trying to sound chic. He felt his penis throb like a thick rope.

'And also, the bulls of Finca las Golondrinas,' said General Arena, 'will outperform all others in Guatemala, for wisdom *and* for speed. That I have proved, have I not, Deputado?'

'The general always said the bulls of Izabel are best,' Deputado Calejes Cruxiero said to Newbury, 'until he bought this ranch down by the coast . . .'

Newbury jiggled the ice cubes in his glass. 'Management. All depends on management.'

Arena's hand slapped the table. Lyman shifted his eyes from the girl in the pink dress to Arena's fat dark fingers with the gold Citadel ring biting into one. 'Management,' Arena said.

'That's why I'm here,' Newbury said. 'I want to improve *your* management.'

Lyman snickered. 'Progress's our mos' importan' produc'.'

Newbury cracked a grin. 'That's why I asked Howie to join us, always says what he thinks. He's your advisor and he wouldn't recommend that you contract for this matériel unless you need it.'

'But isn't it the Japanese who progress,' said Deputado Caleges Cruxiero, 'while the Americans consume?'

'I talk to many people about my bulls,' Arena said, 'but I am the one who decides what to do with them.'

'And Howie's one of our people—'

'How much is he getting?'

Newbury's chin raised. 'Getting?'

'How much does *Señor* Lyman make on delivery of five hundred of these RPG-7 launchers and ten thousand rockets which he thinks I need?'

Lyman sat forward. 'I don't get nothin'.'

'Come on, *Señor* Lyman – I've been to your house. I see what you drive. You don't do that on GS 14 Agency pay.'

272

'Expanding infrastructures,' Newbury said. 'Electricity, roads, access to television, controlling information properly, gaining unanimity through dependence – that's your task here, General. This matériel will help you do it.'

'Give 'em a good tit to suck on,' Lyman said, 'and few people ever raise their heads to look around.'

Deputado Calejes Cruxiero twirled his cigar against the ashtray, breaking off an even section of ash. 'It's those few . . .'

'Give them a little more tit to suck on,' Lyman answered, 'and they'll be eating out of your hand.'

'So your manual says.'

'And it's good advice,' Newbury said. 'So listen up. Same way Howie's telling you, invest in these launchers – you won't regret it.'

Arena pushed out his lower lip. Like a bull's, Lyman thought. Put a ring in it. 'My problem with your matériel,' Arena said, 'is that *I* have to pay for it.'

'Life's a bitch, General.'

'I need more credits—' Arena was watching the bar. A tall, gangly man in a too-tight business suit was trying to talk to the girl in the pink dress, but she was facing away. Grabbing for her wrist he spilled her glass.

'And the ones that won't suck on your tit,' Newbury was saying, 'them you just have to excise. Sounds cruel but you really have no choice. Kindest thing, best thing, for the society as a whole.'

'You tried that,' Arena said. Lyman noticed that his voice made the table shiver. 'Don't you remember,' Arena said, 'Vietnam?'

The girl snatched her drink and handbag, moved to the next stool. The man followed, tripped, tugged her arm.

Arena moved like a cat in one motion up from the table and across to the bar. 'You want to talk to this guy, *Señorita*?'

'Absolutely not.'

'Then, *hombre*, why are you here?'

The man looked at Arena's medals and stripes, his bull neck and round thick face with its crushed-in wide nose and tiny, merry eyes. 'She's here to be taken.'

'Apparently not by you. You have ten seconds.'

The man scowled drunkenly. 'You don' mean it!'

Arena glanced at the soldiers guarding the door. 'Assuredly I do.'

The man steered a course for the door. '*Gracias, mi general,*' the girl smiled.

'You're expecting someone?'
'No. I just told *him* that, to make him go.'
'It wasn't working, your strategy. May I sit?'

57

Murphy slid his back slowly up the wall. Between his feet, on the tiny, night-lit pool eight storeys below, a swimmer trailed a threadlike silver wake.

He reached steadily for the joint between the side girder and the ledge above; it was too far. Wind came up, rocking him; against his fingertips the concrete was smooth, cold and damp.

There was a rush of air out the window of Lupe's room, the curtains wavering. Through them he saw Lupe come into the room, speaking quickly with Pablo. She crossed to the window, leaned out. 'He's coming up! *Stay* here!' She ducked back into the room, checked the Uzi under the pillow, went to the door, unzipping the side of her dress as Pablo slipped out the window and crouched beside Murphy on the ledge.

'Ready, *amigo*?' Pablo smiled, patting Murphy's arm. Murphy's heart went out to him for caring about another's worry more than his own.

'We're going to do fine,' Murphy said.

'We've got one chance in ten,' Pablo said. '*If* we watch it.'

Arena leaned down over them, jiggling the table. 'Making a couple calls,' he said. 'Be right back.'

Newbury was waving for the waiter. 'Order you another round?'

Arena shook his head. Ugly as a bulldog, Lyman thought. 'I'll get a fresh one when I come down,' Arena said.

'I'm serious about this deal, General,' Newbury said. 'I'd like to wrap it up.'

'Put some money on the table.' Arena stood up. 'You don't expect me to pay—'

'The guerillas are your problem.'

'No, Mr Newbury. The guerrillas are *your* problem.'

'She's a nice little piece,' Lyman said.

When Arena winked it seemed to Lyman like an anus closing.

'We'll see if she can fuck,' Arena said. He motioned to two of his bodyguards and they followed him out of the room.

Through the wavering curtains they saw Lupe move to the door. She stood by it, speaking, then opened it. A tall broad-shouldered man in a greenish suit came in, then a second in blue slacks and grey windbreaker. They spoke with her and she waved behind her at the room. They looked round, under the beds, in the bathroom, the closets. The tall one stopped at the door, feeling her up. She backed away, tossing her head. They went out; Arena came in. She closed the door and slid the chain across. He tossed his jacket on the coffee table and opened the minibar, took out two glasses, ice, a bottle of gin and a bottle of tonic. She went to the bed, turned round with the Uzi in her hands. He was busy making the drinks and looked up suddenly. His hands flattened on the bar, he glanced at the door; she shook her head, speaking fast. Pablo slipped through the window and checked Arena for weapons while she held the Uzi on him. Pablo took a small silver pistol from Arena's coat and made him put the coat on. Lupe put her high heels in her handbag. They came to the window, Lupe speaking gently to Arena, as if counselling him. 'You're going to be just fine, *mi general*, just do what we say. We intend to trade you – you'll go free, so don't worry.'

'They'll give you nothing for me.' He shook his bearish head. 'You're lost.'

'Please listen. You're going with us out this window and down one flight to another room. There's a rope so you won't fall. If you try anything silly, or breathe a sound, we instantly kill you. Is that clear?'

Lupe came first out of the window, over the girder and down. Arena stuck his head through the window, drew back. 'You're going to push me,' he whispered.

'If we were going to kill you,' Pablo said, 'you'd already be dead. Hurry!'

Lupe reached the seventh-floor girder, grasped the rope, leaned out and looked up. Arena squeezed through the window, flinched when he saw Murphy and twisted himself against the wall, away from the edge. 'No.'

Murphy single-cocked the .357. 'Quick!'

Like a seal sinking back into the water, Arena slid over the edge, rope clenched in his great paws. Pablo, then Murphy, followed him down. Murphy climbed back up to untie the rope round the eighth-floor girder and went after Arena and Pablo along the ledge and into his room, 708. He shouldered his backpack and took a last glance round the room, strangely anxious to stay.

'We'll have three guns on you all the time, *mi general*,' Lupe said, 'plus others on the stairs and in the lobby and outside. At the slightest wrong move, even with your eyes, it's over.'

Pablo draped his tuxedo jacket over his arm, holding his Colt inside it. He went out and came back. 'It's clear.' They walked Arena down the corridor. At the elevator an old woman waited, her head perched like an ancient bird over a nest of diamonds. They went past her to the service stairs, a bellboy coming up with a tray of Cokes. 'Too long to wait, the elevator,' Pablo said to him.

Windblown grit scurried in the stair corners. They entered the gleaming lobby, other bellboys advancing then turning away with fixed smiles when they saw there was no luggage. They went out of the staff door, into the parking lot, the .357 sweat-slippery in Murphy's grasp, under his jacket, Arena's arms hanging straight at his sides.

It was the Nissan, shiny with polish. Lupe drove, Murphy in the front, Pablo with Arena in the back. In a dark street Lupe stopped and made Arena change into a brown suit and hat. With a tube of glue she fixed a broad moustache to his face. 'Remove this and you're dead,' she said.

She drove east towards La Ermita. 'You have a wallet with two hundred and twenty quetzales in your left coat pocket,' Pablo told Arena. 'There's a driver's licence that says you are Arturo Valdes Moraga; you're fifty-four, born 21 January. Your wife's Jazmín Elena de Sevilla, you have two boys – Arturo and Alejandro. You have an insurance office in Jalapa, 2-47 Calle Doce. You specialize in life insurance. You live with your family in an apartment over the office. Now let's go over it, fact at a time, till you get it right.'

Arena's lips smacked as he talked. Beyond La Ermita the traffic was thin, feeding out into the dark of the hills.

A string of lanterns blocked the road. Lupe geared down, clamping the Uzi between her legs. 'Pretend you're asleep, *Señor* Valdes,' Pablo said. 'Wake up slowly, just act natural. If there has to be any killing you're the one who dies first.'

'Four on the right,' Lupe said. 'They're Pablo's. One in the middle of the gate. Murphy takes him, then helps Pablo with the ones on the right. Two on the left by the guardhouse and two beyond.

They're mine. Make sure, Pablo, that Arena gets it first.'

'No one's going to get it,' Pablo said.

A soldier yanked open Lupe's door. 'Where to?'

'*Solo* Zacapa.'

'Better hurry!' He slammed the door. 'Or you'll miss curfew.'

Beside the road the Río Motagua coiled and uncoiled in the starlight. Cactus waved from the hills like furtive *compañeros*. The moon rose, bigger than two nights earlier, at the beach, Murphy thought, the Night of the Dead, when we too should have set out a share of our sustenance for our dead.

Lupe turned up a goat road into the hills. It was the same one they'd come down, Dona and he and Lupe and Pablo, and now it was Arena instead of Dona, and to Murphy it seemed a hideous barter he'd somehow deserved, and knew he'd never know why.

58

'*Where* were you going with this American?'

Breathe deeply, steadily. Don't look what they're doing. Steadily. Don't look. She was ready but it made no difference, the electric agony darted up her arm, crushing her lungs, seared into her skull. The air afire; tears boiling in her eyes, every last cell begging it to stop.

'I'm no torturer, *compañera*. But I *need* to know . . .'

The current burned faster, a white atomic flash eating through her at the speed of light; air exploded in her cells, her bones screamed. The words were in her throat but she couldn't choke them out.

'I'm trying to *save* you. Once DTI gets you it's over, *compañera*. They'll really *hurt* you. Just give me something, dear, please? So I can keep you out of their hands?'

The G-2 man sighed. His chair legs banged down in front of her face. 'Drop the juice, Hermanito. She's cooked.'

His boot came down on her neck as he reached for an instrument on the table. By the sounds of the instruments against the table she could tell them all apart – the electric probe with its soft thump, the knife that rattled, the bigger one that didn't, the long needle that tinkled, the other long needle with the wires attached, the other wires, their clamps, the drill, its different bits, the cigarette lighter – just a little butane lighter, anybody'd have one—

The G-2 man handed the instrument to Hermano. 'Index left, Hermanito. Come come, *compañera*, don't ball your little fists! That's it, Hermano, get a good hold, twist! Twist! Side to side, do you like that, *compañera*? Gently, Hermano, not too fast! Now, *compañera* – who's the American?'

Cyclone of pain, jaws of agony crushing her arm, a train wheel riding into her body as Hermano in his big white uniform took a better grip with the yellow needle-nosed pliers that said 'Case' on one jaw, phosphorous exploding inside her, and she must have deprived them terribly, these men, for them to do this, just block the synapse, you can do it – it's only integument separating from the lunule, membranes splitting, cells ripping down their walls, electric cries up the ganglia, my brain converting them like a speaker does electric signals, Oh Jesus please help me O Dear Father.

'Harder now, Hermanito! You should see her face ...'

It was coming out now and she begged it to hurry, the fingernail, realized she was choking and made her neck relax against the chain clamping it to the metal frame on which she lay, felt the warm relief of blood welling down her knuckles.

'This grieves me, *compañera*. I'm sick. I hate a world that's forced to do this. Please help me – please?'

The boot that smelled so strongly of cordovan polish lurched back from her sight and came zooming forward but she'd made allowances, told herself stop screaming the cheekbone's not broken, her stupid nose pouring its weakness on the ground – stop pulling the arms back, it chokes the chain. His boot crunched again into her jaw, and she begged dear God please do it quickly.

Hills jumped up from the Nissan's lights, a sawmill's dark windows flickered, a white goat gleamed red eyes in a town named Matanzas – Massacres; the road climbed north into fog then rain, pines teetering out of the black. Even with the windows open the car smelled of Arena.

A man and burro shied from the lights. A few huts, flash of dog's eyes, then jungle, frenzy of tree frogs, thunder of rain pelting billions of leaves, water chanting in ditches, pines moaning in the wind. Another town leaped from the mist – Niño Perdido – Lost Child – a few huts miserably ragged in the rain, brown run-off sluicing between them.

Beyond Cobán, Lupe turned east, away from the Army Base, and picked up the road to San Pedro Carchá, up and down through cut-over jungle, skunks and raccoons scuttling from the lights, down a long hill and left over a bridge, a river and banana trees below, through the main square where topiary shrubs threw leaping shadows across the façade of the ruined cathedral, down a soggy alley of shuttered shops and rats loping for cover, two men arm-in-arm shielding their eyes from the lights, then a weedy track past bedraggled huts and into a stone shed with a tin roof and a rusty garage door.

280

Lupe shut the door and lit a candle on an upended engine block. She and Pablo gagged Arena with her pink silk scarf and took him outside to piss. They tied his wrists behind him and Lupe blew out the candle.

Outside the stars were afire. Lupe turned uphill and Pablo led Arena and Murphy down to the chilled, mushy riverbank. The *río* churned round a half-sunk trunk cab, in its lee a canoe tethered, river chill up their thighs as they climbed in, Arena in the middle, Pablo poling downriver, the stars bobbing on the current, black sandbars sparkling, a chain of cormorants scattering white wakes ahead, occasionally the smell of drying fish, humans and ordure where a hut stood by the bank.

The smoke of morning's first fires came upriver, the river dropping into a deep *cañon*, the jungle gone to raw slopes, lights scattered among huts.

Pablo poled ashore and ran them up a slippery steep trail to a tin-roofed shack, unlocked the padlock, and Murphy pushed Arena ahead of him into the room, shut the door. Holding a flashlight in his teeth, Pablo dragged bundled banana clumps from the middle of the floor, under them a trapdoor with a rope ladder down to a pit hollowed from the earth, rootlets like white earthworms down its walls, on one side a mat and red blanket and a white plastic pail.

Pablo lit a kerosene lantern. He made Arena sit on the rush mat then tied his wrists behind him to a thick root. Cross-legged on fat thighs, Arena rubbed his chin against his shoulder, hunched forward, straining his bonds. Pablo loosened the pink scarf and held a bottle of water for him to suck.

Arena drank some water and spat the last on Pablo's leg. 'Kill me now,' he said. He ran his tongue over his upper front teeth, grimaced. 'They'll give you nothing for me.'

Pablo retied the gag. 'If he does anything, shoot him in the head.' He climbed the rope ladder, opened the trapdoor, climbed out and shut it.

Arena hunched cross-legged, trickling sweat, eyes prowling, trouser knees stretched tight, feet big in muddy, river-soaked shoes.

He jerked his chin: come here. Murphy stood, went closer. Arena mumbled through his gag, nodding his chin down, pointing with it. Murphy moved back, shaking his head. Arena growled louder, eyes wide.

The .357's grooved trigger felt nice against the inside of

Murphy's finger. 'Just give me a reason,' he said.

There were footsteps and the door lifted, daylight dropping in. Lupe came down the rope ladder. 'Go up,' she said, ignoring his smile.

59

Pablo was not there. Through cracks in the walls Murphy watched the daylight grow between the mountain avocados contorted like frozen dancers round the shack, silver sphagnum like torn garments hanging from their arms. From one side of the shack he could see the grey sparkle where the river rounded a brown abutment of cliffs. Below were the glossy crowns of riparian trees, uphill a red-muddy slope, and beyond it a few huts trailing thin smoke, a woman with a burro going down to the river.

White sun flamed through the boughs. From below a rooster called; from above another answered. A mule brayed disconsolately. The air grew hot. A huge black beetle rattled in corner cornhusks. Flies sparkled through shafts of sunlight. Blackbirds chattered, toucans croaked. The tin roof creaked as the sun bore down. Acaris called, 'Fe-liz, Fe-liz'; the incessant wail of tree frogs like the river's steady rustle faded in and out of mind.

Lupe came up and Murphy went down. Arena squatted like an apostate buddha on his mat. The floor above creaked as Lupe paced it. The air stank of kerosene; the dirt walls sweated in the lantern's light.

There was motion upstairs and Lupe came down. Murphy went up and Pablo was there. 'We'll see,' he said.

'They *have* her?'

'Don't know. She's on our list – the ones they have to give us.'

'Will they?'

'If they don't find us first. Dona didn't know this place. She didn't know this part.'

'You mean they can't torture it out of her.'

'That's what I said.'

Lupe came up. 'He wants to use the bucket.'

Murphy and Pablo went down. Murphy loosened Arena from the wall and he stood suddenly and jerked off his gag, rubbing his face and mouth with his big flat hands, swinging his head

283

from side to side. He bent to untie his ankles. 'No,' Pablo said. 'Use it like that.'

Arena pulled the bucket to him, unbuckled his trousers and squatted down on the bucket, his urine spattering in, then great soft plops. Murphy held his breath. 'You have no hygienic paper?' Arena said.

'No.'

'Pigs!' Arena stood and hitched his trousers, smacked out the lantern and knocked Pablo into the wall and Murphy slugged him with the Magnum and Arena punched him in the crotch and the gun boomed, smashing his ears, flames darting up from the spilt kerosene. Daylight leaped down as Lupe jumped into the pit and whacked the Uzi on Arena's head and he fell, grabbing at her, and she hit his temple and he eased down on to his face, blood pumping from his thigh.

'We're cooked,' Lupe said. Pablo threw Arena's blanket over the spilled kerosene, relit the wick. He retied Arena's wrists behind him; he and Murphy turned Arena over and Murphy cut off Arena's powder-burned trouser leg and slit it for a compress, wrap and tourniquet. Arena's thigh was thick as a man's waist, mottled brown. His broken femur crunched.

'He hit the gun,' Murphy said.

'We should go now,' Lupe said.

'Not till night,' Pablo answered. 'How you going to move *him*?'

Lupe went up. Arena's head hammered the floor, his other leg quivering, teeth grinding. 'That was very foolish, General,' Pablo said. 'Now you may die.'

With two planks from the trapdoor Murphy splinted the thigh. He wrapped it, tighter. 'Can you hear, pig?'

Arena gasped, nodded. Murphy loosened the wrapping. 'That better?'

Arena nodded. Murphy wrenched it tighter, Arena's teeth bared. 'No!'

'San Tomás – up on the Río de la Pasión – who attacked it?'

'N'not mine – General Blandia's—'

Pablo stood over them. 'General Blandia's in Santa Cruz.'

Murphy clenched his hand to keep it from punching the wound. 'I'll twist this leg right off . . .'

'Easy,' Pablo whispered.

Murphy waved him away. 'Tell me quick, San Tomás—'

'I don't know. I didn't oh please God stop this pain. You have anything, please anything, stop it?'

'The Americans with your units – who are they?'

'No – oh God Jesus – no Americans!'

'We have *aquardiente* – want some?'

Arena nodded, eyes wide, sweat and tears pouring down his cheeks. Pablo uncorked the bottle.

'Wait.' Murphy took the rum. 'Tell me right, the first time. I know most of the story, just need you to fill me in. Tell it right the first time and you can have rum. Tell me one lie and I pour it down the hole in your leg.'

'You're not even Guatemalan—'

'The Americans – *who*?'

'*Me duele mucho!* Wait!'

'*Who!*'

'Advisors, Jesus!'

'*Who?*'

'Counterinsurgency. The Agency. You know this!'

'Who burnt my village?'

'God it hurts.' Spittle ran down Arena's chin. 'Want to know who burned your lousy little village, wherever in hell it is? *You* did.' He coughed; it sounded like a laugh. 'Your *own* country. God did, then – maybe you like that better?'

'I want the *names*.'

'*Who* pays your taxes? *Who* votes? How many times have we been invaded by *your* Marines? Who changes our government like a whore changes underpants! Who changes your own government, whenever it wants? Kills your president and his brother and gets away with it?' Again the croaked laugh stiffened by pain. 'It's fools like you, make the world such a dangerous place.'

'*Tell* me. Or to hell with it all I'll kill you.'

'Easy, *amigo*,' Pablo said.

'You really *are* a fool,' Arena gasped. 'Don't you *know*, what really runs things?'

'Who's telling you to hit the drug flights?'

'Can't you see – same answer . . . snuffing the independents—'

Wind guttered the lantern; the trapdoor opened; daylight dived down. 'Pablo!' Lupe whispered.

'She's not in here.' Lyman shoved the folder of photos back at Vodega. 'Not the one who trapped Arena.'

Vodega opened a new dossier, tossed another photo across the table.

Lyman sipped his coffee. Beyond the window soldiers were doing

285

an arms drill in the yard. The photo was a young woman, hair cropped, face and lips puffy, eyes bruised, nearly closed. 'Not her, either.'

Vodega smiled. 'This one we've got. Murphy's *chica*.'

'The *doctora*?' Lyman dropped the photo and stared at it. 'Just think – his whole world's come down around his ears. She was all he had left—'

'Sad.'

'—except Arena.'

'They want a Mexico exchange. Theirs released first.'

Vodega peeled down a fingernail, gnawed it.

'Tell them legally you can't. Offer them close to the border.'

Vodega smiled. 'If it's provisional Mexico will get very pissed.'

'Fuck them. Don't you want Murphy?'

'Not like you do. I think you have a screw loose about this dude.'

'We *all* need him dead, Angelo. He's in everybody's way.'

'Yours more than anyone else's. Why?'

Lyman looked at Vodega. Yes, he thought, sometimes you can be frank even with people you don't like. 'I want out, Angelo. The Agency won't let me go until the pilot's done.'

Lyman tipped up the photo, smiled at the swollen gaze of one who knows all that's coming is unending agony then death. He felt his sex stir. 'Suppose he knew her, from before . . .?'

'He was shot up, she fixed him. In that village where we got the priest.'

'He never gave you much, that priest—'

'He's not done yet.'

She could have been pretty, the one in the photo. Nice small tits, slim waist, nice hips and long legs with one thigh half-raised trying to cover herself. Sweet bruised skin. Key to Murphy's heart.

Through a crack in the shed wall Murphy watched the patrol coming house to house down the hill. 'Three more below!' Lupe said. 'No, five.'

'We'll tell them to pull back,' Murphy said, 'or we kill him.'

Pablo came up, took the Uzi. 'Beat it!'

She looked at Murphy distractedly, back at Pablo, gripping his hands. 'At the end, please, let them take you? You'll be on the list.'

Pablo clasped her face in his hands for an instant, like a prayer. She reached for him but he pushed her away, towards the rope ladder. 'Go!' he told Murphy, his eyes fierce.

'Better we cover them from here—'

'There's a tunnel down there and you're taking him through it. Go!'

Beneath the ladder Lupe had pushed aside the dirt to a second trapdoor, a black core down into the earth. 'You're going to have to crawl one-legged,' she yelled at Arena. She turned angry eyes on Murphy. 'You first!'

'What about Pablo?'

'Somebody's got to stay behind, cover this up, stall them.'

With a roar Murphy leaped back up the stairs. Pablo was watching the soldiers climbing from below.

'Get down there!' Murphy yelled. His chest was shaking, he couldn't breathe. 'I'll shoot you! Get down there!'

Pablo ran to the other side of the shack, peered at the soldiers coming down through the huts. 'We've got two minutes.'

'You son of a bitch, I'll shoot you!' Murphy's gun was shaking badly and he held his right wrist in his left hand to steady it.

Pablo looked into his eyes. 'Perhaps it's better.'

Lupe went first, Arena dragging his leg, moaning through his gag, then Pablo. Murphy shut the trap and shoved the loose dirt and straw back over it, scattered dirt and straw over Arena's blood.

'*Hola!*' A man's voice. 'Anyone in this house come out!'

Murphy went up, shut the top trap. 'Men!' The voice called, 'I'll count ten then you fire on the hut. Cut it apart! One . . .'

Smooth snicks of steel as the soldiers readied their guns. Murphy dragged the first banana clump back over the trap.

'Three . . .'

He threw them one on top of the other.

'Seven!'

'*Hola!*' Murphy yelled, stacking the last ones, '*Hola! Hola!*'

'Get out here!'

He shoved the Magnum into the banana clumps and opened the door. Arms up, he went out into the bright hot sun, waiting for the bullets to hit.

60

'You're not going to believe this—'

'Not if *you* tell me, Howie.'

'We have him.'

'Fantastic! Safe?'

'Not Arena, goddamnit – Murphy! His chickie too.'

Merck said nothing, then, 'Where?'

'Right under my feet.'

'Where the Hell's Arena?'

'Murphy may know. Where we got him there was a tunnel – we think some others, maybe Arena, went out it.'

'Where?'

'Goes uphill to empty houses.'

'You mean you didn't *secure* the area?'

'I wasn't *there*, Curt. Be happy with what you get.'

'What's he said?'

'That he was hanging out in this deserted hut.'

'Crush his fucking nuts!'

'He's holding.'

'He made us a lot of trouble in San Francisco, this guy.'

'Soon as we finish talking with him it's over.'

'We *need* Arena back, Howie. They took him right from under your nose.'

'I'm not his bodyguard—'

'You *trained* those two guys! And they're jerking each other off while your friends go out the window with Arena. How you think that looks up here?'

'I'm not your PR guy, either.'

Merck caught his breath, like a puppy, Lyman thought, that's been tearing at something. Pant pant. 'For now be happy with what you got,' Lyman said. 'You got Murphy, his chickie – she's one of their best doctors, a fucking surgeon—'

'I don't *care* from no doctors, Howie. I certainly don't care from

288

no pilot. What I *care* about's Arena. Think what we've invested.
What we have to gain. He's too good to lose, and *you* lost him.'

'He's not lost yet.'

'Even if he isn't, you gotta give up a whole lot of people. People
you ain't finished with.'

'Not if we get Arena first.'

'If you *do* have to trade, Howie – don't fight too much about
the numbers. If they want two hundred people then give them
two hundred . . .'

'Lotta people they're asking for don't live here any more.'

'Give 'em others. Go get new ones and give them to them. Trick
is, get back Arena. We get him back we can ride a sympathy vote
in Congress to more appropriations—'

'I don't know what's worse, Curt. The guerrillas or the Hill.'

'How we talking with the ones who've got Arena?'

'Pay-phones to pay-phones. They're moving too fast to catch—'

'Think of what we been through, this Russia thing. Think
what *I* been through, my family. Seventy years of lost lives,
millions of lost lives. All because, back in '17, we didn't grab
ourselves by the balls and jump in!'

'Like Nam?'

'We *took* Nam, Howie! For over ten years we kept the wheels
turning! Kept a stable balance.'

'I thought the idea was win—'

'Win? That's what we got now, Russia, all that. You call that
a win?' Merck stopped, to sip his coffee maybe, three thousand
miles away. 'Nam taught you all the wrong lessons, Howie. You
go slow where you should run and run where you should hide.
I wonder maybe the Agency's too *into* you. Maybe I shouldna given
you, you know, such a hand-up?'

'It's your nuts I'm saving down here. Long before this Arena
thing. This pilot thing.'

'You're not saving anybody's nuts. You could lose yours. It
happened under *your* nose. You playing for *their* team?'

'You're beginning to piss me off.'

Merck laughed. 'Being pissed off counts for nothing in this
world.'

In the pine grove was a spring between black rocks where blue
sayune flowers, violets, and red wild begonias grew. There were
water-spiders on the spring and the water was achingly cold and
the cool resiny air rose up the bronze trunks into the golden day.

289

'*Tell* me,' said the first G-2 man. '*Where* are Lupe and Pablo?'
'She's stalling again,' said the other. 'Let's do some teeth.'

'You flew slicks for the United States of America! That's your *country*! What you doing tied all up in *this* shit?'

He was tall and very black, trace of southern accent, Levis, muddy running shoes, a work shirt.

'You're the one that hit my village. I know you. You're the one.'

'Man, you're not making *any* sense—'

'The whole village. Little children, old people, everybody.' Murphy pulled himself along the bars till the chain held him. 'The people in the river. A woman and a brand-new baby and a fourteen-year-old boy . . .'

The black man drew up a stool in the corridor, tilted his head to see between the bars. 'I don't know you from Adam. I know nothing 'bout no village and people in no river. I'm just Second Secretary at the American Embassy in GC, and *I'm* the one that gets called when some American gets his ass in deep shit. But in order to get you *out* of this very deep shit you're in, I first need to know why you're *in* it.'

'There was an old woman, Consuela. There were little children—'

'You getting crazy 'gain, brother. I don't know *anything* 'bout none of this old woman stuff.' The black man leaned into the bars. 'But I do know you're in some very deep shit up in the States, in *addition* to the very, very deep shit you're obviously in down here. So what the fuck you *done*?'

'Who *are* you?'

'I told you—'

'You don't even *know* who you are! Oh yes you do.'

'I know I got to hustle to keep the Guatemalan Army from just *wrecking* you. That's understandable, they want Arena. But instead of ripping you apart they might be persuaded to free you, wherever you want to go, with some money to go on. If you help them find Arena—'

61

There were three and they wasted no time. They tied her hands
up to the bar behind her. They stretched her tight between the
bar and the wires round her ankles and two held her mouth open
while the third took a Black & Decker drill and drilled into the
root of one lower molar. He curled the end of an electrode and
shoved it down into the root. He went behind her and drilled a
second hole into the base of her spine and twisted an electrode
into it. They wired her head so she couldn't shake it and snapped
on the grey US Army field telephone clamped to the electrodes,
and turned up the gauge.

'I just talked with the top guy here,' the black man said through
the bars. 'They've got her in custody down in Antigua. They
were going to let her go – you should've kept your mouth shut.
Now they know she's with you, that she's part of this Arena
thing—'
  'Let her go. Then I'll tell you whatever you want.'
  Two soldiers unlocked the door and the black man and a
smaller younger man in a maroon blazer came in, trying to step
lightly in the muck. 'This's Carmen here,' the black man said,
'he's the Embassy translator. My Spanish ain't so great . . .'
  'Jesus,' Carmen said, 'what they do to you?' He bent down,
looked into Murphy's face. 'Oh my God Jesus, what did they do?'
  'We gotta move quick,' the black man said. 'They're going to
ruin him.'
  'Pigs.' Carmen bit his lip. 'Goddamned pigs!'
  The black man knelt down. 'Listen, pal, you gotta come straight.'
He shook his head. 'Otherwise I can't help you.'
  'Have to get him out of here—' Carmen glanced round. 'You!'
he said to one of the soldiers. 'Get a stretcher. We're going to
move this man upstairs.' The soldier backed away, shook his
head.

291

'I've tried,' Lyman said. 'The Guats say no. Their jurisdiction.'

Carmen leaned near. 'You want me to tell them not to hurt her? To be ready to let her go, with you? That you're going to tell them where to find Arena?'

Murphy's words were like chunks of splintered stick coming out of his mouth. There was cool air all over his skin, as if he were going to faint. After a while, he thought, pain is its own drug. 'First let her go . . .'

The black man's face came at him. 'Tell *us* and they'll send you and her to Mexico, Cuba, anywhere you want. They do it all the time, these trades—'

'They'll even broadcast an amnesty,' Carmen said, 'so your friends can give up Arena without bloodshed. So they can go with you.'

'No one knows who you are except us,' the black man said. 'We're the only friends you have—'

'Guatemala's gone through too much,' Carmen added, 'it's on the road to democracy now, it doesn't need this suffering, this reminder.'

'I'm afraid they're going to hurt somebody else,' said the black man. 'I've seen how these people work. If you don't talk.'

'They've got somebody,' Carmen said. 'Somebody you know. You probably shouldn't have told them about that village, where you were . . . Now, I'm afraid, they're going to do him harm.'

'They killed everybody there.'

'When it comes to torture,' the black man whispered, 'the Guats can't be touched. For thirty years they've been trained by the best. Can make you suffer endlessly and never die. Remember your Revelations: how you'll long for death, but death will elude you?'

They dragged her from the white soundproof room down a cement corridor of white solid steel doors through a cell-block where naked women gripped the bars whispering but she could not hear, down another corridor of mould-green damp concrete to a rancid stone room with a steel door in the centre of the floor. One knelt beside her. 'Last chance. We need *names*.'

She looked up at him, and at the end of all things she understood, *him*, the agony he could not expiate. 'That is the problem. I have no names.'

He yanked open the steel door, dragged her over the edge. Her head fell into the hole; she scrambled for the memory that was *all*, made it all true, tumbling down and slamming head- and shoulder-first into icy muck, thinking the steel door shutting was the noise of her head hitting; her head was under, she pulled it up. There was air, mud cool against her skin. Oh God, she thought, I'm saved. I've got away.

The pain was bigger than his body, than this corroded, sweating room. He saw the curve of the earth from the sandspit – the pain was bigger than the sea, the earth, filled all space, erased the stars; you could scream it louder than the universe but it would never go away.

They asked him questions and were very angry and others came and asked the same questions and he begged them for answers to give them, the answers they wanted, these men with their uniforms and white coats and hard hands, but he didn't know the answers they wanted and wouldn't tell the ones he had, thinking they won't know, but they knew, they kept knowing, even when he did not say, they seemed to know.

The black man came in. 'One o'clock,' he said in Spanish. He rubbed his face, a whiskery sound.

The darkness was absolute, the air like mud. A gurgle of new sewage cascaded into the pit; she held her breath, wiped the muck from her face. The sides of the pit were too slimy to climb, even if her hands could do it.

Something moved, a snake, in the sludge. Kill me quickly. Moving – an arm? Yes an arm, a face. Long hair, thick with muck. 'You—' Dona said. 'Speak to me!'

A hand touched her face, the pain intense. The woman mumbled.

'Who are you?' Dona said.

Again the mumble.

'Can I move you, help you?' She slipped her arms under the woman's, pushed her up. 'You've been here how long – tell me!'

'____'

'I can't understand you – here, let me feel your mouth, it's clogged with mud.' She wiped muck from the woman's face; there were no eyes. The woman's head jerked back as Dona felt inside her mouth: no teeth, no tongue. Dona skimmed water from the muck and washed the woman's face, brushed back her hair. 'I will ask you questions, yes or no questions. Make a sound if it is yes. You are Quiché? No? Ladino? Yes?' She tilted back the

293

woman's head, cleaned the mud from her ears. 'Not long will they keep me here. So tell me what I can do for you . . .'

62

They took him to a cell with plywood walls. A child sat on a wooden chair, two men in black hoods behind him. Dark hair, skinny arms, one bright with burns. Ankles and arms clamped to the chair. Jesús.

'You wouldn't do this. Not even you—'

'It's their turf,' the black man said. 'Kid's not American, nothing we can do. Only you can stop it.'

'Even *you* wouldn't do this.'

'We need answers,' said a man with a thin moustache and side-burns. 'You're making us do this. You're the evil one.'

Two men came down the sewer on ropes and tied another rope under Dona's arms. 'Bring *her* up too!' she said.

'Who?'

'Her! This woman whose tongue you've cut out – she's still alive.'

'There's no one here but you, madwoman.'

They hosed her down in a bright, tiled room. One pinned her to the floor while the other felt up inside her, back and front, pulled down his pants, his flesh like stone inside her.

They chained her to the wall and left. Sperm dribbled down her thigh. They came back with a stooped, portly man in his sixties in a white lab coat. He shut the door softly behind him, checked a clipboard, shined a small flashlight in her eyes. 'So! The young doctor!' He had a conscientious manner, smile wrinkles at the corners of his eyes, wire-rim glasses, a little grey moustache and a kindly mouth. A bureaucrat, she wondered, prison inspector – anything, there's hope . . . he nodded at her, her torturers, glanced at his watch. 'Pick up tempo,' he said, and left.

'Arena's in a warehouse above Carchá – an adobe warehouse with a tin roof, banana trees.'

'There's no banana trees above Carchá, Mr Murphy. The

295

elevation's too high. We will now spoon out one of the boy's eyes. *You* choose, Mr Murphy: right or left?'

The man with the thin moustache and sideburns held up the spoon like a magician ready to perform a well-known trick. A soldier unclipped the electrodes from Jesús's fingers and tipped back his chair, the boy's head rolling; the man took it one-handed and with a flick of his wrist dipped the spoon into and under the boy's eye; the boy sat up screaming. 'Tell us?' the man said.

He told them how he'd flown down, stumbled on the village, the boy'd done nothing, knew nothing, just a kid, but they wouldn't listen, refused his lies, refused his truths because they weren't enough, didn't go all the way. The man with the thin moustache spooned out the other eye too; it hung down Jesús's cheek on its connective tissue like a baby squid; Murphy's wrists were bloody from trying to break the cuffs, his arms nearly torn from the sockets, but it did no good, nothing did any good. Die, Jesús, he prayed, urging him along, it's not that hard, child, die quickly now, die from shock, die from pain, die. Over the boy's upraised, pleading face the man with the thin moustache slid his plastic bag, the boy's mouth sucked it taut, his ribs heaving.

In the corner of the floor was a scrap of red Indiana – a Kekchi girl's bracelet. On the wall splashes of blood and the words, 'Boise Cascade'.

'It's on *your* soul,' said the man with the thin moustache. 'This death.'

With rifle butts they beat him along a corridor into a cell. It was too small to stand or lie except diagonally across a sewer hole. Wind down the corridor swayed a bulb hung by its wires, the shadows of the bars sliding back and forth.

From the other cells came moans, weeping, a far-off solitary cough that made it seem for an instant this might be a hospital. In the next cage a man lay with legs bent, an emaciated, white-bearded face. He shoved himself up, wiped dribble from his mouth and squirmed his hand through the bars. 'My God! It's *you!*'

Murphy took the frail, wet hand. '*Hola, compañero.*'

'Don't you remember? It's me, Father Miguel!'

'You got nine hours.'

'The Guats'll stretch it.'

'*Can* you find Arena in nine hours, Howie? That's the question.'

'I'll do my best.'

'You know what I think of people's best? It's never good enough.'

'That's a problem with you, Curt. You're too tight on people—'

'You call this tight, Howie? We ask you to carry on Kit's work, and you don't succeed in raising contributions. We ask you to explain to Arena the tactical value of pulling in the Colombians and you've seemed to fail at that too. Then Arena gets kidnapped on your watch—'

'I wasn't assigned to *watch* him!'

'He's your *baby*. How many times I have to explain this with you?'

'Explain it *to* me, Curt?'

'Call it how you like. But you don't find Arena before noon, Howie, things are going to be bad on you.'

'You threatening me?'

'You know what I'm doing—'

'You don't want to, Curt. Not like you did with Kit. I'm ready for that. You'll all get hurt. Badly hurt.'

'You're back in your private agenda again, Howie. Your private traumas. You got nine hours to find Arena. Safe and sound. Any hope you ever had of getting out of the field depends on this. You don't get Arena back, Howie, you're stuck with us forever.'

Lyman put down the receiver and lit a cigarette. Nine minutes past three a.m. First one of the day. Still keep it at ten. Twelve yesterday, eleven before, but most of last week ten. Normal, hands to shake like this. Too cold. Cold in here.

Three eleven. Feel the smoke like brandy in your soul. Rising fire in your brain. Lovely scented leaf with the power of the sun.

He locked the MACRO room door and went through the three sets of doors and outside. The night hung heavy and cold, the stars like Christmas lights.

'You're lucky,' Father Miguel said. 'It's better to be shot right away—'

Down the aisle a man was coughing, shallow and repetitive. Picking blood from his stubble, Murphy watched a cockroach select its delicate way across the sewage on the floor. 'It's pathetic, the way you try not to hate.'

'We've had our time for hating and wanting and running

around. Now it's time to thank God and live in peace with what's left. You know that—'

'Who the Hell *is* that, coughing? Why doesn't he stop?'

The cough was like a pendulum: cough-cough . . . cough-cough . . .

'It's an old man, Santana. They're shooting him too.'

Through the canopy and rotor blur the Mekong sky is porcelain blue. Five thousand feet below are the verdant, evil hills. Okie scanning right, chewing gum. Always chewing gum. Okie's black helmet with the Grateful Dead painted on one side and the Chicago Bears on the other.

Back on the deck three grunts, an ARVN intelligence man and a Special Forces captain with a woman prisoner and a little girl. Slick riding the thermals, appreciative flutter from the blades, Okie popping gum. The Special Forces captain shoves up between Murphy and Okie. 'These people don't have no feelin's,' he says.

The Special Forces captain has tears in his eyes, from the wind. 'I been asking her some questions, me and Dao here, and Dao was holding her kid out the door, you know, to make her talk? The stupid fucker drops the kid and the woman just sits there, not a change in her face. Fuckin' animals!'

'Take it,' Murphy screams at Okie. He unbuckles and climbs through to the deck. 'You did what?'

'He dropped her by accident, Dao did. Don't get unbent.'

Dao holding the woman by the hair, a .45 against the side of her face. She is looking out the door.

Murphy takes out his pistol; the Special Forces captain shakes his head. 'You're getting out of line, trooper—'

Dao speaks in Vietnamese, turns the .45, ready to fire at Murphy. The grunts stir, reaching for rifles. The captain steps back.

That was it. The moment it all went bad, the moment that led to this. When you should have shot him and you didn't. Then came the court martial but they didn't win so they sent you into the very worst, every time you and Okie, Okie chewing gum, every time a jet was down and Charlie was waiting, every hot LZ, till Okie got it, and they gave you Searles, and then Finkelstein, and when he got it and you got wounded for the second time they gave up and sent you home.

63

'It isn't wrong,' the priest said. 'Trying to make a better world.'

'I wasn't trying to make a better world,' Murphy answered. 'I was trying to please myself.'

'We all do that. Even God did that – inventing us. Though why I'll never know. Or perhaps I shall.' He coughed; it sounded like a laugh. 'You took on too much: the Army, your own government – that's like trying to battle God. I use that word too easily, God. I'm not sure I believe in God.'

'Then why are you a priest?'

'Because here it was the best way to do something, to make a better world. And because I loved Christ, believed in what he said, about how to live and how to treat each other.'

'All I've learned is that the world is evil . . .'

'You were like a bird caught in a hurricane, there was nothing you could do. There was your government supporting a fascist dictatorship, as it nearly always does. And you were smuggling drugs – a role they didn't want to share with anyone but the Guatemalan Army and, as you say, the Colombians. So your intelligence agency, with the help of your Mafia, hunted you down, killing a lot of Guatemalans in the process—'

'That's what I've learned: every attempt to do good only brings more evil. But I wasn't even trying to do good. I cared more about my so-called love than the person I loved.'

Again the priest coughed. 'That's love. Even God does that.'

Footsteps echoed down the stairs to their cells. The black man positioned himself before Murphy's. 'I can stop them,' he said. Murphy dropped his head, uninterested. 'I can get your woman.'

Murphy looked up. 'You could have stopped them long ago. You always could have.'

'I was home in bed with my wife when this village of yours got hit. If it ever did.'

'That's not true.' It was an old, worn voice, Guat accent, the

299

next cell. A small, skinny man, hair tangled and white. 'You *were* there, when his village got attacked.'

'Who the hell are you?'

'*I* saw you. Don't you remember, the helicopter? When you kept the one named Angelo from kicking out my teeth?'

The black man peered down at Father Miguel, chuckled. 'That's what comes of good deeds. I should've dropped you out the door.'

'But you didn't. You stopped him from kicking me. Why?'

'Might have needed you later. You turned out not to be worth much.'

The priest smiled. 'Most of us aren't. How about you?'

Lyman laughed. 'Not much, either. Call it fate.'

'It isn't fate. You don't have to live this way. None of us does.'

'You won't much longer—' Lyman leaned back against the far cell, arms crossed. 'And after you're dead there isn't even going to be a *trace* of you.'

'Think back over all the years and all the pain it's caused you, think of all the love you've had to throw away—'

'I'm down here to ask *him* one last time . . .'

'There's no good in asking. You know that.'

'For *his* sake. Can't you see you've made your rules too strong?'

'The rules are inside you. That's why you fight them so hard. The rule never to hurt people is engraved right on your soul. And every breath you take, you can feel it.'

Lyman stretched, arms behind his head. 'I'm going upstairs, get some sleep. They'll wake me when you're dead.'

Santana's incessant hack through the bars. A man snoring, another gasping in a dream. From somewhere upstairs came faint moans and begging voices. On the cell's concrete back wall so many names carved in the khaki-coloured slime: José Maria Montejos, 4-4-51—11-11-90. Gloria Casales, 19-10-57—4-91, Jaime Aidaño, how many others, names with new names carved atop them, names old in the stone?

He could leave his own body and stand beside them, *in* them, think their thoughts and feel what they felt as they carved the day of their deaths into the damp cold stone. Brothers, sisters – we are all the same body and the same blood. For there's only two human families – prisoners and guards. He imagined them, with sweaty, numb fingers, digging a piece of metal into the stone, thinking how the bullets would feel.

Tick tick ticktick tick as water dripped from the ceiling into

300

the muck of the floor. Did you stare into the muzzles? See the flash?

Curious but timid, a rat ducked its head through the bars, darted over his foot and down the sewer hole. She said to live a good life you have to do as much good as you can. He folded his fingers, felt the pulse between them. Blanched, frightened skin.

A rooster crowed but it couldn't be dawn. Wakened by a weasel, something. Santana's cough was like a man trying to remind you of something. There's no time, Santana, to be reminded. It doesn't matter, your cough.

Stuck on a car fender, little kid. Father gets you down. He could see it, feel the bees stinging, rough grass. Walking by the road, skipping rocks across it. Fingers stuck with cold to the rifle barrel, whitetail diving over the ridge, crack of the Winchester splitting the sky. Girls in the back seat pulling down their pants, windows of frozen breath. Gulls over the sandspit, scream of the sea. Rites of love all come to nothing. Man just another seed eating out its heart to populate the stars.

A truck, starting. Couldn't be. You can live it all in the next two hours. The whole thing. Live it fast. Don't be afraid. Accept it's coming and be ready to meet it.

Bell. Two. Three. Four. Five. Let it not be six, Lord.

Six. Somewhere a generator shuddered, took life. Boots tramping, wail of a gate. Pure water of the Sun River down off the Chinese Wall through lodgepole and meadow, down in swirls of light, red-gilled trout, grass buff like elkhide. Sonora cactus *cañons*, the air a hot knife. Dawn rising over the world at fifty thousand feet. Scents of love and flowers and blood, fresh blood of a kill and old blood between a woman's legs and dried blood of people lying on the ground, one's own miraculous blood spreading over the dirt.

Pain travels at the speed of light.

An officer and soldiers came softly down the aisle. They opened Santana's cell and led him out, confused and disarrayed. Then Father Miguel. 'So you're really going to do it,' he said. They tied Murphy's wrists with rope and led the three of them back up the oily green stairwell that Murphy could not remember descending. He saw everything clearly, every grain of concrete and flake of rust, the scintillating windows and the stars dying behind them, years passing in a moment, a marred boot heel rising on the stair before him, Santana's threadbare sandal slap slap, when he had looked into her eyes and in them had seen the sun in his own. The wall, a cold rail, brushed him, click of opening door, snap of rifles, long lean wall of pockmarked earth, cavitied with stains, three wooden posts before it.

One soldier came close. 'You want the blindfold, *hombre*?'

He shook his head. 'Where do you shoot?'

'Straight for the heart.'

'*Amigo*—'

'*Sí*?'

'Don't shoot me in the head—'

'You'll feel nothing.'

'It's a joke,' Santana said, beside him, 'to end this way.'

Beyond the soldiers checking their magazines was a concrete wall with a tiled roof and above it the early blue of day, the cries of birds and the distant morning clatter of the town, roosters and dogs, a donkey calling. 'It's a shame,' Father Miguel said, 'a Goddamned shame.' A fly buzzed round, warming his wings in the new sun. He rose like a diamond up over the parade ground and flashed away; there was the click of rifles as the soldiers brought them to their shoulders but there was still time for the world in all its glory, *her* flesh soft scented and sinuous, the apple, the wine, the core of the tree red like a beating heart, as we go down the tunnel of our love back to the first days, the first day of all, before time.

Black muzzles pointing with little black eyes. Black hard steel. 'Bless us O Lord for these thy gifts,' he heard himself saying, 'which we are about to receive.' He realized he was saying grace, the oldest prayer, felt a warm, scarred hand grip his shoulder.

Flame spit from the guns, the thunder in one hideous long roar. There was nothing; he floated in an ether of pure perception. It's true, he thought, you just don't feel it.

He would find Clint now, tell him about Sherrie, how she was going to be fine, that Saul would steer her straight, good Saul with his beard and calm reflective manner, he would find Dona now as soon as she passed over and darling come quickly – it's better here.

A loud bang made him jump. An officer with a pistol moved from Santana and fired again, this time into Father Miguel's temple. Blood hissed over the dirt; chunks of Father Miguel's brain stuck to Murphy's face. The officer jabbed the hot barrel into Murphy's temple. 'We haven't shot *you* yet. Want to live?'

The soldiers were lining up again, reloading. A flock of multicoloured parrots burst from a tree.

'We give you one last chance,' the officer said. 'Give us *names*!'

His mouth was too dry to speak. He tried to look into the officer's face but the world was dancing. There was the smell of blood and excrement and dirt and sweat and anguish and burnt powder and seared oil, the calls of men and birds, the soaring music of the sun, the brilliant sky in which all the worlds were coalesced, blood crashing through the streams and canyons of his body. The pistol whacked his jaw. 'Want to *live*?'

64

This time they did not take her to the interrogation block but to a long low basement room with full-body human targets on a sandbag wall. Two of them held her wrists; a third took out his pistol but she would not flinch nor close her eyes, and the shot crushed her hearing and her stomach caved in monstrous pain, awful agony each instant worse, as she writhed in circles on the floor, begging them to kill her. 'Kill you?' one mocked. 'You're going free!'

Back in his cell he stared through the gritty, rusted bars. The other prisoners watched him suspiciously now that he had returned from the dead. *La vida es sueño*, Consuela had said, and death a dream also, for we're dead and dream ourselves alive, hold these bars in our hands and think that they are real.

If I could only tell you now, my love, all I've learned, how much I've learned from you, how I've always loved you from the first moment, the moment I was born, from long before. If I could only tell you – it was *my* mistake, my wanting you, my coming back for you, my thinking I could free you – that's what cost your life. That it's all been wrong since I didn't kill him, the Special Forces captain. Because I've always tried to keep a foot in both worlds, I've never stood in either.

So long I've wanted you, before I knew you; when I was a child I wanted you, have always loved you. I tried to bend the world to my hunger but the world never bends.

Darling, it's charade, acting with our minds *sin saber por qué*. Beneath the charade the heart beats, the body sings, air feels new in our lungs, we touch each other, die.

The soldiers came raging as if they would kill him now, banging rifles on the bars and whacking him with the butts, pushing him and three others down the corridor and up the greasy stairwell to the killing ground. Green GMC trucks stood in two lines; they shoved him up into the back of one, other prisoners crying out as he fell among them. '*Qué pasa?*' he kept screaming.

'They're going to shoot us,' a woman said.

A soldier shut the back. The truck lurched, moved forward, bouncing and grinding, the sound of the other trucks following. Through a space between the canvas and steel he could see a parade ground, then fortifications, then a long road and jungle.

'Who are you?' someone said.

'Just a gringo, got mixed up in this.'

'Sad. Now they're going to shoot you too—'

The grinding gears and diesel smell were the same as his trip down through Mexico, these injured people he didn't know, who were just like the injured anywhere, Nam or Guatemala. Death was coming just like any other death.

Still the trucks did not stop. 'This is the Sierra de Chamá,' a man said.

'We're going to Chisec,' the woman said. 'That's where they'll shoot us.'

Chisec came and went, huddled hovels in ragged jungle under the downpouring rain. A few minutes later the truck slowed again, the others closing up behind. It swung left, the others following. 'Xuctzul!' someone called.

There was a smell of woodsmoke and river and the rattle of a bridge; they followed the side of a canyon, the stream roaring below, down and across another bridge then up through the hills on a muddy track, the truck lurching and groaning, then down the other side. The trucks halted, canvas sides slapping.

'It's the Usumacinta,' an old man said. 'They'll throw our bodies in the river.'

One by one they climbed over the back. The rain had cleared; drops still pattered from the trees. The soldiers tied them in a line and walked them down the slippery trail through wet branches and grass, the roar of the river rising to meet them.

When they reached the river the soldiers untied them. One of the prisoners from another truck came running, calling, 'Is anyone here a nurse, a doctor?'

'I'm a medic,' Murphy started to say, then stopped. Everything you've done's gone wrong, he told himself. Don't start again.

'You?' the man said to him. 'Come then, we have someone dying—'

'Let him go in peace. We're all dying in a minute anyway.'

'She's in pain. Come then, it won't hurt her to see you—'
'Let's go!' a soldier cried. 'Down to the river!'

He followed the man to a huddle of people and a body on a bloody poncho, and saw that it was she.

65

She saw there were dugouts drawn up along the shore.They carried her down to the water and rowed her across, then lay her by a fire whose smoke lowered on the afternoon air between the *palo pinos* and *pimentijos*, a fire of *palo sano* bright as youth, moss on the mottled grey bark flaring with flame, the russet grain of the *palo sano* like a burning heart, blood to ash. And she saw that change is not evil but only change, and death the end, but no matter, for even nothing ends, and no Heaven exceeds one loving touch, one graceful act, one moment in which another's loved, the gift of love is more momentous than time.

They were so gentle, moving round her. I can write a book now for you all, she thought, on the mystery of death, the symptoms of its censure in the body and the brain, but why do we always speak of symptoms and never of the heart? We're so wrong, dear Lord, not to be satisfied with love—

Wood owls called, a blue-crowned motmot tolled the ending day. Smoke sank on the damp air, far away a chopper passed, those men of wood whittled by the Creators, pale-fleshed men who used the Earth but did not revere the Creators, so the Heart of Heaven drowned them in a rain of tar and soot.

How true the legends. I go back now. To the early days. My father's knee in its striped wool suit. Bony: when I sit on it his kneecap shifts. He pushes his glasses up his nose, his smell of pipe. Back to the jungle our mother, the scent of leaves and soil and slumber.

She held her own love's hand in hers and felt the warmth, could clamp her fist in it when the pain was so bad it made her scream. He was beside her speaking in his rough, soft voice like that of a man who has drunk or cried too much, his body warm beside her, not like this fire that glows but does not heat. You, my Utzíl of Panimache who crossed far hostile lands for his beloved, saved then lost her and dived from a cliff to drown in Atitlán. But *you* will live, you and the child Jesús, whom you saved, and a million like him, live on to form the new Guatemala. Utzíl my love, my Guatemala, my beloved quetzal singing from the sacred *amate*—

'Where,' she said, 'where are the soldiers?'

'Across the river. I was in the last truck. This is Mexico.'

Another *compañero* bent over her, a boy with long dark hair and sad eyes. 'The soldiers,' she said again.

'They're gone,' he said.

'They're never gone!' she pleaded. 'Give me a gun?'

He smiled to hide his anguish, the lack of guns. 'I'll give you my knife, *compañera*.' He took a combat knife from a sheath round his neck and slipped it into her pocket.

'We're safe now,' Murphy said. 'Just hold on.'

'Truly?'

'Lupe and Pablo, the others. They traded us, for Arena.'

'How many?'

'Sixty-three, plus you and me.'

She closed her eyes. 'We won . . .'

'They had to send Arena back. He was injured, but he'll live.'

'It doesn't matter. Perhaps he'll change. It's suffering that teaches us to love.'

Fire shadows danced in the companionable chatter of wind in the leaves and ferns, of water trickling down trunks and lianas. They lifted the four corners of her poncho and carried her up the slippery slope towards the trail to Saint Elena and the road the Americans had built to keep out the *guerrillas*, where the car was waiting that would take her to the clinic at Caribal.

The trail came up from the river canyon and there was a broad steep meadow with a white car above it and they carried her up it towards the setting sun, the windbent grass red, the far line of trees and sky of blood, his torn shoulders aching with her weight but no pain could stop him now, and over the river's rumble came another that was four choppers fast over the ridge and down on the meadow. With Dona in his arms he ran for the line of blood-red trees but saw he would not make it, ran back towards the river but the soldiers were there too, Dona crying, 'Put me down! Run!'

The tall black man jumped from the lead chopper, ducked low under the blades. 'Put them in mine!'

'This is Mexico!' Murphy screamed. 'You can't!'

'*Pronto!*' he yelled at the soldiers, 'get them in the chopper.'

They beat Murphy down and lashed his arms and ankles and

threw him in beside her, the cargo deck slippery with her blood, the ancient steel rattling as the Huey took off, nose dipping, tilting back towards Guatemala. 'I'll always love you,' she said, her face drained of all but the red sunset through the open cargo door. 'I'm going now, it's a haemorrhage. Take this.' She slipped him the knife as he tried to lie beside her but the soldiers forced them apart, and he watched her die quickly, her face relaxed, her lips opened, her chest no longer moving beneath the bloody shirt as the wind toyed with a thread of her hair.

The scar-faced pilot seemed familiar, as if from Nam, as if time were compressed, and everything that had happened there would happen over and over for ever, its images serving as lessons to a mystery he would never decode. The last sun sank beyond the mountains of the Río Ixcán, the jungle fading to umber greens, the sinuous headwaters of the Río de la Pasión silver and carmine in the south.

The ancient Huey wailed on an evening downdraught, the rotor shaft grinding at its bearings. He watched the gap between the Jesus nut and the shaft, wondered could he shove the knife into it, break it loose. The tall black man was talking with the other officer, the one who had been Carmen, the Embassy translator. Turned from them, Murphy cut the bounds round his wrists, pulled his legs beneath him, freed his ankles. Keeping the knife and his unbound wrists hidden, he looked up at them. 'I know you,' he said.

The black man grinned down at him. 'Search me, and know my heart? Try me, and know my thoughts?'

'I mean *him*.' Murphy nodded at the other.

'Carmen?' the black man said. 'That was just our little joke.'

'His name's Angelo.'

'What makes you think that?' Carmen said.

'I heard it from an American, a guy named Gallagher. Just before you cut his throat.'

The black man looked at Angelo. 'When was that?'

'The night he wasted my plane, killed my friends. When this all started. Didn't it, Angel?'

The black man took out his gun. Angelo shook his head. 'You're not going to believe this shithead—'

The black man raised the gun, nodded at the cargo door. 'Go.'

'I won't let you do this!'

'I'm not going to hurt you,' the black man said. 'But I want you over there.' Watching Lyman, Vodega edged towards the door.

309

He's the one, Lyman thought. All along. *He* killed Gallagher and blamed it on Murphy because the Guats don't want to pay their share. Because he likes to kill. We've all been used, all of us who fight, by people who move us back and forth, to kill and to be killed. Nancy was right: I'm everybody's dupe. Especially my own. I could let Murphy go, make amends. But not Angel.

Holding the safety strap, Angelo approached the open, wind-sucking hole of the door, but when Lyman fired he fell into the corner screaming. As the black man went to kick him out the door, Murphy rose up behind him and drove Dona's knife into the perfect place between the shoulder-blade and spine, straight into the heart; he fell gasping and Murphy grabbed his gun and saw the scar-faced pilot was climbing back from the cabin; he shot him in the face, then the co-pilot at the controls.

He stood in the cargo door and the jungle was very soft and far below: you could jump but you would never hit. You would float, far away, not thinking, no longer feeling. Epiphany – all pain gathered into one.

Epifanía. The Huey began to drift then slide, the black man slipping out the door. Murphy stepped over Dona, dragged the pilot free of the crew aisle and climbed into his seat, tipped the cyclic forward and swung the Huey round, in a long, easy descent back to Mexico.